For Sandra

"With women of my own rank and culture I have had relations of tenderness, but for me as for them a pressure of the hand has sufficed."

Rex Warner, *The Wild Goose Chase* (1937)

PROLOGUE

It would be an insecure storyteller who began his tale with a story borrowed from someone else. Over to Antoine de Saint-Exupéry, then. The French writer/aviator, much loved for *Le Petit Prince* and inexplicably ignored by modern readers for everything else, tells a story about a party of very wealthy people, "constipated with their possessions", who chance upon a young man reading a love letter. The youth is weeping with happiness. Because the experience of the fat-cat onlookers is limited to acquisitiveness and envy, they can make no sense of his response to what, in their emotional illiteracy, they see as random black squiggles on white paper. But they don't doubt the strength of his feeling and, suspecting that it may enrich them in ways they can barely articulate, they want to feel it too. So they command their servants to write love letters to them. When, inevitably, the letters have no effect they have their servants flogged.

This fable appears in the unfinished *Citadelle*, a long, fragmented assortment of ideas and stories. Saint-Exupéry would have been assembling material for *Citadelle* in the late 1930s. I became an emotional (though not tearful) reader of serial love letters close to 40 years later. Another 20-odd years on, in 1997, Saint-Exupéry and his drawing of the Little Prince appeared on the last French 50 franc banknote (about £5). I wonder if his Davos-like gathering of the super-rich would have been able to interpret the collection of ciphers on a banknote?

If you look at any piece of writing – printed or handwritten – for long enough it begins to lose its sense. The shape and contribution of individual letters start to seem arbitrary, and the myth of Mercury (another story purloined from an authoritative source) inventing the letters of the alphabet from the flight of passing cranes becomes more persuasive. Long, slender necks; angular but fluid wing configurations; spindly legs... it isn't hard to see how notches on a stick and hence runes might follow. Bars, uprights and loops, dots and dashes, knots in a cord. The letters and the sounds they represent are no more than a code and what they transmit is the purpose of the hand that formed them.

In front of me, now, are lines on a page, a sheet from an unmade bed. The writing would commonly be characterised as 'spidery' but that does spiders a disservice. Spiders, formidable architects, would produce nothing so ill-formed and random. Equip a spider with eight spinning ducts and you would expect something exquisite – Escher on a spirograph, perhaps. The lines in front of me have neither vigour nor structure; if, as Laurence Durrell said, poetry is prose in flight, this is calligraphy in a tailspin. But the hand that coaxed the pen across this page (and many more like it) once slid easily into my own and gripped it tightly.

The page in question comes from the last in a series of ancient hand-written letters from my first love. I have been transcribing them (copying via a keyboard), almost as gruelling a task as it must have been to write them in the first place.

My oldest friend is largely to blame. To mark my 60th birthday he presented me with a folder containing copies of the letters I had written to him. They dated from 1975, when our university lives diverged, to the email era. I can't imagine why he had kept them. He was an admirer of Henry Miller and may therefore have been impressed by the correspondence between Miller and Laurence Durrell. Perhaps he believed I would become famous and my letters would hold value for posterity. Regrettably, I neither became famous nor was able to return the compliment; I could find only four or five of his letters to me and, embarrassed, I stored them away in a safe place and determined never to mention them.

Later in the year, however, when I was helping my father move house, I found that I had retained a quite different and far more comprehensive collection of letters. These came from a young woman – a schoolgirl, strictly speaking – of 17. Grace Alexandra

McGoldrick's letters, bound by a perishing Post Office elastic band, were in a dog-eared shoebox alongside such diverse and treasured (if only in the sense of being buried) items as a ticket (value 100Dr) to the Palace of Knossos, a cocktail stick flying the Spanish flag and a pack of German playing cards specifically for the game of scat.

"If I ever met her again," I thought, "I should make her a present of these letters." Before I did that I would need copies; as you grow older, the past becomes difficult enough to hold on to without your giving extensive tracts of it away. Besides, if she were famous they might have value.

If she were famous I would probably have been aware of it. Not having met nor heard report of her in several decades, I could hardly view preparations for a handover of letters as an urgent consideration. Still, if the day dawned when our paths should cross, I would not want to give the wise and foolish virgins occasion to giggle. So I set out there and then to type 28 handwritten letters into the electromagnetic storage systems of the 21st century – from Basildon Bond to Romford-purchased Macintosh.

LETTER 1

I try to picture Grace sitting down to write her first letter to me in the summer of 1972. Because I cannot – the details of her home and its furnishings elude me – time passes and the process of transcription does not begin. Perhaps I am inadvertently replicating a delay on her part all those years ago as she considered how to start.

Unable to produce a convincing image of wherever Grace wrote her letters, my mind lazily furnishes a ready-made one: Vermeer's *Lady Writing a Letter with her Maid*. Almost all of that touching picture seems inappropriate – the writer's puffed sleeves and cap, the stained glass, the maid. In truth, only the discarded first draft at the foot of the table is worth its place. Wool-gathering already, I move on to another study by Vermeer: *The Lacemaker*. This young woman, who might at a pinch be writing if the painting were entitled *Young Woman with Two Pen-like Objects in her Left Hand*, represents my memory of Grace more accurately. There's a hint of Jane Austen about her costume, her concentration is intense and she may be ambidextrous. My mind, fickle as the day is long, also prefers this painting because its title inevitably calls to mind Claude Goretta's wonderful 1977 film *The Lacemaker*. In my fantasy, then, a young Isabelle Huppert is settling down to write a letter to me. Agreeable as this image is, it doesn't bode well for the credibility of my account.

The day, first. It is a Wednesday afternoon – Grace says so at the top of the first page. The postmark, too faded to offer much information, indicates August 1972. The date on her second letter suggests that this Wednesday must have been 2 August 1972 – the anniversary of the day on which Kafka famously wrote in his diary: "Germany has declared war on Russia – Swimming in the afternoon."

Grace began the letter at home – a solid mid-war detached house in a Hertfordshire commuter town – during a break from packing for a family holiday. The stamps have been carefully removed at some point in the past 40-odd years although they could hardly have been very exotic – 90 centimes, if a hand-written reminder where the stamp had been is any guide. The address on the envelope concludes 'Angleterre'.

This first letter is addressed to Mr Stephen Gallagher but begins 'Dear Steve', and there's a jolt to begin with. I haven't been 'Steve' for nearly 40 years.

What's in a name? Does it make any difference to the idea we have of ourselves? If asked, I usually claim to have reverted to my full-length baptismal name to placate my mother. When I showed her the first published piece of journalism to which my name was attached she looked only briefly at the article but concentrated instead on the byline, saying censoriously: "You were christened Stephen."

Alternatively it may have been Graham Greene. Early in *The Quiet American*, Greene talks disparagingly about the American Economic Attaché in Vietnam: "To this day I cannot describe him, except his fatness and his powdered clean-shaven cheeks and his big laugh; all his identity escapes me – except that he was called Joe. There are some men whose names are always shortened." Another objectionable American character in the book is called Bill, who has a friend called Mick. The English narrator, by contrast, insists on Thomas in full. Who, under the circumstances, would want to be a man whose name was always shortened?

Greene, by the way, was a prolific writer of love letters. He is said to have churned out 2,000 (sometimes five a day, as though in obedience to some form of guidance on spiritual nourishment) to the woman he married.

Looking at the script, I am reminded suddenly that Grace was left-handed. There are all sorts of portents and ambiguities in this letter.

Dear Steve,
I woke up this morning feeling as if I had been physically spun

round on a wheel, but my exhausting sleep was worth it when I
told my mother what time I got in & she thanked me (and you).

I have to explain that we had not been a couple for long – a week,
10 days perhaps. Her family holiday to the Dordogne cut off a succession of golden summer days. She was 17, I was 18. We had been
friends (though not notably close) for a few months and were both
pleasantly surprised if not startled to find ourselves taking an
abrupt and unsignalled turn into Lovers Lane, where the holiday
fell like a tree across the road.

Evidently we had been out on the Tuesday night and were not
late home (though late enough for Mrs McGoldrick to have retired).
Where could that have been? I ought to be able to remember – if the
days were as golden as I claim – but cannot. I know that we made
a trip to St Albans to the cinema at some point, although I forget
what was showing. Many fine films were released in 1972 – *The
Discreet Charm of the Bourgeoisie*, *Cabaret*, *Aguirre Wrath of God*
– but I doubt my 18-year-old self would have been discriminating
enough to propose any of them. Besides, I was more interested in
the fact of 'going to the pictures' than in what was showing: 'going
to the pictures' was what you did with your girlfriend. Such was
the sophistication of my thinking and the novelty of my situation.
Ideally, I suppose, we would have gone to see *Here We Go Round the
Mulberry Bush*, the story of a young man's quest to lose his virgin-
ity (in which occurs the best line anyone our age would have heard
in a film up to that time: "This is how the world will end: not with
a bang but with a Wimpy!").

If not a film, it may have been a concert. Also in St Albans, on
that or another imperfectly remembered ancient evening, we saw
a band called Cottonwood. The musicians were US draft-dodgers
playing to raise money to live on. This was 1972 and the Vietnam
War was not going well for the free world. Unknown numbers of
young Americans emigrated rather than be called up to the armed
forces. Conscription ended in 1973, the fall of Saigon took place in

1975 and in 1977 Jimmy Carter offered draft-dodgers a controversial pardon.

The young men on the stage would have been my age or a very little older. Musically Cottonwood were in the Buffalo Springfield style, and I particularly remember that a song called *East England Winter* would have persuaded me to buy the LP. But those were simpler times and assets often remained unsweated. Cottonwood had no LP on sale. They had no merchandise at all. In effect, they played and passed the hat round. I thought they were wonderful, but I was there with Grace Alexandra McGoldrick on my arm, experiencing for the first time those star-bright evenings of unimaginable excitement for which nothing can prepare you. I would have thought Chas & Dave were wonderful.

> Sarah + Rowan asked after you a lot + gave me a mug of coffee with STEPHEN written on the outside which belonged to their father. Without you as a diversion I was torn apart (physically) as of course being a weakling I didn't stand a chance. There were 5 cats inside the kitchen today too, 2 kittens (Lint + Sweepea), 2 red cats (Mother + Tibbs) and 1 mottled one (Cassie). I definitely prefer dogs.
>
> To pass away the time I coloured in four pictures – one of Red Riding Hood innocently picking tulips (?) in the wood, and three of Joe 90 – the famous TV personality. Hum.

If the idea of someone writing a letter seems impossibly dated, here's an abrupt lurch into the present: an adult colouring-in a picture-book. Grace was 40 years ahead of her time.

> About 3 hours later. The phone rang after the hum & it was for me as always but surprisingly it was Maureen. You know, the girlfriend of Tony at Brad's party, who goes to my school. I had the shock of my life because I imagine myself friendless, particularly as regards her. Anyway I was feeling odd & I asked her round 'cos

I didn't want to pack and also as I was secretly touched that she had phoned.

I have never been so amazed by her in all my life as I was this afternoon. You see after I had been corrupted by Craig that time (voluntarily though), for some reason which I really can't get Tony suspected that it had happened & asked me over the phone what I had done, if anything. I was tempted to lie, but being an honest person (as from your own experience you must realise) I admitted that his suspicion was true, & the nosey bastard – I do like him really – told Maureen who went and told her mother. Of course I was furious because our parents are friendly & Mrs Fowler is a right gossip, and so I went to Maureen's with Beth one day & gave Maureen a big blow-up. I can really say that I have never ever been so unreservedly nasty to a friend before, and by the end she was in tears. Since then – last holidays – we have stopped being friendly, I mean I see her at school & we pass the time of day and she tells me some things about Tony but never as happily or freely as before. I just felt that I couldn't trust her any more, and I didn't want to because I hated her for what she + Tony said about Craig to me and to other people. This is a very much abridged version of an event which has had a lot of effect on me, but I hope you get the gist OK. It is also made more difficult 'cos I don't know how much Craig has told you already – if any.

Quite. Craig had not mentioned the episode. Circumstances made it unlikely that he would. I need to do a little colouring-in myself, to illuminate the background.

To begin with, it would be helpful if I could introduce one or two of the characters at this point. Otherwise it's as though we were in the early stages of a Russian novel, where the names are already so exotic as to defy retention without the possibility that half of them will turn out to be of peripheral interest only. Those who make no more than one or two appearances will hardly be worth the effort of memorising.

We can start, confidently, with the writer. Grace was slim and tall, almost my height. Her long blond hair was parted down the middle and lacked only a floral headband had she wanted to look like an archetypal hippy. She was approaching her final year of school. Her most noteworthy characteristic was that she had recently achieved a status bordering on immortality – she was and will always be my first love. I had known her for about six months, through the agency of the Craig alluded to above. Our grace note had changed its character to become musically and harmonically essential a week or so earlier, at a disco in a church hall.

Rowan and Sarah, I'd have to guess, were infants Grace baby-sat. It sounds as though I must have been introduced if they asked after me and I had previously been a diversion. They will be middle-aged matrons by now and may safely be forgotten.

Brad, also known as Brat as though he were a Yorkshireman, was Nigel Bradford, whom I knew from the school I had just left. He is an indistinct figure in my memory: I can picture him against several teenage backgrounds but only ever in a non-speaking role. He introduced me to Craig and was therefore of more significance than my memory accords him.

Tony and Maureen... her name rings a bell in the distant, unhelpful sense of a village church's bell tolling in a valley overwhelmed by a reservoir.

Craig was my closest friend. He had an open, laughing face surrounded by undisciplined curly hair. If I try to project his image forward in time to the present, I arrive at a face like Krusty the Klown's with a similar punch-line. Craig experimented a little with pharmaceuticals. He was in love with Grace, though she did not reciprocate. Recent events made it even less likely that she would. Thus I had no idea what she was talking about in saying she had been corrupted by him, but I'd guess it was drug-related. Unfortunately I was no longer in any position to ask him.

Anyway this afternoon Maureen & I talked for ages about some

serious and some trivial things & then my father came in and told
me to pack. Then Maureen got up quickly and said very fast that
she was sorry about telling her mother & that she hated not being
friends with me. So we sat down again and I said I was sorry too
for being such a cruel bitch etc. Then we both went on about how
we hated last term (because we both felt inferior to the other person & tried to make that so) etc etc. And finally my father came in
again and told me to pack again. So she went and I [indecipherable
– reeled?] up, to pack all the wrong things and forget all the right
ones & now it's too late 'cos they are on the car roof and covered
by a tarpaulin. Phew.

   So now I am frustrated and shocked & flat & dazed all together
& I also feel guilty as well as happy about being friends with Maureen.

I am transcribing this verbatim. Where Grace wrote an amper-
sand, that mondegreen is what you will see. I expect 'v' to stand
in occasionally for 'very' and 'S' for 'Steve' as we advance through
the correspondence. There may also be many more references to
words I can't decipher. I can hardly read my own handwriting now;
Grace was prone to legibility but never consistently. I will hope not
to misrepresent her.

   As for myself, I should probably try to be as scrupulous with my
so-called memories as I am with her script. Yes, it's all a long time
ago, but to be unable to place people and events to the extent I have
found so far is discouraging.

   The main difficulty is that many of these people, for me, had no
life outside her letters. At the swirling tip of her biro they led full,
exciting lives, but that was the only place I ever encountered them
as far as I know.

   My imprecision over the Tuesday evening (and many other outings) is less easily excused. We were not a couple for very long and
our days or evenings out were few. Of the concerts we attended
together I can remember only 50% (ie one) with any clarity. We

went out to the pub together scarcely any more often. We treated ourselves to the cinema once. Such singular evenings should be, if not vivid in my mind's eye, at least discernible in outline. If I can clearly picture unexceptional events from much earlier years I surely ought to be able to dredge up a very rare night out with my first love. But my memories of those evenings are like the glimpse you will sometimes be granted of a kingfisher beside water – when you've realised what that iridescent flash was and you've focused on the place, the bird is gone. It may be that as I immerse myself in those long-lost pre-selfie days, the shades will gain solidity and my accounts will become more reliable. We can only hope...

> Firstly because I have said some pretty repulsive things about her, secondly because I don't know if she really means it (which shows you that I don't really know her anyway) and finally because I had given up wanting to be friendly – which is always an awful feeling. As well, I realise that I have let Beth and Craig down as they can never be friendly with her again & don't want to be anyway. Therefore when they know they will be furious. As my chattel you should advise me on what to do really, but the thing is that it is a stupid situation anyway because I shouldn't want to be friends with her at all. But I do you see. That is why I can't argue much with people that I like – because apart from laziness I am too afraid of hurting and losing them for ever. As it is with Maureen I have been remarkably strong-willed to the point of defeat, & except for her wish to be friends, I would never have made the effort. Now she has, I have given in weakly. O dear me. I had to write all that and I must be boring you round the twist but you see I had to get it out of my system in a rational order to understand it better & of course I couldn't write it to Beth – although I will eventually.

Her chattel... I'm trying to work out exactly how long we had been together. It can barely have been two weeks at the most. But we were comfortable enough to make fun of each other, and 'chattel' is evidence of that, especially since she uses it as a non-sequitur. 'Mentor' would have fitted the context better: as her mentor I might have been expected to advise her, but that would flatter me and build my part up and she wasn't going to do that. It must have been very strange for her, writing to someone she hardly knew, having to rely on the relatively few moments of intimacy we had shared, having to take trust for granted.

I should also pick out the sentence: "I am too afraid of hurting and losing them for ever." There will be more to say on this score in due course.

> Actually it was the best possible thing that could have happened to me really, because it made me think for a period longer than 5 minutes of someone other than you. Which reminds me that Maureen thinks you are goodlooking. But don't get the wrong idea please – it must have been the lousy light at Brad's party, I mean I was completely taken in myself, so...

> About 11.00 at night: I went for a walk because it is such a beautiful and drizzly night. On the way down the avenue I met your old flame Mark Hopkins with Andrew Butcher. Apparently we were supposed to go to the White Horse at 8.30 on Monday night you stupid hum. So I told him that of course he had never said that & valiantly (though without conviction) stuck up for you. He said he phoned up your house too, which if I was you I would appreciate very much.

More incomplete strangers. Andrew Butcher may have been related to Tim Butcher, with whom I played cricket. As for my 'old flame' Mark Hopkins, he went out with Alison Roberts whom I would have been proud to have called an old flame. Alison had won a local beauty pageant and was good value for it. I had discreetly carried a torch for Alison Roberts.

Grace refers to Mark Hopkins in jocular fashion because she knew I thought highly of him. Later, increasingly jaded with life in general in the affected manner of undergraduate students everywhere, I decided that there cannot be very many people whose opinion of you matters. As a logical consequence I pretended to care little about the impression I made on people. Perhaps this conceit began earlier than I thought, and Mark Hopkins was picked out as one of the few whose opinion counted for anything.

The White Horse was in the centre of the town. It looks as though we had been expected on Monday night and I had taken us on Tuesday. Our friends, deciding against hanging around for 24 hours on the off-chance that we might show up, were not there. Our evening had been truncated and Grace had been returned home at a decent hour. She was some months shy of her 18th birthday, so a night in the pub wasn't entirely respectable anyway.

More likely, now that I think about it, is that we have the stress on the wrong word. The night may not have been at issue. Even in those distant pre-mobile days, if you didn't turn up you were apt to get a phone call the following day: "Where were you, then?" It's the pub I can't work out. The White Horse was shabby and no place to take a lady. Well, I had little experience of either pubs or ladies in those days, so that doesn't necessarily mean anything. But I certainly went with Grace one night to the Three Horseshoes in a neighbouring village. I think I must have taken her to the wrong pub. The Horseshoes was a pleasant country inn and further away, thus reducing the chances of her being seen on licensed premises by anyone who knew her. Her mother had serious reservations about me on at least two grounds: one, I was the friend of a known dope-fiend; two, I had a motorcycle. It would have been imprudent to demonstrate a weakness for alcohol into the bargain.

As for the saga about the blabbermouth Maureen, it is too easy – facile, literally – to adopt a supercilious tone. It all sounds a little like the contemporary social media darlings and their volatile emotions, distressing themselves excessively over trifles.

But Grace proved me wrong across the decades. Typing her letter, I reached "it made me think for a period longer than 5 minutes of someone other than..." and, unjustly, was expecting "myself". The fact that "you" was the next word startled me again into the realisation of how blessed I was to have been the recipient of her letter, whatever she chose to say to me.

I have just realised that the only envelopes I have don't match this (cheap) paper but I can't rewrite it because I am lazy and a Scot so you will have to bear it.

Thursday – about 7.0ish.
Hello again. You are the privileged receiver of the first infinitely recorded day-to-day account of my holiday. On the ferry (which we boarded at 10.0) we sat in these maroon chairs which you can sleep on at night if you haven't got a cabin & don't want to go in the lounge. (I can't remember their name.) There were hideous queues outside the duty-free place as that was really the main attraction. In fact it was boring. I read nearly all the time except when I went on deck which was beautiful in 'the sun' to say goodbye to England. I went up later also and listened to an irate French mama argue with her two children over two deck-chairs. I (being a true hippy) sat straight on the dirty deck.
     We drove through Normandy today & it was very like England, all green etc. I can't go on describing it because it sounds so hackneyed & terrible when actually it is just peaceful and foreign. Now we are all lying on air-beds waiting for dinner. My mother has just come in and said that she wishes I was writing to her. So I gave her a suitable laugh (while feeling very sick) and went on. My brother is eating Smarties & he has thrown one at me so I will give it to you. I hope it is not too stale now. How did you get on in your cricket? I kept trying to imagine what it must be like and all I can think of is matches like those on television comedies where they always manage to hit the ball out of the ground etc and

knowing (or rather, not knowing) you perhaps that is right?

There is no sign of a Smartie among the bundle of letters, nor any fragments in the envelope. It was the first gift to pass between us and I appear not to have placed the proper value on it. I probably ate it on the spot, expecting many more gifts.

As for my cricket... again she was making gentle fun of me. I was a sportsman, specifically as in Jethro Tull's exactly contemporary album *Thick as a Brick*; the word 'sportsman' is delivered in a voice oozing disdain among references to Biggles and boy scouts and a generally scornful dismissal of establishment figures of the recent past, proposed then as role-models to young people. My weakness for Jethro Tull was a mystery and a joy to Grace. Little did she know that in my boyhood I had read the works of Captain WE Johns thoroughly.

As for hitting the ball out of the ground, I might if I had connected. Instead I was beaten by the spin and stumped yards out of the crease. A schoolboy error – perhaps I was still a schoolboy. Grace, by the way, was a Scot by birth only.

At that point we went to dinner. It was one of the funniest and most difficult to describe dinners I have ever had. First of all mummy and I forgot that …. meant shellfish & we were given a load of pins stuck in a cork, some black stones and some whole shrimps with both heads & tails hairy and waiting to be removed. Needless to say, having seen the black splodge that passed as a delicacy we went hungry. But as it is near the sea all around us people were digging away with their pins and clacking the shells together etc. It was fantastic & we felt very English. To make matters worse, the lights kept on going out so we could hardly see what we were eating anyway. But after the first 9 or 10 on-&-offs everyone was getting quite friendly & the waitresses were running round like rabbits etc so it was worth it.

Enough. I wrote to Beth a bit in between writing some of this &

told her about Maureen so have no fear (if you ever did, that is).

After you left on Tuesday I really was stunned like I said at the time. I didn't feel any emotion at all, & since then I have felt completely flat, neither happy or sad just indifferent. I think my parents think me heartless, although they never knew what I think about you, but I am glad really 'cos I will be furious if they don't enjoy this holiday. I wasn't going to write anything about you not being here at all, because it seems so pointless & obvious. But it is false to do that I have decided because I think about it such a lot & I can't see why I should consciously try to avoid what I think. That, of course, only works if it doesn't cause me any hurt, and for the moment, still – even now – I feel immune. But I confess that it is wearing off & soon I will attempt not to think about it any more or else I will [indecipherable]. You see what amazing control I have over myself. (It is not true really, but occasionally I can be detached even to the point that it is frightening though not usually in circumstances like these.) I am getting wound up and half of what I have written is rubbish anyway so you can (discriminatingly) disregard it as you please. My brother (insensitive darling, though we are getting on at the moment) wants the light out so goodnight.

This was accompanied by drawings of mussels, winkles, a black splodge and hairy shrimps, labelled, captioned and their colour indicated. Grace made full use of the space on the page.

I know that I was thinking about her all the time, as though there had never been anything in my life worth thinking about before; it was gratifying to find that she thought about me – even to the extent that it might cause pain. There's a good deal of selfishness about first love, isn't there?

The letter resumes in much smaller handwriting.

Friday morning – We are about to start off our 200 mile ride to

Porte-Vine, and we will stop somewhere to get food, where I will post this. It is a fantastic morning and we are waiting in the sun for my father to come back from reading the sign-posts. I went & read them for him but he couldn't decide which way to go from my accent. My brother has now mucked up something in his camera & we are again held up. This is getting tedious & trivial (you really ought to read *Lady Windermere's Fan*, Steve) so I will go I buy my dog OK? Grace XXXX

This last is, as advertised, transcribed verbatim and I have no idea what the final few words mean. An allusion to *Lady Windermere's Fan*? I didn't act on her recommendation to read it then and I won't now, although I believe one of the characters is called Tuppy, which sounds as if it might be a dog's name. On the other hand the phrase may be a parody of a French translation. Or perhaps it related to a private joke between us, but that too eludes me. Perhaps I have simply misread it. None of this would have concerned me to the slightest degree, given the number of capital Xs on the end.

However, there was a postscript.

This will reach you years after it has all happened. I suppose you realise from reading it that I have found it difficult to write to you because it is incredibly unsatisfactory. Perhaps because your conversations are so very unique that I can't reproduce even my half on paper. Of course it will get better.

Give my love to Craig (if you see him) and anyone else if you are writing to anyone, like Drew & Beth of course, and keep some for yourself

It is a prodigious letter to begin our correspondence. It would have gone unanswered, too, for I had no address to write back to. Perhaps I began a reply and waited for a means of sending it. Yes, that is entirely likely. I cannot, however, reconstruct my half of the correspondence. It would be dishonest to try: I would have to make it all up, apart from two or three phrases that have stayed in my mind. Two or three phrases is a poor frame on which to mount a collection of 20 or more letters. I will invent nothing I am not confident of.

More names. Craig has already been introduced. Drew Redmond and Beth Deardon 'of course' will make their occasional entrances and exits. Like confidantes in classical French theatre, they will turn up from time to time, often with news of events taking place offstage. I could leave their introductions to Grace since they were her confidantes. I'm not sure I ever really knew either of them well anyway – they were members of a small group to which I was admitted through friendship with Craig – but I didn't pay them very close attention.

Having acknowledged that I wasn't reading *Lady Windermere's Fan*, it isn't entirely off the subject to consider what I was – this, at least, is something I remember clearly.

I'd like to be able to say *Emma*, because it was being serialised on the television and Grace had asked me to watch the last episode (being screened while she was on holiday) and report to her. Remember, children, that in the days before mobile phones, when people wrote letters to each other, they also lacked the means of recording television programmes. With only three television channels this was not an overwhelming problem. Recording became possible a few years later, in more than one format until VHS finally saw off Betamax in the 1980s.

Even more years were to pass before I fully appreciated Jane Austen. Instead, tackling the other end of the literary scale, I can be fairly confident I was reading a piece of non-fiction called *Playpower* by Richard Neville – my younger self's hand has written May 1972 inside the cover of my copy.

Neville achieved a full measure of notoriety for his central role in *Oz* – the famous Schoolkids' Issue had come out in May 1970. The trial of Neville, Jim Anderson and Felix Dennis for obscenity followed in 1971 and their conviction was overturned on appeal (but not before the law had vindictively imposed severe haircuts on all three). A dozen years later, I found myself contributing to Dennis' prodigious personal fortune as his employee on a computer magazine.

Back to *Playpower*. It's fair to say I had never read anything like it. On the back cover, some of the verdicts of reviewers were listed: 'Coarse, shallow and nasty' from the *New Statesman*, 'Almost totally devoid of intellectual content' from the *Sydney Morning Herald* and, from *Private Eye*, 'The human story of a young Australian who comes to London and finds happiness by bringing out the worst magazine in the history of the world.' Objectively, it set out to be a guide to the counter-culture that grew out of the Sixties; for me, it was a startling revelation of how other young people lived and of the views they held. From an era when politicians proclaimed the nobility of labour and the right of a man to a job, I don't think I ever recovered from reading this in *Playpower*: "A man's right to work is his right to be bored for the greater part of his natural life."

Lest I leave the impression that I was some kind of Beat Generation blowback, nothing could be further from the truth. If *Playpower* influenced me, it did so subtly and over a period of years and despite my nature.

Two other books I know I read at about that time would be more representative of my adolescent self and indicative of how I imagined love to work.

I had recently passed A-Level French and one of my teachers, a young man called Christopher Duke, had persuaded me that it was legitimate to read French for pleasure. Until then I had restricted my reading to Balzac, Racine, Anouilh and one or two others purely to write essays and pass exams. It might never have occurred to me that literature in a foreign language had any other purpose.

André Gide's *La Porte Etroite* was one of my early forays. In summary, young Jerome is so much in love with Alissa that it hurts to think about it. Alissa (a young woman with straight blond hair, according to the cover of the Livre de Poche edition of 1967) returns his love; but her life presents obstacles that she regards as insuperable. They are, of course, nothing of the kind, but poor Jerome respects her feelings. As a result he finds himself treated wretchedly and, ultimately, is dropped by means of a wardrobe accessory – when Alissa appears one evening wearing a certain brooch, it is a sign that Jerome must leave. Grace, be it noted, had straight blond hair.

At the time, I regarded this as the last word in romance – young love thwarted ends in tragedy. Something similar might be said too of *The Man Within*, the first novel Graham Greene had published and by coincidence the first one I read. The central character – 'hero' is not the right word – is a smuggler who has betrayed his companions to the gaugers (this is a period piece). He is persuaded to do the decent thing – give evidence against them – for the love of a young woman he meets under ambiguous and, it must be said, improbable circumstances. Each, it seems, is prepared to sacrifice him or herself for the other; in the event, she proves to be more efficient in this regard, and the reader who has kept faith long enough to reach the final pages is left with the impression that he commits suicide to be with her in the Great Beyond.

Had I been paying attention, these books would have revealed what I might expect from first love. In both instances, however, I mistook incompetence for romantic instincts. Having made that mistake, and being attracted to the idea of romance, I was committed. As Evelyn Waugh said: "If you can't be right, the next best thing is to be firmly and decisively wrong." It's an honest mistake and not at all the same thing as continuing, in a hole, to dig.

LETTER 2

Not many Britons took foreign holidays in the early 1970s. 'Abroad' was expensive and unfathomable. The Wilson Government's devaluation of the pound by just over 14% in 1967, the limit of £50 in foreign currency and a widespread suspicion that foreign pavements were thronging with cutpurses combined to put people off. The McGoldricks were clearly made of sterner stuff: France in particular was known for its surly inhabitants, loose morals and tapwater rich in bacteria. The word 'gite', much less 'second home', was unknown in England.

Grace's progress through France tested not only my knowledge of French geography but also my understanding of the space-time continuum. Her second letter was postmarked Le Lion d'Angers, Maine et Loire, apparently an overnight stopping point on the journey south. But her first letter had given an account of a meal 'near the sea', which would imply a dendritic diversion from any direct route from the Channel to the Dordogne. And the date-stamp said 6pm on 11 August 1972.

Either it had taken the family more than a week to get that far, or the trend-setting McGoldricks took two-centre holidays, or I had to revise my estimate of when Grace began the first letter. A fourth possibility: it was posted on the way back. Still, it gave me an address to reply to in Gagnac-sur-Lot – a Chez Quelqu'un housename in a village called La Teulière. The distance between there and Le Lion d'Angers would be several hundred miles, even à voil d'oiseau. Perhaps – a fifth and vanishingly improbable alternative – the family undertook excursions that most people would have regarded as holidays in themselves.

The letter didn't waste time on preliminaries:

> Steve, I badly want to write to you but I can't write what I want to say. I have begun this letter again & again *[indeed, it is dated Sunday 5, although 5 August in 1972 was a Saturday – such*

were the relaxing effects of a continental holiday in those days]
and each time I read my sick words & start again. That is why
I didn't begin 'Dear' because it sounded so stupid after the nth
time (where n=4). Anyway it has given me luck because I haven't
wanted to begin this again and so I am afraid you will just have to
be resigned to not being dear any more – assuming you ever were
of course.

My writing has been bad because each time I have tried an
airy-fairy description of what this place is like with dismal results.

I imagine I would have taken perverse comfort from this opening
paragraph, seeing her feelings for me as the source of her distress.
To find that the cause lay in a failure of her powers of description
would have put me firmly in my place.

It is also difficult because I don't know you well enough to know
whether you would like it as much as I do anyway. It is a house,
stuck on top of a hillside, built in 1738. It is made of stones &
has small shuttered windows & steps leading up to a balcony and
the front door. There is no garden as no-one would look after it
anyway, but all around there is grass & nettles, with fig trees,
walnut trees and sweet chestnut trees too. Next door there is a
farm which keeps loads of hens & cocks & chicks, cows with bells
round their necks & at least 3 (friendly) dogs. Inside our house it
is really huge; the door opens into the living room which is about
twice (at least) as large as your sitting room at home (which was).
2 steps go up to the kitchen, then a passage with bathroom to the
left, my room to the right & at the end my parents' (huge) room.
Everything is wood everywhere. There are new wooden floors and
ceilings, with some of the beams still left to hold up the roof. In
the living room there is a massive fireplace which is still in use
(when cold). Daddy says we can have a fire before we go, and it
will be like Guy Fawkes I expect.

At the moment I am in my room – Phil could have slept here

> too but he likes having the radio on & I like reading late so he
> sleeps on a camp bed in the living room. I have to be private a
> lot, I find, so I am very happy that I am alone.

Philip was the Smartie-throwing brother from the first letter.
He would have been aged 14 or 15 – too old, surely, for there to
have been any question of him sharing a bedroom with his nubile
17-year-old sister. Didn't the McGoldricks, travellers and Franco-
philes, know the expression 'comme il faut'?

My 'sitting room at home (which was)' indicates a change of
address. While Grace was away in France, my family moved house.
I was due to go to university in the autumn, but the family's move
left me without a pied à terre in the same town as Grace, a difficulty
the severity of which would become apparent quite soon. For all
but a few days at the start, we lived in widely separated places.

You can't help warming to her, can you, for her description of
the holiday home? It would make a useful exercise in French translation, particularly demanding in different categories of specialist
vocabulary – trees, farm animals, architecture.

> This sounds like a big list – but anything is better than the way I
> was writing before, you will have to believe me. It is only because
> I love this so much that I get so ridiculous about writing about
> it. It makes me want to write 50 books on everything important
> in the world because it just feels as if that's what anybody not
> French living here should be doing. Perhaps 50 letters will do?
> You can't do anything here that you normally do on holiday like
> sunbathing & seeing the sights because it would be just like sailing
> a boat along the High Street – you couldn't do it even if you tried
> & you'd make a fool of yourself even if you considered trying. It's
> like being a tourist in somewhere like, say, Liverpool docks where
> you can't concretely go & see anything to remember & photograph
> and pin down as being what the whole place is like.

'Liverpool docks' south of the tunnel have become an unlikely tourist attraction since then. But the fact that they rose to the surface of her reflections, bubbling mephitically, 40-odd years ago makes me wonder... did the family come from that area? Sadly, this is another example not of my memory being inadequate but of my not paying attention at the time. I am sure she told me something about where the McGoldricks hailed from. Liverpool comes to mind, but mind declines to maintain its grip.

I wonder too whether she ever wrote any of those 50 books. Even at 17 she was clearly by nature a storyteller. Anthony Burgess said that literature consists essentially of dialogue and lists: Grace acknowledges the lists but uses them to construct pictures. Much of the time (and this is probably how I read her early letters then) it's as though you're being permitted a glimpse of her diary, but there is so much more to it than that. She has the urge or the instinct to communicate feelings, surroundings and the interplay between them.

The critic coded into Microsoft Word finds her grammar questionable from time to time and inserts its fussy wavy green underlining, but why would we pay any attention to what the programmers responsible for Microsoft Word think? Besides, she was writing to someone she hardly knew. When I consider the matter, our relationship depended in large part on the goodwill and friendly feeling accumulated over the weeks sipping coffee in Beth Deardon's front room and other venues. Trust is a strange commodity, isn't it? Acquired imperceptibly, it suddenly announces itself and you can say whatever you want to someone.

Craig may have taken a different view. When he introduced me to his circle of friends, he probably thought he could trust me not to abduct Grace McGoldrick from under his nose.

Instead you just live there & feel its particular feeling & above all try not to stick out as being different too much. That way you can kid yourself that you belong properly. It is those sort of places

that are the best ever because they make you want to belong
rather than just look in from the outside.

I wish I knew whether you understood me or not, but either way
I had better shut up or else I will die entirely, of frustration. At the
moment I am half dead.

I would tell you properly what I have done since I last wrote
but sadly I can't remember when I finished your letter. I know I
posted Beth's (which was written afterwards) yesterday and so... I
shall start from when we reached here early Sat afternoon.

My brother walked down to Gagnac & I washed up (etc) & my
mother & father fussed about and then we had showers and ate.
I felt very energetic & so Phil & I decided to walk down to Gagnac
again. The road was very narrow & wooded each side & God there
were so many slugs, brown, grey and black ones, and beetles *[this
accompanied by a picture of a 'life size slug']* as well as numerous
other diversions.

We took the short (long) cut on Phil's suggestion & it went
through the wood to a bog & along a river to meet the road again.
At Gagnac we had a go on the pinball machine where I won, of
course, & after a drink we started home. It was 2.5 miles uphill
& by uphill I mean uphill with loads of < bends etc. As well night
was falling... the cars (2) were all going in the other direction...
the insects (slugs) were accumulating... and it was very scary.
We walked very fast and we passed a cross where someone had
been killed in a road accident. Then we heard the cow bells and
this rang out even above the noise of the crickets which was
deafening. Then we saw a bat, which flew close to my face (at
which point Phil started saying how he'd never seen a bat before
(lucky him) & was it a vampire.) Later there were glow worms in
the grass which shone green & bright (like those insects which we
saw at Mark Hopkins', remember?)

No. But I'd prefer to think that we saw fireflies at Mark Hopkins'.
The idea of Mark Hopkins stealing fire from the gods and keeping

it in a small aquarium in his parents' lounge appeals to me very much. Grace was born under the sign of Sagittarius, a fire sign: I had stolen fire from Craig and guilt gnawed ineffectually at my liver.

Perhaps I should say something about Grace's character by way of further introduction. Alternatively, I could allow her to speak for herself through the medium of her letters. But for an independent view, there is the prospect of what might be revealed by her handwriting style and for that, at least, we can call on anonymous but supposedly impartial experts through the inestimable boon of Google.

The hand is tidy but undistinguished. The letters slope slightly to the left, but the ascenders stand barely proud of their more modest fellows and all of them have a tendency towards rotundity. Except the 'i', obviously, and related rake-skinny characters.

Noting that the skilled interpreter of handwriting takes more than 300 factors into account, we can say with some confidence that "a left slant tendency shows emotion and reserve. This writer needs to be true to self first and foremost and can be resentful if others try to push for more commitment from them." The flow of the script – most of the letters linked, but none of the words – indicates a thoughtful, measured person. The words (and lines) are well spaced, a sure sign that the writer is comfortable in her own company (or, possibly, is an artist averse to clutter).

As for the extension (or lack of it) of the ascenders, this is where the analysis increases its demands on our credulity. The area into which the letters 'b', 'd', 'f' etc rise represents our 'higher' selves and thereby gives a clue to our finer feelings on such topics as philosophy and religion. Grace's relatively modest ascenders, apparently, indicate imagination but also a degree of pragmatism. The plunging necklines of her more deeply-minded 'p's and 'q's (et al), by contrast, suggest animal appetites and highly-developed physical force. Because the loops vary in the degree of their decorative style (some straight and plain, others ornate) and the pressure in some cases is clearly reduced as she completes the stroke, "the writer may feel unsettled and unfocused emotionally. Again the handwriting analyst would look for this to be indicated by other features in the script." Her rounded letters show an interest in people. The dots on her 'i's, which are rarely directly above the stroke and sometimes absent altogether, are a sure sign of a distracted mind.

Thank heavens I knew nothing of all that at the time. It would have killed the correspondence stone-dead.

By the time we reached home it was black-dark & Phil had graduated to a thriller/detective story incorporating cliff edges, a jealous wife & being set in the Dordogne, using details like glow worms & cow bells for props. Boy, did my parents laugh when we told them about it. Even now I'd do it again but for those swollen slobbery slugs which turn me almost panic-stricken. When I was little I used to scream & cry whenever I saw pictures of ships at sea, or aeroplanes, rockets & (sometimes) trains (war ones, not civil ones).

I really hated them so much, & even now I would never go to see a film like '2001 A Space Oddessy') because I get too scared. It is the same feeling I have for slugs, although I suppose that is more understandable.

Today the weather relaxed & it poured with rain & thundered with *[an illustration of 'forked']* lightening. We went & looked at a few villages & in one saw this art exhibition of these very famous French painters – cubism or something – which of course I had never heard of. We also saw some rather vicious-looking sculpture like so *[picture of forked lightning mounted on a plinth]* and as daddy rightly said he'd be afraid to have it exhibited anywhere nearby in case he impaled himself on one of the spikes. O and guess what? We saw Liz Hamilton and family in one town. Do you know her?

No again. I wonder if I ever knew Liz Hamilton. Who were all these people who popped up so readily, at home and abroad? And why would she think I knew them all? It's possible, I suppose, that my halting attempts to represent myself as a social success and the last word in non-celluloid cool were more effective than I had thought. But unlikely. Besides, I hadn't seen *A Bout de Souffle* then and wouldn't have recognised 'cool' if it bit me. I was a self-conscious, excitable youth prone to embarrassment.

> Liz goes to Beth's school, lives in the town and is Rob Bramhall's girl.

Rob Bramhall rings a bell. I'll Google him later. And I like the possessive followed by the Americanism – it hints at a subtext.

> I knew she was coming here but never thought I'd see her. It made me feel sick for home. Tonight at home everyone was miserable and it was my fault because for some unaccountable reason I argued with my mother. It was only about me not wanting what they wanted for supper but she got cross 'cos before I didn't want what they wanted for lunch either & it blew up 'cos I was sick of everything and aware that I was being fussy.
>   You should have been there to see me in one of my (few) real rages. It was quite something, though I say it myself & although it left me OK, there was a nasty taste in the air & my mother went all flat, for which I could kill myself.

Here it is, in black and white, or rather on powder blue Basildon Bond – my first intimation that women are a different species. Of the women I've been close to subsequently some have given me fair warning. It took the form of a coy look and a whispered: "I'm a little bit crazy, you know," or words to that effect. This was intended to imply that life with them would be more exciting than I could ever imagine. It later transpired that it was not so much a promise, more a coded alert, enclosing a literal but perhaps understated truth.

Grace innocently describes an early stage in the craziness: a towering rage willed into existence for no obvious reason, and to someone else's deep discomfort. I should indeed have been there to see it. As for it being one her 'few real rages', in her first letter she recounts having torn such a strip off Maureen Fowler that the poor girl was reduced to tears. That suggests an average of one outburst every few days.

At this moment I feel sick for you...

And effortlessly she does it again. I am halfway to regarding her with a degree of objectivity and she reminds me in the next breath of how little prospect there was of that, ever.

... particularly you, & I can remember times when I have had the same feeling. Like when I noticed the interlocking spurs of the hills which made me think of geography & you. That sounds false but it is true. I can't picture you at all, and it makes it so hard when I want to bring you nearer to me. I can remember everyone – Beth, Craig, Drew & even Gordon O, Ben Lauder, Mark Hopkins & Alison, but not you. Can you tell me why?

I begin to wonder if she did it deliberately to impress me with the sheer number of her acquaintances, in the way that Facebook friends are prized by the gross now. Gordon O, our flame-haired Irish acquaintance? Ben Lauder, the third-highest peak in Scotland? I have no idea.

It seems indescribably mean when I want to recall you and can't & the more I try the more you fade away. It must be something simple so explain it if you can please.

Yes. This is a phenomenon well-known to the police in trying to coax descriptions of suspects out of eye-witnesses. They apply what are known as 'estimator variables' in trying to evaluate the reliability of a witness. The variables include any stress or trauma associated with the attempt to dredge up a clear picture. What is first love if not a form of stress or trauma?

Alternatively, we may invoke the Cheshire Cat. In *Alice's Adventures in Wonderland*, you will recall, the Cheshire Cat proves a source of bafflement to Alice: first, in its ability to materialise and vanish at will; second, in its lively and unpredictable conversation. Finally, all that is left of the Cat is its grin. I don't think I'm giving myself airs unduly by identifying myself with the Cheshire Cat: reference has already been made to my 'unique conversation'; and Grace, a wandering heroine with a record of drug experimentation, fits the bill quite well as Alice.

Perhaps, when you're accustomed to being so close to another person that your eyes can no longer focus on them – millimetres away – the question of physical recognition and the conjuring up of a likeness ceases to matter.

It was really funny when we got to France, speaking to the people or attempting it. One woman thought I was French 'cos we only said 'Bonjour' (which you can't tell the accent of, really) & she started jabbering on & on about some caravanners & the weather etc. It was very flattering, I can tell you. My brother met this little girl & all these old people the first time he went to Gagnac & the girl, having found he was English, asked the people what English words they knew – the only ones being 'I love you, darling' so of course she rushed up to Phil & kept on yelling this at him till tears were rolling down everyone's faces. She did the same when I went down with him later, so we couldn't have felt more welcome.
I am going for a shower (truly I am) so goodnight.

Monday morning.
We have just finished breakfast and I am writing amid the crumbs. I wrote your envelope spelling Berks Barks and this was

greeted with roars of laughter because I remembered that I did
it on your last card too. It shows the contempt in which I hold
Reading, anyway. It is still raining but (at the moment) Phil &
I are going swimming – that does not mean to say that we will,
though & it probably means that we won't. I hope you like your
house & the cricket club is up to the standard of your old one
(why did I say that? I don't know but I feel I must get to the end
of the page). I give up. Love to everybody who you think might like
it apart from as well as you.
Grace xxxx
Can you read my writing? If not, who can you ask to translate?

Taking a break from work today I looked up La Teulière, Gagnac,
on Google Earth. It was there in a suitably grainy resolution, as
though dusty and overlooked.

The Google van had not tackled the road up from Gagnac to the
hamlet of Le Teulière so I was unable to retrace her steps through
the darkening wood. But the hairpin bends were there, and wood-
land so dense that the path of the road could not always be followed
from above. The slugs and the glow-worms were easily imagined.

It occurs to me that the torments of young love in even the relatively recent past will be inexplicable to teenagers now. Far from being
frustrated at being unable to speak to each other they would seldom
not be speaking, either on a mobile phone or through Skype or
via text. Unable to picture each other, they would transmit a quick
selfie to make good imagination's deficit. Indeed they wouldn't be
on holiday with their parents in the first place.

They have no idea what they're missing. Whether what they are
missing has any value is a different matter. Was there any virtu-
ous, character-building consequence to the denial Grace and I were
obliged to practise? Perhaps. But another possible result is that an
intensity grew artificially between us because of our separation, in
the manner of pressure building up behind a closed valve.

Today's newspaper carried a feature celebrating the 50th anniversary of *Subterranean Homesick Blues*. To honour the occasion I dug out my copy of Scorcese's *No Direction Home*, a title that defies you not to indulge in nostalgic reflections, and then rewards your surrender by reminding you precisely what the songs sounded like the first time you heard them. It's an astonishing achievement.

I set up the VCR, that being the machinery my copy requires. And that's appropriate too, in a way; ancient technology for a different era, when gratification was deferred if only for the time it took to fast-forward through a tape.

In shadowy monochrome, the Greenwich Village troubadour delivers his angry poetry, evoking a world of injustice and insecurity. Why, against such a troubled background, is the abiding sense one of loss? Is this what looking back necessarily entails? Do all generations experience this? Housman, then:

'Into my heart an air that chills
From yon far country blows
What are those blue remembered hills,
What spires, what farms are those?

'It is the land of lost content,
I see it shining plain;
The happy highways where I went
And may not come again.'

Granted an address, I wrote back. I believe I wrote a love letter. Or, at any rate, I tried for the first time in my life to write a love letter.

It may have been more than a little contrived. I had read somewhere about Persian poets and a device they used called 'kindling', to establish a mood. I attempted kindling. God knows what form this took specifically. I could perhaps piece it together – I may have recruited dusk, twilight, water bubbling through a lock gate, peace. And then, as though we were lying on a blanket in a river meadow with a glass of cider and Mark Hopkin's Disneyesque fireflies to entertain us, I made the declaration for which the mood was essential. I may have gone over the top there, too. If you say "I love you" once, it can hardly do any harm to say it again, with increasing emphasis.

I hope this was how I replied to her first two letters. To have merely sent an account of my cricketing prowess, or descriptions of Reading, or news of people she didn't know from Adam would have been disgraceful.

LETTER 3

When I wrote initially about Grace's distinctions – "a status bordering on immortality" – I was wrong to confine such hyperbolic comments to my own point of view. I see now, having spent more time thinking about her in the past few days than in the preceding few decades, that Grace may stand as a figure of general, even universal significance.

Historic turning points are given handy labels; processes that unfold over thousands of years may be reduced to a single lifetime, to help us identify and relate to them. Thus a collection of fossil remains found in East Africa in 1974 is known for the sake of simplicity as Lucy, and this early hominid (the bones are dated at 3.2m years) has come to be commonly regarded as the Mother of the Human Race. Lucy's fitness for the role is debatable, but it helps to have an identifiable starting point. And if there are traps at the start of the race, why not a winning post to mark the end? Eventually, Lucy may be seen as the first of a pair of bookends, and another convenient individual will match her at the other end of the shelf.

I nominate Grace for this distinction. Yes, it looks like an extravagant proposal on the strength of such modest acquaintance. It occurs to me now only with the benefit of hindsight (6/6 vision in the metric age). But the signs were all there at the time.

For Grace to be placed at an evolutionary pinnacle, where the rising curve ends, evolution must have started to go into reverse. Anticipating objections on at least two grounds, let's consider whether evolution could have such a gear. Isn't the point of evolution that it proceeds, down the generations, to yield individuals ever better suited to their environments?

In 1972 most people would automatically have tended to regard evolution as a one-way street, hoping perhaps that social evolution would gradually take the place of the unforgiving survival of the fittest. But social evolution even then was an uncomfortable line of thought. It might lead with no diminution of competitive spirit to the survival of the fittest society. Then, of course, the Soviet Union and the possibility of nuclear holocaust would come to mind, and the whole point would become moot. Cockroaches would claim the crown of creation and the six-legged would inherit the earth.

Unfortunately, in recent times the idea of social evolution has become even more implausible. The inequalities in society indicate that looking after the unfit is not a high priority among the ranks of the fittest. Not a day goes by without one or more items on the news decrying the decline in woefully underfunded public services.

By the same token, most news bulletins will also offer the contrasting picture of people who clearly have more money than sense and possibly more than is good for them. Not long ago, for example, there was a piece about young people buying, using and sharing DIY tattoo kits.

But the obvious answer – taxing more heavily people who can easily afford to do without their Nissan Qashqai, or their replica strip, or their multiple annual foreign holidays – is never proposed. When was the last time a major political party entered a General Election campaign on a programme of increasing taxes? It seems unlikely ever to happen again, and this must be a serious if not terminal flaw in Western democracy. People – voters – seem unable to detect, beyond their own self-interest, a greater social good. It doesn't augur well.

Even without calling on the 15 to 20 different species of early humans, many of which found evolution simply too challenging for them, it seems plausible to argue that evolution is not a linear process. How, then, might Grace be installed as its highest representative?

Her handwriting is the key. The ability to write well and beautifully is a fine human accomplishment and one that is on the verge of dying out. Why will future generations bother with handwriting? In Finland, a civilised and admirable nation, the schools are already dropping cursive handwriting lessons in favour of keyboard skills. Elsewhere the same thing is happening informally.

That's in the name of convenience and practicality, but surely it is also a regression to a coarser, less reflective phase of humanity. The earliest keyboard instruments were 'played' with a gloved fist. From there to Chopin represents progress, doesn't it?

Handwriting exemplifies the ability to conceive of, create and use tools. The keyboard alternative, tapping with one or two fingers, is primitive by comparison. It's possible, too, that the end result is less sophisticated but we'll come to that in due course. Let's stay with typing for a moment. It doesn't need an opposable thumb – much more primitive creatures than us could have done it. Even Homo Habilis, our distant precursor, had an opposable thumb. "In the absence of any other proof, the thumb alone would convince me of God's existence," Sir Isaac Newton is supposed to have said.

The vital importance of the thumb is that it allows us to grip and manipulate objects: branches for descending from the trees, clubs for protecting ourselves against sabre-toothed tigers, charcoal for drawing on the walls of caves and, eventually, Bic biros for writing love letters. Yes, the ability to write – and with either hand – might be the single conclusive proof that Grace McGoldrick in the second half of the year 1972 stood at the high-water mark of human evolution.

You don't need a thumb for a keyboard or pad. People continue to use their thumbs, of course – its position vis-a-vis the palm of the hand makes it ideal for tapping rapidly at a keypad. But tapping is far less sophisticated than gripping and guiding.

The beauty of the thumb isn't simply a question of holding and directing a pen, of course. That's an estimable talent but the results can be reproduced by other means. What's important are the various skills involved in learning to write: motor skills, concentration, coordination, aesthetic appreciation... simply hammering away at a keyboard requires none of these to the same degree and some of them not at all.

Even the results achieved at a keyboard, as alluded to above, may be lower grade. When you set out to write anything in the old, handwritten fashion, you're apt to think carefully about what you're going to write first. Otherwise you risk crossings-out, insertions, marginal notes and other untidy intrusions. With a keyboard, a computer and word processing software, there is no need to think about it at all. Any alterations can be made without leaving a trace, any radical changes of mind effected with little inconvenience.

This distinction will be particularly sharp among journalists whose careers spanned the transitional phase between typewriters and word processors. With a typewriter, you began a piece of writing by taking two sheets of white paper, inserting a sheet of carbon paper between them and winding the resulting wad on to the cylindrical platen. You thought very carefully how you were going to begin your piece, to avoid going through that rigmarole repeatedly. Not necessarily as a direct result but perhaps through the same discipline, you considered how the argument would develop and how the structure of your piece as a whole would bring it to a satisfactory conclusion.

It may still be true that journalists try to construct an article in their heads before beginning, but there is no longer any penalty for not doing. Further, there is never enough time. The introduction used to be the part that took the most thinking about, but now you can dive in and promise yourself that you will tidy everything up when you've finished; and once the words are there on the screen and they make sense and the red wiggly lines indicating spelling errors have been accounted for, there will be a strong temptation to say: "Done. What's next?"

Grace Alexandra McGoldrick in 1972 was beautiful and smart, and she could write with either hand. Do those attributes necessarily place her at the high-point of the evolution of our species?

Statistically, no. Young people have been growing steadily more accomplished since then; according to A-Level results we've had decades of consistent improvement. Although Grace might have been fairly knowledgeable in her day, she'd struggle to hold her own against the hordes of A* holders and First Class degree achievers now.

Or not. You wouldn't be comparing like with like. Grace needed no artificial aids; she could hold knowledge in her head and produce it in appropriate places and associations on demand. What she couldn't supply from her own memory, she'd probably know where to look up. No context-sensitive help, no online forum, no electronic or cybernetic aid of any kind. She may have been able to use a slide-rule but I couldn't swear to it.

The contrast with the advantages 17-year-olds enjoy now brings us back to the matter of the thumb. The opposable thumb enabled primitive man to make and manipulate tools, giving him an early digital advantage over his less dextrous competitors. As the centuries passed, his tools became more sophisticated. His technology now spares him the trouble of acquiring and developing all sorts of skills: memory, mental arithmetic, writing, navigation and, since modern technology seems to have been hijacked by the entertainment business, the ability to make his own amusement. Modern man will eventually have no resources of his own. If a power cut prevents him from recharging all his fancy gadgets, he will find himself at a complete loss.

When I think of the young people I know personally – nieces and nephews, mainly, but also work experience students and others – I have to acknowledge that they are very bright. Their high academic attainments do not surprise me because they are impressive young people. In their case the exam system and its grades do not seem over-generous. It's just the luckless gigglers ripping open their envelopes and jumping for joy for the benefit of the TV news cameras once a year who seem ill-suited to a life of cerebration.

Besides, that * attached to the A makes me suspicious. You could only need an A* grade if the A grade was becoming over-populated. The purpose of grades is to enable universities, employers and proud parents to distinguish between candidates. If everyone has an A, how do you tell one from another? So you establish a new upper level of achievement to which the cream naturally rises. But what's left is not merely milk... these people have an A – they must be exceptional. It would not surprise me if further subdivisions between A* and A were devised, to permit finer distinctions. Forty years ago they would have been labelled A, B, C and D grades. Forty years ago the Football League was split into Divisions I, II, III and IV. We still know where to find the good teams.

Grace's third letter was postmarked Bretenoux on 16 August. Puzzlingly, she gave Thursday 17 August as the date on which she began it. Reinforcing this sense of inverted sequence, the letter begins with a PS in the top left-hand corner of the first page, in very small handwriting:

Written Friday morning having re-read
PS As far as the two halves of this letter are concerned, one must feel full of falsity since they are filled with such completely different emotion. I assure you that when writing both I experienced both emotions consecutively – strange as it must seem. To avoid too much of a nasty shock I should pause a bit (like I did) before the half headed 'Later'. love Grace

Dear Stephen James,
Thank you very much for your letter which graced our mossy doorstep (& was accompanied by loud hoots from the post van) this morning. When I first read it I smiled & smiled, and even now (having lost count of the times I have read it) I smile because parts of it are very witty.

It's a promising opening although not the mood I had hoped to kindle. Either I had shed the firewood for another day or introduced it with something a little less ambitious – metakindling, they would call it now. Still, smiles from Grace and the French facteur finding it a hoot aren't to be dismissed lightly.

I did hate writing to you, because I don't know how to either – it shows how little we know each other, doesn't it? In fact I was almost nervous. I read your letter second because I wanted to save it up (excuses). And I got the only two letters so far delivered here (the other being from Beth) so everyone was very jealous. That I enjoyed also.

Before writing this, I went into a very big 'HUFF' about 'Emma', but as you say I am weak (and anyway it's no fun if you aren't here to fold your arms as well). I am also – I have to confess it – rather jealous of your dog and in desperation nearly attempted to hail a black one of similar intellect & appearance to yourself, that I saw walking along in Gagnac, as 'Stephen sweetie'. But then I remembered the French vocab required and my accent and thought it not worth the breath. Those slight drawbacks alone will prevent you from experiencing the hurt that I now feel... I have to go now because we are going to a concert of Bach music, where I will meditate on you.

No love letter, then. Still, whatever I sent, it doesn't appear to have done any damage. On the contrary and completely by accident, I seem to have struck the right note. That would have been the result of careful consideration – I was not an especially spontaneous youth.

A Bach concert on holiday, by the way, illustrates what different worlds Grace and I lived in. Had I been on holiday there with my family, dad and I would have been going to see Racing Club de Gagnac play Olympique Cahors in the local grudge match while mum and the sisters went shopping.

Hello again. It is about 12-ish and the concert was good in places. But even in the good bits I thought of you (so it can't have been that brilliant). I had better give you a quick rundown on what I have been doing in the past few days. ('Ah-ha' thinks S. 'Tough' says G.)

> As usual I can't remember when I posted your last letter. But
> I think it was Monday. Yes, it was Tuesday, and it was a card of
> stalactites & stalagmites, right?

This paragraph was in blue ink. She subsequently switches back to black. I mention this only for the sake of thoroughness. What it might betoken is beyond me. As for the card, I didn't keep it. Strange, isn't it? I hold on to letters for decades but a postcard might have been in the bin by the end of the week.

Letters took the better part of a week to reach England from France at the time. While absence was undoubtedly making my heart grow fonder, her words plumped up the cushions of my fondness even further. It was clear that I was on her mind much of the time, and never as a less than agreeable distraction.

Well, we will have to pick our way through the waterlogged timbers of her shipwrecked daydreams soon enough. I hope I enjoyed this as much as I could at the time. It is difficult, isn't it, to conjure feelings from the distant past. Sometimes a smell will prompt this kind of memory, sometimes a noise (and in the case of a steam locomotive, both), and the sensation is fleeting. But to look at words on a page and to try to retrieve the feelings they generated two score years ago is a task only the hopelessly sentimental will approach with any optimism.

> Well on Tuesday I felt ill in my stomach, not sick, just ill. So while
> the others went to a chateau I slept in bed. Then they returned for
> lunch (of which I didn't partake) & went out & Phil swam in the
> rain. I wrote a letter to Beth, I think.
>
> On Wednesday (yesterday) we went to more caves - & I thought
> of you a lot because they were caves with an underground river
> & lake in, at Padirac. I thought of you 'cos of geography (like
> the interlocking spurs). It was very good except for I still had a
> stomach ache. We went in a boat along the river to a lake which
> we had to climb up steps to see. There were stalagmites & tites

but not so impressive as those in the other caves. (My geography mistress will love me if I tell her, but I will save it up for when I want to give in an essay late, I think.)

Then we went home & out again to dinner at Carenac (where I saw Liz the first time). It was quite good but I wasn't hungry & nobody near us ate snails (which was what I really went to see).

Ah ha, I have not told you. I ate a mussel. In fact at least 15 mussels, at one of the hotels we had dinner at on the way. I ate more than anyone else of the family (swank) because I wanted to tell you I had. Frankly they weren't very nice, & what was terrible was picking them out of the shells. They were yellowish & sticky almost, and stuck on to the inside of the shells by little white stumps. I was so pleased that I saved three of my shells & I will give you one when you come to stay.

If an exam grade had depended on it, perhaps I would have read Grace's letters a little more closely. You might think that a putative lover would have scoured them repeatedly for subliminal meaning. But I recall few details from these early letters and I suspect that the reason is I only read them once. Even a moderately attentive pen-friend would remember more than I do.

I don't remember ever asking her whether the stomach upset on the Tuesday might have been related to the consumption of 15 mussels only a few days previously. Perhaps I did. But if she ever gave me one of the shells it has gone – metaphorically – the same way as the Smartie.

Which again reminds me. I asked my mother if you could and she said "um" which is pretty good as she has rather slow reactions to things. Then she said "I expect so" which is brilliant. I think it would be best if you came quite soon after I go back to school (6th Sept) so that the essays etc haven't piled up too much by then. Also because my brother goes to Vienna about then, and you can have his room. (Really it's because I want to see you

SOON.) When do you get back from holiday? I will give you a better idea of days (if you really want to come, of course) in a letter which you should receive when you return from holiday.

Where was I on holiday? At the time I might have stood on my dignity and insisted that it was not, strictly speaking, a holiday but an educational visit. It had been organised by the school – the very establishment whose already gloomy doors I had just darkened for the last time. Education was so much more generously and carelessly dispensed then: no longer an inmate and planning no further French studies, I was awarded a 10-day trip to France by the school. No wonder it was referred to as a liberal education.

The destination was Thonon-les-Bains, a spa town on the southern shore of Lake Geneva. We stayed at the Palais des Jeunesses et de Quelque Chose – the Internet can't help me complete the name, indicating perhaps that the palais is a victim of the steadily ageing population. By 'we' I mean a mixed group of 18-year-old students from the UK and France. It was the first time I had been on holiday without the family and only the second time I had been abroad at all.

Like an Intourist party in the Soviet Union, we were closely guided and chaperoned. Some of the outings made little sense: visits to local craft workshops might have had some educational value but we had no money and the artisans would earn nothing from us; at the wildlife sanctuary the wild boar refused to show themselves, prompting obvious puns; and a night on the town in Geneva showed us only that Geneva was an unusually tightly-laced city. "Mais où se trouve l'action?" one of my fellow students cried, exasperated, to a Geneva gendarme.

It was a pleasant enough diversion; I would rather have been somewhere else, but since Grace and I no longer lived in the same town this was a non-specific longing. It became a theme, however: where, once, nothing more complicated than walking down the road had been involved in seeing one another, henceforward in order to be in the same place we had to make more or less elaborate arrangements.

My parents moved house while I was in France, and on my return after a hard day's travelling I left the suburban Waterloo to Reading train at the wrong station and walked several miles to their new home.

> If my parents object (which is possible but not likely) I will tell you
> that in the letter too, so either way you will hear then, OK? Will
> your parents let you come? (I never think about little things like
> that till afterwards but I suppose it could be a drawback if they
> mind.) Could you phone me sometime?

And that brings us to 'Later', and as instructed I'm going to go and do something else for a while. The kitchen sink needs cleaning. In truth it has needed cleaning since I moved into this house some months ago, but to do it now gives it a purpose above drudgery.

Three hours later. To leave the kitchen sparklingly clean for as long as possible, I treated myself to dinner out. The most extravagant treat in town is a French restaurant at the far end of the High Street; to commune with Grace and to prepare for a long day's work tomorrow, I took myself and several sheets of proof-reading to the Lanterne Rouge.

They sat me in a distant corner, took my order, delivered a large glass of wine and left me to it. I worked on the copy for a while. The piece was a socialist critique of modern socioeconomic thinking. Its primary thesis was that 'we' (the West, the First World) owe our prosperity to the deprivation visited on the rest of the world. Some day (with a nod to the tides of human misery lapping at the Mediterranean shores) the bill will be presented, the writer said.

Sitting in an expensive restaurant in the Home Counties, I was in no position to argue. Taking a fortifying sip of red wine I looked over the room. Life goes on. A couple in the opposite corner holds hands across the table, shortly after the young man has licked an excess of salad dressing off his fingers. Two women are transferring fruites de mer from one plate to another like chips on a gaming table; between them, an ossuary is developing. The young woman with socially-transmitted salad dressing thrusts her hands hygienically into her sleeves, although the room is very warm. She will need to take care – those acute ongles could snag her threads. One of a threesome – portly steak eaters – at a table for six rises to greet a couple and their daughter: shaking of hands and much cheek-kissing. They might almost be French. I return to my meal, which is not moules, and reflect upon the nature of my debt.

I wonder if I observed her instructions so scrupulously the first time around. I doubt it. Apart from anything else, I liked the first part of her letter: it was chatty, friendly and it looked forward to us being together again. A second part inspired by a different emotion didn't sound like good news. I would not have wanted to defer its arrival.

> LATER Hum… hum… hum (just 'cos you aren't here I haven't given it up, you know.)
>   That was just to sober you down for the miserable part of this letter which is going to come. I really do mean that Steve, it is very sad and it concerns Beth.

That would have come as a very considerable relief to me. I was in love – what would I care about Beth? I am certain that I would have approached whatever was to come with the confidence that I could cope with it. Besides, there was the recent example of the Maureen kerfuffle to sustain me. That ended well enough, didn't it?

> I did not want to tell you, and even now I am unsure whether it is best to or not, so of course I am going to. The letter I received this morning from her was quite short and it stunned me so much

that I immediately wrote back, an equally emotional one in reply
– parts of which I now, of course, regret. I would send you the
letter, for it concerns you also, and for all I know you could have
been sent an equally curt one, but I assume not, as she did not
say she was writing to you. I will quote some bits from it to give
you a general idea, and I assure you that I am in no way taking
them out of context or making them sound different by picking
them out like this.

I would have had a fairly clear idea what was coming. An incomplete geometrical figure had formed in our little group: not so much an eternal triangle as a provisional polygon. Craig would have been proud to carve his initials into a tree-trunk alongside Grace's; Beth likewise with Craig; and it's possible that Drew panted like an endearing puppy after Beth. None was ever going to be gratified, but being unable to see that sort of thing is part of the agony of adolescence, isn't it?

Beth, however, was sure to regard my abduction of Grace as an act of the greatest perfidy and would leap to Craig's defence. Later, when she realised the opportunity it gave her, she would soften her opposition. For now, however, Grace and I must be reminded of our treachery.

Did I know this at the time? I can't be sure. Craig, when I asked him about her feelings for him, generously described Beth as a complicated person. I felt I could approach the second half of the letter with equanimity. To paraphrase Keats, here lies one whose name is writ in mud.

It is better to do it like this than by sending you her letter or by
writing it out fully because that would really be unfair to her, I am
sure.
    "Your letter [mine] was so basically unthinking and naïve, if
I hadn't realised it was that and not your nastiness, I might not
have replied – either that or I would have written a bitter, cutting

letter."

In my letter I talked about Craig & your relationship & how I felt that I was breaking it partly because he might possibly have wanted to go out with me

I'm not a fan of exclamation points but if ever several were merited in close formation, there it is.

but mainly because of his liking for you, & him being hurt.

"You tell me to think of Craig, think of his situation. Could you just think of me & my situation?

"I have been deceived by many people & hurt by many – as most people have – but I thought I could rely on close friends. First Craig (ie their arguments before), and now you and Steve?"

She says that she has been "disposed of in this heartless way, and disregarded". It goes on like this for about 4 sides, and I assure you it gave me plenty to think about. I read it once through & truly couldn't understand what she was getting at. I really couldn't understand it, I couldn't believe that she could write like that. In the letter which she had received from me, I wrote about Brad's party and after that – about Craig, & him being hurt and how I hated myself for it.

The scales have fallen from my eyes. Brad's party, referred to several times now, was not (as I had thought) some routine Saturday evening social event at which we had made our debut as a pair, smug and self-absorbed. No, it was the night we *became* a pair. What I had taken to be just another disco in the church hall was Nige Bradford's 18th birthday party, and hence Craig was the DJ. From this dawning, shafts of light might be followed to uncover more substantial material. We shall see.

Anyway, I read Beth's letter a second time, and I realised that she felt deceived and terribly, terribly hurt & disillusioned because she

must have thought that we had just been waiting to "get her out
of the way". That is honestly the only way I can interpret her letter
& I have read it over & over again. She says things like "Why was
I the pawn to be pushed around in something that was yours and
Steve's?" which shows that she must think that our going out was
planned long in advance. I don't know about you Steve, but for
my part although I liked you before (particularly that time at your
house with the fire) it was on the Wednesday only that I realised
it. It gave me the shock of my life, and from what you said then
about expecting to get me with Craig – I am sure that goes for
you too. This is a muddle. But how can we have "pushed her
around"? God I feel guiltless, Steve. I really do. But I can see
what she must be feeling & sympathise terribly. It makes it even
worse when I remember that I didn't mean to tell her about it to
begin with, and all that stuff about "it would never have
happened if Beth had been there" etc etc – I feel very very guilty
about that, and it is that which must make her feel deceived.
Anyway when I wrote back I mentioned what I have just written, &
said that it must have appeared as if we were deceiving her. I said
that as we have no proof that it was not a pre-meditated act (so
to speak), and as I for one can't really decide why I didn't want to
tell her, that I would admit that it could look like a big deception
if you believed that. But I also said that I loved her (which I do
very much) and that she could decide whether to believe that or
not herself – for in her faith, one way or the other, lies the crux of
the whole thing. I said from my point of view that I was incapable
of wilfully hurting her, that any 'deception' over the letter we sent
was the result of shyness – I didn't know what else (can you tell
me?)

No. But 'the letter we sent' catches my eye. Was I party to this?
Did we compose some sort of joint declaration to poor Beth before
Grace went away? I hope we weren't too pleased with ourselves.
Unable to remember anything, I have to regard myself as capable

of pretty much anything too. Her reference to 'the Wednesday' is also intriguing – would anyone have their 18th birthday party on a Wednesday? If not, what else have I forgotten?

An analysis of that paragraph would make an interesting study. The root words 'deceive' and 'hurt' are discouragingly prominent.

> Steve I can't stand this, I really can't, because I love Beth & my affection for her will never be broken. I can't bear her to believe that we have been really nasty to her & hated her & that is what she believes at the moment. I must be feeling now what you feel about Craig – Beth in her letter places us me/you her/Craig in parallel positions as regards hurt.

There. Beth has already glimpsed the new realpolitik. She identifies herself with Craig where no such equivalence exists. For her interpretation of all our relative positions to be legitimate, Beth would have had to have designs on me that were thwarted by Grace. Incongruent triangles, indeed.

> I can't believe it has happened like this, can you? Why is it so terrible? I can't understand why we are still so much worth it, but we are. If you ever needed proof this is it as far as I am concerned. But can you stand it yourself? Please, please tell me if you can't, because I detest toleration above nearly everything. And I couldn't bear to be 'kept on' by you out of pity or obligation.
>
> When I wrote to Beth I laid myself at her feet, basically told her that I valued her friendship above everything (which is a lie I suppose but who cares?) and that it was up to her to believe or disbelieve me as she pleased. I told her I realised it must look what she thinks it looks like, so I didn't expect her to change her mind. O God why can't I talk to you? That is all I can say about Beth's letter, and it is enough.
>
> You must be worn out & sick with shock. Like I was this

morning I suppose. I feel almost mean having written all this,
since it can do no good & may actually do harm. But you are part
of it whether you are informed of it directly or not, so I suppose it
to be OK.

  I miss you so much, particularly now, now is the first time I
have cried since you left.

  Grace XXXX

Heartlessly, I was neither worn out nor sick with shock. I may
have been concerned that Grace was so upset, but I wouldn't have
regarded it as an irremediable problem. If I had believed, however,
that the world loves a lover, this would have put me right.

  I entertained the conceit in later years that love was unlikely to
strike me so forcefully ever again because I had been a nicer, gentler
and more receptive person then. In the light of the evidence presented so far, that looks an implausibly indulgent verdict. I cared
for Grace but I treated most of the other people who will feature in
this account shabbily to varying degrees. I seem to have regarded
Beth as an annoyance; Drew I hardly noticed until I needed something from him; as for Craig, we've already seen how careful I was
of his feelings.

My belated identification of the central role of Brad's party has
granted me a sudden access of something like memory.

  I can clearly remember how I saw things that night. It's almost
as if Craig had treated me to something mildly mind-altering, so
that I can glimpse feelings and events. It's as if the shades of all
the people who had ever occupied a certain church hall were to
congregate there, restlessly, with all the irrelevant ones gradually
subtracting themselves. This is how Brad's party is coming back to
me.

  The first thing to acknowledge is that whatever I had said to
Grace, there was certainly an element of premeditation. Beth was
away and Craig was busy jockeying his discs, so I escorted Grace to

the party. Along the way, in broad daylight, moved by who knows what impulse, I held her hand... for the instant it took her to realise I was holding her hand and for her to remove it, gently, without giving offence. It was a momentary contact between two friends.

Why would I have done that? Because the previous night I had kissed her, briefly and drily. This had come about when I walked her home through a dark, damp, calm evening. We maintained an even space beneath a barely adequate umbrella. On turning away from her at her door, with goodnights exchanged, I heard what sounded like a minor throat clearance or a catch of the breath. It was similar in timbre to that emitted by Ian Anderson at the end of *Thick As a Brick* (and, for that matter, at the end of *Wind Up* on the preceding Jethro Tull album, *Aqualung*).

That kind of exhalation, then, held a depth of meaning for me. It was scarcely to be ignored. Its meaning, I divined in a split second, was that she wanted me to kiss her goodnight. I turned and did so, to her evident surprise. When she had recovered herself (which didn't take long) she observed tartly that I had been making off with her father's umbrella.

It would be instructive to consider the implausibility of someone so gauche embarking on an adult relationship with hopes of happiness, but I need to get back to the church hall before the memories fade again.

I can see Craig in a corner almost concealed by his speakers and decks and a trestle table, like a manic paper-hanger. I can partially populate the hall, thanks to Grace's references to one or two people who were not unknown to me. Oddly enough I can't see Nigel Bradford, but there was always something subfusc and vaguely nefarious about him.

Most of all, though, I can see Grace, and I can remember how I characterised her appearance to myself at the time: she flitted like a flower from bee to bee. But she repeatedly returned to me. It was as though we were together. When, after a brief interchange with one of the drones, she returned and firmly took my hand, I was not entirely surprised. Neither of us let go. "Dance on, ye foolish ones. Ye sought not wisdom, neither did ye find it."

Presently we went outside. Across the car-park from the hall loomed the parish church, contributing depth and solidity to a night in whose shadows angels' voices whispered. A line of slender buttresses embraced the western side of the nave like a ribcage, and the ground rose into a confused darkness of shrubbery and hedge-row.

We found sanctuary behind a buttress and took the opportunity to kiss properly, carefully at first but with growing abandon. We clung tightly to each other as though we hoped to coalesce. We spoke soft, encouraging words to each other and took heart from them with wandering hands and slow. Stained glass saints, arranged in twos and threes in the church windows, looked down upon us for want of anything more interesting going on within.

On the summer night's air, in my mind's unreliable ear, *Maggie May* drifted out of the church hall. But that is probably invention: you didn't go to a party at that time without Every Picture Telling a Story at some stage. Ideally, Craig would have been playing something featuring cracked bells and washed-out horns. Had there been silver saxophones, I would have ignored them.

When I think about that evening again it is as though the fact of us being a couple was suddenly there, where no such thing had been before. Like Athena springing fully-formed from the forehead of Zeus (a messy and, in the post-*Alien* era, deeply troubling image), Grace and I had created a third party – us.

Quite by accident, I had side-stepped most of the clichéd agonies of first love: steeling myself to ask her out, unsure whether words would emerge when I opened my mouth to talk to her, apt to babble banalities, uncoordinated and unsteady – none of those torments afflicted me. I should think myself fortunate to have escaped so lightly.

I should add that no alcohol was involved. Yes, it was an 18th birthday party and someone would have smuggled a bottle into the place, but this was a church hall in the early 1970s and there would not have been a bar.

I am still not sure about the degree of premeditation. Had either of us thought it through, our behaviour would have been almost perverse. It would be good to know exactly when Brad's party was – a Saturday, surely, so either five days or 12 before Grace's departure for France on Wednesday 2 or 9 August. If it were more, Beth would have had to have been away for three weeks to have missed the party and our subsequent inseparability, and that seems unlikely because few people took three-week holidays.

In other words, if we had been able to keep our hands off each other for just a handful of days, we would have spared ourselves a great deal of trouble later on. Grace would have gone on holiday with one correspondent fewer; I would have moved house several times with little to draw me back to Hertfordshire; and our lives would have taken their separate courses.

Such hypotheses are pointless. We could not and so we did not. And whatever courses our lives subsequently took, I would not have had it otherwise and I hope she can say the same.

I have asked old friends for recollections of their own launches down the slipway of first love and their replies have been disappointing. They seem apt to confuse love with reciprocal pawing. Perhaps the intervening years – or their sense of manhood – have left them cynical and deadpan.

Ian, for example, a man of Celtic blood and unpredictable moods if not passions, denied any specific memory, admitting only to breathless fumblings after midnight in the car-park of Kings Langley railway station. I might have asked whether any cars were involved – Ian never learned to drive, and the idea of breaking into a car at random for the sake of privacy seemed far-fetched. But he was sceptical anyway. "I expect you want to over-complicate it," he said. "You're a bit afraid of physical directness, aren't you? Oh no, what if I go too far? What if I offend her? There's no great mystery about it: you both want it so it happens."

"Doesn't there have to be more to it than that? Two people so well-matched that they can suddenly share thoughts and impulses, how is that going to happen?"

He sighed. "It happens all the time. People go on about how important it is to read the signs properly – some signs are unmistakable."

"But I'm asking you about first love," I said, "and you've jumped straight on to sex. Wasn't there an intermediate stage where you weren't sure what was happening? After all, when it's the first time, you're trying to interpret unfamiliar signals for the first time."

"You mean what was permitted. Woman want romance, men want permission, that sort of thing?"

"It's nuanced, is how you would express it nowadays," I said. "It's like, in a cricket match, when you're fielding and the ball's coming your way and there's a split-second when you realise it's catchable. You might still drop it, but you know you can get to it. In the same way, there's a split-second with a woman when you know it's going to happen."

"You're the romantic one, aren't you?" he said. "Woman as a firmly struck cricket ball; I doubt if the sisterhood would take kindly to that."

"The images merge, sometimes," I said. "The night I started going out with Helen [at which point he groaned theatrically] I'd put a fielder in hospital that afternoon. He was at backward square leg and I pulled the ball hard straight at him and it went through his cupped hands into his face. After the match Phillip Dunkley and I went to the Willoughby Arms, the pub the other team used, to ask how the fielder was. Helen came in with some friends. She invited us to join them. I'd been pursuing her in an increasingly desultory, tentative way for weeks, but right then I knew it would happen."

Ian gave me a look of infinite patience. "First, we seem to have moved away from first love to third or fourth. Second, how long had you been in the pub when you had this revelation?"

"Nobody was drunk. I can't explain how it happens – body language, chemistry, dilated pupils, who knows? We hadn't got changed – I was still wearing my whites. Perhaps she couldn't resist a man in a uniform."

Ian sighed again. "But we don't know what she felt about it, do we? This is all based on your perceptions and your pursuit which, I might add, you have characterised as... I think 'desultory' was the word you used. Had she ever expressed the slightest interest in you?"

"She invited us to join her party..."

"In your whites. She was being polite," he scoffed. "Had it been a hot afternoon in the colonies? Did you look and smell your best?"

"Naturally, we went home to get changed and to collect Phillip's wife and we joined them for dinner."

"So it was a cricket ball that brought you and Helen together? And didn't that go well?"

"For a while, yes, spectacularly well." It was no exaggeration.

"For a very short while, yes," he said thoughtfully, evidently regarding a year as a mere bagatelle. "And what of the stricken fielder? Dilated pupils there too?"

"Detached retina. Beyond that I don't know."

"It sounds like the Big Bang theory to me," Ian suggested. "You have this tiny, tiny ball of compressed potential, and the next second it's expanding all over the place into a fully-fledged affair within which your perceptions of time and reality are fundamentally altered. To put it another way; you're at backward square leg, the ball's heading towards you growing bigger and bigger in your line of sight and then it explodes into your head and a new world of pain opens up."

"If you must. Or consider the princess and the pea. The pea represents the same thing – a kernel of pure potential, which she can sense through hundreds of mattresses, and the happily ever after is what the pea grows into."

"Yes, after it has been soaked overnight."

Ian later claimed that he too had an umbrella story. "I wonder if there might be something to be made of the influence of umbrellas on the course of young love," he said. "I was walking up Charing Cross Road with the ad sales manager, Ilse, you remember her? We'd been to dinner at Chez Something or Other off Shaftesbury Avenue. It was late. Also it was raining and naturally we couldn't find a taxi. I had a brolly but it was one of those ridiculously small telescopic ones. I asked Ilse if she was getting wet. She said: 'Only my groin.'"

He paused briefly, then went on: "So we stopped and kissed, in the doorway of an Anne Summers shop as it happened. Just kissing. It was one of the most exciting nights of my life. I couldn't believe she'd said that to me."

I asked him whether the evening had been leading up to it. He said no, not at all; they'd gone out to talk tactics, about how to stop the members of the editorial team – his colleagues – pairing off with the ad sales girls – hers – because they thought it was likely to be bad for morale when, inevitably, it ended in tears. So her remark, which made all manner of endings to the evening possible, took him entirely by surprise.

"Did you stay the night with her?" I asked him.

"No..." His pause lengthened. "I was living with someone else at the time."

"Ah."

"We found a cab eventually and delivered her to her flat somewhere north of Kings Cross. As the cabby and I headed off to Euston, he said to me: 'You should a' stayed wid de chick, man.' He was probably right but it was an impertinence. I considered withholding his tip to teach him to mind his own business. But you don't want to spoil a night like that with a fit of mean-spirited pique."

"The girl you were living with, did you love her?"

"I had thought so," he admitted. "But I broke it off with her and took up with Ilse and you know the rest."

Our mutual friend George Lord offered a tale from the celebrated Lord Byron's formative years. "What does everybody know about Byron?" he began, as though addressing a tutorial group.

George, through the coincidence of his name, had made a study of Byron, and his friends had been exposed to some of the results. Any one of us could have supplied the answer he expected. "That he was mad, bad and dangerous to know," I replied.

"Quite," said George. "The verdict of Lady Caroline Lamb, but she was literally madly in love with him so we must take her judgment with a pinch of salt. Besides, he was about 24 at the time of the affair with her; by then he had at least 15 years' experience of dealings with the opposite sex to draw on."

George watched me doing simple mental arithmetic and was satisfied by my astonishment. "How many?"

"As I say. You might think, in the light of his reputation, that it would be no surprise if Byron had been a sexually precocious child. But it's worse than that. Being a member of the aristocracy the young Byron had a nurse. Some biographers claim that when he was nine years old his nurse, May Gray, indulged in some inappropriate touching."

It is difficult to picture Byron as a small, vulnerable boy. Quite apart from his dashing reputation, two of the best-known portraits depict a heavily armed man. He called a gentle Lakeland contemporary Turdsworth, and 19th century gossip accused him of incest and sodomy. He may not have been very congenial.

"Getting into his bed and 'playing tricks with his person' is how it was described," George went on. "Before that, though, at the age of eight, he had intense feelings for his distant cousin, Mary Duff. Who can say he didn't lead May Gray on? Not long afterwards, he was writing love poetry for another cousin, Margaret Parker. At

15 he was in love with yet another cousin, Mary Chaworth, and refused to go back to school because it would take him away from her."

The young Byron seems to have been mysteriously drawn to girls whose names began with an 'M'. I mentioned this and was ignored.

"But my point," George said with a palm-up hand gesture, "is that he never got over Mary Duff. Some years later, the news of her marriage almost sent him into convulsions. According to the collected letters and writings he said something like: 'I certainly had no sexual ideas for years afterwards; and yet my misery, my love for that girl were so violent, that I sometimes doubt if I have ever been really attached since.'"

"Mad, bad and unsatisfactory to know, then?"

"Very possibly. By the way, do you know where the family's barony was, where he was Lord Byron of?"

"No," I said. Who does?

"Rochdale. It makes him seem a good deal less glamorous, doesn't it?"

In the parish church of the town I now live in, there is a brass plaque of a knight and his lady. They are known locally as the Crusaders, though it seems improbable that they are quite old enough to have spent any time in Satan's little Acre.

On the contrary, there is one charming and bucolic touch: just above the lower hem of the lady's skirt the artist has skilfully picked out irregular strands of grass, as though she had recently been strolling through their park.

But the key feature of this couple, or, at least, the reason I mention them here, is that they are holding hands. They have been holding hands since the 15th century and will continue to do so into eternity.

I am aware of a certain coyness in my account of Nigel Bradford's party. Hand-holding, for example, is prominent. So here's a note to the prurient: hand-holding into eternity was one of my early hopes for the unexpected bounty that had come my way, and if it is not mentioned in accounts of events from that point onwards it can usually be taken for granted. Anything more – I was, as has been noted, gauche – will be described more fully only if the artistic context demands it.

It probably won't. This is another realm of experience in which the successive silty strata deposited by life make it difficult to locate and mine any one seam with clarity. What you did and how you felt, particularly where physical contact is concerned, eventually coalesce into one evanescent touch that can best be described only in mystical terms: Michelangelo's *Creation of Adam*, perhaps, in which the extended fingers imply a charge about to leap across the gap; or Gerard Manley Hopkins' line: "Over again I feel thy finger and find thee."

What I said about 'hand-holding into eternity' may not be completely honest. In the first days of first love, all you want is for tomorrow to resemble today, and if you think about the future at all it is only in that sense of a lengthening series of such tomorrows. Tomorrow and tomorrow and tomorrow, as it were. As Norman Mailer said: "There are few occasions in life that are free of the sense of irony." This is not among them.

Love is a flame easily snuffed out. It brings with it insecurity. It is the most wonderful thing that has ever happened to you and it might be snatched away at any moment.

So you don't plan ahead. You hope to be worthy tomorrow in the mysterious way that has proved sufficient today. In the first few days you are particularly vulnerable. Her own reactions, those of other people, the simple change of perspective that daylight brings... all these serve as a kind of cooling-off period, as though you were an unwise insurance policy she has taken out. No, insurance is the last comparison to make. You can't insure against this. It's a speculative non-financial instrument. That is, when it's not a delusional state induced by hormones.

I may have been aware of all that in the following days. Not immediately. I walked her home from the party, slowly and with many pauses. A journey that should have taken no more than a dozen minutes took 60 or more, many of them spent in the sheltering darkness of the delta of a public footpath, where the sodium streetlights didn't reach. We kissed as though we had a lifetime's deprivation to make good. It's possible too that we tried to make the most of each moment in case, with the new day approaching, it dissolved in daylight.

Lest this all sound too much like love's young dream, I ought to admit that there were moments of embarrassment. We both wore glasses and there were repeated glancing clashes, as though we might physically generate a spark. Our noses also got in the way occasionally.

But if what we were doing amounted to bonding, to some form of imprinting, it worked. The following day might have been suffused with anxiety. Ideally, I would have taken up where we had left off with the darkness for concealment, but there was a whole day to get through first. In the event, on the phone and later face to face, there was no embarrassment, no suggestion of dreaming and no doubt that we were fully committed. I believe the word for a day like that is 'frabjous'.

In an optimistic frame of mind, I just tried on an Armani shirt I bought for £1.50 from a charity shop last year. Medium in size and 19% silk (81% viscose), it is still too small. Or I am too large. Since the shirt is not going to expand, I must continue to try to shrink. In 1972 I would have been just a little over 11st; now I'm 11st 11lbs. It can't be beyond my compass. If I were to succeed all my other clothes would become too large but we'll cross that bridge when we come to it.

LETTER 4

I began this session's typing by entering Grace Alexandra McGoldrick's name into a search engine. It would be disingenuous to call it idle curiosity.

On the other hand it doesn't mean I'm seeking her out. I would be interested to know how her life turned out, but no more than mildly. Could she cook, could she sew? Her practical talents or life skills were never very important to me. As the years have passed, I have tended to think that what matters is fidelity to the idea of love rather than love of any specific person. In any case, I don't know what name she goes by now, nor what she looks like.

The Internet obligingly delivered her up to me within a few minutes.

Exhibit A appeared on a company-checking website. "Ms Grace Alexandra McGoldrick holds 0 appointments at 0 active companies, has resigned from 1 companies and held 0 appointments at 0 dissolved companies," it asserted briskly. The report continued in a tone of greater familiarity but no better grammar: "Grace began their first appointment at the age of 41. Grace is not registered as holding any current appointments."

This could have been another Grace Alexandra McGoldrick, of course, but among the director's details was Exhibit B: "Date of Birth Dec 1954". Precisely the same name, and the right month and year of birth; there could surely be little doubt that this was the Grace I knew.

The directorship related to what was evidently a dwelling converted into three flats. The name of the company was an address in Hampstead with 'Limited' tacked on to it. Grace was listed as a director; she was appointed in 1996 and resigned in February 2004.

Would it necessarily have been her home, or might she have been a landlady? I couldn't say. I don't know enough about why people set up companies to administer properties.

And that was just about that. No related directors were named, there was no indication of what became of the company, and the subsequent career of the director was not explored. Although it had been an intriguing half-hour I had learnt very little.

So let's get straight into the fourth letter before the impetus is lost. Let's remember, also, that since posting her third letter, Grace might have been in receipt of a bundle of Persian kindling, tinder-dry and volatile. Another of the many difficulties of pre-cybernetic communications was the possibility – indeed the likelihood – of messages passing in the post. I can seldom (if ever) have been so conscious of that possibility.

   Grace's fourth letter was posted on the 19 August and apparently written that same day. It was a good deal shorter than any of its precursors.

> Dear Steve, I knew that I would have a letter from you this morning, and I thought that I might from Beth also. When my brother brought them to me I was asleep. But I found them on my bed when I woke up a split second later and he drew the curtains for me to read them. I decided to change the order of reading, hoping that your letter would give me strength enough to face Beth's. But I was so completely drained by it, that as usually happens when I try to calculate with people, my plan failed. Yours was a beautiful letter. I will never forget having had it ever.

Perhaps those old Persians knew a thing or two. All I can remember about it, apart from its contrivance, is that I freely confessed what I was trying to do. I did not confess that I knew as little about Persian poetry as I did Persian carpets or Persian cats. I hadn't even encountered the old tent-maker at that stage, nor his Victorian promoter. With more wit than piety I seemed to have hit the right note. 'Yesterday, today's sadness doth prepare…'

> It came just when I needed it very much, and it made me so

very happy I can't think how to tell you. You are right in what
you wrote, of course. I felt that as well, and regretted intensely
writing like I have been. The last bit of my last letter to you was
really the nearest I have ever reached to you, and that not nearly
close enough. You were in one way wrong about the first letter I
received, though, because you shouldn't regret it so much. When
I received it & read it I was glad, because although it didn't give
me all that I needed, it was enough then. It will never be again
though, and I pity you having to follow up a letter like your last
one, although just one like it is plenty.

How much constitutes enough? Is it inevitable that, having moved
the bar to a new level, a young man not by nature a high jumper
should seek to surpass it? The reward lies in a handful of words
scattered carelessly across the previously fallow field. "Just one like
it is plenty." No, it must not be, or a lifetime of settling for second-
best would follow.

I feel terribly calm now, so much so that I can't think what I
should be saying. One thing I am convinced of, and have been
since I have dared to think about it, is that I need to know you
very much. At the moment I know you so little – you admit that
yourself. I expect you understand far more of me than I do of
you. I cannot love you unless I know who I am loving. I love you
now because I feel that it is possible for me to know you a bit
more eventually. And possible for me to like what more I get to
know of you. But that is only a little bit of the reason, of course.
And all the time I am writing this I am afraid that it will not be
understood properly, or that you will not be able to respond to
it how I need you to. I can't rely on you. I can't rely on anybody,
and about things like this I suppose it must be the same for most
people. Of course Beth & Craig acting how they have acted has
lessened my faith even more (and vice versa I suppose). But it
still seems wrong that I should find it like this.

This is going to be very short, because it is all I need to say to you now. But before – I will say about Beth's letter, to save you any useless wondering (although I don't want to include it in my thoughts of you).

She still wants to be friends, she says that she saw you & Drew & that it was like a pretence, so from that I gather you know nothing of what I have been writing about concerning her sadness. Her letter seems flat and half regretful. She says she regrets ever having informed me of mistakes about which I was so obviously unaware. Now it seems to be over. She remains hurt but a little healed, and I remain puzzled and guilty because that is what I feel I should be. But I don't understand it really at all. So our relationship sounds as if it is staggering back to its feet again. It will heal in time if I am careful – and that is nothing new, I know. I hate being mediocre friends, which is what it will be for a time, but I will be because I am convinced that it should get better. Compared to what has happened with you and Craig it is great, so why am I worried?

If this letter sounds flat, it is not. It is merely calm. I can't write again because they won't reach you (what a terrific system this is) anyway I feel struck dumb. Have all my love that you want to return, and more. Grace xxxx

Re-reading this wonderful letter 44 years on, I am struck by how carelessly I misread it at the time.

I was looking only for signs that my love, of which I had thoroughly persuaded myself, would be returned. And there those signs were, joint and several. If she attached any qualifications they were eminently sensible. Eventually I would hope for more than 'sensible' but the word 'love' broke cover more than once and seemed to be heading in my direction.

Invited to begin a sentence with the words: "Love is…" how would you continue? You might opt for the classic: "Love is not love which alters when it alteration finds"; the succinct: "Love is blind";

the religious "Love is patient, love is kind"; the Hollywooden: "Love is a many-splendoured thing"; the purple-tinted: "Love is the colour this place imparts..."? There are many possibilities. My love was selfish. Introduced unexpectedly to a sample of the transports life might have to offer, it sought a season ticket. This involved it in a base assessment of values – its own, particularly, and the trade it might command. Could I be worthy of her? The doubt could only breed anxiety.

Had I read the letter more closely and taken her at her word I should have laid in a more balanced course. Grace was by nature cautious and reluctant to commit herself. I don't believe she was unduly afraid of being hurt; rather, of being mistaken, of giving herself too readily to the wrong person. It was not so much that I needed to prove myself worthy, but that it would be a good idea not to reveal myself as unworthy.

That may look a flippant distinction but it makes a world of difference to the thinking of a sensitive and unworldly young man. Where I chose to offer proofs, I would have been better advised to allow her to imagine them. But that's another thing about love, isn't it? Love does not calculate. Nietschze: "And I love him who throws golden words before his deeds and seeks to outdo them, for he wills his own downfall."

It is also apparent from Grace's letter that she was aware of a tendency in herself to withhold trust. To be untrusting is not uncommon; to be conscious of it suggests an event on which the issue turned. Had I explored this at the time I might have been able to apply the honeymoon effect: love conquers all, but only in the early days. Unfortunately I did no such thing.

Almost exactly 10 years later, I was the recipient of a similar but very much shorter communication. A telegram (telegram! – this is turning into a review of prehistoric communications media) from Sydney to London, it read: "I love your words and I love you. Mrs Boong xxx". Again, in response to a letter. Again, I had decided that faint heart ne'er won fair lady. My view of relations between the sexes was 600 years out of date and, it seemed, impervious to experience. Mrs Boong, God bless her, (she had adopted the name from *A Town Like Alice*, casting me as Peter Finch) thought rather less of me and my words six short months later and I haven't seen or heard from her since. If only I had confined myself to imagining and expressing in words. The attempt to translate those ideas into action proved repeatedly futile.

The Cat has entered the room. She sits in the doorway as if unsure of her welcome. In the act of sitting, her fur arranges itself over her back legs and feet like a hovercraft settling on to its skirts.

"Hello, Mrs Cat," I say, cheerily. Sometimes we are less formal in our greetings, sometimes more, but I seldom ignore her entrances. I'm all the company she ever gets, so I feel a responsibility (like a hitchhiker to the driver providing the lift) to try to find something to say to her, stimulating or otherwise. "Hello, Mrs Cat" is seldom the end of the conversation. And the Cat responds by finding something in urgent need of attention in the fur on her shoulder.

Where once I might have hoped to make Grace McGoldrick my life's companion and the consolation of my declining years, that role has fallen to a long-haired tabby. Named after Audrey Hepburn's Cat in *Breakfast at Tiffany's*, the Cat has seen off two serious rivals for the job and, at the age of 20, shows no sign of regarding her work as done.

I talk to her partly because it would be rude not to and partly, as I say, to assuage my conscience. The Cat has spent most of her life alone. She has never had a little friend and I have shielded her from male admirers. As a result and, by virtue of early surgery, she has never had kittens either. The two human rivals might deserve sympathy on the same basis, though without the surgery. The result, however, is that I have been the Cat's main source of entertainment for most of her life. She enjoys chasing screwed-up paper, is mystified by a clockwork mouse and will reliably pounce on shadows or reflections – it's possible she includes me among such diversions.

An undemonstrative animal and not obviously bright, she inspires teasing. But as she grows older I worry that the affection behind a mocking tone of voice might elude her. For example, last night for no obvious reason she slept downstairs on the settee rather than upstairs on my duvet. As I was taking a bath this morning she sloped into the bathroom and I couldn't help myself: "So, you've decided to show your furry little face up here at last, have you?" Generally, though, I try increasingly to talk to her in a friendly, even tone. This becomes repetitive. "Good little Cat" is a staple of our conversation: 'good' to reinforce the sense of approval, 'little' lest she develop body-image issues and 'Cat' for its two-fold contribution to her sense of identity.

Sometimes she sits with a purpose and sometimes she just sits. This morning she has a purpose. I'm spooning down a bowl of Special K in between typing, and the Cat is aware that if she makes her presence known early enough I will save her some milk. She takes up station in the doorway, so that if I'm going to take the bowl back to the kitchen I can't overlook her. Actually, she invariably sits in doorways anyway. She has no sense of being in the way.

As I approach the last few spoonfuls I try to entice her into the room. This involves getting on to my hands and knees and gesturing with the spoon towards the bowl. She watches, immobile. Sometimes she will drink from the bowl, but more often she likes me to present her with a spoonful of milk at shoulder height (her shoulders) from which she will lap untidily. This being a rented house and my deposit being at stake, I would prefer to keep milk off the carpet as far as possible. Of course, the spoon can be presented above the bowl, but she is messy in her habits and I'd rather she drank from the bowl in the kitchen.

"Well, what I'd rather is neither here nor there, is it?" She doesn't move. I'm going to have to move to her. And I do, and she drinks, and a point has been made or, rather, reinforced, because it has been made many times in the past 20 years.

Most of our interaction concerns food. Long in the tooth, or at least in the very few teeth she has left, the Cat is low-maintenance. I talk to her and try to engage her in mindless activities, but we both know when she is humouring me and her only spontaneous responses occur at mealtimes.

These – the responses – can be surprisingly elaborate. She recognises breakfast time either by the arrival of rosy-fingered dawn or the abrupt babbling of the radio alarm, whichever is the earlier. Sitting like an Easter Island statue close to my head, she waits for a weak will or a full bladder to force me out of bed, and then she dogs my steps until they take us to the kitchen. I set out a bowl of food for her and a cup of tea for me and I return to bed.

She follows some minutes later. Out of the corner of my eye I see her padding past the bedroom doorway into the bathroom. More minutes elapse. She begins to wail. Not normally a vocal cat, she produces a noise that a timber wolf under a full moon would be proud of. The first few times this happened I flung the duvet aside and hurried into the bathroom to save her from her tormentors. I found her sitting calmly on the bathmat. No further wailing ensued. "You cheeky old Cat, you want your bathwater, don't you? Yes." I have to reply on her behalf, but I don't believe I put into her mouth any words that she would disapprove of. "It's too early, damn it, Catty. Let Stephen finish his tea, at least. Come back to bed for half an hour, for goodness' sake."

The business of the bathwater is slightly troubling. When the Cat first became a member of the household she drank nothing at all as far as I could determine. A variety of bowls – metal, plastic, earthenware, Dresden – and a similar variety of soft drinks – tap water, bottled water, milk, cold tea – seemed to make no difference at all to her.

Eventually the Cat took the initiative and showed me what she wanted to drink. She would join me in the bathroom at the start of the day and jump on to the side of the bath, apparently to watch. On several occasions she showed off by teetering along the side of the bath, but after falling in once she confined herself to sitting in an elevated avocado corner... until I pulled the plug, towelled myself off and let the water drain away. When enough dry plastic was exposed in the emptying bath, she leapt on to it and began lapping the disappearing water.

In the past couple of years she has lived in a bungalow where the shower in the en suite exerted a similar attraction. When it was vacated she would step in daintily and have a drink.

Now, in her new home, she is too old to jump on to the side of the bath and there is no shower. So she sits beside the bath and finds new ways to make her wishes known. After a few false starts – trying to get her to lick water dripping off my foot over the side of the bath, failing to lower enough in a cupped hand – we eventually find an acceptable solution. I install a shallow dish in the bathroom and at bath-time the Cat drinks from it. The only real progress I have made is to get her to drink clean water occasionally, but it is still perfectly obvious that she prefers scum.

LETTER 5

There was a hiatus before the next letter. I'd guess I received the fourth one, posted in France on the 19 August, on about the 23 August. The fifth was posted more than two weeks later on the 4 September, back home in Hertfordshire.

It would be gratifying to be able to record, if we weren't writing letters, that we were spending time in each other's company. Sadly, we were not.

With a self-indulgent flutter of melancholy, I always thought of my first love as an affair of a few months only; and so it was, according to the calendar. But it would be instructive to work out exactly how many *days* we spent together. A handful between the party in the church hall and Grace's departure on holiday; another handful between my return from Thonon and my departure for university; and then, a weekend here and there until the end. I'm getting ahead of myself, obviously, but it seems entirely possible that we were actually together for fewer than a score of days.

Time may pass with the appearance of nothing happening; but the earth rotates, the seasons advance, trees grow silently towards maturity. The sand trickles through the hourglass.

Writing about the distant past presents particular difficulties, especially where intervals are concerned. Grace's letters are the fixed points here and they relate some of what she did in the intervals. They have little to say about what we did together; partly, I suppose, because we spent so little time together, but partly because when we did, both being present, we had no need to tell each other about it.

That being the case, it would be heartening further to be able to record that we made the most of every minute. Again sadly, I cannot. What did we do? I promised coy protection of innocence but the fact is I can remember almost nothing, incriminating or otherwise. We passed long, late evenings in her lounge, listening to music, stretched out on a sofa. Since the family had gone to bed by that time we must have spent the earlier parts of the evenings elsewhere, but I can't retrieve any of them.

My claim, then, that almost everything was new to me must be regarded as suspect. Novelty, you would think, would find a more retentive anchorage. Impressions alone remain. Love's alchemy failed to transmute all the base metal – the discovery of unexpected and easily accessible erogenous zones, for example, and the potential for your own body to embarrass you in unforeseen ways. But mainly I remember lustrous intimations of gold. How easily, in retrospect, I was satisfied. It was intoxicating to feel Grace fall asleep in my arms on the sofa. I lacked the imagination to realise how much more so it would have been to watch her wake up beside me, with the sparkling morning light streaming through the blinds.

The fifth letter finds both of us back home and September has begun. A month has passed since we saw each other.

> Dear Steve,
> I never asked for your address. Drew & Beth both expressed surprise when I said that I didn't know where you were.

This would be a reference to my parents' new home, but I took it to be a mystical hint. Having discovered where Grace may have lived between 1996 and 2004, I set out to find what else the Internet might be able to tell me, particularly where she might be now.

I acknowledge a change of attitude on my part. Having idly wondered what might have become of her, I am now thinking methodically of how I might find out. At this remove, more than 40 years having passed, I see no harm in it. The years have produced no evidence that she yearns to see me, but her preferences are her business.

If you ever looked for anyone via the Internet you will be aware of the difficulties, most of which are associated with the superfluity of information the Internet will swamp you with. An uncommon name at the focus of your search will help but it is no guarantee of success. There only needs to be someone more prominent with the same or a similar name, or indeed an energetic nobody with those attributes, and your search results will be inundated by them.

Looking for a woman presents an additional difficulty: you can't be sure what surname she will go by. If Grace was still Ms McGoldrick in 2004 it seems reasonable to assume that she would not have changed it. She may have remained single; or have married and kept her maiden name; or she may have married since then, but being generally known as McGoldrick would have held on to it for the sake of convenience.

Still, I looked at those records I could find of marriages. The source I consulted, on a free eight-day trial, was not particularly helpful: it provided summary information only. That meant the names of the groom, the bride, the date and the venue.

As matters stood when I knew her, I would have expected Grace to opt for a white wedding in the local parish church. No such ceremony took place there at any time, according to the files I was consulting.

The only marriage involving a Grace A McGoldrick in the south-east of England in the decades between then and now was in Ealing in 1987. The groom's surname was Smith. That could hardly have been less helpful and therefore more discouraging. Meanwhile other Grace McGoldricks, not insisting on the middle initial, married men of less commonplace names in Didcot (1986), Greater London (1990) and Luton (2000).

So I began to look for Grace McGoldrick in the free scans of the electoral register. A few possibilities arose, although nothing with a matching middle name or initial. One in particular that caught my eye was associated with an address in Bedfordshire and had been since 2004.

Zoopla indicated that the occupant of the flat in Hampstead sold it for just over £250,000 in early 2004, when Grace resigned her directorship. The buyer of a detached house in Beds paid just under £250,000 in the middle of 2004.

The postcodes hint at a contrast and Google Earth confirms it. The building in Hampstead is a distinguished Victorian terraced townhouse with mullioned bay windows and, discernible through them, blinds. At the front, neatly trimmed trees shade the pavement and fully-occupied residents' parking bays conceal it. Hoists indicate urban renewal; 'To Let' signs hint at turnover. Not far away, around the traffic-calmed corner, there's a Czech restaurant, a 24hr florist and a tube station.

The house in Bedfordshire would have been a new-build in 2004. It stands on a modern, gratuitously curved close, characterised by plain architecture, orange bricks, uPVC and an occasional immature tree. No parked cars litter the close; the houses benefit from generous off-street parking. No cables disfigure the roofline. There may be a view of farmland for some of the residents, but most will have a view only of houses exactly like their own. This Grace, the Google camera van reveals, has a burglar alarm.

It may seem unlikely that someone should exchange a distinctly urban, implicitly cosmopolitan way of life for such a bourgeois suburban one. But Grace would have turned 50 in 2004. Perhaps there was silver in her long, blond hair and a new style was indicated. Perhaps the life and energy of the capital began to feel wearing. A flat in a three-storey terrace might give you many neighbours only a few feet away through the walls, floors and ceilings; a new detached house in the sticks would give you peace and fresh air on all sides. I can see plenty to recommend it.

Besides, a more fundamental change might have taken place. The new address is that of a family home. Perhaps Grace had acquired a family by 2004, having married in Luton in 2000.

What else might Bedfordshire have to recommend it? Proximity to the M1, a reasonable commute to London, on the same vector from London as the town in which she grew up (and perhaps where her parents still lived)? Who knows what other possibilities a 50-year-old woman might consider: the WI, book clubs, a local chrysanthemum growers' association...

No other occupant is listed at this house. At one of the electoral roll's other nearby possibilities, however, the various Graces had company.

In Watford, a Grace McGoldrick in the age range 50-54 (which need not exclude mine – it would depend on the date to which the register referred) occupied a house for eight years from 2006, and in the later part of this period shared it with two much younger people of a different surname. Perhaps she took in lodgers. Perhaps she had a daughter who brought her husband to live with them. This too is a modest house on a suburban street of Edwardian terraces. From above and at street level it is apparently a two-up, two-down with a long, thin back garden. The house last changed hands in February 2006 for £166,000. It looks as though this Grace had encountered hard times, or perhaps was downsizing having taken early retirement.

I catch myself wondering at what point such speculations might become intrusive or voyeuristic. Inclined to be indulgent, I conclude that for the moment it is hardly any different from watching people in the street and inventing lives of improbable glamour and excitement for them. Or drudgery, as the case may be.

I am furious of course, but realise that it is typical & am resigned. I wasn't going to write until the weekend, but I couldn't wait that long, so this is the result of my impatience (PARADOX). I have never felt so dispassionate about writing to you before, so this may turn out rather impersonal.

This doesn't look good. Why is she so dispassionate? Had I taken her, ignoring her stated aversion to the genre, to see a war film in St Albans? When we saw Cottonwood, were they playing support to Hawkwind? Having no clear memories of anything we did, I am prey to all sorts of anxiety. Anything might have happened!

Perhaps she will explain. Indeed I will be mightily surprised if she doesn't.

> In which case it will probably be torn up. I have got millions of things to say, But I feel as if I have told them to you already, as I have been collecting since I last wrote which was years ago.

My deduction earlier, to the effect that although deeply in love we hardly ever met, begins to look more persuasive. By this point we had not seen each other since the eve of her departure for France one whole month ago in early August. If she was collecting things to tell me, it sounds as though we didn't set much store by the telephone either.

> Perhaps I should use numbers? It could be shocking, or alternatively it could make everything seem unimportant. Either way you will be cross with me for not saying more about each thing so that should be fun.
> 1. Beth is fine to us.
> 2. I haven't seen Craig yet – he has been staying with Roger in Berkshire.
> 3. Drew is better. He came to my house this afternoon & it was OK. His father had an accident in his mother's car in London & it was a write-off. His father is miraculously alright.
> 4. My mother has a slipped disc so I will be able to write ironing, hoovering & peeling potatoes on my UCCA form amid my other consuming *[illegible]* (if there's room).
> God it's me who can't stand this, not you. Why am I so flat? I think I will give this up and read 'The Idiot' instead.

Yes, I remember reading *The Idiot* at about that time and at her bidding. I don't remember earnestly discussing it with her, but I know I enjoyed it. She was an improving influence on me, I don't think there can be any doubt of that. On the other hand, when I showed her a sample of the whimsy in which I specialised at that time, she said: "It's funny, but you can do better than that." To the extent that I have remained "profoundly unpublished", in the words of Iain Banks, I have not done so.

Back to Grace. I should add that her handwriting was becoming very much smaller. If I measure it with my depth scale (a gauge used in newspaper offices in the days before the Apple Macintosh) it is roughly 10 on 11pt, which would be clear enough on a printed page – the text on this page is $10^{1}/_{2}$pt – but in handwriting is tiny and cramped. It isn't always easy to read. Instances of the [illegible] above may become more common.

My own handwriting was, like so much else about me at the time, affected and embarrassing. It survives in the pages of a sturdily bound A4 exercise book identified by a label on the front as belonging to me at the University of Sheffield Department of Geography. The capitals are particularly flowery, although occasionally the writer forgets himself and something more natural and almost elegant emerges. The lower case letters are slightly flattened but otherwise undistinguished. The contents of this book are moderately competent maps (produced with £30's worth of drawing equipment) and associated verbal explanations. Alongside them, the Geography Department's senior staff has written 'S' for Satisfactory, ominously 'S-' and eventually 'U'. If there was a mark above 'S', I never achieved it.

Saturday night
I have just read your letter and felt like writing. I want to write all the time but am only capable in flashes of about $^{1}/_{2}$hr each, & saying anything remotely understandable. I can't decide how to write this. Shall I say what I have done today? Or shall I say just anything?

It will have to be today. Today I went to Crystal Palace and saw (in this order) Capability Brown, Wright's Wonderwheel, Mahavishnu

Orchestra, Lindisfarne & Yes. I took this paper so I could write about it to you while I was listening, or in between. But as it happened I didn't. 1. Because we were so close together it wouldn't have been a private letter, more like a proclamation. 2. I talked to this French au-pair girl. 3. I talked to a girl from school. 4. When I wasn't talking (and all the time during Yes) I was imagining that you were there too. By Yes, I was really believing that and it made it superb. So I enjoyed it loads and have come home wondering whether the music was good or not, which is a bit worrying.

I can't speak for the extensive supporting cast but I'm sure her instinctive response to Yes was reliable. On the morning *The Yes Album* came out, in February 1971, I was in a record shop on Watford High Street to buy it, and on a whim I asked the man behind the counter to put it on for a moment. He played it to the shop at large, rather than for me in a booth. Everybody stopped what they were doing and listened to *Yours is no Disgrace*. I took their attention to mean they had never heard anything like it before.

It's strange, now, to reflect that there were specific days on which things happened – everything seems to happen indiscriminately, all the time, now. New albums always came out on a Friday, for example. The programme at the cinema always changed on the same day – Wednesday? I can't remember. The new week's Top 20 was revealed at tea-time on Sunday. Does any of this still happen? Perhaps it does, but I doubt anyone sets their clock by it. As for 'tea-time', I apologise for using such a dated term; it's simply that I can't remember whether it was 5pm or 6pm.

I saw Yes twice in that era and they were not everyone's cup of tea. Some of the best bands of that period became pompous and overblown (others were to begin with) but for a short time they produced outstanding music and put on great shows. Talking of pompous, I suspect that when I say I saw Yes twice in that 'era', I mean in fact 'year'.

Exciting things happened on my journey both ways. Going, I met Maureen Richards (did you know of Ross?)...

No, inevitably, nor of Maureen for that matter.

... and we talked about James Bond 'cos she is going to be one of those sexy girls in the next film, among other things. (My English mistress would have a fit.)

Was she talking about *Live and Let Die*, which was released in summer 1973? There is no Maureen Richards in the cast, although several lesser names are identified in such roles as Beautiful Girl, Sales Girl, Tribal Dancer etc. There is also (not an obvious glamour girl's role but too precious to overlook) Fillet of Sole Waiter. Perhaps Maureen found a career more to her English mistress's taste, although I suppose it's always possible that she had a stage name.

On the way home I met (& got picked up by) Maureen (driving), Tony and Boz. They were coming to my house (it was around 10.30!) and so I asked them in, like the martyr I so consistently show myself to be. But Tony felt ill, & after a graphic description (lasting about $\frac{1}{2}$hr) of his feeling, they left. Then, with great restraint, I had a bath and washed up the coffee things & went to bed before reading your letter.

It made it even better though. It has been one of the better days since you left, but only 'cos you have been with me more tangibly & less painfully therefore than usual.

When I was on holiday I had a very weird dream about you, and it was set at school too. But the school (mine) was being bombed in the war. I was forced to drive a skewer through my own neck until it could be seen the other side. When I had done that I was told that I was supposed not to be dead, that I would have to do it again and die later. The strange thing was that I couldn't decide whether I was dead then or not. I kept on asking myself 'Am I dead?' I can't remember what you did but you were the only other person I knew there. It was a very violent dream.

Like so much of what she wrote, I doubt I took this up with her. I didn't exactly skim her letters but I tended to be in a hurry to get to the next section in which I might find soothing words about her feelings for me.

Besides, although it was indeed a very disturbing dream it was hardly a dream about me, as billed, was it? I should have shown more interest. People who tell you their dreams generally want something from you. Attention, obviously, but some kind of response beyond merely taking notice. Sharing, perhaps, in the modern argot.

It occurs to me that I never dreamt about Grace, before, during or since. Nor, in the way that dreams have of introducing familiar characters in disguise, did she infiltrate a dream behind a mask. This seems to contradict the idea that dreaming is the mind's way of absorbing and processing the more mystifying events of the day – Grace provided plenty of them but never turned up after lights out to explain herself. On the contrary, it might support the contention that life is nothing but a dream.

Last night we went to 'Hamlet' in Southwark. My mother couldn't go, of course – and it was supposed to be for her birthday too. But Beth came instead. It was very interesting & good in places. Beth liked Keith Michel as Hamlet (Henry VIII) but he had a beard so I was prejudiced from the start, of course, and never fully recovered to enable myself to get the most out of the performance.

Look if you want to know about all these things (like Yes, 'Hamlet' etc) I'll tell you later, OK? I can't tell you now because immediately I start trying to describe them I either change my mind about what I think/thought or else begin to dislike them.

Monday
My writing has decreased in size very recently. I noticed it
particularly when signing Terence Doyle's leaving card. It is now
getting bigger again.

The line from *White Rabbit* comes to mind. I like the idea of Mrs
McGoldrick giving Grace pills that don't do anything at all.

As for Terence Doyle, he was a curate at one of the Anglican
churches in the town – I know this through the good offices of
Google, naturally, not because I knew him. If a name comes and
goes without explanation or comment, as with Boz a few paragraphs earlier, you may take it to be that of a character who is
unlikely to appear again.

When I was about 15 or 16 I got complaints at school & one
mistress refused to mark my exam paper as well as another one
who lowered my grade. So you see it is a big difficulty. When it is
small it is so small you can't read it & when it is big (like this or
larger) the letters are so badly formed that you can't read it either.
I hope you understand. Anyway, I don't expect marks from you.
I just thought I'd better explain it all to you so that you realise
the trials I have had with it. Yours is very easy to read and to tell
when you are getting emotional also. But apart from that it is very
hidden, like you.

This I should definitely have given more thought to. As explanations go, it is opaque.

She talks about her handwriting as if it were a handicap imposed
on her by a wilful third party. If she notices the coincidence – that
at 15 or 16 there were O-Levels on the horizon, and now she faces
A-Levels – she chooses not to say so.

Schoolwork aside, she was the most prolific writer of letters I
have encountered before or since. The school essays she refers to
could only have been hand-written. Today schoolchildren neither

write nor type essays but cut and paste them in another pleasing example of the labour-saving contribution of technology to all our lives.

As for my being 'hidden', I can't deny that I was a guarded youth. I was keen, naturally, to prevent Grace seeing me for what I truly was – a clueless, inexperienced and excitable adolescent barely out of short trousers. To that end I practised a careful form of restraint which she charitably interpreted as unfeigned.

That was a risky strategy. The most damaging criticism you could apply in those days to a person or to an artistic endeavour was that it or they were 'pretentious'. For example, fans of The Who (and of Pete Townshend in particular) often wore boiler-suits, and they were dismissed as pretentious on the grounds that they had never been near a boiler in their lives. Authenticity was prized. My attempt to disguise my true nature might have been seen as pretention as a way of life.

At the time I felt there was little alternative. My dilemma had a regional component. I had lived in the south of England for only three years at the time I am recalling – the rest of my life had been spent in the north-west. There, if I was gauche, people had known me all my life and would make allowances; in Watford they would make fun. I changed the way in which I expressed myself, from my accent to my demeanour. At some point this personal development became a natural process but in the beginning it was wholly artificial.

Because Grace was neither clueless nor unduly excitable, I regarded her as more experienced. In truth I had no foundation for this belief. We did not exchange personal histories. In my case that was to conceal the fact that there was none, and uncovering hers would have left me insecure about meeting some previously established standard. Perhaps she felt the same. In any case, by acknowledging no history we gave ourselves a clean sheet to start from, an unblemished page on which to write our story. We were the first lovers in history and the world itself was young.

At the age of 18 I had nothing that might have been called 'baggage'. It is, in any case, an inappropriate and ill-favoured expression. If anything, baggage should be something to be proud of. Touch my baggage, that is life. Thanks to the era of budget airlines and 40lb limits baggage has acquired a bad name, as though it would be advantageous to be rid of it. Before the Pearly Gates perhaps there is a pre-paradisal antechamber encircled by a carousel, clanking around for eternity, on to which the souls of the blessed can ease their burdens by finally getting rid of all their baggage. Those destined for hotter climates must carry the load a little longer, on trolleys with unstable wheels.

But baggage in this sense is simply the contribution of loved ones past and present. It would be a betrayal of them to diminish or distort their memory; such episodes represent the rings of the tree, the branches beneath which we shelter, the confidence on which we draw. The fact that Grace McGoldrick once loved me should be regarded not so much as baggage, more as a proud boast and an enduring source of comfort.

I am now in Pat's, having just been to Beth's for a long time. It is about 3.10 and I have to go home to do some hoovering for my mother. She has been absolutely amazing about loads of things that have happened recently, which I never expected her to be & the best thing she has done to date is letting me ask you to stay. Will you come this weekend? If you can't I am furious but I can't blame you. You had just better come, that's all...

You could have come as easily as anything before, I think, but you see as she has this slipped disc it means that everything is in a mess & she is miserable. Anyway as I say she is being unbelievably nice about it all, & I have told her that you won't mind the chaos. I hope that is OK?

I tend to be dismissive of Mrs McGoldrick – how typical, I found myself thinking a moment ago, that Cinders is having to do the

Hoovering every five minutes.

Aside from being a slave-driver Mrs McGoldrick may have been something of a snob. In one of our first conversations the subject of my mother's car came up. "What does she drive," Mrs McGoldrick enquired, perhaps in an innocent spirit of enquiry. "A clapped-out Mini," I replied modestly on my mother's behalf. Mrs McGoldrick heard 'Clubman' for 'clapped-out'. Even allowing for my vestigial northern vowels, only an extremely posh person mistakes an 'a' for a 'u'.

But a guilty thought sends a quick shiver up my spine. I spent any number of nights under her roof, and I can't remember ever buying her flowers or offering a gift in return for her hospitality. She was a strait-laced, difficult woman, but she deserved that much at least.

What she made of me is easy to guess. Apart from being egregiously ungrateful, I was a friend of the infamous Craig Lofthouse, corrupter of minors, and I owned a motorcycle. I'm not sure I had any redeeming features from her point of view. Even my harmless Nana Mouskouri haircut was beginning to grow suspiciously long. I was indifferent boyfriend material.

It might have been better had I started going out with her daughter just two weeks later, having first applied myself seriously to the business of playing cricket at county level (albeit under 19s). I don't think it would have made an ounce of difference to my cricket career. But from Mrs McGoldrick's point of view I would have been a member of a kind of county set. On the other hand, putting aside our importunate desires for two weeks would have meant Grace setting off on holiday with no thought of me in her mind.

Having shaken off one unwanted admirer I seem to be saddled with another. He won't say his name but signs himself 'Potato & Radish Salad'.

I believe this to be an acknowledgement of a parody of a short anonymous letter I sent her, with the letters and words clipped from various sources. Tinned potato and radish salad sounds like the sort of label that would have come out of my mother's larder. Those were the pre-*Protect and Survive* days that post-1990 generations must regard as comical. But Mutually Assured Destruction was a constant if low-level background threat in the early Seventies, and few householders expected the official government advice (coat your windows with a solution of milk and eggs) to impede the first strike. My mother, however, laid in a store of tinned goods in case we survived the initial exchanges. Not likely, with Aldermaston just down the road... and the aptly-named Wargrave, where there was supposed to be a bunker complex for a regional seat of government, close by in the other direction.

> You can't say I have any secrets from you, anyway. (I have just taken up cricket too.) I think Drew thinks I don't understand how brilliant you are, but of course I do. I knew it all along and am enjoying being right. I don't expect you to believe me, naturally.
> I hope you had a good holiday a little bit, but what you said about things to come is interesting my hopes more at the moment (I am not expressing myself properly I realise but...)
> In the same way as your unconventional letter openings have dried up, so have my endings. But you know what I would say anyway, don't you,
> Grace
> I am sorry the paper is so curly – it is 'cos I have been carrying it about for such a long time.

I imagine I took nothing but comfort from that letter. We looked happily into the future together. We were both brilliant. We knew what we would say at the end of a letter, and it wasn't 'Yours sincerely'. She wanted to write to me all the time but when she actually sat down to do it, found she couldn't say what she wanted to. From that I deduced that she could not yet overcome her native caution, but I felt certain that emotion would eventually carry her over the line. I'm sure I would have expressed it in just such hackneyed terms. No troubling signs clouded my horizon.

It also appears that I'd been writing more than I give myself credit for; or, at least, I'd been composing amusing opening sentences. I imagine, having taken the plunge, I simply repeated my pledges of undying love in various guises. I think I wrote from Thonon. I wonder if I attempted any kindling from the Dent d'Oche? We were taken up a mountain to spend an evening in a cabin complex, eating fondue and draping cheese over our faces. We slept in a communal dormitory and, rising early to dramatise my solitude, I watched the sun come up over the mountains. Successive horizons were revealed, lines of mountains like theatre flats, as the sun slowly rose into the sky. "The sultan's turret in a noose of light."

In looking for my depth scale – it hasn't been the kind of equipment even a professional sub-editor would keep handy, in case of urgent need, since the mid-Eighties – I uncovered my photograph of Grace.

Very few people our age had a camera in the early 1970s. Writers of science-fiction in those days may have anticipated mass camera-ownership, but I suspect even they would have dismissed as absurd the idea of cameras capable of making phone calls. Craig, a perpetual early-adopter, took up photography at a young age and I suspect I owe this singular photograph to him.

A 6½ by 4¾-inch monochrome print, it shows a group of teenagers on the grassy verge of a road significant enough to warrant a freeway sign with 'End' beneath it. It may be a sponsored walk: most of the young people are on their feet, though not actually walking, but in the distance another small party is disappearing up the road. A brutally clipped hedge to the right promises thorns under foot, and the trees are bare. An inexplicably long, thin shadow suggests either that it is early in the morning, late in the day or that someone hidden from view is carrying a bishop's mitre. The season is spring or late autumn but nobody is feeling the chill. Nobody seems to be wearing so much as a woollen jumper, although Grace is about to tie one round her waist.

It is clearly a picture of Grace, since she dominates (albeit reluctantly) the foreground, but a dozen or so other people are visible and three are recognisable. Indeed Grace is not in good focus; she is moving, turning to her left, her long blond hair flicking out, her eyes half-closed either in contemplation of Ian Anderson's vocals or because she would prefer not to be photographed. Her face is 20° into the turn, giving neither a full face nor a profile. It is similar to the attitude of the Mona Lisa, although Grace's glance is in the other direction and the Mona Lisa's eyes are fully focused on the artist.

With that paragon of female beauty in my mind, I call up an image on-screen and set it alongside the now digitised photograph of Grace. There are certainly points of resemblance: both have full cheeks, a high, broad forehead, long, straight hair, a hesitant but slightly mocking smile. A decade ago, analysis of the Mona Lisa by the University of Amsterdam's computer experts concluded she was 83% happy, 9% disgusted, 6% fearful and 2% angry; Grace looks happy and forbearing in equal parts, as though there were a fool on the other side of the lens but she is prepared more or less gladly to suffer him.

Neither face is marked by time, but there isn't much insight in that observation; time has not yet had much opportunity to leave its imprint on either. There may be intimations of privilege or good fortune. Leonardo's model – Lisa Gherardini? – would have been of good family. He is known to have spent a long time over the painting and would hardly have done so for an impoverished peasant girl dolled-up for the occasion. But she may still have been considered fortunate to have attained adulthood without the disfiguring scars of smallpox or syphilis. Perhaps that is why her smile has a hint of smugness.

Grace is not smug, which is a mighty relief. The risk is there: she lives in a substantial house on the leafy slopes of a Home Counties commuter town; she attends a fee-paying school; financial considerations seem not to inhibit her social life. With those advantages, smugness would have made her insufferable.

It would be an outstanding photograph that revealed all this of its subject, but I am able to draw on other sources – primarily, my own observations. In truth the photograph reveals very little of her, which makes it a suitably accurate representation. She was a private young woman.

One of the great and gratifying surprises of first love is the revelation it gives you of another consciousness, a view nobody else has of another person. Just as a hardback book's dust-cover protects the contents and projects an idealised image of them to the reading public, everyone constructs a face to present to the world. A trustworthy lover is awarded the inestimable privilege of seeing the true face.

And in the process, a comforting possibility emerges from the psychic antechambers of childhood, screwing up its eyes against the light. Up to a certain age, a small child believes the world revolves around him. When he realises his mistake the consequences are severe; his sense of self swings to the opposite extreme and he regards himself as cast adrift and alone. "Nobody understands me," is how he will typically express his unease. In love, he will find that the world can be compartmentalised and that the compartment he now inhabits is not necessarily heliocentric.

Privileged access to another individual's self is obviously first cousin to sex. Sex is a symbolic celebration of the lifting of the veil, of the readiness to expose body and soul to another human being; at the same time it brings two people as close as they will ever be, physically, to that privileged other. For a while, two become one or, quite possibly, in the forgetfulness of the moment, none.

There may be a price to be paid for failing to complete that equation. If lovers leave the sexual world imperfectly explored, can trust and faith be complete? And this privileged access to Grace's innermost thoughts that I am making so much of, could I have been reciprocating if she regarded me as 'hidden'? But the digression has lasted long enough. Back to the photograph.

No, she was not smug. Rather, Grace looks self-conscious. Caught off-guard, she has had time to do no more than reconcile herself to the idea of being photographed, with an indulgent dismissal of Craig's tiresome attentions forming in her mind. Given more time to respond, she would have found a mocking word for him. And possibly for me, for still possessing this image of her. Forty years on the photograph would have been posted on Facebook, where it would have been lost among billions of others.

To my mild alarm I realise I recognise her clothes. I could tell you what colour her jeans are, and of what material. The photograph, I need hardly repeat, is from the black and white era.

She is pictured from the waist up; below the waist she would almost certainly have been standing with her legs crossed at the ankles, the left foot sliding behind the right – it was a characteristic pose.

Slender, tall, with an enigmatic half-smile as if she were reflecting on something beyond the notice of mortals, she is very pretty. When the romance finished my mother tried to comfort me: "Well, she wasn't exactly Amazing Grace, was she?" This was (a) not what I wanted to hear and (b) not remotely true. Grace was extraordinary and beautiful, in my eyes and no less so when I try to imagine her through anyone else's. Perhaps her cheeks were a little too full, her nose a fraction long, her hair lank when unwashed, her John Lennon glasses something of a pose... But I am deliberately trying to find fault. None of the above is fair.

Because Grace is the fulcrum of the picture, the three other people looking at the camera appear to be looking at her, almost paying homage. Most prominently, and in slightly sharper focus than our heroine, is a brunette with an expressive face and a quip interrupted by the shutter. I don't know her. Perhaps it is Maureen, risking the fresh air and discovered for once without the equally sickly Tony. To Grace's left and a little further back is the face of Drew Redmond as he would have looked five years earlier. Drew was the youngest of our group but he wasn't that young. In this picture he appears to be wearing short trousers; they could be shorts, I suppose, it being a sunny day. More likely, it is someone else entirely – it looks, now that I examine the photograph closely, like a 12-year-old Peter Noone of Herman's Hermits.

Most of the rest of the people are either looking away or otherwise engaged, but at the left-hand margin of the picture, kneeling and therefore looking up at the camera from beneath a darkly suggestive fringe, is none other than Alison Roberts. She, I believe, is looking at the photographer, rather than at Grace or at the camera. Perhaps Mark Hopkins took the picture.

One final anomaly persuades me after all that Craig was the photographer. Further away from the camera, perhaps 20 feet down the road, is another recognisable face. It belongs to Evie Durham, who three years later was Craig's girlfriend. He didn't know her then but inadvertently took her photograph anyway.

I've tried to reconstruct in my head what I knew of Grace before the realisation dawned that we were meant to be together.

Craig came first: I had become friendly with him through Nigel Bradford, and Craig and I took to riding out to a pub along the A5 and playing bar-billiards.

He introduced me to the circle that comprised Grace, Beth and Drew. (Yes, 'circle' is something of an exaggeration; 'pentagram' might be more accurate, if slightly sinister.) We would meet in varying numbers, usually at Beth's house (it being the most central and having the most extensive record collection), and listen to music and drink coffee in her front room.

What we listened to depended mainly on Craig and on Beth Deardon's elder brother, Jeremy, whose LP collection was vast. Craig operated a disco called Ars Longa and was therefore professionally committed to listening to a lot of music. This might have meant that we had to listen to some very indifferent stuff but democracy prevailed in our little group, and everyone made a choice. I associate Nick Drake and Jonathan Kelly with Grace.

A couple of days ago I was in my sister's kitchen enjoying a Sunday roast dinner. In the background something distantly familiar was playing. I said: "Is that Nick Drake? I think I recognise the voice, but not the song."

My brother-in-law said: "Yes, being shuffled by Spotify."

I said: "I knew *Bryter Layter* well but it was a painful time in my life – I never felt strong enough to explore the rest of the oeuvre."

He said: "You should. You should listen to *Pink Moon* especially."

I demurred. "I'm not sure. It was a difficult time for me."

My brother-in-law paused and then replied: "It wasn't the best for him."

What did we talk about in Beth Deardon's living room? I imagine Craig and I tried to amuse the young women but succeeded mainly in amusing each other. Besides, we may have been more exotic to them than we realised, without needing to try so hard. I was on the verge of university while they were both a year of sixth form away; and Craig was on the threshold of a working life that began, I think, as a salesman with a company that sold forecourt equipment to filling stations – not glamorous, but impressively independent in the light of the family business he could more easily have moved into.

I don't remember feeling anything for Grace one way or another at that time. She was, after all, the object of my friend's interest, and I listened sympathetically to his laments on the unlikelihood of Grace McGoldrick returning his love. In one of her letters she recalls a party at my house and a coffee table. I remember that too: the open fire was dwindling and I amputated the coffee table's legs to keep the fire going. Apparently people do that sort of thing at AirBnB rental properties now – then, we foraged for our own coffee tables, careless of the prices G-Plan furniture would command 40 years hence. My parents must have been away. But I don't remember Grace being there, which is as good as admitting that I hardly noticed her. Our love lacked both prelude and postscript.

LETTER 6

In trying to piece together the details of my life in the early autumn of 1972 I have consulted almanacs and found that historical forces were in play. The Munich Olympic Games degenerated into violence and tragedy at the beginning of September 1972. Palestinian terrorists (the word used then was 'guerrillas') took hostage 11 members of the Israeli Olympic team. None of the Israelis survived, and five of the eight hostage-takers died in a shoot-out with West German security forces.

That was an early episode in what has broadened out to become an Orwellian conflict: one part of the world constantly at war with another, and with no indication of how it might ever end.

One significant feature of the Munich debacle was the fact that it unfolded on television. At one point, the guerrillas watched on TV as the West German police prepared to storm their bolt-hole. There had been hijackings and hostage-taking before, but with the role of television and hence of publicity, Munich might be regarded as a turning point in modern history.

My own reaction must have been widely shared and it does none of us any credit. An armchair Olympian, I would certainly have followed the drama. But the Games, after a pause, went on, and I similarly returned to my own preoccupations.

Did I spend my first weekend with the McGoldricks? The next letter, dated 13 September, begins with another short prologue squeezed into the top left-hand corner of the first of two pages. Her letters were becoming shorter but she was certainly shoe-horning more words in per page.

This is called the 'nth' letter, only the final sentence of which is really relevant and even that is unoriginal.

Dear Steve,
I was interested to witness your leaving yesterday. What dignity.

Betty once told me how a man had both legs amputated failing
to catch a train at our station. But of course your success is just
one minor drop in an ocean of qualifications enabling you to be a
student. (You can tell I have other things on my mind now.)

It sounds as though I'd been trying to be cool and failing. Even at
that age I should have realised that if you have to try, you aren't. She
was making fun of me again. Well, it's no bad thing to be able to
amuse people. As for Betty, I wonder if this could have been a pet
name for Beth? It has a domestic sound.

I also wonder why I was catching a train. Had I parked the Tiger
Cub at the next station down the line to avoid disturbing the neighbours and thus to curry favour with Mrs McGoldrick? When I rode
over to see Grace I certainly used to wheel it around the corner
from their house before I started it up on leaving.

Thank you for coming to stay was how I really wanted to begin,
but on reflection I thought it sounded a bit unusual and so I said
the first thought that came into my head when you went, which I
couldn't then tell you, instead.
    This is an ideal place to talk of nothing or the spirit, because
you can't possibly want to know what I have done since you left,
and as it is nothing I couldn't tell you anyway. (Chaucer has
obviously gone to my head.)

Is that Chaucer – 'nothing or the spirit'? The friend I might have
asked is dead. So much time has passed. Since Chaucer's time hardly the blink of an eye, of course.

'Hamlet' with Ian McKellan is going to be on television on Sept
23, so I read in 'The Times' today. *[An indication of stardust
sprinkling around The Times, in capitals.]*
    God I am giving up you know. I can't think what to say to you.

This rapid descent into despair at finding nothing to say is becoming a regular theme. When we were together, how on earth did we pass the time? Kissing and holding hands, of course, but not all the time, surely; perhaps I held up my end of a conversation better than she could unaided.

> If you were here it would be a trivial conversation easily forgotten.

Exactly. From unique conversationalist to master of small talk in just six weeks.

> It makes me feel as if I am nothing, this complete blank. I feel characterless with a hackneyed mind filled with useless rubbish. All that I am thinking someone else could be thinking, and not even several people thinking a different one of my thoughts, for it could even be one person exactly identical to me.

What to make of that? She implies that her grip on her sense of identity is slipping. There's no indication of what has brought it on. Introduced (as not infrequently) by the disclosure that she is struggling for something to say, she shifts down an octave and reveals a much more sombre humour. After my disingenuous attempt to generate a mood in the alleged manner of Persian poets, perhaps she is setting a scene. I can't believe this is Chaucerian, though. She might have found French more congenial than English. Sartre: "My memories are like the coins in the Devil's purse; when it was opened, nothing was found in it but dead leaves."

> If you happened to find that other person, it would be no good, would it? Does that worry you?

No, it wouldn't be good. But also no, it didn't worry me. Unable to understand what she was talking about, I chose to pass over it and hoped that she would too. It's possible that the weekend had been a disaster but this is a very circuitous way of saying so.

> I am being completely honest, you understand, and you disbelieve
> me at your own risk. Perhaps it is just momentary because of
> school & lack of sleep & everything else which decays people
> mentally (if I'm not careful I really will begin to talk about the
> spirit and I assure you that that was not my intention).

I expect I did not so much disbelieve as blithely ignore what she
was saying. There was always so much in her letters – I couldn't be
expected to take it all in. In those days, I was unaware of the black
dog's secret life, much less capable of recognising it.

> Tuesday: It's OK I have got over that mood now, you will be glad
> to know. It is 5th lesson and I am in the commonroom (as it is a
> free). Everyone near me is talking and working at once & about
> 6 people are smoking noisily & wickedly which is no longer as
> embarrassing as it used to be.
>   Apparently Pete Seward is going to go to Barnet College after
> all, cos he has had a job as you know & is realising how much
> nicer work is at school (no comment). He was the one who went
> out with Carrie, not Drew, so you are learning a lot from me today.

As it happens, no, and I doubt I did then. Who was Pete Seward?
Or Carrie? And I'm uncertain of the transcription of Barnet Col-
lege but that's what it looks like and I can think of no association to
confirm or correct it.

It's possible that I once knew all these people quite well and
have simply forgotten them. You reach an age where each new fact,
in order to be retained, pushes out an old one – like making room
in a bookcase for a new purchase. That would account too for why I
remember some clearly and others not at all. But the truth is almost
certainly that Grace assumed I knew them and I, reluctant to reveal
the narrow confines of my social life, neglected to put her right.

The idea of people smoking noisily is intriguing. She may simply have meant that, being young and inexperienced smokers, they were coughing and spluttering with each life-giving drag; but the possibility that they sucked and blew and generally tried to draw attention to their wickedness appeals to me more.

> I haven't written this for a long time (about 20 mins) because people keep on talking to me. You see I am in demand even at school. This letter is mainly so you know I am thinking of you. Because I am except for when I get distracted like now and even now you are in the back of my mind while I am talking (Tina Black got her O Levels). Apparently Tir-na-nog was good. I won't send this… well, perhaps I will otherwise you will never know that I wanted to write even though it didn't quite work out.
>
> Wednesday: But you do know because you phoned last night and I told you then. Afterwards I spoke to Beth about you coming which was not very satisfactory. I also read about Mr Wilson, and the reply from Uganda today returns his compliment along with a fittingly juvenile piece of added abuse. I will send you this so you will know that I love you which I can't say especially on the phone. Grace.

It's possible she affirmed her love because she grew tired of not doing. It became impossible to find any more ways of filling sheets of paper. Naturally, as instructed by the prologue, I paid complete attention only to the last sentence and was deliriously happy.

The Cat has devised a new game. An encouraging development at the best of times, this is inexplicably kittenish in an animal in her 21st year.

When I'm getting dressed I sit on the end of the bed to put on my socks and shoes. It's an elderly man's concession to his lower back, a point of occasional weakness. The Cat sits on the floor alongside my left foot. When the socks are safely on, she moves into a crouch. I pick up the left shoe. She begins to quiver. As soon as a lace moves in front of her face she pounces. At this point, I can either insist on putting the shoe on or I can play along for a while. Being self-employed I have no need to worry about punctuality and have time to play along. I dangle the lace in front of her, or over her ears. I draw it slowly across the carpet. Holding the shoe above her, I whirl the laces around in front of her face. She demonstrates that she is ambidextrous: with the laces moving anti-clockwise she deploys her right paw; clockwise, the left; so that the laces and the claws are converging, and she is not obliged to chase the lace.

Her excitement is a treat to behold but her concentration is unreliable. She is prone to lapse into a different game that has been a popular favourite down the years – this happens if the hand holding the shoe moves across the light source in such a way that the shadow distracts her. She has always loved to chase a shadow, especially one created by waggling fingers. She flattens herself to the carpet and lashes out with a paw from time to time. The shoe-lace is forgotten. But tomorrow she will be in position, as she has been for the past week. The Cat's memory is a thing of mystery to me.

This morning she could not disengage her dew claw from the shoelace and began to fret. Unable to flee with a gentleman's shoe, size 8, attached loosely to her paw, she began to shift visibly from agitation towards panic. It's an odd thing, isn't it, for an elderly cat not to understand the mechanics of claws? I was able to free her by unhooking the lace, suffering only minor lacerations. She stalked off and performed a little furious grooming in the doorway.

It may be too late to try to recreate this and film it for YouTube. Cats doing cute things on the Internet – it's heart-warming, isn't it, the valuable uses to which advanced technology is put?

If the Cat's first language were English, what would I say to her? I tried this on the landing just now, after screwing up some paper, batting it to and fro and failing to lure her into taking part. We crouched there, I on my hands and knees, she on her feathery haunches. I said to her: "Mrs Cat, if there were to be just a few minutes in which you understood English, I'd want you to know how my life has been enriched through your being in it, and how privileged I am that you have made me your life's companion." At this point she moved away to lollop down the stairs, pausing at the fifth from the top. Here she sat again, but not to encourage me to continue. No, her attention was on a beige cat called Charlie, visible through the banister posts and the window and the length of the garden, in gathering gloom. "I've always loved you, you old beggar," I finished, carefully stepping around her to resume normal life.

LETTER 7

There's a gap of three weeks before the next letter. Its envelope bears my third address in three months, a temporary residence while the student accommodation service at Sheffield sorted itself out – I spent a week in digs, as though being fostered, while a more permanent arrangement could be made.

I must have gone north at the beginning of October. Two September weeks devoid of letters suggest that we spent some time with each other. Grace came with me to Reading at some point but that might as easily have been in the Christmas holidays. In other words, as so often in this account, I can't be sure.

I do remember the poached eggs I tried to make for her when we arrived, too late in the evening for me to call on my mother's help. I got the eggs into the poacher and set that off well enough but I didn't realise that the lid was necessary for successful poaching. So our eggs remained uncooked, as far as you could tell by looking at them from above, for 20 or 30 minutes. When I finally scraped them out of the containers they had developed an oddly green-tinged mother-of-pearl base.

Dated 5 October, the letter is written in a bold right-hand slant on lined paper, in marked contrast to the tiny, hesitant scrawl on the envelope. It begins:

I have to write like this 'cos I am now (apparently) holding my pen properly. My character remains amazingly unchanged.

Dear Steve,

I have just come back from babysitting and have decided to begin a new letter to you. I don't know why I am writing for I have nothing to tell you. Whenever I think of you, and want to write to you – which is often – all I can think of is you and not what I should write. Do you see? I don't want to concentrate on irrelevant things to tell you, I just want to grab hold of you. The best way to feel you nearby used to be letters – it worked quite a lot in France, but now seems different. Now you are with me in a less unreal way than you were then, I feel more sure of you in some ways (& less in others of course) but it means that you feel more a part of me, to such a large extent that telling you things outside ourselves seems pointless. I think that some of the time, which is when it is worthless writing, & when I am more detached and in need of you I can tell you more.

I hope I was some use in helping her keep this sort of anxiety in proportion. I like to think that despite the number of letters that passed between us, our most successful communication was, simply, a form of communing. Words were unnecessary. But I doubt I reassured her because the theme – a hopelessness consequent on finding nothing worth saying – recurs.

Besides, my move to Sheffield made no practical difference to the dominant feature of my life in those days. When I wasn't with Grace I was simply passing the time, and nothing that happened was at all interesting in comparison. Any reassurance I might have offered would have lacked conviction.

I saw Beth & Craig yesterday (you know) & Mark Hopkins & Beth today. Maureen & Tony came round – she had scived off school & they had been to St Albans where they went to the Record Room & saw Jeremy & heard Pete Townsend which Tony wants to buy. Tony is going to live with a relation in Southampton until he can get digs or a flat. Lucky guy, I thought, and then of you.

Mark Hopkins, who turns up quite often, is always referred to by both his forename and surname. It's as though he were a character out of Jane Austen: Mr Frank Churchill, perhaps. Newspapers and magazines have protocols governing such common occurrences: often, people are identified by their full name the first time they are mentioned in a piece and by a title and surname thereafter.

So when every other newspaper in the country was full of stories about firebrand student activist Danny the Red in the late 1960s, the *Times* wrote calmly about the activities of Herr Cohn-Bendit. I believe it was also the *Times* that once published an article about Meat Loaf and called him, second time around, Mr Loaf.

> Maureen gave me a lift down to Beth's where we discussed Craig
> & I told her you phoned me. I didn't want to tell her but... I was
> v glad you phoned. Before when I said don't I hadn't realised
> what it would be like that evening – my imagination then became
> too vivid because I could see you very clearly at Reading. (It was
> helped greatly by having stayed there of course.)

We did go to Reading, then. It is troubling to have so few clear recollections of what may have been her only introduction to my home – but then, it was no longer my home by that time.

Apart from the fiasco of the eggs, she was also treated to a glimpse of my father in his vest and underpants, hurrying across the landing between bathroom and bedroom. Perhaps, if that is the quality of my memories, it's no bad thing they have faded.

I try to reconstruct mechanical aspects of the visit to see whether memory can be nudged. For example: how did we get to Reading? I was not by that time qualified to drive a car, so the answer can only be by train or motorcycle. Either would surely be an exciting escape from the prosaic staging within which our love had been contained, you would think. I tend to agree, but that doesn't mean I can see it any more clearly, if at all.

Let's hope, though, that if it was the train we made an excursion of it and enjoyed a day in London. Perhaps we even bumped into Maureen and Tony, or Eileen and Russell, or Mark Hopkins (but not Alison, who I can't help but notice is seldom mentioned).

And if it was the motorcycle, please let it be that I took her by a particular road. In those distant, pre-M25 days, the most direct route would have involved country lanes as well as A roads. I became particularly attached to one somewhere in the vicinity of the Chalfonts. The lane was minding its own business, proceeding between hedges and sunlit fields, when quite abruptly it ascended a gentle hill and plunged into a deep wood from which almost all sunlight was excluded. In my mind's eye I can see a copper-coloured carpet of pine straw, slender trunks with few low branches, a vaulted canopy, a sepulchral light and no sound at all.

The reliability of this vision is called into question by the idea of my Triumph's four-stroke engine making no sound at all as we negotiated the wood. No, I was never there with Grace.

So the most likely answer is: train to St Pancras, Circle Line to Paddington and then another train and a bus. I wonder what sort of a day we had. I can't even remember how Grace felt about public displays of affection. It doesn't seem likely to have provoked any.

I switch off when people begin to talk about unreality because it always seems so futile. Steve you would be frightened if you understood how unreal my journey home was. Everything about it was so hard or else very blurry, it was like doing the right thing the wrong way, or else the wrong thing and thinking it was right while wondering why people thought it was wrong and not understanding. I wanted to make everyone being in the train important, because me being there was revoltingly so, but instead to them it was totally natural & unimportant. They acted normally while nothing, to me, was normal; therefore they were the mad ones, not me. But really of course, it was me.

Sarah-Jane (not abbreviated) woke up and coughed tonight. She wouldn't stop it or have any milk. Apart from that I don't remember you being out of my mind for longer than 5 minutes together. What a maternal instinct. (Don't start smoking, by the way – not 'cos I care whether you kill yourself but because I hate to be unable to want to as well.)

Thursday morning: I have to finish this and post it otherwise you

won't get it before Saturday which is a long time to wait for proof
that I miss you. I hope very much you find somewhere to live
soon, and when you do don't forget to send the address, OK? V
good luck – I meant to say it on the station & then on the phone,
but forgot both times (along with many other things).

　StephenllyGrace – not very spontaneous because I have too
much time to think about it at the moment.

I was out of my depth. Grace had a heightened sense of social
dynamics, of the people around her and the psychic relationship
they had with her; I saw the words and recognised them as English
but could make nothing of them. I find it hard to imagine what
people I know quite well might be thinking; Grace could apparently picture the inner lives of complete strangers, in numbers, and
more to the point was acutely aware of what they made of her. It
must have been noisy and unsettling, like trying to file out of a
packed entertainment venue unseen in the dark.

　It is plain to me now that this strange letter presents more evidence of Grace McGoldrick's higher standing on the evolutionary
ladder. Her elevated sensitivity is prefigured in *Middlemarch* when
George Eliot writes: "If we had a keen vision and feeling of all ordinary human life, it would be like hearing the grass grow and the
squirrel's heart beat, and we should die of that roar which lies on
the other side of silence." Grace dwelt on the other side of silence,
where peace of mind is not to be expected.

　I, by contrast, well wadded with stupidity, read her letter at the
time to mean that we had reached an advanced state of confidence
in each other; each could rely on the other understanding what
he or she meant without it having to be explained at great length.
Which was just as well: unless my mind worked along less rigidly
linear lines in those days, I surely found much of what she writes
scarcely intelligible. With her in a less unreal way than previously,
I am nonetheless warned that she'll switch off when people begin

to talk about unreality. Didn't Byron have something to say along these lines about 'systems'?

I might have baulked at the qualification of 'I feel more sure of you in some ways (and less in others, of course)' – why 'of course'? But she trusted me, and I had found a way of doing the right thing even by accident – phoning when expressly asked not to, for example. We were going to be separated for long periods but it did not seem to matter.

Sarah-Jane not taking her milk worries me. I'd assumed she was an infant to be baby-sat; perhaps, instead, she was one of the many cats.

In short I filtered out what it suited me to take from Grace's letters and allowed the rest to evaporate. And in one more illustration of Mailer's First Law of Irony, not six months later I was a smoker.

LETTER 8

This morning I spoke on the telephone to Grace McGoldrick. She is an acupuncturist working at a complementary therapy clinic in Rugby. Her age is in the range 55-59 – a detail supplied by the Electoral Register. I didn't ask her exact age: the question would have been impertinent when it became apparent that we didn't know each other.

She was returning a call I had made, earlier, to the clinic. For a little over a day I had been in the unsettling position of knowing every time the phone rang that it might bring a voice from the past. I need hardly have concerned myself; the phone rings less often as you grow older.

I had left a message with a receptionist rather than with a voice-mail system, and not much of it had found its way to this Grace. She was under the impression that I was in need of acupuncture. I felt guilty as well as self-conscious, explaining that I was not a potential client. "I'm looking for somebody of your name that I used to know," I said.

"What did you say your Christian name was?" she asked. It was a pleasant voice with no particular accent or, for that matter, intonation.

I told her. She audibly 'Hmm'd', but then added: "No. But I used to work with an Andrew Gallagher."

I said: "Then I apologise for bothering you, and thank you for taking the trouble to return the call."

Grace McGoldrick the 50-something acupuncturist said: "That's all right."

The Electoral Register had one more entry I wanted to check before I returned this Grace to the discard pile. "By the way," I said, "and to perhaps save another phone call, you wouldn't happen to run a graphic design agency in Loughborough, would you?"

"Yes, that's me too."

"Your days must be busy and varied," I said. I was on the verge of asking whether she had ever considered tattooing as a career, but remembered in time that this was a complete stranger. We parted on good terms.

I found that I had enjoyed the phone conversation. I resolved to step up the search, possibly in the Home Counties.

The next letter was dated 11 October – in ancient Rome, the date of the festival of Meditrinalia, when new wine was offered to the gods and enjoyed by mortals in combination with an older vintage. The blend supposedly had medicinal qualities. At Sheffield University, where the hangovers from Freshers' Week lingered, it would have been a useful addition to the calendar.

The letter found me at yet another address but relatively settled. I had moved into lodgings with a Mrs Jablonski in the Brincliffe Edge area of the city.

I hadn't deliberately opted for digs. At the time, Sheffield University had one mixed hall of residence and four single-sex halls. I applied for a room in the mixed hall, having spent the previous seven years in boys-only establishments. On finding the mixed hall oversubscribed I chose to go bush by looking for a room off-campus. It proved to be an outstandingly good decision, though not immediately.

Immediately, Sheffield reduced me to a state of penury I had not previously experienced. Mrs Jablonski charged £6.25 a week. That sounds modest enough until you look at the income from which it was to be deducted. My parents were sufficiently well-heeled to provide most of that income; their contribution, referred to provocatively as an 'allowance', amounted to £30 a month. Then there was the local authority's grant of about £120 per 10-week term. In other words, after rent I had £13 a week to live on.

The Geography Department, revealing an unexpectedly predatory side to its nature, reduced those meagre resources by £30 for 'essential' mapping and drawing tools. It also issued a reading list, and I was close to my wits' end until it was pointed out to me that buying the books was not obligatory. I thriftily discovered the library and later, the second-hand bookshop. Even so, after living well all summer on my income as a supermarket shelf-stacker, belt-tightening came as something of a shock. I chose Economics as a subsidiary subject in the first year quite by accident.

Other students found ways to supplement their income. From Brincliffe Edge to the university was about 15 minutes' walk through the Steel City's leafy suburbs; however, to make the journey by public transport involved one bus into the city centre and another out, as though down and up adjacent spokes of a bicycle wheel. The total distance covered made it legitimate to reclaim the bus fares from the local authority. I doubt the local authority demanded tickets as evidence. I, enjoying the walk and particularly the names of the streets and passageways (Frog Walk, Brocco Bank, Stalker Lees Road etc), remained uncompromised but poor.

Mrs Jablonski and her husband Marion were Polish émigrés who had reached the UK in the 1950s. I once introduced a copy of *Socialist Worker* to the house and she asked me politely but firmly not to do so again. They had come out of the Soviet bloc hidden in a furniture van, and in Sheffield they found a home from home and a thriving Polish community that seemed perfectly integrated into South Yorkshire.

I shared my room with another first-year student called Ron, from Essex. He was in the Engineering Department, I think, so we saw little of each other except at the ends of the day. At the weekends I either went south or pined.

On this letter the lined paper was deployed again:

Dear Stephen (originally a *[indecipherable - Greek, probably]* word meaning 'garland' and then 'crown' generally)
    Thank you for your letter, and Hannah for her present. You seem to have a way with young girls. Huff. I have not begun this before now because I have not had time.

1. Friday evening babysitting for S&R (Essay: to what extent is it true to say temperature varies with latitude – unfinished)
2. Saturday – St Albans (alone) in morning
    Drew came round in afternoon
    Went out with Beth in evening
3. Sunday (today) morning – To what extent etc; finished a book by one of your heroes – Gide.

[Alongside 1 & 2 she wrote: 'Read It's a Battlefield.*']*

That was very concise and has probably given you a totally wrong impression of what I did. Perhaps I should begin an analytical isolation of moods. Drew came round to ask for the Reading prospectus (which I didn't have) – really I suspect it was because he wanted your address, which I lovingly gave him, of course.

Drew's interest in the Reading prospectus must have been some sort of subterfuge. In the first place, it was a walk of close to two miles from his end of town to Grace's on such a speculative errand; in the second, he surely wasn't thinking of applying to Reading.

In those days there was a good deal of snobbery about tertiary education. Polytechnics were treated as second-class citizens and even certain universities were regarded askance. Reading was known as a university you went to if you weren't good enough to get in anywhere else, unless it was to study geography. I'd be surprised if Grace had considered Reading seriously enough to acquire a prospectus. She told me once that the girls at her school had to ask the headmistress' permission if they wanted to apply to Hull, and I imagine Reading would have been in a similar category.

Last night Beth wanted to go out, and to shake off her accusation of lethargy (made the previous Thursday) I went. It was a type of disco thing in St Albans done by Jeremy. Strangely enough I think Beth must have hated it even more than me, because she was there all the time whereas I wasn't at all. At one point I took out

'Isabelle' and indeed tranced through two chapters before being
accosted by an irate Jeremy (equally *[indecipherable]*).

If she made her way far enough through *Isabelle* she would have
come upon this: "Rien n'empêche le bonheur comme le souve-
nir de bonheur. Hélas! je me souviens de cette nuit." Or was that
L'Immoraliste? So she might have had to trance all the way through
Isabelle and into another book entirely. It would have been quicker
to dispense with *Isabelle*. Luckily, she hadn't asked my advice and
been sent off on a wild goose chase. I wonder if she was reading it
in French?

"Nothing stands in the way of happiness in quite the way that
the memory of happiness does. Alas, I remember that night." I
believe it means there's a danger of setting the bar too high by getting carried away in the first flush. Once you've experienced the
intense excitement of the coup de foudre, if you don't get it into
perspective everything thereafter might seem second-best or even
mediocre. Fortunately, I can hardly remember those nights at all,
and I am not therefore prey to anxiety about meeting an impossible
standard. But I'm talking about 44 years later and I imagine Gide
had something a little more immediate in mind.

Freud defined happiness as the deferred fulfilment of a primitive desire. Thus, the argument proceeds, money cannot buy happiness because money was never an object of primitive man's desire.
Apart from wampum, of course; and barter; and, when you think
about it, all those exchange mechanisms that predated the mint-
ing of coinage. The quest for happiness can then be regarded as a
form of computer game in which the player collects assets or tokens
and disposes of them in ways that will bolster his security. Security
might be required to protect him against poverty, hunger, lovelessness, acts of God and more besides; a man might count himself
happy if he is covered against only one of those eventualities. Money will help with all of them except lovelessness.

How are we supposed to evaluate our memories? I have spent most of my working life in an environment where memory depends on the on/off state of an electronic switch, valve or digital successor. It seems an inappropriate medium for preserving anything more emotive than Accounts Receivable or Sales Order Processing. If I were looking for an analogy, temperamentally I am disposed to prefer an organic alternative: the ring of a tree, perhaps, where everything that happens to that tree in any given year is recorded; all the nutrients the tree draws in through its roots, the pollutants it struggles to neutralise and, implicitly, the life it sustains in its bark and its branches – yes, a tree might be said to have lived a good life and it could be measured in the rings in its trunk's cross-section. They would reveal its age, of course, but also perhaps something of the character of the tree and the contribution it made, and so a picture of the tree and its context would emerge.

But the valves, the transistors and all the digital paraphernalia are much more convenient than a tree and utterly reliable, we are urged to believe. As long as we have the appropriate peripheral devices we will always be able to retrieve those memories.

It's a substantial proviso: it isn't difficult to envisage a world dependent on C90s for its memories and no VCR to play them on. Besides, media decays. Even the most sophisticated storage of the Information Age might be subject to degeneration. Take a look at those photos you burned on to a CD 10 years ago (if your computer still has a CD drive); aren't they slightly foxed, the colours overcooked? Yes, of course, it may have been the camera you were using then. But the prints you took off a roll of film 10 years earlier aren't in the same state, are they?

Coincidentally, in the past decade computer technologists have been looking at the possibility of pressing organic materials into service as memory media. "Like brains," suggests the IT press, choking back its disappointment that its vision of a sci-fi future has failed to materialise despite 40 years of uncritical promotion. In fact such memory devices would be no more like brains than something carelessly ordered from a foreign menu and pushed under the lettuce leaves in the hope that the waiter will not see it as he or she takes the plate away.

Memory, love and life create and reinforce each other. If I fail to remember many things in the course of this account, it doesn't mean they didn't happen – simply that too many other things have happened since and the earlier treasures have been thrust aside. They aren't eliminated but, like rings in the cross-section of a tree, they are relegated to an inner circle. There, you'd like to think, they continue to constitute part of the tree's character and strength. If ever writing has a wooden quality, here's the explanation.

Besides, remembering what you did and remembering how you felt are two different things. My recollection of events is fragmentary, an incomplete collection; my sense of how I felt throughout the period is complete and consistent and therefore entirely suspect. If you can articulate how you think you felt in the distant past, does that cast doubt on the authenticity of your memory or of your feelings?

I had difficulty with *Isabelle* on one other count.

I was in a Parisian book-shop, browsing, when a sharp-nosed shop-girl approached me. There was something in her manner that made me think of the shop assistant deceived by Bogart's famously improvised impersonation of a wimp as he flushed out Arthur Gwynn Geiger, one of the minor characters in *The Big Sleep*, from his hidden pornography business. I was slightly intimidated when she asked in brisk French if she could be of any help.

I replied in kind, perhaps hoping to impress her, that I was looking for something by Gide, *Isabelle*. She heard not "*Isabelle*" but "qui s'appelle…" "Why would this crazy English be asking me the title of the book 'e seeks?" she may have asked herself. To me she merely repeated, with a quizzical lilt: "Qui s'appelle…?" I tried to say *Isabelle* again, with verve, but it sounded like "qui s'appelle" to me too by then. She looked blank and asked again what it was calling itself. Flustered, I could think of no way to explain myself, so I changed my order abruptly to *Les Caves du Vatican* and spent many francs on a book I already owned.

I'm sure that would have amused Grace and I would have enjoyed presenting it to her, but it is a memory that belonged to the future from our perspective, as do almost all others.

I have superb capacities of detachment, but two things affected me: one was that Jeremy was drunk, therefore many repetitive, noisy and inaudible conversations which were eventually embarrassing. Also the complete contrast between his friends – who were putting on a go-go show – as compared to the stolid sportsmen who thronged the bar in braces and polo necks (it was at the Verulamium Sports Club). The record I now remember most vividly was 'Virginia Plain'. Balancing on the piano I could see Beth sitting on a chair miming 'How to be hip in 10 easy lessons' (totally unoriginal but crudely amusing if the senses are already dulled by overdoses of alcohol, smoke & decibells) and then the sportsmen (& about 4 women) who literally stared at J's friends and were probably condemned as everlastingly unaware (and vice versa naturally).

In fact it works three ways almost.

I can't say I think Gide is v good at the moment. The ending was OK – in that it wasn't happy – but it seemed too short to be particularly meaningful considering the simplicity of the theme. Drew said you were unusual in liking him, but I will reserve my judgement until I have read some more.

Yes, do, and read *La Porte Etroite*, *Les Caves du Vatican* and *Les Faux-Monnayeurs* if you have the time. But especially *La Porte Etroite*, if you want a miserable ending.

My brother is watching *The Big Match*. It seems v far away from last weekend today.

What you are doing sounds like what happens at the beginning
of our lower sixth year. They called it 'settling in' then, but it does
just make you wish you weren't there. It can't fail to get better,
anyway; if my mother was here she would be muttering darkly
about background reading that you'll never have time to do again,
but of course (goal) she cannot know the supreme creativity of
your mind. Which reminds me, if you ever want anything published
(I am being v serious) I would love to get it put in 'Cob's Pen'
(our termly mag) which seems to have had only junk written for
it so far*. It would have to be anon of course but you would raise
it above its present seedy level. (Which sentence explains why
maybe Use of English is a good idea.)
* I have seen the unpublished work 'cos some of the committee
are friends.
NB it is gym-shoes, not pumps or plimsolls.

It occurs to me that I never thought of Grace as a schoolgirl. I never
saw her in any item of school uniform, which in those days might
still have been de rigeur even for students in their final year. In
truth I was a little hazy over where she actually went to school. It
was an all-girls fee-paying school in the vicinity of Edgware, easily reached by bus or in Maureen Fowler's car. More than that, I
couldn't be certain.

The reason for this neglect on my part was simply that she
seemed more grown-up than I was. Hence much of my concentration was focused on disguising my immaturity. I doubt this was
very successful. In the beginning, evidently, she found me brilliant and creative. But I knew exactly how little experience I had,
of life, of women, of anything worth mentioning; I suspected she
could not have less, despite the slight difference in our ages. And
in person she was calm and cool and measured. She was clearly an
intellectual. These were qualities I admired and aspired to while
conscious of a certain shortfall in myself. Gide! Hélas!

It is about 7.0 and I have given up with 'To what extent...' I know the answer but am too bored to write it. I will change to English when I have written you a few lines. While I was pondering over the refraction of clouds (25%) I wrote another lot of drivel. One would have thought that as you are a geography student *[the word surrounded by asterisks, as though indicating top billing]* I would have been inspired. I suppose it is comforting since it shows how I rely on you alone without any material benefit. Yet books on the perfectability of love are unconvincing, and having recently read so many cynical ones it is no wonder I feel strange – ethereal?

My mother is going to have a bath, my father is putting away the car, my little brother has gone to the '72 group meeting and my big brother had a good time in Vienna.

Apart from you, I have another constant – or semi-constant – thought which is so obscure I cannot help wanting to tell you it. I walked to school one day (from the bus stop) and it was a beautiful morning. There are these green park railings along the road and two men, dressed in navy blue boiler suits, were painting them with grass green paint. One man stood inside the park, and the other outside. The next day I didn't have a lift home, and there they were again, a little way down the road. By the end of last week they had turned the corner and one of them smiled at me. That is all. I am going mad, I promise you – but I really am obsessed with the whole idea. It is making me worried because I can't understand why something so trivial should be so important. It isn't important at all, but it seems all the time to be terribly symbolic, and I want to make it be that, but I can't fit everything in. It's like reading a book & knowing that something vital is there which has the power to change you even, and however much you think, you can't find out what it is. I don't know why I'm telling you at all. When I think of things like that I am so glad to love you because then I know that I am valuing something that really is important, and I can be sure that it is. But then when you know that love finally cannot work.

I am still transcribing this verbatim. There may be some punctuation missing in the last sentence. With the careful insertion of a comma or two, it almost makes sense.

I can't imagine that I had anything very helpful to say in reply to this sort of anxiety attack. I remember the story of the park railings, which perhaps means that I attempted a response. Now, however, my only comment would be to recall the difficulties some of the left-leaning authors of the 1930s had with formal Marxist explication, apparently because they knew so little of what working people did or felt.

What Grace meant by "books on the perfectability of love" is anyone's guess. They sound like American self-help texts, perhaps appearing under a specialist publishing offshoot of Readers Digest. That would explain them being unconvincing. Had she written "novels and poems exploring the perfectability of love" it would have made more sense; the difference may be slight, but she was educated to make that kind of distinction.

> I want to scream with fear, I suppose, because nothing can be certain. I used to think that it was better always to have to believe in things being OK, rather than knowing. God, what innocence.

What a pity she had just read *It's a Battlefield*. In *A Burnt-Out Case*, she would have found this: "God preserve us from all innocence. At least the guilty know what they are about." It would have stayed with her.

> And what is worse is that everyone is ultimately totally alone. I cannot help you in things beyond a certain level – and you cannot help me. So once you begin to feel the smallest bit hopeless in yourself, and once you analyse it properly, Bang. That is split-second hopelessness which I hope I don't believe. Probably it is logically all wrong anyway but I refuse to take it back once written, because it is what I was thinking. About 5 mins ago.

Anyway of course we all thrive on uncertainty…

The split-second hopelessness she writes about is a not as bad as you might think at first glance. It contrasts with the enduring hopelessness which later began to seem so routine as to be a part of the human condition. It is tolerable, presumably, because although alone, everyone is broadly the same. I can't remember the full quotation from St-Exupéry again but it runs along these lines: "A man should not expect to emerge from his loneliness through his own efforts. A rock cannot be other than a rock. But enough rocks together can be a cathedral."

Tuesday: I have not forgotten you. I just didn't want to write yesterday. Today I have news and it's really worth waiting for… the amazingly intelligent author, editor, agitator extraordinaire (etc), Richard Neville *[again with asterisks]* is coming to speak at our school. The daughter of our Russian mistress in the 5th year is going out with him (occasionally) and so we've got it made. The Current Affairs society committee are in raptures and from all accounts feverishly swotting up 'Playpower' etc ready to quote at him if by any slim chance he is as eloquent as suggested on the First Programme. What will be amusing (if any amused people could be there to see it) will be when he has to take tea with the headmistress before the happy event – as is customary treatment for all guest speakers visiting school. You see I am now profoundly affected by what is going on around me & that is a very good sign. I am beginning to push sickness for you into bearable proportions. I do not love you any less, and I suppose I can be happier loving you now than I could say, last Monday, or even yesterday. Having said that, I am missing you intensely now, and loving you more. Grace ('blessing' – what irony)

An overdue question bubbles to the surface and sits there, heavier than air, demanding to be inspected: What sort of man keeps

25 or so love letters through four decades, several important but ultimately impermanent relationships, multiple recessions and the Information Revolution?

The short answer is that I kept them unwittingly. During the clearance of my parents' house, a year or so ago, the bundle came to light in a shoe-box in an attic cupboard. They would have been there (or in another such cupboard at another such address) since 1981. In 1981 I went to live overseas and left many of my household goods in informal storage. On my return two years later, I retrieved some but, evidently, not others.

Had I been aware of them I'm not sure I could have brought myself to throw them away. It's not a collection of beer mats we're dealing with here, is it?

I knowingly kept the letters for eight or nine years. At first, for perhaps 12 months or more, anyone would have held on to them. Events might have taken a different turn. Had we patched it up and fared forth a new way, I and Grace withal, I would have been mortified to have had to tell her I had destroyed tens of thousands of heartfelt words in a fit of pique. Dante Gabriel Rosetti ordered Lizzie Siddal's body to be dug up so that he could retrieve some hastily discarded poems. There is no telling how attached people might grow to their emotional output.

A year on, when it was clear that Grace would be open to no suggestions of further faring forth or, indeed, was unlikely ever to talk to me again, I might have thrown them away – but there was no need to. Stored away, they were doing no-one any harm. Held tight in a bundle by a Post Office elastic band, they were no larger than a small packed lunch; they took up no space, disturbed no tidy minds and were forgotten.

Completely forgotten. As I was transcribing the first letter in the series it occurred to me that I had not read it in full since the day the postman delivered it. The letter is, admittedly, very long. I may have set out to read the correspondence, in the manner of a miser counting his hoard, but halfway through the opening letter I would have been discouraged by its length and set them all aside, never to be retrieved until a prince hacked through a hedge of thorns.

Life brings a continual succession of new priorities and relegates older imperatives to a particular form of abstraction. It isn't difficult to remember that something was important at one time, but times change. The letters are tokens of a bygone era, part of the fossil record. They merely existed, in a box, compositions on the way to decomposition.

Their final transformation, it now occurs to me, took place in the millennial year. One of my closest friends died and I was granted an unwelcome insight: with his passing, doubt was cast upon parts of my own past. It wasn't that the things I remembered hadn't happened; rather that I could no longer call on Ian for corroboration – there was no third-party confirmation of my memories.

Grace's letters constitute a similar reserve. I realised that until I found the letters I hadn't given her a moment's thought in decades. Tonight is a Thursday evening: somewhere in the world she may be wondering whether to put out the green or the grey wheelie bin, listening to *The Archers*, enjoying a glass of medium sherry with the Channel 4 news; but I have never thought of her in such contexts. I have never thought of her, full stop. I behave as though she were dead, and her letters are the last surviving evidence that someone of her name ever meant anything to me. So the letters remain, defused by the endless succession of the seasons, and part of my life is authenticated. Paradoxically, the more time that passes, the more that life seems to belong to someone else entirely.

LETTER 9

Over the past few days the pace of my typing has slackened but my admiration for Grace has grown hand over fist. I have been obliged to become ambidextrous.

My own carelessness is to blame. As you age, you are apt to forget that certain physical exertions are probably beyond you. Taking delivery last week of a dozen cardboard boxes full of magazines, I lugged most of them from the pavement to a spare room and put the rest into the boot of my car. This morning, my right elbow is letting me know it will stand for no more of that sort of abuse. It will tolerate no load; I can grip nothing with my right hand; and the arm is almost useless unless braced against my ribs, protruding like a Dalek prosthesis.

The shortcomings of the left hand don't take long to declare themselves. The left hand may grip things and bear weight, but it is very far from being dextrous. (Well, it wouldn't be the left hand if it were dextrous, so let's say, rather, it isn't very handy.) Simple, everyday activities like chopping up the Cat's breakfast (lacking teeth, she needs the chunks to be reduced) take longer and quickly turn messy. Worst of all, though, is shaving. Manipulating a sharp object close to your face, in the reflection of a mirror, with a shaky, untrained hand, is frightening. Unless you exercise superhuman patience it's not unlike shaving with one of the whirling hub attachments off Boudicca's chariot.

Grace's achievement in writing legibly with either hand is not only impressive in the light of my difficulties: it's remarkable. The only writing I need to do, if I plan my day carefully, is the crossword and the Sudoku, one painstaking character at a time. Even then, any character that involves more than a single stroke – a 4, for example – or any kind of loop – most of the alphabet – is subject to distortion to varying degrees. Attempting a crossword, I give the impression of pondering my answers carefully. Writing a full-length letter in the old-fashioned way would simply be beyond me.

In the end an accident with the tin-opener persuaded me that my right arm had rested for long enough. I am slowly rehabilitating it.

University is commonly regarded as some sort of rite of passage, this being the first time many young people will be away from home for any length of time. One of the noticeable features of Sheffield University when I was there was the high proportion of undergraduates from the Manchester area. It seems they were happy enough to be away from home but preferred not to be too far away.

The question didn't arise for me. I wasn't sure I had a home. I didn't need one: all I needed was a letter-box. This prefigured the Internet age, when a journalist can make a living from just about anywhere as long as he has a power supply and a telephone jack socket.

The next letter is postmarked just one day after the eighth, 12 October 1972.

Dear Steve,

I have just read your letter, and it is one of my free afternoons (at home) so I thought I would shock you by replying quickly for a change. In my glorious burst of enthusiasm I forgot I had nothing to say (pause)

Do you feel nervous when you open my letters? I do often when I read yours in case you have changed since the last one. What you said about making yourself better was strange. I read about personality yesterday – I haven't finished it yet but will quote: "Is there a real, natural or undisguised personality? Even when B is performing before a completely trusted friend, or before no-one at all, is he not his own audience, putting on behaviour which approximates to his own internal standards and values, in just the same way as he acts to others' expectations?" Therefore if you want to do it (ie change yourself) you may be able to – or even be doing it already. But beware because this book then says: "Despite variations with different audiences, is there not a fair

degree of consistency – a personal style which he cannot readily
disguise?" I love you you. It is worrying to think that you aren't
you at all, or even that 'you' doesn't properly exist. What a lot of
truth there is in the existence of non-rabbits, then.

This is exactly how Alissa (never quite 'Jerome's Alissa') would have
written, except that, being religious, she would have been unable to
keep the Almighty out of it. Grace instead could not keep Jethro
Tull out of it – non-rabbits celebrated silflay in the elaborate album
cover of *Thick as a Brick*.

I can imagine what I would have done to have provoked those
comments. I would have been carelessly reflecting on those aspects
of my character that could stand improvement and considering
how I might address them, with a view to becoming less unsatisfactory to myself (and, implicitly, more worthy of her).

Alissa would have admired the commitment while lamenting
its target. Jerome should try to make as much of himself as he can
to make a gift of himself to God, not to Alissa. Render unto Cae-
sar etc. Indeed, writing that down makes me wonder whether she
didn't actually chastise him on those very grounds.

Grace's objection that she loved me as I was, not as I hoped to
become, is nit-picking. At that age, in that era, we were all little
more than potential. Knowing very little of life, we were unformed
(I am speaking for myself, of course). For example, I was on the
verge of a revelation that would colour my attitude to love and relationships for the next few years of my life, but that day I knew nothing of it. I feared, which according to the Gospel of St John meant
only that I did not love perfectly.

I begin to find the subject tiresome suspiciously quickly. Her
objection is perfectly valid: you want to be able to rely on the character of your beloved, and perhaps there are certain characteristics
that are so laudable you would want to preserve them. On the other
hand, it's unrealistic to expect someone to resist change entirely.
What you need to be able to do, then, is rely not on the character

of your beloved but on his judgement. Let's allow John Steinbeck in *The Winter of Our Discontent* to sum up: "And I remembered thinking what a hell of a man a man could become."

Sometime later, an image with which I might have replied to her came to mind. It draws on a device common in the children's puzzle books of my early years – perhaps they still have them. You are presented with a pair of apparently identical pictures but there are 10 differences for the eager young reader to find. The first three or four are easy and almost jump off the page: the bicycle's front wheel has a spoke missing, there are more seagulls in the left-hand picture, the boy's pullover has a V-neck on one side and a crew neck on the other, that sort of thing. Another three or four differences demand more careful scrutiny. Then you're left with just one or two, and to find them you might have to call in a friend for a second pair of eyes.

So, perhaps, with our sense of ourselves. Most of us sustain a few harmless affectations and if pressed we might be prepared to admit to them. But there are some aspects of our characters that we can't be quite sure of and others that we hadn't even suspected. It takes someone else to see them and to bring them to our attention. This is not a question of ourselves as we see ourselves, or as others see us, or indeed as we actually are, but of how we might begin to make the distinction.

That wouldn't exactly have answered her point, but it would have given her something to put in her pipe and smoke, if she were so disposed.

In all that I answered the phone & left my biro downstairs so I wrote in black (grey). Now I have just answered the door to our new phone directory, and a man who said he had ringed his number. What consideration, I thought (still thinking of non-you) so I said 'thank you' and he looked annoyed and then laughed. And then I looked amazed & laughed also in realisation. You have a numbing effect on my brain, & perhaps I think of you so intensely it gets clogged up.

    I liked your letter a lot. You have an interesting 'turn of phrase' and I liked the way you wrote viz: because I use it also for my own selfish amusement which is therefore not selfish anymore. And the stars. Germain would have an unemotional fit if she knew how I am crawling to your ego. But the chances are you won't be able to read it anyway; if you can (oh dear, I'm at it again) I suddenly feel very happy, so I'll finish. Grace.

There follows a line of xxxxxs forming a cartouche round the word 'bath', at the end of a line that reads:

hoping to transmit some of it *[arrow to 'happy']* to you. By the way, what does 'corriente' mean? How long is it since you had a bath?

And at the top of the page, small drawings of a boy and a girl, holding hands, with five-pointed stars (the pentagram again) above their heads.

Sir Ian McKellen was on the radio this morning. Apparently he had told Oprah Winfrey about his first love, a holiday romance at the age of eight. She was called Wendy Cadwallader and they stood beside the sea holding hands. Later, having returned home, they wrote letters to each other. They met again by chance more than 60 years later, in the West End. She told Sir Ian, he recounted, that she had kept his letters... until the day of her wedding, when she'd burned them. Hah! I'll bet she's sorry now.

    As for bathing, there were showers in the Students Union building. It was hardly a country club set-up; the showers were in a secluded part of the Gents, not so much behind the scenes as behind the urinals. Many students will have used the Gents intermittently for three years without appreciating their full extent. Mrs Jablonski had a bathroom, of course, but it had to serve six adults. Once I discovered the Students Union showers (which were hot and powerful) a daily problem was resolved, leaving only the question of what to do with a damp towel for the rest of the day.

'Corriente'... the only context in which I have ever known that particular word is in the expression 'vino corriente', which I believe means 'house wine'. Red wines produced by such master vintners as Don Cortez, Hirondelle and the makers of Bull's Blood and sold in bottles of 1.5 litres didn't become a regular part of my intake until at least the second term; in October, I was still restricting myself to a half-pint of dry cider when yielding to an impulse to live it up.

LETTER 10

That impulse had to be firmly controlled. Three years later, when I was unemployed and living on a very tight budget, I had cooking facilities and understood the nutritional value/basement price of meals involving tinned mackerel and dried beans. In the first term at Sheffield, with lunch and dinner to be found, I dined out almost every day and with great care. The refectory in the Students Union building was a reliable stand-by; fish and chips was another. I didn't put on weight.

Grace's next letter is postmarked 16 October (a Monday), at 2pm.

Dear Steve (you pedantic wretch)

Thank you for your very long letter. Why are yours always longer than mine?

That would be because I had nothing else to do. Four out of five mornings I had 9am lectures, which I attended, studiously, knowing no better. That left long hours in the middle of the day when nothing much was required of me. I spent time in the upper refectory if I could afford a coffee and in a comfortably furnished lounge if I couldn't. The Geography Department's library was also nicely upholstered, and along the corridor was an ad hoc coffee lounge in which the vending machine occasionally returned your money as well as dispensing coffee. Equally, it would occasionally withhold both; and the coffee was thin and tasteless; but life is flawed.

I hadn't discovered the basement, known as the 'stacks', of the main library at that stage, but when I did it soon became my favourite place in the whole city: warm, dark, deserted and home only to tons of ancient newsprint in the back-copies of newspapers stored there. Perhaps my career choice was made there too.

It surprises me that my letters were longer. I find it hard to believe I had much to say. Hers, on the other hand, were especially long for someone who found writing physically challenging. In the back of my mind there's a comment by Stendahl, I think, about the importance of paying attention at all times to what a woman says.

I read it yesterday. Here is a formal invitation for next weekend – or some of it anyway. You may come. OK? I haven't told anyone yet, except my mother, and the strain is killing me. By the time you have read this I will have though. Frailty thy name etc.

Everything is horrible here, it is either downright revolting or else flat. Beth is fed up. I haven't seen her except for Friday when my parents went out and she and Drew came round. They talked about people they knew in town when they were small – it sounded amusing. But it was a nothing evening.

The television is gabbling downstairs. It is 'The Third Man' and out of love for you I should watch it. But I'm not going to. Or the programme on Van Gogh, which I would like to see. My parents are in bad moods. My mother lugged an expensive (& ugly) glass lampshade for the hall light all the way back from Lewis' in London and my father has just dropped something on it and broken it. Unfortunately, my mother just isn't an 'accidents will happen' type of person.

Jimmy Reid is all very well but where have you disposed of Ian?

I had attended a lecture by Jimmy Reid and must have allowed a little hero-worship to creep into my account of the meeting. A week or so later, Sir Keith Joseph addressed a similar crowd and was even more impressive. Reid, after all, was preaching to the converted; Sir Keith encountered a hostile audience and dealt with it adroitly by playing one faction off against another.

Such ficklety is disgraceful in one so old (and a student), my parents pay taxes to support people like you. You are right about Richard, he is rather irrelevant & unconstructive in his ideas I must admit, but he is an interesting person and I enjoy his offensive arrogance. I saw Jimmy R on television ages ago talking

> about UCS, and he said that thing that you quoted like he always does.

That would be "A rat-race is for rats". Grace obviously thought it sounded trite. She may have been right. That doesn't filter all the sense out of it, does it?

It surprises me that we had this kind of discussion. Perhaps, in the wake of the 60s, ours was a more politicised generation. It is more likely, on reflection, that the young people I know in their late teens and early twenties seem less politically conscious because they avoid that kind of conversation with me, fearing that I will set off on a 30-minute celebration of Mario Savio or some other figure from 50 years ago, overlooking the fact that I have thrown my body on no gears in the meanwhile. Still, we knew what UCS stood for. We read the papers and watched the television news. It was, I repeat, an era in which all was potential – and nothing came of it.

> Of course it is true. But not everybody is socialist because some people really do think they are superior to others and deserve more, starting from birth. Even nice people like my father. And people like Mrs Fowler say (& she did, too): 'The trouble with this government is that it's too left wing.' There hardly seems any point in being anything.
>
> I love you very much but I can't write more because I want to go to sleep now. I will write before I see you next.
>
> Grace XXXX

I should have told her that she was right: that the purpose was not to 'be' anything but to concentrate all the time on 'becoming'. And, what's more, to determine that if you accidentally succeeded in becoming something, you should then aim to become better at it.

LETTER 11

Another quaint peculiarity of this historical period is that there were at least two deliveries of post on weekdays and multiple collections. Pillar-boxes displayed tokens that indicated the hour at which the next collection was due – the postman or woman inserted the appropriate token as they emptied the box. The tokens are still there but now they are more likely to indicate which day a collection might be expected.

If we had had modern communications technology at our disposal, how much use would we have made of it? Grace's output (and my response, taken as read) suggests we would have been enthusiastic early adopters, with one important qualification: she regularly referred to the emptiness of her days and I carefully disguised the emptiness of mine. That wouldn't necessarily have inhibited us: much of social media is devoted to people exaggerating the glamour and excitement of their lives, isn't it? But the element of honesty would have been lost in the process, and with it the entire point.

Do people still write love letters? If they want to be in tune with the times a little emotional incontinence will go a long way. Love doesn't go out of fashion and the means of expressing it are hardly in decline. On the contrary, 21st century love can be communicated more briskly and economically than ever.

But would lovers write a letter when the love-letter emoji is available? The idea of a digitised picture (international code 1F48C) to stand in for a love letter seems insensitive or even crass. Consider also the banal nature of the symbol itself: it's a drawing of an envelope, with a bright red heart where a seal might have been impressed. In more sophisticated versions the heart is bevelled for three-dimensional effect and decorated with reflected light, suggestive either of a swollen heart overflowing with emotion or, less comfortably, of Roman Catholic statuary.

A website devoted to emojis declares: "We love emojis – they speak to our souls! Sometimes we feel like they express our thoughts and emotions better than words ever could." Quite. Another site explains with charming simplicity: "Prior to smart phones and emails, people used to send letters to one another." Love letters, it continues helpfully, were especially valued when they came from someone you were fond of. It is reasonable to conclude from this that the economy of the gesture – one click to insert a symbol into a message, as opposed to several hours agonised handwriting – is unimportant. What matters is the feeling that already exists between the writer and the recipient. To express that, only a symbol is necessary.

But in the jargon of technology, an emoji is an 'icon'; in conventional English, an icon is a means of expressing ideas (often complex and abstract, invariably spiritual) through a simple picture. For once the two vocabularies coincide.

When not making disobliging remarks about full-grown Americans with little boys' names, Graham Greene had plenty to say on the subject of women. Somewhere – perhaps *The End of the Affair* – he wrote that a man might love women or he might understand them but he should not hope to do both.

I had chosen which fork of that road I would take but I was next to no distance along it. The limits of my worldliness were not far-flung. It would not have taken many steps into the unknown for me to fall off the edge of the world.

Arthur Koestler offered the analogy of a canal to illustrate the difficulties ordinary people have with technology. Getting used to a particular device or technology is like entering a lock, he said; when the water level has risen and you emerge, fully competent, at a higher level of understanding, you find that there's another lock to negotiate straight ahead of you because the technology has moved on in the meanwhile. I believe this image might apply to the stages a young man goes through in his dealings with the opposite sex.

The theory, based on a means of transport that has outlived

its original commercial purpose, is almost certainly as outdated now as our exchange of letters, but there may be eternal verities in human affairs that technology leaves untouched. It begins, naturally, with a relatively straight section of canal:

● Complete Indifference. Small boys grow into big boys with a view of girls as being, not to put too fine a point on it, a bit girlie. Can't run, can't catch, can't throw and prone to burst into tears. Practically useless, girls nonetheless receive preferential treatment in many important social contexts because adults regard them as cute. That annoys boys and leaves them even less disposed to give girls the benefit of the doubt.

● Dawning Awareness. Up to a certain age (and this is impossible to pin down even within a generation, far less across a gap of 44 years, so let's just say 'the teenage years') having a girlfriend will be an occasion for teasing. Abruptly, without an obvious boundary having been crossed, having a girlfriend without being teased becomes possible and, as a mysterious consequence, desirable.

● Growing Pains. One by one, as your friends acquire girlfriends, it will be increasingly urgent that you find one for yourself. There may be any number of candidates from your childhood if you haven't alienated them too deeply with your dismissive early views. Or you may have to start from scratch – if you have moved to the other end of the country, for example. Either way, the fact of having a girlfriend will be more important than the identity of the girl or any qualities she may possess. This is a sensitive time and you don't want to blight your chances by being too picky.

● Discrimination. On the other hand, there is prestige in having an attractive girlfriend. I'm sure everybody enters this phase; I suspect many men get stuck here; perhaps women too. If you regard looks as being of surpassing importance you risk missing the point. Also, you make yourself vulnerable; your relationship will be tested every time a door opens and somebody new walks into the room – somebody new might be better-looking, and people who are susceptible to that kind of thing are sure to notice.

● Maturity. Eventually you'll stop thinking of a girlfriend as an accoutrement or a trophy. You don't need to read Aristophanes to understand that the right partner will make you feel complete. You will start to look beyond a face or a shapely body or, heaven forbid, wealthy parents. At one level everyone is the same, but that's the shallow end; at the other end, where inexperienced swimmers may get into difficulties, everyone is different and you need to get to know someone quite well to discover whether she is the one. If you make a mistake from this point, it is at least an honorable mistake.

I was not very far along this stretch of inland waterway. In fact the canal network might have become redundant while I was negotiating the lock staircase, but fortunately canals found a second role in the 20th century as recreational resources.

First girlfriend? Before Grace there hadn't really been one. I had spent a desultory evening or two with a girl from one of the schools that picked up students to transport them to St Albans, across the road from where my school bussed us into Watford. The bus makes it pre-motorcycle days – age 16 or so. Even she was a second-best; her prettier fellow-student, when I asked whether she would go out with me, asked: "Are you doing this for a dare?"

First kiss? At a party, with the head-girl of the neighbouring girls grammar school. Again, one or two inconsequential outings followed but no sustained kissing. The outings involved trips to her home several miles away and can therefore be dated to the Triumph Tiger Cub days – 1971-72.

First crush? On a very beautiful girl who worked at the embryonic supermarket-style store where I was a part-time shelf-stacker. Anne accepted my declaration of love graciously and suggested I might be better off asking Maddy, who like me was part-time but, more to the point, was regarded as somewhat complicated. Maddy and I went on the Tiger Cub to see Jethro Tull at the Gaumont State Theatre, Kilburn, on Sunday 28 February, 1971. Ian Anderson wore a jewelled cod-piece, and ice-creams were served in an intermission. The ticket price was 60p. It isn't just letters that I keep – a ticket stub was among the buried treasures. Maddy gave me no kisses but she did donate a leather jacket with a Suzuki badge on one elbow. She maintained that the owner had died in the jacket in a pile-up on the North Circular Road. What became of Maddy I do not know.

Two other crushes should be mentioned because they were influential in unexpected ways. One was Cynthia, whom I met on the train coming back from my first visit to Sheffield. I had been there as a sixth-former looking over the university, in a half-hearted sort of way because I had more or less decided I wanted to go to Bristol University at the time. But Sheffield offered the memory of Cynthia and Bristol didn't. So I went to Sheffield and never saw Cynthia again.

The second was Helena, who belongs to the era immediately before Grace. My regular circle of friends and acquaintances at that time comprised two contemporaries from school, two more from the town and the girlfriends of two of these four. Helena was one of the girlfriends. Her family was very wealthy. Many people in the town were rich but few had an indoor swimming pool.

Apt to go weak at the knees in the company of Helena, I was attentive but lacked the confidence to become much of a nuisance. It was enough to snatch a moment alone with her from time to time. On one occasion I shipped the entire group home one at a time on the back of the motorcycle, from a party not far off, solely to have Helena on the pillion for a quarter of an hour. On another, four of us took part in a sponsored 24hr table-tennis marathon, 2hrs on and 2hrs off, and she dozed with me beneath the table during one of my breaks. After that I was dropped from the group and became available to join Craig's.

In summary, I was unsuccessful with girls and very wary of them. I could talk to them but required help to take the next step, or even to visualise it.

It's probably fair to say that I expected to fail, in the same way that, 40 years on, I expect to be defeated by the technology of mobile phones or TV handsets. And I became acquainted with the idea of a self-fulfilling prophecy.

I didn't share any of this with Grace, naturally. Candour is an over-rated quality.

The leather jacket reminds me... Grace gave me an ARP (Air Raid Precautions) great-coat dating from the Second World War. A label inside a flap identified this garment as being for a female warden of medium build. I took it to be a very generous gift; it didn't matter that her mother had probably badgered her to get rid of it from the moment it entered the house. It certainly re-entered a number of times on my back.

Other items of clothing from those times: an orange woollen jumper that I ruined by not knowing how wool reacts to high temperatures in a drier. In the Students Union building there was a launderette where, away from home for the first time, I benefitted from a university eduction by learning how to ruin clothes – the jumper came out looking as though a chicken had just been roasted in it.

I didn't own many clothes and Grace saw only a sample – I wanted to look my best when I was with her, which meant being very selective about the cheap pairs of denims and several more or less brightly coloured loon pants (jeans without pockets or belt-loops but with vast compensatory flares), one decorated with embroidered butterflies. Also, inexplicably, I owned two velvet jackets, one green and one purple, but seldom wore either. I didn't have an extensive wardrobe but until winter arrived I didn't need one, whereupon the great-coat and leather jacket would fill that gap.

The 11th letter, of 18 October, featured the lined paper again but a more furtive, reduced script. It's almost as though she were whispering, an impression reinforced by the way she begins.

Dear Steve,

Everyone is working very hard. I am in the library surrounded by loads of studious people. Luckily as I write on this I appear to be working also. Someone has just switched on the light. The girl opposite me, wearing a pendant saying Pisces, is scratching her eyebrow with a very long fingernail. People are talking now in discreet mutters as Mrs Mullery has gone. The girl opposite me has just looked at me (her fingernails really are colossal). I came in to find a book on Indonesia because my father said it was interesting & I am badly in need of something to keep me awake. I am going to Genesis and Lindisfarne (or Lindisfarne [surrounded by stars] and supporting groups depending on how you look at it) tonight so wish me a good time. Beth phoned last night as her mother went out but we said little 'cos I saw her on Monday afternoon anyway. Everyone at school is very flat at the moment and wanting to leave. It is hot and sleepy and there is the sound of the boiler underneath me which reminds me of crossing the Channel on that goddamn car ferry.

A girl has dyed her hair bright yellow. It is permanent but she says she hates it & is going to dye it back. Will you tell me how you did your T-shirt?

When you write for *Cob's Pen* can you write an article or story please? It is OK if you do a poem but we have more of those & people tend to read them less also. The bell has gone which means history. People are talking out loud now & laughing in happy expectation, poor fools.

I had a vg history lesson. Then break then geography & it was the best lesson we have ever had this year because we talked instead of writing. Now it is Modern History. Mrs Goldman insists on calling Mussolini Mossolini, which is excrutiating after the third time. I normally read, because she is quite inoffensive and sometimes amusing. But of course I will write to you instead. Someone has just asked her if she can darn socks. The answer is yes which shows that I haven't lied. They have written things on the board and Mrs G has read them and is accusing people. This happens each lesson with fatal regularity. We do Franco next week. I can't go on like this because it is not worthy of me, and worthy for you to read. But I do.

I read this book (it is Michael Quoist, you know? He makes me mad) to a woman and in it it said that 'adolescents' who say they love each other are either ignorant or liars. My parents deny that they think that but I am sure they do. Everybody (including me) seems to think they know everything. They are now (in the lesson) slating middle class socialists as having never known poverty. But that is easy to do. Christ I cannot write, so instead I addressed the envelope & stuck on the stamps very ostentatiously. I hate the colours of the stamps but my father didn't have just a blue one *[royal blue for 3p, pink for 2¹/₂p and sky blue for ¹/₂p]*. The only reason I send this is because I said I would. If you weren't coming (are you coming?) I would never bother to show you my weaknesses like this. They are not weaknesses in real life, only as regards letter writing, so don't believe this is me at all.

I wonder again if she was religious? What on earth would she be doing reading Michel Quoist? Why would she read him and not expect to be mightily annoyed?

Quoist was a Catholic priest whose *Prayers of Life* (published in 1954, translated into English in the early 60s) sold in extraordinary numbers. He was the youth chaplain for Le Havre for many years and worked closely with young people for much of his career. He may have known what he was talking about. On the other hand, the sample of young people with whom he came into close contact in the 50s and 60s may arguably be regarded as unrepresentative. He seems, incidentally, to have spent much of his life in Le Havre, where in an earlier time the nun-manquée Alissa of *La Porte Etroite* would have been one of his parishioners.

I believe I essayed a rebuttal of Quoist; in the back of my mind, the expression 'deck Quoist' tolls dully. Not having read any of his work and, indeed, having no more than a vague idea who he was, I can only speculate on the form my response took. I'm almost certain I pompously weighed eros and agape in the balance (and wasn't there a third?) My clinching argument, I suspect, was to ask rhetorically how Quoist, not having been in love with Grace McGoldrick, could know anything at all about the subject.

It isn't really a rebuttal at all, is it? Insisting on the validity of a single particular instance doesn't advance our understanding of human nature very far. On the other hand, all general propositions are susceptible to exceptions and I, like lovers throughout time, believed that our case was exceptional. The position is not devoid of logic.

Why, in any case, should there be an age limit? All right, Byron's weakness for his cousin at the age of eight may be stretching credibility in this context, but he became known as much for his amours as for his poetry. "The heart has its reasons that reason knows nothing of." Pascal's famous observation is followed by this: "We know the truth not only by the reason but by the heart." In other words, it isn't always possible to explain something that appears to be perfectly simple. I don't know whether he said that before or after his abrupt conversion. Either way, he seems a most suitable figure to oppose to Quoist.

Grace obviously objected to the designation 'adolescent' – the inverted commas indicate her distaste. She, then, sidestepped Quoist's judgment by denying membership of the category to which he referred.

Neither of us, though, felt secure enough to aver that he was, simply, wrong. Surely it's possible that first 'adolescent' love is stronger and more pure than anything that comes afterwards; it is unpolluted by the spirit of compromise that inevitably permeates all subsequent relationships. Later, when you know what can happen, you make adjustments, you hold just a little bit back – but not the first time.

My case may appear to be undermined by what I have already

said about my own immaturity. At that time, though, I was at what Carlyle called "the conflux of two eternities"; everything preceding Nigel Bradford's party belonged to a different order to what followed. The realisation of potential – in both senses, ie understanding what might be possible and setting out to achieve it – is not contingent on age.

I went down to Hertfordshire by train that first time. Apparently I stayed with the McGoldricks on Friday night only and went on to Reading to visit my parents on the Saturday.

LETTER 12

I have quoted Thomas Carlyle out of context and incompletely. The point he was making was that any day might be regarded as exceptional. "Is not every meanest Day 'The Conflux of two Eternities'?" Grace's next letter was posted on 26 October from St Albans. By coincidence, on 26 October 110 years earlier the Goncourt Brothers also had fissures in eternity in mind: they described in their journal an eccentricity of the Emperor Napoleon III's attendants and commented: "There are two infinities in this world: God up above, and down below, human baseness."

> Dear Steve,
> I am in the library again. It is first lesson and I cannot work because I feel tired having stayed up last night to the preposterously late hour of 11pm. I tried to watch 'The Cherry Orchard' but failed dismally. It was because I went to a debate after school – 'Hell is Other People' which as you know is a quote from Sartre. It could have been good but it wasn't. The first speaker (a male from Habs) used loads of long words just like you. Apart from that it was boring.

When, many letters ago, I proposed Grace as the pinnacle of human evolution I was not being fanciful. Here is more evidence. In the quest for diverting ways of passing the time, Man tries to justify his existence but only demonstrates its futility. He makes Grace tired in the process.

The futility should be no surprise. The rhythm of the earth is cyclical while a man's life is distinctly linear. He is born, lives a while and dies. Meanwhile the earth, to all intents and purposes, dies every winter and is reborn in spring. The explanation for old people feeling irrelevant becomes immediately obvious: their frame of reference is the world as it was some dozens of its cycles ago. It has renewed itself several times since then, and the cycles with which the elderly were most actively engaged belong to a disappearing past, like the rings in a tree-trunk. Young people may understand the world; for a short time they may even impose themselves upon the world to make it what it briefly is; but the middle-aged and elderly can only expect to be increasingly confused and anxious.

The idea itself, of pursuing a straight line while the mother ship orbits, is distressing. It leads (directly, as is only suitable) to the inference that man is an aberration, a creature that has evolved into a cul-de-sac untenanted by all the rest of life on earth. All other creatures are obedient to the changing seasons and sensitive to the earth's cycle; women too have some susceptibility to regular natural rhythms. But a man has none. He deploys technology to try to bend the world to his mysterious purpose and fails to notice that he is merely distancing himself from life. It was technology, in the first place, that disrupted his response to the world's cycle.

Men have used technology through most of human history to compensate for their physical shortcomings. They built machines to make them stronger, quicker or more deadly in their execution of various tasks: steam engines, flying shuttles, multi-role combat aircraft and the like. From the 70s onwards, the emphasis has shifted to mental shortcomings. Computers took over a lot of the drudgery and people, in theory, were freed to be more creative. But computers are becoming capable of more and more, and the demand for creativity seems finite if not actually diminishing. If, as is often asserted, the brain needs exercise like any muscle, it will need to find itself under disciplined ownership to thrive. There's a human tendency to do as little as possible and let the machine pick up the slack.

Meanwhile the uses that most of us put computing devices to have become increasingly trivial – computer games, selfies, cheeky photo-montage apps. The radio this morning has been agog at a breakthrough in virtual reality headsets. Virtual reality, indeed... here's an image of the near future: a youth lies sprawled on a sofa, wearing a headset that gives him the experience of lying sprawled across a sofa. In *Charley Varrick*, Joe Don Baker silences a roomful of giggling prostitutes by announcing: "I didn't travel 600 miles for the amusement of morons. Is that clear, ladies?" The computer industry has travelled 50 years for the amusement of... well, morons is harsh, but there's a hint of Huxley's epsilon-minus class about it.

How far must one go back to find the origins of this fatally divisive susceptibility to technology? One of the most interesting periods in human history must have been when man realised for the first time that he had a part (so to speak) in procreation. Before that, how would he have had any idea? Counting the months? What months – and what's counting, anyway? Detecting a family resemblance? How – by looking in a mirror? According to Robert Graves, this transition can be dated thanks to the known habits of the ancient Greeks and their architecture. Ionic columns are regarded as feminine: they are smaller in proportion, their fluting represents clothing and the decoration between the volutes might be taken as curly hair or more intimate elements of female biology. The Ionians, worshippers of a goddess, were displaced in perhaps 1200 BC by the Dorians, whose Doric column is austere, squat and strong – an altogether more masculine order whose chief object of worship was the sky god Zeus. Troy fell in about 1200 BC. Grace was directly descended from Helen of Troy.

That is a very decisive full stop and marks a pause *[and a transfer from pencil to blue ball-point]*, during which I pretended I was thinking what to say but didn't really. I have to be honest with you or else you would never know. The fact that it was useless anyway is naturally irrelevant. When I began writing to you last night I was for some obscure reason very contented; however I didn't finish the letter and so when I read it this morning, having changed my mood totally, it seemed incongruous and grated my sensitive ear miserably. That is a mouthful of rubbish.

When letters with this sort of paragraph arrived, I'm sure I took it to be mild banter. She was being playful. Perhaps she over-egged the pudding slightly in droning on about the dullness of her life, the unpredictability of her moods and the impossibility of finding anything at all to say. But now I wonder whether she was not, as she says in this strange paragraph, simply being honest, because otherwise how would I know? How would I know what? Your guess is as good as mine.

> As far as people go I am very happy indeed. Everyone is being excessively right.

Does she mean 'nice'? It would be an odd word for Grace to use, but no more odd in this context than 'right'. What seems probable to me now is that she was thinking of something else entirely, and 'right' popped into her mind just as her hand reached the end of 'excessively'.

> This applies at school only to my life at the moment you see. (I have not seen Beth since Sunday afternoon, and tho' Drew phoned on Monday I didn't go out.) But I can't talk to you about school because you wouldn't find it interesting. At home – I mean home home – the best thing that has happened recently is our television, and really I am indifferent to it. I am seriously worried about my mother who is entirely lifeless – but then, I get out of that by saying 'who isn't?' Of course you can't really. Christ I haven't read this through yet but you must be finding it awful. I refuse to apologise, because if I do not write like this I wouldn't at all. You must tell me which you prefer.

Not at all, I think would have been my instictive reply, but I'm sure I would have kept it to myself.

I wonder whether I had made any progress at all since her first letters. They contained long, descriptive passages through which

I would hurry in the hope that the next paragraph would contain something about us or, better yet, about me. Now the descriptive passages had given way to interior exploration and I approached them in the same selfish spirit. It would not have occurred to me to read her words closely and wonder if there was a cry for help to be decoded.

It must be an ego trip this – or something similar. It is I I I all the time, but I assure you that I intend to write for you and not myself.

My friend has said something to me. She is looking up in an important Latin dictionary. I cannot decide whether you would like her or not. She is a very lonely person due to her genius – for that is undeniably what she is. You said Beth seemed lonely also didn't you? What about yourself? Perhaps all my friends are. Doesn't say much for me, does it...

You going on Saturday made Sunday morning lovely because I woke up thinking it Monday and found out I was wrong. Thank you. Everything is sometimes good. (I consciously avoided the cloud [?] then.) Did your journey go OK? It got warmer here in the afternoon. How are your family?

The bell is going to go. This has taken me 40 minutes – if you wanted to you could work out the number of words per minute, or even per 5 minutes, or even per second. It went when I wrote '5'. Goodbye.

Home again: the endless cycle. Maureen and I read to Mrs Waite out of Michel Quoist again, and again I find it hard to express my anger. What a lot of 'agains'; that should tell you something. I went to Beth's for a while. She was bored as it is her half-term & she is alone. Frank came on Monday & they both went to Drew's.

I have got to the bit in 'Emma' where Churchill (Frank) says: 'How often is happiness destroyed by preparation, foolish preparation.' Just as often they aren't, I agree with you. I cannot get away from you, thank God. Now, I return to difficulties in development in early Tudor English literature – at the moment I can't find any – but if Mrs Bowers says there are some, then there are. If necessary I'll have to make them up. What a life.

I thought I'd wait until I received a letter from you before sending this, so that I'd have something to say. I did. And look what happens. It doesn't matter that you were bending over because I feel all the time. That is very important indeed so don't forget. Thank you for your letter, I thought it was a great day too, but it couldn't not have been. XXXX Grace

It is often very frustrating to be unable to remember a word of what I wrote. To that, now, I can add "or a glimpse of what I did". 'Bending over'? What can that mean? Figuratively, perhaps, bending over backwards to be nice to Mrs McGoldrick? On top of which it was very important and I wasn't to forget it. I can't believe I deciphered it with any more assurance 44 years ago. Perhaps I clarified it on the telephone.

With the task made easier by modern word processing technology, I counted the number of her words. She wrote 541 words in 40 minutes – almost 14 words a minute. This may explain why several of the words are difficult to decipher – 'cloud', for example, and perhaps also 'bending over'. It isn't enormously rapid by a skilled typist's standards. But the best I ever managed, in extreme circumstances imposed by deadlines, was 1,000 words an hour which is not much more – about 16 words a minute. And that was for a readership probably more interested in the adjacent recruitment advertising. Hand-written to my beloved, I doubt I'd ever have managed so many.

As for Frank Churchill, wasn't he untrustworthy, self-satisfied and something of a wide-boy? I imagine I passed a comment about the treacherous appeal of spontaneity. Grace and I had to make preparations or we would never have seen each other. As it was, that Saturday was our first day together in three weeks.

Jonathan Kelly played at Sheffield University on Saturday 28 October. I wonder if I told her? Perhaps not; I hadn't been in Sheffield a month at that time and Grace's failure to visit was not yet an issue. On the other hand Jonathan Kelly was our favourite folkie singer/songwriter, after Nick Drake, and it might have seemed furtive to go to see him without mentioning it. Besides, Grace went to a concert every other evening to judge by her letters.

Jonathan Kelly... Craig or Beth made me listen to him first. I doubt I would ever have heard of him otherwise. He perpetrated some truly atrocious rhymes, notably 'kisses' and 'Mrs' in pursuit of his adulterous ambitions. Through the miracle of YouTube, I can now listen to *Madelaine* while I type... and find as a result that I cannot type at all.

LETTER 13

My search for the 61-year-old Grace has moved on to social media. I've started with Facebook and LinkedIn, since these are clubs of which I have membership.

They open up a world, literally, of possibilities. To the half-dozen or so contemporary Grace McGoldricks disclosed by UK websites, I can now add a score or more international ones: a McGoldrick diaspora. Many of them may well have married into the name and can be discounted but there is no immediate way of telling.

On Facebook, about half the candidates include a photograph – their Profile Picture. They look improbably young. Grace McGoldrick appears to be a named attached mainly to teenage brunettes in the New World. Is it possible some form of nominative determinism operates: that if you're born with a certain name, you develop a particular look? The look might change with the years, of course, but cosmetics can help an earlier generation of Grace McGoldricks keep in step with a more recent one. The idea that the young woman I knew has a Botox habit on top of high-quality reconstructive surgery seems unlikely.

LinkedIn is slightly different in that none of the candidates includes a photograph. This is surprising, since the majority of them are regional representatives for a well-known cosmetics company, and you might think their looks would contribute to their commercial success.

If all else fails I will send messages to these people, but for the moment they can go into the folder marked 'Unlikely'.

A helpful cicerone going by the name of lifehacker.com adds a number of further options. "Google isn't the only game in town," she announces, offering zabasearch.com, pipl.com, wink.com, zoominfo.com and others. Lifehacker coyly points out: "Stalking is a serious business. When we say 'stalk', we're exaggerating, not recommending."

Testing lifehacker's theory, I found two previously undiscovered

Grace McGoldricks in distant lands. One is a quilter in a stitch-and-bitch group in the Pacific Northwest of the United States. The crafters are mainly women of a certain age, and their blog is colourful and appealing. They aren't shy of including pictures of themselves, either, as they draw inspiration from visits to the studios of nearby artists or from neighbouring beauty spots. This Grace looks as if she would be somebody's favourite grandmother; a halo of short, curly hair that might be silver or blond, a twinkling smile and a weakness for mauve cardigans.

The other is more elusive. She may live on the South Island of New Zealand; she owes her barely perceptible Internet footprint to a single Instagrammed photograph with an @rspca tag and a location descriptor attached to it. This Grace, perhaps a volunteer at an animal shelter, is either hugging or restraining what might be a Staffie cross – would they have Staffies in New Zealand?

Although both would fall into roughly the right age bracket, I find it unlikely that either is the one I knew. Examining their pictures, I find myself speculating on the lives they lead. That in turn prompts me to reflect on how unwelcome Grace might find the unlooked-for return of such an old old flame into her orbit. I dispose of that objection by considering my own likely reactions; if the boot were on the other foot, I'd be fascinated to talk to her. I would not find troubling an approach from any of her successors, either, although plain speaking might be necessary in one or two cases.

Grace's next and 13th letter was postmarked 1 November, All Saints Day, and carried a Christmas stamp – an angel with a lute. Grace had reverted to Basildon Bond or whatever her unlined paper was. Now that I hold it up to the light, 40-odd years later, I find that it is indeed Basildon Bond. While we're on the subject of detection, how is it that all her English letters are postmarked St Albans? Apparently, she wrote many of them at school. Between the school and the bus-stop, opposite the freshly painted railings, a pillar box

has been available since the days of George VI. Perhaps she finished them off at home and took advantage of a household stock
of stamps before posting them locally – at 2pm on a Wednesday,
in this case.

> Dear Steve,
>   Thank you for your letter. I was pining for one. I don't know
> when it came because I was away. How can you forgive me for
> not writing? Don't even try to I wrote to you many times includ-
> ing the *[indecipherable: Isolde? Fecund?]* one mentioned on the
> phone. What I wrote then is too personal for me to tell you & not
> be there to see your reaction. As for my other letters written at
> Cambridge – they have been too fragmentary & unsatisfactory. It
> is better to tell you about it now it is all over, then perhaps I can
> be objective. It was v interesting but I wanted you very much –
> mainly because it was so totally free but also because for obscure
> reasons which I can't pinpoint I thought about you more positively
> than usual. Perhaps one reason was because we saw different
> people to those I know & they were still unlike you in many ways
> (only judging superficially of course).

She must have visited Cambridge as part of the university selection
process. She was, as you will have noticed, what her school would
have called Oxbridge material.

I doubt I paid much attention to the letters that were never sent.
Here is the one that was and it makes clear she wanted me; who
cares if a few days had gone by without a letter?

On the other hand, she rarely thought positively about me. I
could only interpret that to my advantage by regarding it as a reference to the general frustration of being so much apart.

As for the phone conversation, that would have been initiated by
me. I don't mean to claim undue credit; it's simply that Grace had
no means of phoning me, except perhaps through prior arrangement and split-second timing around a public phone-box. I don't

think Mrs Jablonski had a phone; even if she had, I would have been reluctant to ask for the privilege of using it. Instead I phoned from the Students Union building, in the foyer of which there was a bank of kiosks, none of which took incoming calls. Our phone conversations, then, were limited by the amount of loose change I had. They were seldom completely satisfactory.

I wonder whether the florin was still in circulation then. It would give the account a suitably historic tone. Now, it would be perverse for us not be in almost perpetual communication, texting, posting, Tweeting, perhaps even talking to each other on our smart phones with generous contracts. The early 70s seems by comparison like an era when rationing was still in force.

> You see I tend to relate everyone I see & talk to to you instinctively (bad?). As I feel I am gradually meeting most types that exist I grow more happy. Because I feel more sure that you are unique. I used to worry that I built you up to be more than you are, through lack of judgment and ignorance. But I don't, I feel sure. I am sure I shouldn't be writing this because you are bound to get an impression different to what I want you to receive. If you don't then you will understand that I have made progress in my ideas of you. If on the other hand you are at a loss – don't mind, & I will explain later. Suffice for the moment to say that I am contented because I don't feel that I have a false idea of you in relation to other people.

All this would have been profoundly worrying. It hardly mattered that she was feeling positive about me, what with me being unique and all. The point that would have caught and held my attention was that she compared me to other people and, in this instance, Cambridge undergraduates. Sooner or later, I would come up short. I could easily see that happening sooner.

If I had read the passage properly, as I had been trained to do by 15 years of good state education, I would have noticed that we were very much alike in our evaluation of ourselves and each other. There was nothing in this letter for me to be anxious about. On the contrary, Cambridge had given her a glimpse of what life might have to offer; Grace not only took pleasure in it but she also wanted me there too.

Now what have we done. Some things were boring and others stimulating. Apart from the boring bits, the best thing I gained from 4 days alone with Meg is an unusually good feeling of understanding. Of course I am glad, and it is what I hoped would happen.

We stayed an extra night to see a play with Ian McKellan in it. Then we talked all night and gassed ourselves on the fire in Meg's room because it leaked. It was on all night and when we rose from our chairs around 6.30am Meg was nearly sick etc etc. The effects lasted all day (she being worse hit than me) but I feel better now. It was worth it and I love you which I nearly wrote was irrelevant but it is never that & if I don't say it I burst.

Thank you for phoning me – all that long time ago. You sounded very sad. Were you? I hated going more than usual.

I want to talk to you above everything now. To tell you what I feel for you. To make you laugh because I have done things that will interest & amuse you. They do that to me but always in an ultimately unsatisfactory way because I have to wait to share them. It becomes very frustrating at times.

I have bought 8 books. One is on Dostoevsky by Gide. What more could I want. You have removed the innermost root of my independence – but in a way which couldn't be more beautiful.

Remember to phone me from Hendon. This is becoming too illegible to be worth continuing. Luckily I am secure in the belief I will see you soon now – so even if something prevents it happening I am momentarily glad. Forgive my writing and incoherence stemming from too many ideas. You are complete to me. Grace

This must have been the high-water mark. I certainly never received another letter like this. Towards the end she was writing diagonally across the page, so urgent was it to get the feelings into words and on to paper. Her name, finally, was penned into the bottom left-hand corner by a tumbling torrent of words.

Hendon. Let's return to something earthy. The reference to Hendon marks an exciting change in my travel arrangements. The train was expensive and, owing to the necessity to go to St Pancras to get back up the line to Grace's home town, tiresome. The motorway coach was cheap and involved less doubling back. It stopped twice: at Leicester Forest East, briefly, for refreshments, and at Hendon Central for dropping off. I dropped off there at what felt like the dead of night – a little before 10pm – and walked down the hill to Hendon railway station, to catch the train north. It was cold on Hendon station and I would not have been surprised to hear wolves howling. But a dozen minutes down the line, love was suffering similar privations.

Grace met me at the station. I drew her towards me and folded the flapping great-coat around her and we kissed and, to all intents and purposes, that was how we spent the weekend.

I am conflating several Friday nights into one: the coach, the cold, cheerless kiosk on Hendon station, the wolves and, finally, Grace meeting me off the train. I can't remember how many such Friday nights there were. She never let me down. We ascended the steps from the station parade slowly, through being locked together at different points: now cheeks, now flanks, pausing to be face to face, and proceeding in much that way up the hill to her home.

On the Sunday afternoon of that weekend I accepted a lift from Craig to the roundabout at the base of the hill that led up to the King Harry in St Albans. To the left the road – then known as the M10 – made the short journey to the M1 and headed north. Here, for the first time, I became a hitchhiker. It must have gone well on that gloomy, chilly day in November 1972 because I continued to thumb lifts on and off until 1981. More to the point it was even cheaper than the train and the motorway coach, although not entirely free. At the junction for Sheffield I treated myself to a bus into the city from Swallownest.

Back in Reading a Triumph Tiger Cub was attracting dust in a garden shed. I didn't think it was up to the journey – it struggled with the Chilterns, so I was reluctant to test it along the spine of England. But the true reason for my neglect of the motorcycle was that winter was approaching. The bike was a mode of transport intended for short rides to a country pub on a warm summer's evening. So strong was that image in my mind that I could see no other possibility. I should have tried harder. The motorcycle represented freedom and in its absence I meekly accepted constraints.

LETTER 14

Grace switched between lined and unlined paper at random as far as I could see. There may be something to be read not between the lines but actually in them. Were they a restraining influence? The lined paper reappeared in her next letter, which is postmarked Wednesday 8 November, 2pm, and again from St Albans.

> Dear Steve *[this within a circle traced around a small coin or perhaps the cap of a biro – it looks as though a cartouche, yet another device to contain her writing, is intended]*
> I can't use the paper we bought from Jane D on Saturday because it has no lines on it & is therefore impossible for me to write on with my right hand. This has a printed margin also *[of which she makes no use]*…
>   I have another interview at Leicester on Friday week. Would that be easier than York? I will look on the map. Anyway I don't know whether I will be going to it, because it says you have to take 3 recent essays and (a) I have only ever written one (apart from exams) and (b) that one will still be at York from the Tuesday interview anyway.
>   Meeting you was one of the first things I thought of; I am glad you did also. Really I don't think it is a very good idea.

This looks hesitant but is in fact emphatic. Normally she would have abbreviated 'very', and possibly 'good' too.

> I badly want to see you but I can't make myself think that it could be satisfactory then. I haven't been able to say this without hurting your feelings, I know – and as you can see I have not made up my mind whether I want to see you or not. Between ourselves it would be beautiful, but after an interview with perhaps only two hours to spare before being pulled away from you again I don't think I could bear it. Do you understand?

I did. I was prone to obedience where a clear preference had been expressed. No violent films, for example.

But enough of that. She had only ever written one essay? I wonder what the Secretary of State for Education would have made of that. I was incredulous. In any case, her letters are littered with references to essays, either in the process of being written or in preparation. Surely she meant that she had only ever written one that was up to the standard she imagined would be demanded by a university.

> For that selfish reason, I am bravely & madly going to try to make you come closer to me & bring myself closer to you through this letter. Your letter felt very close to me indeed because you said what I hoped you would say and expressed my own inadequacy for me. It is not you who should have written that letter but me[1].
>
> I don't properly know how to go about explaining why that is so. Especially as every word takes so long. Basically from your letter I feel that you think I am dissatisfied with you. It is not you that applies to but myself. It goes back to me – all that I found less than perfect last weekend. The reason why that is so is because I find it virtually impossible to concentrate on you and give myself to you as much as I would like. Because of that I am always fighting myself. Just take as examples these things – v different but both important: leaving the pub on Sat night and my continual worries about my work (made worse by interviews etc).

It is true that her handwriting was now barely recognisable from the confident cursive style of August. The letters look as though they are individually formed, slowly, and as though no part of the hand rested on a solid surface.

If, by the way, a footnote was supposed to be attached to the [1] a couple of paragraphs back in the letter, it never appears.

> I hate myself because inside I have such a muddle of thoughts. I

can never detach myself from them at the best times. Everything seems to pile up and I rush from one to the other when I know that I want only to concentrate on you. That is what I wanted to say when I said that thing about some of our kisses being meaningless. It was due to my miserable inability to concentrate on you and cut myself off from irrelevancies – not because you aren't enough for me. How can I explain? You are everything to me, but other things constantly demand my mind. I hate them so much – and the more because they distract me from you – so I tie myself into a bundle of frustration. You are the entity on which I want to focus all my feelings and hopes and emotions and thoughts. Things conspire to prevent me from so doing, leading to misery.

I am asking too much of myself as regards you, perhaps? But surely that is what love is?

For God's sake, S, know that you are blameless in my eyes, if when we are together it is imperfect. I can't go on writing now.
Grace

'I hate myself'. Not knowing how to react, I would probably have chosen to regard this as hyperbole and ignored it, or said something trite and unhelpful – 'Why would you hate yourself? You aren't hateful. I love you'. She almost certainly meant it literally, however. She was a serious-minded young woman and apt to be hard on herself. At the same time, we've seen enough of her writing by now to regard it as possible that her hating herself was not a permanent nor necessarily a long-lasting state of mind. How often it would recur might become important but I would hardly trouble myself with thoughts of what might happen, as long as I was 'blameless in her eyes'.

Where she signs off, the capital G of her name is inscribed within a circle. It occurs to me at last that these geometric shapes, one at the beginning of the letter and the other at the end, are by a distance the steadiest, clearest elements in the letter. She may have used the cap of the biro by way of compasses. Two circles, echoing across the paper.

(my mother bought one of the raffle tickets from me at her own suggestion...)

I am sorry about the beginning of this letter. It sounds false mainly because I was finding it hard to get going.

1hr later I saw this lying on my bed and wanted to talk to you again; at least I can tell you that I wanted to. I will write again very soon. If this hasn't made you any better in your mind about me then we can meet in York, I won't be martyring myself, I promise you – it is only fear that makes me say I don't want to see you then. Love G.

It will not have escaped your notice that there's no sign of Sheffield on the list of universities she was applying to. I wasn't particularly upset about that: I didn't look forward much beyond the next weekend, far less the next three years.

Later in my undergraduate life, when I had begun to take more interest in Sheffield University, I found something rather unsettling about couples who had known each other before university and had carried their relationships forward into it – as though they were protecting themselves from a deficit, insulating themselves against the experience in some ill-defined way. York or Leicester, I thought, were admirable compromises. With direct rail connections to both cities we could see each other at the drop of a hat without being in each other's pockets.

In other words, I did not tax her on the subject. In any case we had known each other no more than three months and had spent precious few days together. The idea that we would be a good fit for three years was optimistic, and it made no sense for her to gamble her future on it. Besides, I would have happily settled for her spending just a weekend in Sheffield. A counter of minutes, I was content to let the years look after themselves.

LETTER 15

Grace had a self-contained quality that provoked a complicated response. Despite her comments about my occasional knack of reacting in just the way she needed me to, it was seldom obvious that she actually needed anything. In person she was often serene. It is noticeable, too, that in her dealings with her friends she invariably gave the impression of being slightly aloof, or perhaps less emotional.

And yet she wrote about her feelings with clarity and candour. The ability to distinguish between 'need' and 'want' would have served me, not to mention a greater attention to what she wrote. As it was, I often pictured her to myself in a religious context, wearing a lot of white and emitting a celestial aura. Chastity was leaving a radiant brand on our relationship.

Her next letter arrived just a couple of days later – a surprising turn of events, given the evident difficulty she was having writing, not to mention her various anxieties. The handwriting was small again but more even, although it deteriorated from time to time.

> Dear S
>   Thank you for your letter which I received this afternoon. I read it very quickly & then again slowly. This will be a more newsy letter also. Craig drove me home & I talked to take my mind off you waiting by yourself & not understanding me. Then I had to go to Beth's & it was really awful & she was v upset about Saturday. I don't know why I am telling you all this because it is the past now. Anyway I felt bad & said all the wrong things as usual and in between pity felt angry at her as well as myself.

In other letters she writes in great detail about her activities when I am not there; when I am, her references are mysterious (eg bending over) or tangential. It would help me if she were to say a little more about what we did with our weekend. Why was Beth so upset about Saturday? I ought to know without having to rely on Grace to remind me. It's possible that I didn't even notice at the time, so accustomed had I become I to the idea of poor Beth being moody.

Monday was OK. On Tuesday I couldn't face school and so I didn't go. I read all day & talked to my mother who changes so much about everything. I don't know what to think of her any more. Maureen is going to stay at Southampton this weekend, at somebody's girlfriend's house (which is why her mother let her go) & she is therefore v happy & so it rubs off on me & I enjoy her company tho' it leads to rather one-sided conversations.

Thursday. Hello. I am babysitting at the psychologists' house as usual. The children have gone to bed. 'Top of the Pops' was the best it's been for ages – and even then I didn't positively like any record on it. Did you see the programme on China? I thought it was v interesting. Parts of it sounded ideal (eg the relationship between officers and men) but bits did seem dubious & rather inhuman. Now it is the news and it is really boring as usual – I can remember the time when I used to find it interesting… My mind is relaxing so much now that I am in danger of forgetting it is you I am writing to. It is because now you seem very far away – nearer always when I read one of your letters – but otherwise cut off from everything else in me, in a separate box. I still relate much of what I do to you, though. So you do influence me, but in a different way to how you did before.
    I am finding this v hard to say because it takes so long to write & by the time I have written it I have changed my mind. So you can disregard most of what I have just said.

What a curious young woman. If I'd been a few years older – 44 years older, give or take – I might have wondered whether medication was involved. The insecurity, the profound uncertainty of mood, the handwriting difficulties… I wonder what sort of pastoral care a private education bought you in 1972. Being able to take a day off when you couldn't face it sounds like an enlightened regime.

I did not see the programme on China. I saw very little television of any description in my early days at Sheffield. Mrs Jablonski's lounge was part of her living space and although I was invited I didn't want to take advantage. Besides, what sort of undergraduate would be sitting watching TV with his landlady on a regular basis? And while there was a television lounge at the Students Union I didn't start to use it with any regularity until the second term. I was, simply, studious. I wrote letters. And, unlike my poor friend in the south, I wrote many essays.

> I went to Beth's yesterday & we talked about school almost all the time.
>
> I am home now. I suddenly wished that you lived just round the corner & I could go & visit you. But that is not to be. All the people I know best have some effect on me – but you are a part of me which now I feel I can never cut away. Even at my most cynical when I imagine – or try to imagine – our relationship dissolving into indifference – you can never totally leave me because you have even now changed me so much. We must go on working & moving forward *[three words obliterated here]* to infinity only, of course. The thing is never to pass it & come down the other side. Ultimately – at this moment – we are together and facing each other which is the right way to be. Long may it continue my love.
> Grace

This may be as moving a declaration of love as anyone could hope for. It expresses much of what I felt too, and 'I suddenly wished that you lived just round the corner & I could go & visit you' could be straight out of *The End of the Affair*, Bendrix contemplating Sarah inaccessible across the Common.

But my shrivelled sub-editor's soul, 44 years later, hoists its spectral hand and raises an objection. Do parts of that final paragraph sound a bit stilted? 'But that is not to be'… 'together and facing each other'… As for 'working & moving forward', that might have come out of a party political broadcast.

My soul is churlish and I hope I did not allow it to express itself. Instead, I would be very surprised if I had not quoted Milton to her by then:

"The world lay all before them, where to choose
Their place of rest and Providence their guide,
They, hand in hand, with wand'ring steps and slow
Through Eden took their solitary way."

Perhaps, after that, it is hard to say anything moving and original in your own words.

INTERVAL

This section deserves some sort of fanfare, or at least a drum-roll and an over-excited voice-over: "At this point in the account, the mists of time part and we emerge, hesitantly at first, into the sharp spotlight of the historical record."

But the figure of speech faces the wrong way. The historical record is almost all we have had so far, in the form of Grace's letters. What we have been noticeably short of is the oral tradition. Prehistory becomes history when someone makes a record to hold information other than in a human memory – by incising a wax cylinder, making notches on a stick, baking a marked clay tile or by writing letters and figures on hide, papyrus or Basildon Bond. Herodotus, the Father of History, takes over from Homer, the Memory Man. Here, the tale has been the wrong way round; my hitherto blank memory suddenly makes its contents available to complement Grace's written record.

The log-raft of the letters, being chronological, has been gradually drifting downstream towards the present. It's only natural that memory should improve the closer we come to the here and now. But one day in November 44 years ago is not very much closer than the previous day in November 44 years ago. There must be more to explain my sudden access of memory. And there is. The 14 November 1972 was a special day. I need the Internet only to confirm that the day of the week was Tuesday.

I can remember the weather unaided. It was a bright, mild autumnal morning in south Yorkshire and I was up and about in it for a 9am lecture. A tutorial followed at 10am and this yielded an essay, returned and marked. At 11am I took this unexpectedly influential piece of work to the coffee lounge to consider at leisure.

In writing the essay I must have been struggling to stretch my material to a respectable length; it was even more long-winded than usual. Against one of my preferred pseudo-scientific circumlocutions – "the truth of this assertion might be demonstrated by recourse to Buys Ballot's Law" or some such – the tutor had written: "As Jerry Rubin would have said, 'Do it!'"

Thanks to *Playpower* I knew who Jerry Rubin was. I also knew that his original remark would almost certainly have been intended to urge a vigorous act of civil disobedience, not the cautious demonstration of a scientific proposition. But reading it in a Sheffield coffee lounge that morning I was struck by the urgency of its tone and by the way in which it might constitute a general call to action. I reread it and saw that it was an unambiguous message from the psychokinetic beyond. Its clear imperative could easily apply to one specific deed: it was Jerry Rubin telling me, by no means his disciple but prepared to listen to his far-flung voice, to go directly to York, where Grace was visiting the university that day.

Had Jerry Rubin, the Menelaus of the counter-culture, been there in person we might have discussed it. Since Grace's 14th letter, treating the possibility of a meeting in York with notable caution, we had broached the subject again in the course of an increasingly tense telephone conversation. Grace had repeated her reluctance to see me in York and a second, perfectly valid reason, had emerged: she was going for an interview that might determine the next three years of her life, possibly more, and I would be a distraction. The University of York must have first call on whatever concentration she could bring to bear on the visit. We could meet anytime – the following week, perhaps.

Jerry Rubin was not there in person. Instead, I had his simple exhortation, written by one admirer for the instruction of another. His words gained strength from their timing. It was as though Ian Anderson was clearing his throat all over again.

It dawned on me that if I went to York and intercepted Grace at the end of her visit, I could do no damage to her concentration on the events of the day. In reasoning thus, I overlooked her main objection: initially, she had been worried not about concentration but about spending a couple of hours with me before being whisked away. I gave that no thought at all.

Instead, as though my brain could operate on only one aspect of the project at a time, I realised that this was the only way I could see her there anyway. I knew nothing about the arrangement of her day. For example, I didn't even know how she was getting to York. The likelihood had to be that she would travel by train. If I went to York and waited at the railway station, I reasoned, I would eventually intercept her.

It was about 11.30am by this time. I didn't know how much time the train journey from Sheffield to York took. More to the point, I didn't know what time Grace's day at the university would end. Not before 2pm, I decided, trying to remember the days I had spent visiting various universities around the country a year earlier. Well, I had nothing better to do with my taxpayer-subsidised time: I finished my coffee, tucked the essay away and headed for the bus-stop to board the number 60 coming in from Crimicar Lane to the railway station.

It would be dishonest not to mention a short diversion on my way to the bus stop. I went to a strange, all-purpose grotto of a shop run by a scaly troglodyte of indeterminate gender. And purchased three condoms. They were not boxed and could be purchased singly, like cigarettes in an earlier era. In any other shop this would have been an embarrassing transaction; here, it almost raised the tone. The proprietor's complexion hinted at a lack of condoms at the crucial moment some years earlier.

I never mentioned this purchase to Grace. It was simply a matter of being prepared. I expect Frank Churchill would have had something dismissive to say about such preparation; or, like many wealthy Georgians, he may have had secreted about his person a section of sheep gut, ready for use not at short notice but after prolonged soaking to make it malleable.

The day was less sunny than earlier, but the gathering anti-cyclonic gloom was not going to dampen my mood. I always enjoyed a train journey and this one had a more princely purpose than most. The excitement carried me as far as York and only began to dissipate when I arrived and finally began to think the idea through.

The layout of York railway station has changed since 1972 but some of its key features – from my point of view then – remain the same. Most of the trains to London leave from the platform closest to the station entrance. Some, however, leave from the next platform island, accessed by a footbridge. I needed to find a position that gave me a view of the foot of the footbridge steps where the concourse emerged into the station proper.

There is still a bench in the position I chose. It looks north from the end of platform 1 (now unused). I wonder if I thought platform 1 needed to be covered as well, in case she was thriftily taking a stopping train that began its long journey along a suburban line. The bench gave me a clear view of the footbridge steps and the main station concourse. It was about 1.45pm when I installed myself there.

Harvard students enrolled in classes with the art historian Professor Jennifer L Roberts were apparently invited to submit to a singular form of initiation. She instructed them to nominate a piece of art and then to go and look at it for three hours. At least York railway station gave me a moving, changing, living tableau to enjoy. As for the three hours, I had no means of knowing how long I would have to study it.

In later years I became adept at passing the time. Hours on end, in airport lounges, railway stations, long-haul airliners; I could beguile them away effortlessly as long as I had a book and a newspaper. Later still, I added napping to the repertoire of ways in which the hour-hand could be coaxed around its perimeter.

Raymond Chandler, referring (I think) to a night Marlowe spends in a cell, talks about "the kind of time they don't make in watches". If they did, you would ration yourself; you would carefully restrict the frequency with which you checked the time, so that time ticked away in chunks of 10 minutes or more, and every so often another hour would have gone by and the waiting would be appreciably diminished.

On York railway station I had a newspaper, a book and an annotated essay to pass the time. The newspaper was the *Guardian*. That Tuesday afternoon may have been the first time ever that I attempted a cryptic crossword. It certainly didn't go very well – in my mind's eye I can see no more than four or five answers filled in after hours of intermittent effort. Again, this was a skill that I began not long afterwards to develop, though usually in company. It could have been worse, I suppose – a crossword that yielded within minutes would have been of little use to me that day.

The book was something by Steinbeck – *East of Eden*, I think. Yes, it was *East of Eden*; I remember a lurid Pan cover and the words: "The book that introduces Kathy – the most evil woman in fiction." I wonder if Steinbeck thought that was what his book was about.

The essay had no further interest for me and indeed at some point in what remained of the day I mislaid it. Well, its work was done. It had become expendable.

At about 2.15pm I began to consider the question of lunch. A kiosk plied its trade away to my right, but to use it I would lose sight of the concourse for however long I stood at the counter. I worried over this for some time. It would be absurd to travel to York and miss her for the sake of a sandwich. The same anxiety attached to the idea of coffee and how long a trip to the Gents might take me away from my post.

Eventually the temperature made up my mind. Sitting still on my north-facing bench, I began to feel chilly. It was a mid-November day but it had opened, as I said, in bright sunshine in Sheffield. When I left the house I had been planning no northerly journeys. I was wearing a navy blue corduroy jacket of the kind known as 'safari', with panel pockets above and below and a belt at the waist. It was not particularly thick; presumably, being a safari jacket, it was intended for the kind of climate I might have found in Kenya. Below it, my bargain-basement denims were even cheaper and thinner.

I walked over to look at the destination boards and, reassured that no London-bound train was due in the next 10 minutes, I bought a pastie and a coffee and, to remove any lingering odour of pastie, some chewing gum.

Lunch (and tidying up afterwards) takes us through to 2.45pm. You see? An hour has passed by already. Nothing has happened. Few crossword clues have been solved, no pages devoted to evil women have been turned, but an hour has passed and that can only mean that however long this vigil proves to be, it is now an hour shorter.

That is assuming, of course, that she is leaving by train this afternoon or evening. There are other possibilities: the McGoldricks might have come up en famille, in the car; she might have a friend in York to match the one in Cambridge and intend to spend the night; she might have called the visit off. I begin to consider the possibility that this is a fool's errand and that I should impose a time limit. No, I decide; either she shows up or, accepting a sign similar to Jerry Rubin's earlier in the day, I will acknowledge defeat and leave.

On the other hand, the open-ended nature of the commitment appeals to me. I am conscious that what I am doing might – indeed should – be regarded as romantic. Patience and durability were romantic qualities in the stirring tales of yore; dragons or agons constituted one kind of trial but not the only kind. Was it Jacob who waited seven years for Rachel and, on discovering he had been tricked into marrying her sister, worked another seven years for her? He must have been cream-crackered after all that.

The railway station contributes to the fluid passage of time. People emerge on to the platform in an almost unbroken stream. On a weekday afternoon they are not so numerous as to make identification difficult, should anyone in need of identification appear, but they provide a regular diversion. I find that the book is superfluous – it demands continuous attention, whereas a crossword clue may be glanced at and considered while gazing elsewhere.

The rhythm of the station also establishes itself and helps to advance the hour. Regular services come and go and the names of some of the destinations remind me that I am in a region unfamiliar to me. Perhaps someone better travelled than I would be similarly impressed by a station announcer in, say, Budapest, directing passengers to trains for Sofia, Vienna and other cities; in York the names of Scarborough, Durham and Selby seem exotic enough to me.

But time drags, there's no denying it. And the afternoon gets no warmer. As darkness begins to fall – I can just about make out the arched opening of the station to the north, around the elegant curve of the platform, but the artificial light on the concourse makes the same point more sharply – the temperature falls with it. I risk a trip to the Gents and another to the kiosk for a coffee. No-one takes my seat. It is as though the station has accepted that this is my bench for the rest of the day. Besides, anyone waiting long enough to sit down now will almost certainly head for the waiting room in preference to the open air. I consider making periodic circuits of places a traveller might sit while waiting for a train, like a nightwatchman checking premises, but there really is no point. If she turns up, she will sooner or later be visible from where I am stationed.

Grace appeared eventually a little after 5pm. I can still see her in my mind's eye: she was looking around for a departures board; perhaps she wanted to check that the 5.30pm was on time. If so, she was going to miss it.

She was dressed sensibly in a duffel coat and her hair was tucked down inside the collar. She didn't see me when I rose from my bench for the last time, nor as I moved towards her. I was quite close by the time she realised she was being approached. And in that instant her face, which had been slightly pinched whether by cold or traveller's anxiety, was flooded by a smile and a gasp that promised to turn into a laugh.

"Speechless, eh?" I said. "That's good. I'll settle for speechless." I'd had some time to prepare what I was going to say, and that wasn't it.

We embraced and held on to each other as if one of us had just returned from the trenches. The life of the station made room for us and flowed around the small island we created. We were interlaced. Time may have stood still, briefly, within the bubble that contained us.

Eventually she drew back and said: "What a wonderful surprise!"

"I wasn't sure you'd be pleased. In the end, I couldn't stay away."

She smiled again and said: "I've been thinking I've been a bit mean to you about it. Putting you off, I mean."

"No, you shouldn't worry about that. You have enough to think about on a day like this without lovelorn teenagers importuning you."

She squeezed my forearm. "Let's go and get a coffee. How long have you been waiting?"

Coffee of indifferent quality was easy – my kiosk served it by the carboy. I was more interested in an alcoholic drink, but in those days pubs and bars didn't open until 5.30pm. A decent cup of coffee would do. We set off, hand in hand, with wand'ring steps and slow, towards the station entrance. There would be a hotel close by, with a lounge. "I've been here long enough to check the local facilities," I said, "but I didn't dare move from my bench in case you slipped by when I wasn't looking."

"Have you been sitting there for hours?"

"Not all that long. It was a last-minute decision to come. How has your day gone?"

"Let's leave that until we're sitting down. It's been all right but I feel as if I've been on my feet for most of it."

Having turned left at random out of the station we came to a pub that looked too scruffy to be considered. Beyond it was a rather elegant hotel. Grace was dressed for an interview so it would be I who would let the side down. We entered, located a lounge and sat down. It was unnecessarily well-lit but comfortable enough.

"Will they come to us?" she asked.

"I don't know. I always assumed you had more experience of the high life than me."

"High life? The Station Hotel, York? Perhaps I do if that's your yardstick."

"I'll go and see what I can see. What would you like?"

"Just a coffee, Steve, please."

I left her with the plastic bag that contained my book, newspaper and, perhaps no longer, my essay. A bored young woman at the hotel reception desk took my order. Back in the lounge Grace had *East of Eden* out. I crouched beside her and we embraced again and this time kissed, too. Nobody said "get a room" in those days, though we were in a hotel. It crossed my mind to importune her. She said: "We did *Of Mice and Men* last year. I didn't really get it. So I haven't read any others."

I said: "*Sweet Thursday* was the first grown-up book I ever read. It was on a shelf in a holiday cottage we were renting on Anglesey – I would have been 13 or 14. I doubt I understood very much of it – I wouldn't have known what a flophouse was, or what profession the girls at the Bear Flag followed. But I've had a soft spot for Steinbeck ever since and also a superstition about Thursdays. Good things happen on Thursdays. And on Tuesdays, because here we are. Tell me about your day."

I was content to look at her and smile and stroke her hair and cheek as she talked me through her visit: a tour of the campus, lunch in the students' union, fellow interviewees, two more or less informal interviews in the English department separated by empty 'free' time. I said that she had written more enthusiastically about Cambridge after her days there; she replied that she doubted whether anywhere would quite measure up to Cambridge viewed from the perspective of an undergraduate's lodgings. How had I chosen from the universities I'd visited?

I didn't want to find an extra chair at the table for the ghost of Cynthia so I spoke instead of the mystical appeal of Yorkshire. I praised the Dales on the one hand and the North Sea coast on the other without ever having been to either. I tried hard to make industrial decline sound glamorous before contrasting York with such blighted cities as Sheffield, Leeds and Bradford. Sheffield, I'd been told, produced very little table cutlery any more but had turned its hand to plastic picnic cutlery – I mentioned this in making a case for ingenious, resilient and surprisingly warm-hearted Strongitharms. If Grace wouldn't come to Sheffield I wanted her in York. I'm sure she knew what I was doing. In case she didn't, I told her explicitly.

"You aren't disappointed that I didn't apply to Sheffield, are you?" she asked.

I didn't know where to begin answering that. She must have noticed my difficulty, because she stepped in herself. "Look at how we were on the station: you're concerned not to upset me by springing a visit on me, I worry about how you must have felt not to have been invited. We're considerate. We care for each other. I don't see that much can go wrong while that's true."

I said: "I won't deny that I daydream about you being in Sheffield. Just for a weekend, now, but if a weekend is good, years at a time must be better."

That produced the first "Hum..." of the day. She went on: "When you were doing the UCCA circuit last year, how did you go about it?"

"Originally I was set on Bristol – I struggled through Maths A Level because Bristol was in the vanguard of the quantitative revolution and its course was heavily statistical. Then I decided on Sheffield anyway just from the feeling I got from the place."

"I didn't mean that. I meant you were free to go wherever you wanted to, yes? And away from home, you could live more or less as you chose?" I agreed. She went on: "If I went to Sheffield, I wouldn't have that same freedom. You wouldn't want to restrict me, would you? And if I went to Sheffield and it didn't work out between us, how awful would that be?"

I said: "You're right, of course. In my daydreams, nothing interferes with the course of true love. Even to consider the possibility seems like a hostage to fortune. I can't imagine my life without you now."

"Me neither," she said, "but until three months ago we managed quite well, didn't we?"

"Three and a half. And yes, I suppose we did. But you've shown me something I had never suspected life might have to offer. It's all-consuming, Grace. It's as though all the colour has drained out of everything else in my life and only you…" I failed to finish the sentence. "I can't see beyond it," I managed eventually.

"Is this what you meant by a lovelorn teenager importuning me?" She raised us both above my discomfort.

"No. Importunate would be suggesting we book in for the night" – I motioned in the direction of Reception – "and you phone your parents with a white lie." This was unfair and I should have withdrawn it straight away. We had speculated on how we would spend our first night together and had agreed that only somewhere very special would do. A railway hotel in a random provincial city would be dishonourable. In the shadow of a lie, nothing good could possibly come of it.

She must have thought so too, because she said: "I'm sorry, I can't," without a "hum" to soften the negative.

"I know. It's not what I want either. I was being facetious. Besides, it's hard to see how the lie could have been anything other than Bible black."

I wonder what I did have in mind for our first night. It wasn't going to be Mrs Jablonski's, and my home and hers were out of the question. Like so much else, I doubt I had even thought much about it. With Grace the moment was always sufficient unto whatever the expression collapses into. When I was with her I simply wanted the clock to stop. I tried to express some of that to her. She said she felt much the same way.

We talked about getting something to eat and discarded the idea, since she had eaten in the middle of the day and wasn't hungry. We also rejected the idea of a drink; roaming an unfamiliar city in search of a pub in which we could feel comfortable seemed unappealing. Besides, the clock was still ticking and her return home was going to be late.

We made our way back to the station, arm in arm. The next London train didn't stop until Peterborough; some called at Doncaster in between, and I would have gone that far with her. Although a Geography student, I wasn't entirely sure how far it was to Peterborough and therefore how far back to Sheffield. So I put her on the train, when it came, and installed her in a compartment, and pulled the door back across one of the more extraordinary days of my life.

Nothing had happened. I had spent a great many hours sitting around, and more were in prospect. When I returned to Sheffield I would make my way back to the room in which Mrs Jablonski's Dandelion & Burdock awaited, and tomorrow another day devoid of Grace would dawn.

Lord Byron, a latecomer to keeping a daily record, wrote on 14 November 1813: "At five-and-twenty, when the better part of life is over, one should be something; – and what am I? nothing but five-and-twenty and the odd months. What have I seen? the same man all over the world, – ay, and woman too."

To feel that the better part of life is over is sad, at whatever age. But that need not conflict with the temptation to attach more significance to some days than to others.

The cost of a return ticket, off-peak, with student discount, Sheffield to York, was £1 in 1972. If I ever become famous enough to be the subject of one of those quick-fire Q&A interviews in a

magazine, and one of the questions is: 'What was the Best £1 You
Ever Spent', there's the answer.

LETTER 16

You might reasonably regard it as deeply suspicious that a man who can barely remember what school his beloved attended should suddenly recall substantial extracts from a conversation he had with her 44 years ago.

I ask for a little latitude on three grounds.

First, I believe I have been faithful to the spirit of what was said.

Second, all direct-speech dialogue in novels and plenty in nonfiction is invented to a certain extent.

Third, at least I was there. Some of history's most famous speeches were carefully inserted into the orator's mouth by absentee historians many years after the event. Pericles may very well have said, in his famous funeral oration: "The friend who is familiar with every fact of the story may think that some point has not been set forth with that fullness which he wishes and knows it to deserve." Equally, he may have said nothing of the kind. Thucydides blithely asserts that those were the words the situation called for.

I confess I am hazy on details of the precincts of York railway station in 1972. The hotel lounge in which I claim we sat and talked and drank coffee may actually have been an early form of fast-food outlet; bright lights and tacky furniture intrude into my memory of the evening. It's something of a palimpsest: memories of other conversations from subsequent eras overlay their contexts and make it difficult to see clearly. This happens to sounds as well as images: if I try to remember Grace's voice, it invariably emerges in my imagination with an Australian accent.

Where I am in no doubt is in what was not discussed.

We did not talk at all about her handwriting problem, and whether it might become more severe as exams approached in the following year, and what I might do to help. In a relationship based largely on letters this should have been an urgent consideration.

We did not talk about the hopelessness she periodically falls prey to, nor the flatness that so often pervades her mood. I expect I wanted time spent together to generate warmth and light. I was too simple to see that unless we addressed the darkness we should expect to spend more time in it.

By my lights it had been a very successful day. I imagine I felt inordinately pleased with myself on the train back to Sheffield. I probably congratulated myself on what an unexpectedly romantic fellow I had proved to be. What I didn't think about, I can guarantee, was the unusual mutation of my idea of love. I can guarantee that because it only came to me as I was going over our conversation in my mind and writing it down.

I had come to regard our love as a distinct, thriving entity. It demanded respect and consideration. The trouble was, of course, that because it was kept in a cupboard most of the time I was beginning to regard it as cake that might be had but not eaten.

When, for example, we looked forward to the circumstances in which we might make love for the first time, I thought we owed it to some specific quality of our love to do it full justice. Well, you might concede, the first time would only happen once; it isn't unusual to want it to be perfect. To which a number of objections might be raised: approached in the right spirit, every time might feel like the first time; taking excessive care will defeat the object – this is an occasion for spontaneity and loss of control; in any case, according to the Law of Primacy and Recency the last time is just as likely to be remembered as the first; that being the case the important thing is just to get on with it.

Instead, I was beginning to treat our love as though it were an organism that we had to maintain in a carefully controlled environment – monitoring the levels of temperature and humidity, adjusting the flow of nutrients. The purpose would not necessarily be to encourage growth – growth is the natural tendency of all living things and, for that matter, feelings, until they come to term and die – but to keep the thing at a certain pitch.

Grace and I were the stewards of our love. It was Eden, and what dwelt within it was our responsibility. Where that analogy leads is immediately obvious – Grace could hardly be other than Eve, the most misunderstood woman in non-fiction.

She began the next letter the day after her trip to York, Wednesday 15 November, but did not post it until Sunday 19 November.

Dear S,
I am sitting here thinking of you. I have a muddled mind at the moment but I want to write. Tuesday seems such a long way away that I have had to write. That shows you that much of the time I write from selfish motives. Well, I do – but never totally. On the way home from York I met the girl who I disliked and talked to before the interview. She was really quite nice. By the end of the journey we were talking quite personally – because we agreed that as we'd never see each other again it didn't matter. So it was very odd altogether.

On Wednesday Maureen's car broke down halfway to school. We phoned her mother & as neither of us wanted to go to school and I only had two lessons anyway, we didn't. Thursday was confusing – Maureen phoned & then Beth. Maureen should have had an interview at Bognor Regis TTC but when she got there it was horrible – opposite Butlins etc – and so she didn't go in. Beth has been ill with a cold, headache etc & she had 2 days off school. I was a little cross because I missed the programme on China & I was thinking of watching it with you. Anyway. (I felt bad about not ringing her too.)

It was generally mediocre at Leicester, very cold but the town was rather pretty.

Did Leicester in 1972 have an ancient medieval heart that has since been bulldozed? My impression of Leicester, from a visit four years ago, is that there are some very attractive buildings and each of them is ruined by its hideous neighbours. I can't help wondering whether Grace went to the right place. Leicester? Pretty? After dark and through an alcoholic haze, perhaps.

They took a day off at the drop of a straw boater, didn't they? Perhaps that is how it was/is at public school. And yet the schools achieve high grades when it counts. I knew how smart Grace was and I'm beginning to warm to Maureen – to go all the way to Bognor Regis and then not to go into the interview because there's a holiday camp nearby. It's priceless. Perhaps if Butlins had premises in Leicester, Grace would have seen it in its true colours.

The programme on China makes a second appearance, suggesting a series rather than a single documentary. When she talks about thinking of watching it with me she must have had some form of telepathic communing in mind – perhaps I had undertaken to be in the Students Union's television lounge at a particular time. This was the year Nixon visited China, wasn't it?

Her handwriting had deteriorated again. This letter was a scratchy scrawl. When I compare it to the first letter she sent me, from France back in August, it seems barely conceivable that they were produced by the same person.

There were 4 odious girls and 2 meek men outside the door when I got there. Running late as usual. I don't seem to like people very much, do I? What sort of an attitude is that? On the way home I had another intimate conversation in the station buffet. It was with a woman all about her boils (treated with penicillin), being sterilized, her foster child and her daughter in care who she is fighting a court case over, & her boyfriend – an unobtrusive guy of about 40 who bought her a Lucozade and disappeared into a fog of steam surrounding the fruit machine. Her former husband died in an operation.

(Major interruption as Maureen phones. She told me she saw Craig in Watford today & that he mentioned you in connection with Genesis being like Yes (or vice versa). Tony has bought 'Close to the Edge'.) They may be coming round tonight – I told them to if they have nothing better to do, mainly to stave off my guilt. Beth has gone to see East of Eden in St Albans with Pauline. I could have gone and had a lift, but I already have a headache and am settling more than comfortably down to a nice, quiet evening at home. I can't think why I don't mind not going out; before, I would always go, however bad I knew it was going to be beforehand. Perhaps it is the beginning of a more mature/lazy/cynical attitude? Who knows.

Who indeed? But it does not carry the punctuation that would make it a formal question. The preceding sentence, by contrast, has a question mark but is more in the nature of wondering aloud. It is reminiscent of the cover notes to *This Was*, the first Jethro Tull album; they conclude: "This is how we were playing then – but things change. Don't they."

East of Eden makes a second appearance within a few days. The East of Eden Beth went to see, though, was a band that had a brief moment in the spotlight with something called *Jig-a-Jig*. I doubt they would get away with that today. East of Eden supported the Sensational Alex Harvey Band that night. The Internet is unbelievably well informed on long-forgotten gigs by long-forgotten bands.

Drew phoned last night & I spoke to him today. He mainly wanted to tell me that you were coming, which was nice of him. He has an offer from Leeds (& Beth has one from Hull (no interviews)) which pleased him. He babysat tonight, and that was all we talked about.

I am trying to transcribe these letters verbatim, with all their occasional eccentricities and errors faithfully reproduced. The software thwarts me from time to time, automatically inserting its own 'corrections'. Unless I notice them at the time they will survive into the final draft, because no proofreader alive will be keeping a sharp eye open for accurate copy that he or she can sprinkle with errors.

Grace's nested parentheses, however, have evidently won Microsoft's favour. I saw plenty of these in my days as a computer programmer – it is a way of determining the order in which coded instructions will be executed – but her use of them in plain English prose is boldly innovative. It looks, too, as though she were approaching the technique in a spirit of trial and error – earlier in the letter there is a closing bracket without an opening bracket to balance it.

Beth has an offer from Hull without need of an interview. I wonder if she had to ask the headteacher's permission.

> I went to Beth's this morning – always a dangerous thing to do. She gave me your letter to read – I didn't want to because of the resultant necessity of taking 'sides'. We agreed that it probably wasn't condescending. She is not coming, though, because of what happened at the 3 H sh's. I want to shout but I can see her viewpoint. She really isn't being as petty as this is making her sound. She just goes into things too deeply & one-sidedly, that is all. I would do the same but act differently outwardly, I expect. It will all resolve itself in the end, I suppose.

Apparently I had been busy. I'd taken up an invitation to spend a weekend at Drew's. I would be going south to see Grace, but by staying at Drew's I eased the burden on Mrs McGoldrick and, thereby, the rest of us. And I had written to Beth. If Beth detected condescension she was almost certainly accurate.

The 3 H sh's was the Three Horseshoes in Letchmore Heath. This, from one of the earliest letters, was where I thought we may have gone when we stood up Mark Hopkins and his party at the White Horse. Needless to say, I have no idea what happened at the 3 H sh's. I had not at that stage in my life encountered Arthur Balfour's comment: "Nothing matters very much and few things matter at all", but I believe I was ready for it.

What on earth would have possessed me to write to Beth? It

was plainly entering a minefield, to have anything more to do with her than was absolutely necessary. I can only assume that there had been a misunderstanding involving her and Grace at the Three Horseshoes – someone's failure to buy a round, I shouldn't wonder – and I had written to try to put matters back on an even keel. I hope I was sober at the time. I doubt the dry cider at the Three Horseshoes was as seductively cheap as in the Students Union bar (where, as I may have said, it cost 9p a pint and sweet cider 10p; a rare instance of economics coinciding with intuition – the extra ingredient, sugar, adding 1p to the price).

A flash of memory pierces my glibness: Beth was upset because she felt Grace and I were making a gooseberry of her that night. Since she would almost certainly have been in the right, I hope my letter was one of apology but it doesn't sound very much like it.

> Since I am thrown from problem to problem it is no wonder I am becoming so indifferent. I am very aware now of when friction is going to start & why. But each crisis is so laughably similar & seldom fatal. My sensitivity is becoming restricted to the analysis rather than being poured into feeling (what the hell am I talking about?) God I hope Maureen & Tony don't come round…
>
> At that point I went downstairs and spent an agreeable 15 mins with my parents discussing the new lampshades in their bedroom and the immorality of men. My mother has the usual bee in her bonnet, but I wonder if she speaks from experience. Impossible sometimes. I really like my parents as people (why do I sound so amazed?) This is one of those times. Don't worry. It will wear off very quickly.

Grace freely makes assumptions about my attitudes to people. She must have taken it for granted that I would think along the same lines as her. I was deemed to be ill-disposed towards her parents. In truth I tended to be indifferent to them.

This being first love it was also my first close contact with a completely alien family; how much simpler life would be if, on fall-ing in love, you just had the object of your love to deal with. In the early days, before the McGoldricks' own attitudes (and Grace's understandable preference for a quiet home life) became such obstacles, I was keen to get into their good books. When I was an occasional weekend visitor I don't ever remember them making me feel at all uncomfortable – there was the standard call down the stairs of "Grace, it's time you were going to bed" but that was to be expected. If I try hard I can picture us all round the table for agree-able Sunday lunches. The only aspect of those occasions that strikes me as at all odd now is that I must have been a very confident hitch-hiker; even approaching the dead of winter I didn't mind leaving it until the darkening mid-afternoon on a Sunday before setting out for Sheffield.

I wonder what they made of me? There is a marvellous passage in *Decline & Fall* where Waugh speculates on the feelings of a par-ent for his or her daughter's beau: "He is not the son-in-law I should readily have chosen. I could have forgiven him his wooden leg, his slavish poverty, his moral turpitude and his abominable features; I could even have even have forgiven him his incredible vocabulary, if only he had been a gentleman." I doubt if either of the McGol-dricks had read much Evelyn Waugh but I wouldn't be surprised if he caught something of their mood.

One of the lecturers in Sheffield told me I was "a trite revolu-tionary". That would be the weakness for Richard Neville, Jimmy Reid and épater-les-bourgeois gestures like sticking maps into my Geography practical book with Christmas Sellotape. The very word 'undergraduate' becomes adjectival to cover such shenanigans. As for 'revolutionary', he was simply wrong. 'Revolutionary' suggests a programme, a coherent alternative once the status quo has been swept aside. But the status quo had served me very nicely and I was not about to fly to Germany to join the Baader Meinhoff gang, however attractive Ulrike Meinhoff may have appeared to an over-wrought English teenager. Or am I confusing her with Gudrun

Ensslin? Had I done so, would the newspapers have said I had been radicalised?

At the McGoldricks, in any case, I was on my best behaviour and, having been brought up properly, I might have been reasonably convincing. There would certainly have been no cheap shots at soft targets: the *Daily Telegraph*, the bridge school, the detached house on a leafy avenue of a Home Counties commuter town. Besides, apart from the bridge school, the same sitting ducks were lined up at my own family home. And now, 44 years on, I'm living in a detached house on a very pleasant street in a Home Counties commuter town. My window looks out over a valley in which trees outnumber houses and most of the houses are large. Down the middle of the valley runs the railway line on which the prosperity of the town now depends (or, at least, its property prices). In the place of undergraduates I now associate with town councillors, golfers and other pillars of society.

The trite revolutionary doesn't change his spots completely. Instead he proposes further evidence of evolution going into reverse. It stems from an abiding view of the world and how it works.

There are two kinds of people: the conventional and the subversive. People of a conventional disposition keep the material world ticking over. They constitute a very large majority. Failing to detect the defective logic at the heart of the system to which they subscribe – that a world of finite resources can provide perpetual growth – they aspire, they consume and they make endless small accommodations to the world without noticing that they are being manipulated. As Gore Vidal put it: "Hypocrisy and self-deception are the traditional characteristics of the middle class in any place and time."

Any number of examples would serve to demonstrate how this works in practice. Any car advertising would do the job; or, a personal favourite, the replica strips of football clubs. Football clubs have a home strip, an away strip and a third strip, plus others –

a pink strip for charity matches, on occasion. They change all of these in subtle details every season. They charge a small fortune to fans who buy these articles because, allegedly, the fabric has been developed at huge expense: "Moisture management technology is engineered and designed to aid performance, by dispersing the moisture absorbed during play." And people buy them in large numbers, year in, year out, man and boy. This isn't even a confidence trick, since nobody's confidence is abused. It's simple extortion against which parents are powerless because they too buy the shirts.

Who gains? The answer, generally speaking, is the Biblical aphorism: "To him that hath shall be given." The have nots, primarily the peasants in their distant sweat-shops, are simply exploited. The purchasers' gain is factitious. The sense of identity a replica strip gives them is false, and the millionaire players must be laughing behind their hands at their gullible fans. Indeed it's arguably a pretentious display to wear one. The Australian baggy green cap can only be acquired in one way, and that is by being picked to play cricket for Australia, which is exactly as it should be. But by feeding the vanity of people, the system creates a demand and thereby generates an income stream where none existed previously. And pushed along by money, the world continues to turn like a whipped top.

The time of year at which the football season begins clinches the deal. The acquisition of the replica strip, annually, towards the end of the summer, is nothing more than a modern harvest rite. The crop is gathered in and instead of a corn-dolly or a loaf in the form of a child we buy a football shirt.

The emergence of economic growth as the gold standard of a functioning society is quite recent. It might be dated back to the early Seventies, when Grace McGoldrick took her place at the top table of human evolution. Before then, governments measured their success in the number of houses built or jobs generated. No doubt more of each would occur in a growing economy, but the emphasis was not on quarterly percentage points but on homes and jobs.

Growth is a recent fixation but it has taken hold remarkably quickly. Hence the anxiety now that the emerging generation will find their lives more difficult than did (do) their parents. The idea that economic growth is linear and eternal is being exposed as a fallacy, but the mass of people and their leaders are reluctant to believe so. Instead, they argue that technology will make good the deficits. What the world cannot supply – a perpetually growing standard of living for all its citizens – technology will. They prefer not to notice that it is precisely this faith in technology that has brought them (us) to the present straits.

The subversives, on the other hand, hold back from full engagement with the life offered to them by the world as it is. They delight in snide remarks and schadenfreude. Nobody represents them and as a result they feel excluded and resentful. Many grow half-hearted, lacking not only the courage of their convictions but also convictions themselves. This natural balance prevents them from becoming dangerous.

It will be apparent that I never quite threw off the undergraduate mentality. But having become bourgeois, I no longer feel the need to épater them.

Mr and Mrs McGoldrick grow more interesting the more Grace writes about them. Whence indeed did Mrs McGoldrick derive her jaded view of men, and how did Mr McGoldrick fit into that picture? It seems odd that Grace didn't know or wasn't willing to speculate. Well, I doubt I would have wanted her to. But the distance between the two subjects of their discussion – lampshades and men – is intriguing. I imagine Mr McGoldrick said something that demonstrated how little he knew of soft furnishings.

There are compensations in being schoolchildren eg Monday. I thought the day would be *[indecipherable]* to everyone – but I

suppose it would accelerate even further the ruin of our economy.
Why not students also, tho'? They could always exempt Stirling
U if feeling petty. Do you want my pity? I told Pauline at school
about you coming to York & she was amazed. Her being amazed
made me feel it all over again – and it still hasn't really worn off,
although the actual event is now a mere and misty haze,
interspersed with a few clear flashes of course.

Phew. Grace records the event as 'misty' only a day or so later. I feel
vindicated in my failures of memory. Perhaps if I'd managed to
offend Beth it would have made more of an impact on both of us.

I can't provide a social context for the start of the paragraph.
It looks as though schools were closed for the day – might it have
been the Three Day Week? No, that was later. But after the past
couple of decades of industrial peace it takes an effort to remember
when power cuts were almost routine.

As for Stirling University, perhaps she was having a senior
moment and believed that was where I was. This is before the days
of predictive texting, remember. It's possible, I suppose, that she
meant someone else, or that absent-mindedly she was confusing
me with someone else. But if she meant me, my appearance in York
on a day-trip from Stirling was not merely romantic but heroic.

When you think about it, or notice it, will you watch out to see
how quickly your moods change (ie in the course of an outwardly
stagnant period like walking down a familiar road or just sitting
alone in your room – how quickly do you feel happy or sad & how
long does each feeling last before being replaced by another?)
Please notice & tell me because I would be very interested to
know.

If I played along with that I might have had to invent a few moods
to make it more interesting, but it was a simple enough request.

Walking down a familiar road was always a pleasure in the city's leafier suburbs, especially at that time of year. Kicking through piles of leaves on Brocco Bank, even in the days before dog-owners would tidy up after their animals, was thoroughly exhilarating. On those Saturdays when I was not in Hertfordshire, I used to walk down Eccleshall Road to Bramall Lane, with a bag of chips, to go to watch Sheffield United on their three-sided ground: again, a pleasure then as it is now to look back on it. I had always been content in my own company. I had plenty of time to myself but that would largely be spent mooning about Grace McGoldrick, either writing to her or thinking about her.

The idea that university life was passing me by simply did not occur to me. My mood was relatively unchanging. And however cheerful I might represent myself, I must acknowledge that my focus was generally on the next time I would be able to go south, and my enjoyment of Sheffield was increasingly compromised by the fact that I could not share it with her.

I will see you in 5 evenings' time. That is remarkably near & by the time this reaches you it will be even nearer. Maureen tells me she always works it out in evenings – and she is right that it does make it seem sooner.

My writing is definitely becoming quicker even if the content of my letters is deteriorating. I can feel both to be true. I can only say what I have said before in so many different ways. I am afraid if I say it too often you will stop believing me or else (worse) take it for granted. But I love you and I would more if you were here to respond in front of me. No that is not a possibility. I wait. I can't ignore the difficulty of you being at Drew's, not here – but let us acknowledge it and transcend it. We will have to reconcile ourselves to not seeing each other all the time, then. When we do *[two short straight lines at a divergent angle as though to indicate an explosion]*. And even if it isn't (which probability you have to allow for) we exist. How do we exist through such mediocrity, I wonder? I think possibly it is due to things like you coming to see

me at York. A dream only of course – but when shadows come up
to your hopes perhaps perfect reality is not a futile ideal? Grace
XXXX

Anybody glancing at this would think me v schizoid. Only you
know the truth. I enjoy watching all the sides of my character
come lumbering out anyway.

I wonder if Grace, once again ahead of her time, practised mindfulness? No, because she was also aware of what might be going on
in the minds of others around her, and I believe the contemporary
vogue for mindfulness is very much more self-absorbed than that.
What an extraordinary young woman she was; what a difficult
mind it must have been, at times, to be at the whim of. Would 'at
the mercy of' be a more suitable expression? Perhaps 'in thrall to'.
And no birds sing.

LETTER 17

At about this time there was a considerable change to my life in Sheffield. For the remainder of the autumn term I had the room at Mrs Jablonski's to myself.

This came about through drunkenness and misfortune on my erstwhile room-mate's part. Mrs Jablonski had three pets: a small, listless and rather dim dog, Penny; a cute white cat called Dinky; and a budgerigar whose name escapes me – let's say Pilsudski. The night-time sleeping arrangements of these creatures – as opposed to daytime, since they all slept round the clock – were very particular: Dinky had to be kept away from Penny, whom she would goad into a frenzy of barking and foaming at the mouth; she also had to be kept away from Pilsudski, whom she would have tortured and eaten given half a chance. So Penny and the bird slept in the living room and Dinky stayed in the kitchen, with access to the yard through a cat-flap in the back door. The door between the kitchen and the living room had to remain firmly closed when no-one was there to supervise the cunning Dinky.

My room-mate was a student and occasionally he came home late, the worse for wear. On one such night, he went into the kitchen to make a coffee and wearily left the door open behind him when he brought the coffee upstairs. Some time later, with the house in darkness, uproar erupted in the living room.

It can't have been a first offence. For Mrs Jablonski to evict him she must previously have issued some sort of verbal warning. She was a very fair-minded woman and experienced in the ways of first-year students. Whatever the case, she gave Ron notice. He didn't need it, apparently; he packed and left almost immediately, leaving me in sole possession of the spare bedroom.

It shouldn't have made a great deal of difference to me, but I had had my own room since I was eight and sharing a bedroom had not been easy. The loss of half her rental income must have made a serious difference to Mrs Jablonski but her generosity to me only increased from that point on. I was invited to join the family for Sunday lunch, on those weekends when I wasn't imposing myself on someone or other in Hertfordshire. I was introduced as a friend of the family at the Polish Club. A bottle of Dandelion & Burdock was placed and, when empty, replaced in my bedroom.

And crucially, she made it clear to me that if I wanted to invite anyone to visit for the weekend, I should feel free to do so. This was a notably liberal and kind-hearted concession which I could not have expected from my own parents or Grace's. Mrs Jablonski knew all about our distance-defying relationship. The postman arrived early in the morning and I was rarely first to the front door; Grace's letters were usually waiting for me in a carved wooden letter rack attached to the wall in the dark, narrow hallway; the household began to anticipate them no less than I.

On 23 November the sun had moved into the house of Sagittarius, Grace's birth sign. The Archer is one of three fire signs; I had been playing with fire for four months and was unscathed. The 17th letter arrived with a Friday 1 December postmark and stamps to the combined value of 5p. Grace had begun it on the preceding Wednesday.

> Dear S,
>   Again I write in my modern history lesson. Franco & Spain now, with exerpts from 'Homage to Catalonia'.
>   3 other people are writing letters also. But none so beautiful as this. Maureen has been away these last few days with a feverish cold.

I begin to feel as though, far from not remembering Maureen, I know her quite well: her lively social circle, her unreliable car, her aversion to proletarian holidaymakers, her delicate health. I expect Tony will make an appearance soon.

I wonder if they have moments of doubt? Of the few fixed points in Grace's letters, the constancy of Maureen and Tony is one. It would be heartening, if only I could picture them. At Sheffield I had become acquainted with a couple who had been childhood sweethearts and continued to be so at university. There was something cloying about them. I can picture them, in a few years time and at the age of 65, celebrating their diamond anniversary.

> Tony didn't go back to Southampton becos' of the fog on Sunday. How were you? It must have been revoltingly slow by coach. Will you write me an essay on 'The course and importance of local winds'? She *[the teacher, presumably]* has just asked Meg to read out what she is writing & Meg did – it was a letter in which she made some derogatory remarks about the content of the lesson = v funny (luckily). Now they are talking about grace before meals, now the spiritual meaning of marriage & compromise. But if you realised that before you married you never would. Mrs G agrees. Now marrying one's father
> 　& now back to Franco – the point is what will happen in Spain? Nothing. We have been told to inform our correspondents that Mrs G is going to read extracts from Orwell. OK? She says she feels sick after our lessons (sarcasm is wasted). She is Jewish & is gabbling on about the season of goodwill. No-one feels guilty.

She was right about Spain insofar as Franco lived on for another three years. Meanwhile, however, Juan Carlos had been nominated as his heir, Franco gave up the role of prime minister and ETA blew up his successor in that post.

I wonder if her lesson also disclosed how limited were the prospects for a bright young woman in Franco's Spain? Management of a woman's life passed from her father to her husband on marriage, and as late as the 1970s a woman needed a responsible man as a co-signatory to have a bank account. In the 1980s I was there as a journalist, reporting on an international banking conference, and everything had changed. The rapidity of such change (and, for example, in the case of the collapse of the Soviet empire not 10 years later) should make us less complacent about aspects of life we tend to regard as permanent.

> Thursday – Thank you for your letter & forgive me for not finishing this one. Can you?
>   It is 10 *[am? pm?]* and Maureen has just phoned – she is still away. Did you see the Strawbs on T of the P's? I like that song v much now. It reminds me of you in exactly the same way as 'Virginia Plain' does. What a lucky person you are.

I'm not so sure. The Strawbs song must have been *Lay Down*. It makes me melancholic to this day. The idea of lying down has always been congenial, but in the Strawbs' lyrics the Biblical echoes suggest a prostration more terminal than merely restful. The singer anticipates lying down for the Big Sleep.

   Yes, a website confirms that the Strawbs played *Lay Down* on *Top of the Pops* on 30 November 1972, just before the song peaked at number 12 in the charts. Or perhaps they mimed to a recording of it; there's a story to the effect that one tape of a Strawbs appearance on the show, long-since wiped, showed the band 'playing' with two guitars plugged into each other in protest at being told to mime. Also on the show that night was Little Jimmy Osmond with *Long-haired Lover from Liverpool*. I suppose it could all have been a lot worse. As for Roxy Music, was I a fan? Apparently – or perhaps *Virginia Plain* was associated with a particular memory that, in common with so many others, now escapes me.

> I went to Beth's today for about 30mins and Mrs D was very rapturous & suggested me to tell mummy to buy knitting bags made of tapestry work with cane handles for her aunts for Christmas. What can one say?
>   This is the question Meg & I have to talk about in 'discussion' tomorrow: 'In what circumstances & why would the following

excuses be a reasonable defence:
a) the agent was obeying orders
b) the agent didn't realise the consequences
c) the action wasn't illegal
d) the action was done under duress.'
 I dislike making a fool of myself which is what it'll be, & boring too.
 On the way back home from Hendon Craig drove very danger-ously & we very nearly had an accident. I went to Cathy North's for about 45 minutes & then walked home alone in the fog. It was v wet & gloomy & loomy.

I was prepared to claim that I always hitched back to Sheffield and that Grace's earlier reference to the coach journey being delayed by fog must have indicated a Stirling-style misunderstanding on her part. However, the only reason Craig could have been driving her back from Hendon would have been after dropping me off there at the coach stop. I presumed a good deal on the good nature of a man whose girlfriend I had appropriated. No wonder he drove badly.

(How was Drew?)
 This letter is making me guilty because you will be sorry it is so long from when I saw you. But I only write when I want to which is theoretically the most fruitful way.
 I can't go to Southampton & am half glad because it would have been v complicated. Partly because of work, which I wish I could make myself not care about. (I got two B's from lousy-interview Kent.) But of course that is impossible. As well parents. They won't let me go at the moment. I doubt they will in the future either, which is a great pity. God come & stay on the 10th if you can and don't think how far away it is 'cos it isn't. No more.

The trip to Southampton would have been with Maureen, to visit Tony. I doubt I gave it a second thought, but the fact that it would have been 'v complicated' should have served as a warning to me. If a visit to Southampton was difficult, how much more so would Sheffield be?

I haven't made much of the degree to which we missed each other. Grace makes it plain occasionally, and from my point of view it was a constant, like π or perhaps more appropriate, ∞. I wonder if I was so restrained at the time. It would have been tiresome, would it not, to rattle on all the time about how much I missed her? On the other hand she would have wanted to hear it from time to time.

The 10th, by the way, would have been only a week away by the time I received this letter. A week would look like no time at all eventually... but I'm getting ahead of myself.

> Beth was cross all the time I saw her today which is partly why I left her so early. She made v pointed comments about how long ago it was since I had seen her which I meanly ignored.

And rightly so. Numerate readers will be able to work out the elapsed time for themselves. It could be no more than two weeks, and probably less. And we don't hear much about Beth struggling up the hill to visit Grace. We hear nothing of Beth applying balm to Grace's wounded feelings. It seems to have been something of a one-way friendship.

> Having said that, you must know I am no longer the kind, forgiving, beautiful person you have built me up to be. OK I will shatter your mad illusions still more because Stephen I tell you officially and (at the moment it seems irrevocably) that I have totally given up with Beth. I have so many other things I would prefer to waste my conscience on, like you, that I am just burning myself out & lamentably turning into a big hard. I badly regret this but I can't seem to be able to go on controlling my worse nature. There it stands. Of course I will soon change my mind but you will always be able to remind me if I do.

Enough of these little girl problems. Is that what you regard
them as?

I doubt it. But now, yes, they seem to me to foreshadow the Facebook generation, to whom slights real or imagined are felt so deeply
and smoothed over so rapidly. At the time, I should have paid more
attention. After all, there was always the possibility that I too could
fall foul of her uncontrollable worse nature.

Grace's assertion that I had built her up to be kind, forgiving
and beautiful contains the seeds of just such a possibility since it
contains three separate misapprehensions. She was mistaken in her
understanding of how I viewed her: beautiful, yes, though her loving me was what I mainly required of her. Kindness and a forgiving
nature were neither here nor there to me. She was also mistaken
in how she saw herself: it was becoming increasingly obvious that
she was very hard on herself. And third, she ignored altogether the
possibility that we shared stewardship of a third entity as discussed
above, to wit our living, breathing love, and that the rest was more
or less irrelevant.

I know my parents do – when they notice, at any rate.
I wish I could see you now, for just 5 minutes. Just 5. (I am
lowering my standards in everything, it seems.) This week I have
almost allowed you to forget me. Well don't. When you read this
I shall be looking after Sarah & Rowan while Mrs B has her hair
done. I will specifically think of you then my love me.
Grace [with a dramatically exaggerated descender on the G, from
the lower end of which she had written 'How flash'. Over to the
left-hand side, a short postscript:] 'This is all my right hand so you
are improving me already – thanks.'

LETTER 18

I find that the rate at which I am transcribing these letters is slackening. Not that the first flush of enthusiasm for the project has receded. No: it's more as though some kind of historic cadence is asserting itself. Each letter is completed and saved with accompanying comments to the hard disk every few days. That is similar to the intervals at which, 44 years earlier, they had dropped through Mrs Jablonski's door.

It is a sinister thought, and a vague unease is unavoidable. I imagine a form of sympathetic magic whereby the letters, once again entering my consciousness at the rate of the originals, would have the same effect on me as they did all those years ago. Flaubert apparently said that, while writing the passage describing Emma Bovary's death by poisoning, he had felt a pain in his stomach and had vomited repeatedly.

I don't mean to compare myself to Flaubert. All I'm saying is that words (singly and in ordered groups) have mysterious properties. It crossed my mind to head off any ghosts by changing my method: if I were to treat the transcribing simply as a typing exercise and add my reactions and comments later, I could complete the letters much more quickly .

I was no more than a paragraph into the 18th letter before that resolution was shelved. I type so slowly that it is almost impossible not to think about the letters as I'm entering them, and hence not to comment on them. I wonder if some of the wilder pieces in the letters were Grace, obliged by her wrists to write slowly, supplying her own commentary.

This letter was posted from St Albans on Tuesday 5 December.

Dear S – It is 7.30 in the morning. I got up specially to write to you & all I can find is this green biro. But I was not deterred. Thank you for your letter which I have just re-read. I didn't understand it v much at all, which is worrying because it was

important. What happened on Sunday afternoon to you? & why?
You can tell me when you see me if you want because then I am
bound to understand I hope. Whatever it was, & though I don't
understand, you did make it OK because of the intention behind
your letter. As for Saturday, mine was not so complete as yours
because if you remember I didn't see you much to begin with,
but after that it was. This all sounds very pedantic and laboured,
because I have thought it a lot and because I am still half asleep.
Never mind.

This is all a reference to the weekend I spent abusing the Redmonds'
hospitality. There must have been another misunderstanding that I
sought, no doubt in a laboured, long-winded way, to straighten out
through the post. At least this time I had resisted any temptation
to include Beth in the round-robin of my explanations. As for Sunday afternoon, I'd hazard a guess that Craig doing me yet another
favour had something to do with it.

She goes on to write about the succeeding weekend:

My weekend – nothing exciting happened except for a violent
stomach ache on Sunday morning.
    I was not at school yesterday because I was finishing an essay.
Beth phoned on Sat & Sun afternoons of which the latter was
better. She went to her brother's party on Friday which was v good
& the rugby club ditto. What a raver, eh?

Yes. And is it less than a week ago that Grace had 'totally given up
with Beth'?

Drew wanted to see Velvet Underground but I don't know if he
did. As I have implied I am a hermit. I am waiting for you, of
course. I am no longer convinced (if I ever thought it) that not
seeing you makes me not get sick of you. That sounds bad so I'll
rephrase it by saying I wish that I could see you more & preferably

now. My letters are repetitive. If you wait till Friday I promise I will
send you a beautiful, original one. Then I won't be under pressure
to get up. I see 'Hamlet' with the school tonight. If this sounds
anything other than you would like it to be you have got the wrong
idea because I love you. Grace

LETTER 19

Hard on the heels of that odd, slightly troubled text came the 19th letter, posted in St Albans the next day – Wednesday 6 December, at 6.15pm. In his diary Byron had written on this day in 1813: "God knows what contradictions it [the diary] may contain. If I am sincere with myself (but I fear one lies more to one's self than to any one else), every page should confute, refute and utterly abjure its predecessor."

Dear Steve,

Here I am (or was, depending on which way you look at it). Please excuse my last letter. You do not deserve such treatment and I am very sorry.

At the moment I am being driven mad by Alan Freeman. My god he is playing Deep Purple. It sounds superb after the Osmonds, D Cassidy, Peter Skellern etc.

Last night I saw 'Hamlet' as I told you. I went to Meg's and then to the Cockpit Theatre in London. It was v op art & full of trendies. We laughed all the way through, no kidding. A whole row of us sat there being v juvenile. The King was a moth & Hamlet was a spider, they twisted themselves up in intense contortions. Half of Hamlet's soliloquies were delivered from the floor. The Ghost spoke as if he was giving a sermon & Laertes' tights (he was standing in for someone who was ill) were embarrassingly small. They had to keep on turning out the lights so that various members of the cast could clamber up ropes to give the words more [indecipherable]. In the dark music was played – groans & moans on 2 notes.

(I spoke too soon. It's 'Crazy Horses'...)

I am going down to Beth's in a minute – it is my free afternoon and I came home at 12pm 'cos I couldn't stand waiting until 2pm. I met your friend Mark H on the train. He likes geography too, and he asked me when you were coming. (Procul Harum –

what has happened?) Those are the main things I remember he said, which just shows.

How are you? I intended to ask at the beginning but I forgot. It isn't a stupid question because loads of people are ill. My big brother had tonsillitis and a temp of 104° so he said when he phoned last night (poor thing). Miss M told me to go home if we weren't feeling well, in prayers today, as it is standing room only (literally) in the sick room.

As if the idea of a romance conducted by letter is not dated enough, Grace adds to its documentary interest with the glimpses she offers of her school life. At private schools in the 1970s, they still had prayers and a sick room. I wonder she didn't call it the san; and how can it be that the tuck shop has not been mentioned?

I couldn't stand to think of you so far away & ill. I waited for a bus for 50mins today (as Maureen is seeing 'L'Etrangere' in London) and 2 women next to me talked non-stop about the badness of the buses. After the first 10mins I felt [indecipherable]. Then I began to analyse the different ways they produced of saying the same thing. Then finally I joined in and argued so convincingly that lunch-time buses are the ones most often cut out that they changed their minds (before they had been saying that it was bad between 4 & 5). It was silly, really, but it stopped me from getting mad.

Get it off your chest. God I can't stand it any longer.

The last sentence encapsulates everything that doomed us. The microscopic ambiguity of that urgent imperative – to whom is it addressed if not herself? – is followed immediately by a perfectly clear cry of pain. How could I not have responded?

But I can recall tackling neither with her at the time, on the phone or by letter. As I have said, I absorbed from her letters only those words that nourished my idea of 'us'. Grace, by contrast, wrote letters that revealed herself to me to ever increasing depths, had I only troubled to them properly. I can find no way to excuse myself.

In the admittedly controversial translation of the lyrics to Canteloube's *Shepherdess's Song* (*Baïlèro*), the shepherdess teases the shepherd across the river: he doesn't look as though he's having much fun, his flock aren't getting the best fodder, why doesn't he join her? But then the mood changes abruptly; the water divides them and she can't cross, the shepherdess sings with a first hint of panic. And words that may be the shepherd's come in reply: he will cross lower down to meet her. His grasp of geography is poor: lower down, the stream will be wider. My almost wilful incomprehension reminds me of that. As far as I was concerned, the purpose of our letters was to fill in the gaps between our weekends together. Having discovered beauty, I found various forms of waiting to accompany it. I was much less interested in examining it for flaws.

I intended to make this longer but I will send it now in the hope of it reaching you tomorrow. If not it is a pity. I don't forget you. Grace XXXX

The pathos of it – I just addressed an envelope to your old address.

Having contemplated adding my comments later, I find I have nothing useful to say to this anyway.

LETTER 20

The end of my first term approached and with it, the Christmas holidays.

I can remember approaching them with something like dread. They promised no material change in our circumstances: we would still find ourselves living in two different places. Thus the set-piece occasions – Grace's birthday, Christmas and New Year's Eve – would have to be accommodated but I couldn't see how. The image my anxiety produced of Christmas dinner is strong enough to have stayed with me. The McGoldricks and I sit round their dinner table, which differs from any Sunday lunch only in that the chicken is replaced by turkey. Festive cheer and paper hats cannot quite overcome the habitually lugubrious disposition of some of the diners. Presently, as darkness falls, I make my farewells to disappear into the night, thumb optimistically cocked. The streets, highways and motorways are completely empty.

My imagination was running into the sand. There must have been more attractive entries in the diary: parties, concerts, outings of any kind. The social whirl outlined in Grace's letters would surely not have been suspended for Christmas. But I was bogged down with thoughts of her home life and I'm sure that is exactly how I characterised her situation as well – bogged down at home.

Unsure how a lover should behave, I did what undergraduates do. I took a holiday job with the Post Office.

Grace's 20th letter was evidently written and posted on Sunday 10 December, again from St Albans, where the Sunday collection was at 5.15pm.

2.10 Sunday afternoon
Dear Steve,
   I have just been talking to Drew about you. I love doing that because it always renews my feelings and makes me like you

more. I felt very happy because of you before lunch, and because there is so little time before you arrive home. No time at all.

Why would I have worried? She could make everything sound so easy. Only one thing mattered, really, and there it was.

Drew wanted me to ask you whether you wanted to go to the review at school on either Friday 15th or Saturday 16th. It depends when you get back for the former date I expect. Will you phone one of us to say when? If it is me to be so honoured can you make it Tuesday as I won't be home on Monday night (going to a play with Pauline). If you want to go, Drew will get tickets. (I seem to have put this very badly – my mind is still where it was at the beginning of the letter.)

Yesterday night was appalling. We tried to go to Stackridge. Drew had a ticket but Beth & I didn't get in. Apparently it was v good & a good atmosphere etc etc. B & I went to Jeremy's disco – do you remember me telling you about one we went to before? Well it was the same one and equally terrible. Going home was 'exciting' because Jeremy was drunk & the car deviated from the left to the right side of the road etc. Enough. I want to tell you what I do in case you ever want to know. I realise it isn't v stimulating but refuse to apologise. At least this way it means we won't have to waste time talking about it later on. (How can what I do without you be interesting? It means that only half of me is doing it. You see?)

Thank you for the Hawkwind badge & your letter. I laughed when I saw it. Unfortunately the essay arrived too late for me to use it. A pity. Perhaps you could try your hand at comparing & contrasting the W & E coastlines of India?

Hawkwind always had a special place in my eardrums. They were the first band I ever saw live. That was at the American School, Bushey. Time stood still when Hawkwind played, although not for the concert organisers. The band went on for much longer than planned and someone effectively unplugged them. The evening ended in a dark, silent shambles.

This was, of course, long before their success with *Silver Machine* – I had not been lured in by some tawdry *Top of the Pops* appearance. I expect Craig was involved in some way, or perhaps the head girl.

The gift of the badge is worth noting only for the memory it prompts of what I didn't give her. I owned (and held on to) a Jethro Tull poster that found its way to me from Ian Anderson's aunt; she was among the old folk a group of schoolboys visited on Wednesday afternoons as a gentler alternative to rugby. The poster didn't leave my possession until 1981, when I left it on the wall of a bedsit in a careless house move. If only I'd given it to Grace or, better yet, left it in my parents' safe hands.

I asked Drew to bring Andy over here sometime next weekend, you will be able to meet him then. I hadn't realised until Drew said it that you have never met Andy before. I hope you can be able to stay there very much. You can't fail to make a good impression, anyway…

This is your best letter for a long time. Not because of its length or content but because of the way you wrote. I wish I could put my finger on why particularly it is good. You sound very remote – why do I like that?

(At the moment, the one thing, the only thing in my mind is that I want to see you. That is all there is. It is amazing because often I feel distracted.)

That was a fit which has passed. It is hard to be single-minded especially – you add – for fickle woman (Germaine shudders).

It is 3.15pm. This has taken me 1hr 5mins which is very quick. My right hand is seizing up now.

A whole page to write goodbye. What luxury. Especially as it isn't.

All our letters are prologues as you rightly pointed out, my love.
Prologues to when we are together. Mere preparation and that is
enough of course.
   Grace XXXX

However I might feel about all this, it looks as though I made an
industrious correspondent. The essay would almost certainly have
been something geography-related – I could dash off that kind of
thing from the top of my head in those days, at least to 'S' standard.
As for 'my best letter for a long time', my first term at Sheffield had
been tedious and I looked forward to its ending, which must have
added a certain élan. I can't account for sounding very remote, nor
for why that might have appealed to her. Once again, the only thing
that mattered was that she wanted to see me.

   Apparently I stayed at Drew's twice. Odd, isn't it? I mention
him hardly at all and yet I enjoy his family's hospitality as often as
Grace enjoys mine. And this Andy I was to meet, in the hope that I
could "stay there very much"... I wonder who that was I was about
to impose myself on. I can't believe I did; surely I'd remember if I'd
billeted myself on a complete stranger.

   Grace had an older brother I never met. It was in his room that I
stayed when I was chez McGoldrick. I remember heavy, dark-wood
furniture, no personal items to speak of, a view over the bosky back
garden. The similarity with my own bedroom now, a few steps from
where I am writing, is surprising; there, if you overlook the Cat and
a wardrobe full of clothes, the only thing that says anything about
me is the station to which the radio is tuned and the book I'm halfway through.

Grace's 18th birthday fell just a day or so before my last visit of
the year. I gave her the Jonathan Kelly album *Twice Around the
Houses*. It begins with *Madeleine*, alluded to affectionately above,
but it went down very well nonetheless. It wasn't much but there
was nothing feigned in her delight.

If the name means nothing to you, look for Jonathan Kelly on YouTube. There are a few videos of the man performing relatively recently, including *Madeleine*; he's a silver-haired, agreeable-looking elderly cove, and although the reproduction is poor, the audience singing along is poignant. But if you're only going to listen to one song, try instead the one called *Ballad of Cursed Anna*, uploaded from the album. It is as chilling now, from the first chords, as it was 40-odd years ago.

Her letters make it look as though Grace hardly ever spent an evening at home. The accounts of her visits to concerts, theatres or just friends' houses are dizzying to try to follow. I'm sure the bands she saw are all on YouTube in one form or other. Stackridge, for example, are represented by albums from the 70s and live performances through the decades, including Glastonbury in 2008.

Conversely, the strongest image I retain of the two of us together is in her parents' lounge, on the settee, listening to a record (as they were known then). This must be a false memory; surely the family didn't vacate the lounge for hours on end at peak viewing times to accommodate us. But where we went and what we did at other times remains a mystery to me.

My first term as an undergraduate ended and my introduction to working life began. The job, at Reading Post Office as a Christmas casual, turned out to have a more lucrative and comfortable option than I had expected: instead of cold days trudging around Reading with a heavy bag, I joined the night shift in the sorting office.

We clocked on at 10pm, whereupon we promptly left to go to a pub on Friar Street and returned to begin work at 11.15pm. This disgraceful behaviour was not slackness on the part of the Christmas part-timers – I doubt we would have had the nerve. No, it was the practice of the old-timers, a privilege no doubt gained through the sacrifices made by generations of working people in the struggle against oppression. The shift ended at 6am.

The job and its anti-social hours had consequences, one of which (in retrospect) is that the Christmas holiday was a significant turning point. Not having seen much of each other during the university term, we didn't during the holidays either. My contribution to the nation's merriment, ensuring that its gifts arrived on time, was one factor; the approach in January of Grace's mock A-Level exams was another. The likelihood of Grace actually sitting them seemed remote. That did not draw their sting, however, nor diminish their utility as a means of keeping me at arm's length.

Perhaps I traduce Mother McGoldrick with this insinuation, or not. Were the mocks already being used to remind Grace of her priorities when I was offered an extension of my employment into the New Year? Once again, I can't remember. But I did accept it because the money was very good. Quite suddenly I became a wealthy man. I was paying no rent, buying no meals and raking the cash in at the generous night-shift rate. My supervisor's habitual greeting was "All right, kid?", but when Saturday night clicked over into Sunday morning he replaced it with a cheery "Double-time, innit kid?"

Grace and I exchanged no letters for almost a month. I imagine we made more use of the telephone, not being restricted to outgoing calls only, but did we exchange visits? The only indication I have is a reference in a subsequent letter. We certainly didn't spend Christmas Day together and on New Year's Eve I worked a revised shift.

Back in Sheffield in January 1973, change was literally in the air. A smoker moved into the bed vacated by Ron at Mrs Jablonski's.

Gavin was doing a combined Geography and Economics degree; I had been vaguely aware of him from lectures. He was a shadowy figure shrouded in a duffel coat and rarely seen before midday. In fact the first thing I learnt from him was that 9am lectures were not obligatory.

In this as in many other respects, he was a vital new element in my life. He too left Sheffield at weekends, but to pursue a grown-up relationship with a girlfriend in Derby. During the week he spent time with a group of five young women who shared a house. Eventually he fell hopelessly (éperdument, 'lost', in Jerome's terms) in love with one in particular. He attended lectures on an ad hoc basis. Summoned by his tutor in the third term, he passed the tutor in a corridor and they didn't recognise each other, never having met during the passage of an entire academic year. Gavin smoked and drank and when Kevin Hector took the field for Derby County, he stood up and waved, if only at the television set.

We hit it off immediately and within a few days I had a life in Sheffield that consisted of more than passing the time until the next journey south. I also had someone I could talk to about the several aspects of first love that mystified me. This may not have been an unmitigated boon.

LETTER 21

When you start to intrude on the timelines of Facebook subscribers, you may notice an unexpected reciprocity. They begin to appear on your home page, in the 'People You May Know' banner. Presumably this indicates that, having noticed your interest, they are looking you over in return.

Neither of the Grace McGoldricks among the People I May Know looks at all likely. One is simply too young – I wonder if she is the Maryland cosmetics magnate? The other is associated with licensed premises on Humberside. I amuse myself for a moment imagining Grace asking the permission of her headmistress to marry a publican from Hull.

Reluctant to scatter-bomb Facebook with messages to the global community of Grace McGoldricks, I have sent postcards to the two closer to home.

Ms McGoldrick in Watford, if she is still living at the address recorded in the Electoral Register, will have received a card bought in the Gemäldegalerie in Berlin. It is a portrait of one Hieronymus Holzschuher, by Albrecht Dürer. This is another small item of stationery I have been holding on to for many years. I would have looked at the painting initially through an interest in and admiration for Dürer; but the startling resemblance of Herr Holzschuher to Martin Lancelot Barr, Jethro Tull's guitarist, would have persuaded me to buy and keep the card. Its main recommendation in this instance, though, was that it was a neutral kind of a card to send to someone who would probably turn out to be a stranger. My message simply asked her to phone me or email me if she was the Grace McGoldrick I used to know.

The Bedfordshire Grace was sent a similarly bland message, but the painting *Coalbrookdale at Night* by PJ de Loutherbourg has vivid drama and a vaguely geographical theme.

If I have to send out any more such messages, I may have to stock up. All the other postcards I have saved down the years, from gallery shops, seem entirely unsuitable to go to women whom I don't necessarily know: almost anything by Klimt, several works by Schiele, Correggio's *Leda being ravished by Zeus in the form of a Swan* and Toulouse-Lautrec's *Femme à sa Toilette* are notable examples. Even if one such card happened to find the Grace McGoldrick for whom it was intended, I'm not sure any of these are appropriate images.

Grace's first letter of the New Year arrived with a 22 January postmark. The six-week break had not been sufficient for her wrists to recover. There were two very different styles of handwriting in the letter, as though a paragraph here and there had been contributed by someone else.

Dear S,

Thank you for your letter, it arrived yesterday but from the postmark it should have been Thurs. So much for 3p stamps. I am halfway through wasting my weekend again, like the last one. It is likely that I'll look back & see this letter as my only concrete achievement since returning to school (aren't you proud to be able to give me such a sense of fulfillment?)

I enjoyed your story. It seemed very like a complete story. I think you misunderstand what I say about Beth tho'. Your writing about her sounds very veiled, I don't understand the thoughts or feelings that provoke it, I'm afraid. But I do understand her much more than I ever used to, there is method in her madness just like most people's, and in fact as it is so distinctive with B I am finding it increasingly easier to clarify. Do I sound swanky? It amuses me how you don't commit yourself in your letter – but that is what I have to expect & actually until you brought up the subject again I was accepting it. This is my fault becos' I mould too much of what I say to you (& other people) around what I know already they think. That applies to everything, not just B, & probably shows something base & basic in my nature. Who cares?

> Anyway, having effectively confused you I shall say either 'forget it' or 'don't worry', take your pick, on second thoughts have both.

You bet I misunderstand what she says about Beth. Obviously, I would be guarded in what I have to contribute on the subject because Grace will have changed her mind again by the time the first-class post delivers my view. "What a little minx that Beth is," I will offer in sympathy with her latest expressions of frustration and confusion at her friend's behaviour. And by then she will be seeing Beth's passive-aggressive posturing as perfectly reasonable. Had she offered 'I give up' to my list of options, I suspect that is the one I would have chosen.

I have given up trying to remember what the context might have been. Just as Grace, at the time, had accepted it and put it behind her, whatever 'it' was, what I find startling is my readiness to step once again into a quagmire so obvious that RD Blackmore would have scorned it as a plot device. Such upsets were very small storms in disproportionately large teacups, and the ripples never quite reached the rim.

I'm intrigued by the mention of a story. *Cob's Pen* fodder? Apparently not.

> Why do you want me to have a huff when you can only guess as to whether I am or not? The biggest huff I had was in Reading & that is over, so you are thwarted, Stephen, becos' I have changed.

A huff was a stylised gesture of annoyance – Grace would go into a huff, I would fold my arms and we would laugh out loud. If we were arguing, a huff would have indicated that everything was all right again. If I had to guess, she wasn't laughing, and the upset was genuine.

One of the things young lovers have to work out for themselves is how to negotiate an argument. Not the least startling feature of first love is the idea that someone else sees the world exactly as you do. The first disagreement undermines this notion – and no bad thing, you might say, since the notion is ridiculous. But you still need to handle it with care.

A row is supposed to clear the air but I'm not so sure. I suppose it depends on the degree to which the people you've grown up around were hot-tempered. If you have wide experience of friends, siblings or parents flying off the handle at the drop of a hat it may be possible to take calumny calmly. If, however, you're used to words being employed to mean exactly what the dictionary says they mean, a shouting match can be a very disagreeable experience.

I've known arguments of Biblical proportions, where the word 'disagreement' is hopelessly inadequate as the storm rages for 40 days and 40 nights.

Mrs Noah in one notable case was the Australian single mother Helen Hewitt, encountered earlier in this account in the Willoughby Arms, New South Wales. Helen was exceptionally beautiful. She was the kind of woman whom strangers importune in bars. Such a woman, you instinctively feel, must develop a distorted view of men as creatures driven by opportunism, insincerity and a high idea of their own merits. Would she also notice that such men must be inherently unreliable? If they'd approach her in a bar, why would they not approach the next slightly prettier stranger they saw? They would not, one imagines, be looking for someone to settle down with.

Helen drew me into her web without too much difficulty 10 years after the Reading huff and the arguments I had with her were noteworthy for their uncompromising tone. You have to care about someone to have a blazing row with them. Grace and I cared, no doubt, but in retrospect we never had anything much more than a misunderstanding and/or a difference of opinion. It's very much more difficult, of course, to have an argument by letter.

Helen's style of argument was didactic. She began by identifying failings in my character. If I would only acknowledge my faults, together we might be able to correct them and I would grow as a human being. In relation to Grace I've mentioned just such a dialectical process as being natural and possibly desirable, a view that looks increasingly implausible now. Times had changed. By the time I knew Helen, my faults were neither few nor trivial, and in tackling them there was no time like the present.

That will have been why she chose an evening on an exotic holiday to begin. We were in a Bangkok restaurant, on a stopover back to Sydney after a few weeks in England and a fortnight in Greece. We had the place more or less to ourselves and we were winding down, talking about what we'd seen that day, in the way you do on holiday. Out of the blue, she said: "But I wish you'd stop perving."

That was an Australian expression meaning 'ogling other women'. I wasn't immediately alarmed because I couldn't think she was serious. I said: "I'm sorry, I didn't think I did that." As a defence it was feeble but accurate.

She said rather more sharply: "Well, you do. You were perving all the time on Crete."

I looked at her across the Lazy Susan. There was a flush on her face that may not have been caused by the temperature in the restaurant. In her eyes I imagined anger glittering. I tried to think back to any particular episode that might have been taken the wrong way. "There's a lot of flesh on display on the average Greek beach," I said. "I may have passed comment on it. I may have appeared to be ogling, but I wasn't, honestly." My pedantic attempt to replace the Australian idiom with an appropriate English verb illustrates how badly adrift of her mood I was.

"I don't just mean on the beach," she insisted. "You were perving all the time. On the beach, in tavernas, in the street, on the scooter, you were doing it all the time."

"For God's sake, on the scooter you were on the pillion. How could you tell where my eyes were?"

Objections of that order were beneath her notice. She said: "It was humiliating. Some of the time it was as if you weren't with me at all. One night when we were having dinner you were so engrossed in the other women in the place, there was a guy sitting at another table asking me with his eyes if I'd prefer to join him. I could have done; you wouldn't have noticed."

What she was saying called for a firm response but all I could think of now was the solitary diner with the eloquent eyes. Who was he, this lonely Lothario, and why was he unaccompanied in a Cretan tourist hot-spot? He must have been a lecturer in archaeology, I decided, who could find no partner to brighten his vacations and therefore took his holidays in places that could be considered part of his work. I tried in vain to recall a fellow diner with intense eyes and a chunky-knit cardigan with reinforced elbows.

I knew I had a tendency (as above) to drift off into what I thought of as quiet reflection, which to another may look like daydreaming. From Helen's point of view she might occasionally feel abandoned. I said as much. It exasperated her. "You were perving. Why won't you admit it?"

I replied carefully: "I'm sorry, I don't think I do that." This was barely a change of tense away from my first reply and as firm a response as I could manage. After all, who among us could be absolutely sure?

"Well, you do, and I wish you wouldn't, because it's very offensive."

You don't have to have seen much of the world to know that further argument can serve no purpose. You might as well ask the waiter for some birch twigs, give yourself a sound thrashing and ask to be forgiven on the firm understanding that it won't happen again.

On the other hand... If you concede on a point as absurd as this, what damage do you risk not only to the balance of your relationship but to your sense of yourself? What irreparable psychic rent might suddenly open up? In other words if the accusation isn't justified, and it isn't going to be withdrawn, is pretending guilt for the sake of a quiet life a possibility? I decided it was not. The dark clouds gathered accordingly, and presently torrential rain began to fall.

The metaphor is not entirely inappropriate: in Bangkok at that time of year, torrential rain fell reliably in the middle of the afternoon, daily. Our storm took the form of additional accusations or, from my point of view, outrageous slurs. The floodgates opened the following morning at breakfast.

I'd had a disturbed night. I had passed reflective small hours in the dimly-lit night-time foyer after finding the bar closed; this was well in advance of the 24hr economy. Curious that they should be called 'small' hours – they're easily the longest on the clock.

At a neighbouring café we'd chosen for breakfast, I began: "I think it might be a good idea if we didn't spend today in each other's pockets."

Helen didn't reply immediately; she was having difficulty with some boiled eggs. In the first place, she had ordered scrambled; in the second, the boiled eggs delivered to our table were raw. The one she topped sprayed the surrounding area generously with albumen.

I waited for her to tidy herself up with a serviette. When the repairs were effected I went on: "We could do with a break from each other." But I was still talking to myself; Helen was now engaging a waiter and drawing him to our table as though with a tractor beam. The waiter surveyed the debris cheerfully – a ready smile was the first requirement for the job. Helen said to him: "These boiled eggs are raw."

Blank incomprehension replaced the smile. Perhaps the waiter's English was good enough for him to be baffled by the nonsensical juxtaposition of 'boiled' and 'raw'; perhaps eggs are considered boiled in Thailand after the merest introduction to warm water. What seemed more likely was that the waiter spoke no English at all. He certainly made no move to explain the state of the eggs to Helen's satisfaction, nor did he seem in any hurry to remove them.

I said: "Then we could get together for dinner and it wouldn't be as though we'd been doing the same things and seeing the same sights all day."

Helen looked at me bleakly. "What?" The waiter began to sidle away. She said: "Here!" and handed him the plate. "I would like scrambled eggs, please." The waiter's face broke into a huge grin, as though she had delivered a wonderful joke with perfect timing. He hurried away with the plate.

She turned back to me with a quizzical expression. I said: "I was just saying…" but it was too tiresome to repeat myself. "I'm just trying to make the best of a bad job. The whole deal seems like a bad job this morning."

She appeared to have no comment to make to that and picked at sections of an uncommonly crusty roll. Neither of us spoke for a short time. Eventually I said: "There's a bus going to Pattaya from the end of the street. I thought I'd go and have a look. You might want to do something different – shopping, stay by the pool, I don't know…"

She was clearly forming a question that had to be set aside as the waiter returned, bearing two intact eggs on a plate. I was not sure that four and a half minutes had elapsed since his departure from the table but I kept my suspicions to myself. Also, the eggs being in their shells cast doubt on the amount of scrambling they might have undergone. Helen greeted them with no comment; she seemed prepared to give the waiter the benefit of the doubt. Perhaps she was assessing the possibility that the English word 'scrambled' might sound like the Thai word for 'uncooked'. But the eggs were at least warm. Helen whipped the top off the first one and a good proportion of the contents, glassy as a jelly-fish's phlegm, followed.

"You don't love me, do you? You're tired of me," she said. "If I was a blond with big tits you'd love me. You never pay me any attention, do you? Look at you today: 'I'm going to Pattaya, to perve the women there in peace.' You make me sick."

On which note she rose from the table and disappeared in the direction of the hotel, perhaps to return to our room to be sick. The egg regarded me like the Lidless Eye of Sauron.

Neither Helen nor I would yield. To each of us, the view we held of events, words and feelings – of reality, in short – was so important that we could not compromise any part of it. The initial cause, after a while, was barely relevant.

We returned to her home in Sydney, where we had planned to begin a new life together – the purpose of the visit to the UK had been to renew my visa. Alas, the old life would have been preferable.

A kind of inflationary spiral developed. In happier times, lovers might seek to outdo each other with the ingenuity and intensity of their declarations of love; unhappy, Helen found new grounds for complaint. I was unfaithful, devious and wholly unreliable.

Rather than clearing the air, the storm grew in intensity and unpleasantness, and the atmosphere in the house echoed with undischarged static electricity. In the end, I attended to the foul air conclusively by provoking her in a childish way. We were on our way out of the house to go to a party when I quite deliberately said something of an incendiary nature – something to the effect that she would need to keep an eye on me because there would almost certainly be women at the party and I was, after all, always perving. From that hackneyed opening there was no holding us back.

The row rolled back and forth across her sitting room like a thunderstorm that cannot climb out of a valley. It was soon obvious that our unhappiness would blight nobody's party that night, and this realisation seemed to remove any remaining restraints. After a couple of hours tossing around on waves of accusations, recapitulation of past error and name-calling, I steered our vessel into its natural harbour. I said: "It doesn't look to me as though there's anything left between us."

Helen said: "No."

"Then I'll be going now."

She said: "The sooner the better as far as I'm concerned."

A week later I was back in England. It was late January and there was snow on the ground. From the air, the countryside looked like a map from which all the information had been erased. In that regard it matched my brain, where no viable points of reference to important human issues remained. It was as though the final page of a book was left blank. The air – and everything else – was indeed thoroughly cleared.

Does everyone experience these moments? When the mind slips out of gear and runs on with an unexpected momentum, like a needle skating across a scratched record (that's vinyl, of course). Such moments issue no warning, creeping up stealthily through the barrier of fatigue, and they usually pass quickly, leaving barely a shudder. But for a second the lid of Pandora's Box is lifted and pandemonium clamours to get out. It is sobering to sense the border between order and chaos, and to learn that it might shift surreptitiously with no regard for the sovereignty of the mind. Madness must follow when such moments extend themselves into minutes or hours. The turntable mechanism fails and the stylus arm, unable to return to its dock, continues to make futile charges at the spindle, like a moth at a candle.

The root of the argument is always the same. Two people see an event differently. If it matters enough to one of them, that version must be accepted as the truth by both. What makes it matter, to whatever degree, is the toll taken on the ego. You always have the choice: you can make an issue of it, or you can try harder to become the person your lover hoped you were. To that extent the argument is always the same.

It may be so at a second level. If a parting were effected without a final, air-clearing, elemental row, is it possible that the row would be visited upon a luckless successor? To put it more simply: if all men are the same, they will be equally guilty of the same misdemeanours and must be chastised for them. In advance if necessary.

After the storm the skies clear, the sun beams down, optimism returns and you begin again... repeatedly, until you get it right. Getting it right means simply making better choices. There is always choice.

> Sunday
> I read your letter again. I love the word you used – enigma. It makes me think of a beauty in something which is sad because I went out last night. To see Home & Fumble in St A. I went with D & B. Maureen & T went also. Fumble were quite fun, but paled in comparison with ShaNaNa – who I know you adore anyway so...
> The best thing Home did was 'Roll over Beethoven'; apart from that surpassed unheard of lows of mediocrity.

Grace moves from people I can't remember to bands I can't remember. The mists of time have closed over Home and Fumble in my mind, if they – Home and Fumble – ever lodged there in the first place.

Reassuringly, the gang was all there. Shouldn't T have been studying in Southampton? Was Maureen well enough to be out after dark on a chill January evening? And St A is generous – many would have abbreviated it 'Snor'.

This was clearly a section written in haste – the number of abbreviations leads me to that deduction, but also the lack of punctuation. Grace's gloss on the word 'enigma' may be missing a comma but an explanatory clause would be even more helpful. Why would going out be sad?

> Drew was delighted with your letter I think, although his mention of it was artificially blasé. When Craig phoned to ask about Al St he sounded mournful on hearing that we had had letters and not him. But of course I only mentioned it unintentionally (how many ways can you take that?)
> About Al Stewart: I said I wanted a ticket, although I previously

hadn't intended to go. The reasons why I hadn't were because:
a) I wanted to see him with you
b) I felt mean at not going with you, but am unable to ask you to stay because of the usual grind.

However C said you wanted me to go, so I will, although I am sure my reasons for not going still stand really. Oh well.

Everybody is well; as well as can be expected, that is. Beth is doing exams, Maureen is having a 'nice time' with Tony, Drew is prob working hard. I am having chats with my headmistress about dictating my A Levels – just imagine. You are missing nothing. D said you were indifferent; well, so am I. But we cannot afford to be, my sweet S – how that trips off the tongue, totally unintentional. You will be desolate to hear that the fatale Christine has got rejected from York. I am afraid my own sentiments reveal my rottenness. Please don't hold it against me.

She provides plenty to ponder here. It's noticeable that there is no mention of mocks. As for dictating A Levels... well, somebody had to stop pretending she could sit them in the normal way. A Levels were tough enough without them becoming a speed-writing test. This had obviously been on her mind for some time – she had twice made a point of measuring the speed with which she got words down on paper in letters to me. It occurred to me to wonder again about her intimation months earlier to the effect that she had only ever written one essay – had that been a dispensation in recognition of the physical challenge of writing? Surely not.

As for my indifference reported by Drew, that can only have referred to university life. The improvement wrought by my new friend in my circumstances was too recent to have made much difference in the stream of letters. What hers referred to (in a clear tit-for-tat style) is more uncertain. Life in general, from the look of it.

Al Stewart played in Sheffield on 8 February 1973. Before the concert Gavin and I encountered him in the pub across the road from the City Hall. Something in his manner inhibited us; where in similar circumstances I bought Ray Dorsett of Mungo Jerry a drink, we left Al Stewart to his own devices. Events proved us right. His performance that night was cut short, with a hint of petulance: a guitar string broke and after a bit of grumbling he carried on. Then a second string broke and he called it a night. Apparently the man who later became famous for *The Year of the Cat* had embarked on a national tour with just the one guitar and an inadequate supply of cat gut.

> I was about to say goodbye some lines ago but became transported on wicked ecstasy (the wrong word).
> So farewell & see you next time as Matthew would say. Take care & don't let me forget you & remember me. How could we fail? Grace.

We haven't had an unexplained new character for a while. So let's just put it on the record here that I have no idea who this Matthew might have been. It sounds like something a television host might say, so it was probably the apostle she had in mind.

LETTER 22

Forces of the kind known as 'countervailing' were acting on me in January 1973: first, if I was spending any time in Hertfordshire I can offer no evidence of it; second, through the agency of my new room-mate I was beginning to appreciate Sheffield and to enjoy university life.

On second thoughts these were not countervailing but congruent, nudging me in a consistent direction. Finding the Steel City in January surprisingly attractive, I would have wanted more than ever to show it off to her.

Grace's next letter arrived towards the end of the month, having been posted in St Albans on Sunday 28 January.

Dear Steve,

I enjoyed your letter very much. I have just finished it and am preparing to get up. But I will write a little first, far more spontaneous than normal. Last night was v g but I said I'd let Craig tell you about it, but* I will say he did forget his words but seemed v nice & not as sarky as you'd said. But perhaps I am too hard. I felt as if I wouldn't wish you had been there, and began by not wallowing in sentiment etc. It worked until he played ones I'd heard before (esp the fated 'Swiss Cottage Manoeuvres') & then all I wanted was to hear you catch your breath. Enough. I said I wouldn't tell you about it so I won't.

There has been a long pause during which time loads of wooly things have drifted through me, none of which I can write down but all of which are important in a v minor way.. O yes, Craig gave me a photo of you. There, I knew you'd be cross. I haven't shown it to anyone else, tho'. It has caught you in mid-expression & as I know what the rest of it would have been (as it is a characteristic half-smile, half-lip curl) I can realistically continue it on in my mind. An action movie Christ this is a trifle illegible yes? Actually – before I leave you to go to the library – I will tell you that I would have minded if you hadn't written – not merely my base instincts of pride either. But also I realise it is better you don't write so much – firstly 'cos it means I get fewer complaints from your other lovers & secondly because I really have been valuing your letters more. That is rather stupid.

Craig blazed the trail for our little group in so many respects. He was the first to learn to drive, for example, and owned an Escort van for plying his DJ trade. He also led the way, as noted, in experimentation with drugs. And he was the first person I knew not of my parents' generation to own a camera.

The photograph of me would have shown a clean shaven, boyish face below shoulder-length hair parted down the middle. NHS black-framed Nana Mouskouri glasses compensated for myopia; they sat at a slight angle to the face, nudged out of alignment by a kink at the bridge of a rather sharp nose. The mouth had served as an example in a distant French lesson: "Monsieur Gallagher a une petite bouche." I wonder which of my classmates had provided the model for "une grande bouche"? Grace's friend Maureen might have been "une grande gueule".

It being better not to write so much would have sounded ominous to me. From her point of view it made good sense: she often lamented her inability to find anything to say, and the physical act of writing was difficult.

But it sounds as though it was I who had proposed writing less. How could I have thought that would be better? I'd find myself with more to say at greater intervals? Writing often and with nothing to say beyond repeated declarations of love had been fine as far as I was concerned.

Besides, I had been using words that she loved, like 'enigma', had produced what may have been some sort of well-received short story and only recently had achieved my best letter for a long time. It was never a duty. I wrote enthusiastically because I thought it was the one way I might keep her – I saw attentiveness and mild amusement as my unique selling propositions many years before encountering the expression.

I can't imagine I ever had very much of substance to say: my enjoyment of Sheffield in the first term had been limited and, in content, repetitive. Unfortunately, I had not been making the most of the opportunity. Gavin was hardly an improving influence in many respects, introducing me to a life of idleness that I found perfectly congenial. We absorbed re-runs of *Callan* on daytime television. We discovered snooker tables in the Students Union. In order to make the time to use them, we commissioned a charming and complaisant fellow student to take copious notes for us from the three-hour practicals, from which we would subsequently write up the required reports.

These, be it noted, were afternoon activities; in the mornings we allowed the *Guardian* crossword to stand in for a university education in the matter of improving our minds. A pastime that had defeated me for half a day at York only a couple of months earlier was now the work of an hour or so on most mornings.

> It is now the evening, 6pm to be exact. What are you doing? I can't think. (If you called Ronald Ron, why don't you call Gordon Don? Or doesn't he like it? Or is it a return to propriety?)
> Will you come down to stay on Feb 23rd?

From time to time, Grace's letters contain details I am genuinely astonished to have forgotten. Here is such an item: a date for a weekend close to the end of February. How could I have forgotten this? It must have hit me like a truck. In addition to suggesting we write less often, surely I hadn't proposed that we never see each other either?

In my admittedly unreliable memory of those days, I see myself shuttling up and down the motorway almost weekly. In fact it appears that I didn't make the journey at all from mid-December to late February. We weren't to see each other for the better part of six weeks, even assuming a snatched couple of days around New Year.

Objectively, now, although that sounds a long time, it isn't very much longer than the separation at the beginning of our... What to call it? Romance, relationship, love, correspondence? 'Separation' itself is not a bad description. The previous summer, we had not seen each other between 2 August and 9 September. Since then we had become much more sure of each other and separation should have been more tolerable. I doubt I found it so.

On the contrary, I am fairly sure the prospect of another month apart would have agitated me beyond measure. I wonder if I restrained the urge to point out that she would be able to picture perfectly clearly what I was doing at any given moment if she could bring herself to visit me.

I hope the writing less was a joint decision to spare her wrists. But if it was my suggestion, might I also have said that if she wanted to see me, she was going to have to come to Sheffield? Perhaps not, in the light of the next paragraph, but I can't be entirely sure.

> Perhaps it is silly to ask you (now why should I think that?) I want you to come very much, although it sounds silly asking so far in advance (ah, that is why) if you want to come we can look forward to it.
>
> I need to look forward to it very much. Also, the Strawbs are on in St A then, if you want a ticket raise your hand etc. Also Genesis are on in Dunstable on Monday 26th. But is it likely you could stay that long? Your wish is my command anyway.

What sort of turn might events have taken had I opted for the Strawbs in St Albans on Saturday 24 February? The visit would have assumed the pattern and length of the previous term, which had served us well enough. Also the Strawbs were just another band to us, whereas Genesis added to our expectations of the weekend.

And if I had gone to see the Strawbs, I might have seen them play the song that almost contains the following lines:

"Where one man's search would surely cease
The irresistible wild geese
Led Hero in search of the peace
That she alone could offer

"Thus he knelt before her feet
Wary lest their eyes should meet
He knew his life was incomplete
For he had yet to suffer."

In the event I turned my nose up at the Strawbs. I thought of them rather sniffily as a singles band. I could hardly have been more wrong, and my error (of judgment, of classification and of reasoning) had one immediate consequence. It added a day to the separation to wait for the Genesis concert. No, I could not impose myself on the McGoldricks for four nights – but if I didn't arrive until Saturday 24 February, I would hardly be outstaying my welcome.

Perhaps you would like to know what everyone is doing tonight? Well, there I'm afraid I can't help you. Maureen & Tony are going to Southampton to see Colin Blunstone & FAIRPORT CONVENTION. They asked me to go but I said no. Then they asked Beth. She got all ready & they phoned to get tickets & heard that it was sold out. That was this afternoon. Craig is doing a disco with Roger in Oxford. Drew is silent & mysterious.

Fairport Convention is in capital letters because in the first term I had met and spoken to Sandy Denny. The band played at Sheffield University in my first term. A group of people I took to be their roadies was setting up in the lower refectory/concert hall of the Students Union building, and when I drifted in to ask what time they expected to be on stage that evening I was referred to the young woman at the piano. Star-struck, I may subsequently have dropped her name a few times.

> I should be attempting to fill this letter with interesting news,
> or ideas, or even clever nothings like yours. That goes for all the
> letters I write to you. If you leave out the probability that I am
> incapable of doing that, I wonder why it is I don't? I am ashamed
> (& hopefully wrong) to come to the conclusion that it is laziness.
> If it is not that it is 'cos we are basically incompatible. Are we?
> I remember in one of the more terrible periods of our unity, you
> saying that we are less alike than you thought. Of course that is
> not a logical follow-up as regards compatibility but it is interesting
> 'cos I used to think us very alike in many ways.
>   I don't know why I have waited until Sunday to say goodbye. My
> mother will post this on the way to church, take care of yourself,
> Grace.
>
> * God so many 'buts'

I was on the point of writing: "This is the least troubled letter for quite a while" when I thought to look again at the two that preceded it. They too contrast sharply with the abrupt descents into despair of many of the previous autumn's letters. Since the turn of the year Grace had written in a bright, chatty style. Because I failed to notice the difference at the time, I made nothing of it.

In any case I had other things to worry about. Clever nothings... I imagine that caught my attention, but I would have been much more concerned by the emergence of compatibility as a factor in our relationship (or 'unity'). I regarded compatibility as an argument against which I might easily find myself defenceless, simply because I thought it a ridiculous idea. A man and a woman, both heterosexual, what further compatibility could you want? Grace thought about things like character, taste, disposition etc much more systematically than I. If she put her mind to it she could find evidence of incompatibility almost anywhere. I lived in Sheffield, she didn't; by some standards that might make us incompatible.

Still, her reflections on compatibility were my fault, it seems. I recall going through no 'terrible' periods, which confirms how lazily I read her letters; but if I had said I found us less alike than I had once thought, the hostage to fortune was my own.

I doubt I was discouraged by the 'clever nothings' comment. I set out to amuse her. In the process I often amused myself. I think there came a point at which this order of priority was reversed and I overbalanced into self-indulgence.

This is a timeless risk, isn't it? When you consider the difficulties that people get into with comments on social media – the Labour Party front-bencher with her photograph of white-van man's home before the 2015 election, for example – it's clear you're never quite so vulnerable as when you're trying to be clever. And in evaluating how clever you are, you are apt to be generous.

LETTER 23

My postcards have prompted no response. I may yet have to extend the campaign to Facebook.

My experience of exchanging messages via Facebook is not encouraging, but I have known this particular kind of search to produce results of a kind. Three or four years ago I received a message from someone whose name meant nothing to me, asking whether I was the Stephen Gallagher she used to know, born in Malta. Her photo showed a cheery, attractive face in middle age beneath an extravagant hat. I replied immediately in the negative and wished her luck. Her Facebook timeline shows her still 'active' in the sense that she posts occasionally, and she has 50 friends – but none of them is called Stephen Gallagher.

Grace's next letter arrived a week after the 22nd, postmarked Sunday 4 February.

Dear Stephen,
   Thank you for your letter & card. It was a v long letter & a v short card (in which my mother was v interested). The letter arrived on the day I went to Bristol & it consoled me greatly (except for when I realised I had made a mistake about your friend called G). What imaginative Sp homework you have.

Did I mention I had chosen Spanish for Beginners as another subsidiary subject in the first year? I don't recall any homework being set – it was an exceptionally undemanding course. This may, then, be a reference to a clever nothing.

I have seen Silverhead twice – did they do that one about the Rock 'n Roll Band? Craig saw them when B, D & I went to see Home; they are getting around – due to popular demand no doubt. Maureen & Tony thought Colin B the best ever. They didn't stay for Fairport… My brother has bought 'Pictures at an Exhibition' – it was budget price tho', so we are still speaking. I understand you about your record, but I'm sure Ian would be furious. It seems rather blasphemous to play such a damaged reproduction.

I had found and bought a copy of an early Jethro Tull single called *Love Story*. The main distinguishing feature of this song is that, contrary to what the title might lead you to expect, it deals more with the sour aftermath of love than with the hearts and flowers. Its driving, harsh chord sequence and bitter words anticipate thrash metal. Released late in 1968, its B side was a Christmas song of sorts called… *Christmas Song*. This too was lost in storage eight years later.

I liked Bristol. The railway stn was properly depressing & the bus properly late. The Wills Memorial Building really soars into the air doesn't it? One of my interviewers was cross-eyed & the desk added greatly to the general air of intimacy & friendliness. When I got home mummy was at bridge (don't you dare say how bourgeoise because that is unoriginal) & I watched Nastase & Orantes play tennis.

Beth went to see Jeff Beck at Dunstable who she said was good. I haven't seen her for ages, but she did v well in her exams & has an offer from Bangor so she sounded quite happy on the phone. I spoke to Drew twice last week & he sounded a bit fed up – but that could be just me. The gay round continues…

(That wasn't what I was going to say but I began with a 'g' & am not a naturally messy girl so…) Are you going to watch that programme on the mysterious Andy Warhol tonight? Think of David.

My brother is going to Ethiopia in the summer. He wrote a very long letter which pleased my mother. My father sounds tired. He is in Japan now. He forgot his toothbrush (so I am told by reliable sources).

Please tell me exactly when your driving test is, then I can prepare the necessary prayer & sacrifice etc. But of course I am seeing you before then! I forgot. How could I? It is Craig's birthday that weekend by the way so you will be able to congratulate him for it in person. That is something to look forward to. Adieu, adieu, adieu, remember me.
Grace

[with an 'x' at the top of the 'G', and a rule ending in more 'x's beneath the name.]

The letter, neat and controlled but once again in two different handwriting styles, was accompanied by a clipping from a newspaper – a translated extract of the speech Alexander Solzhenitsyn had been unable to deliver on accepting the Nobel prize. Grace had highlighted these sentences:

"It is like that small looking-glass in the fairy stories: you glance into it and you see – not yourself. For an instant you see the Inaccessible. You will never be able to ride there or fly there. But the soul cries out for it…"

As usual, I allowed my focus to alight on the wrong subject. Like a photographer who glimpses the possibility of the shot he should take but makes do with an easier, motionless subject, I overlooked the Inaccessible. A place she would never be able to ride or fly to, indeed. It is the iridescent day-glo light show of a knuckle ground into a closed eye. It is the coordinates for the second star on the right, and straight on 'til morning.

Instead this letter, alone of its many companions, became known by name. It was the Daddy's Toothbrush Letter.

Why the question of the toothbrush should have concerned me to such a degree is unclear. This was by no means the first of Grace's letters to include material of questionable interest. Indeed the letter extended the series in which she struck a lighter tone than we had been used to, and I could have taken it at face value. Perhaps I valued moody intensity above an increasingly brittle levity. Perhaps the banality of the forgotten toothbrush and her attempt at jocularity bothered me more than searingly honest soul-searching.

I must, at any rate, have been quite crestfallen to have shown it to Gavin. He responded with derision. "Don't they sell dental equipment in Tokyo?" he said. "And if her father didn't know the word, couldn't he just point?"

Dicing the phrase and studying it under the microscope of my anxieties, I found much more in the letter to worry about. "But of course I am seeing you before then! I forgot. How could I?" Quite easily, since we no longer saw each other. Heavy-handed was her irony in suggesting that Craig's birthday gave me something to look forward to in a weekend with her. As for the quotation from the ghost of Hamlet's murdered father, it was probably no more than a light-hearted way to round off the letter, but I found it unsettling.

I phoned her, in need of reassurance. I'm not sure I got any. At least I had the sense not to tell her Gavin found the letter very funny.

On reflection I would have been better advised to ignore it. Making an issue of it put several clichés in play: Pandora's box, a can of worms, hares running in all directions and the cat among the pigeons. In short, from that point on Grace must have been obliged to reflect on whether what she was writing would strike me as prosaic or tepid. Given that writing anything at all was a struggle, it might not be a large step from there to wondering whether it was worth the trouble.

LETTER 24

I must have spent some days fretting over the Daddy's Toothbrush Letter before finally calling her on the telephone to try to explain my anxiety. Grace's next letter was sent from St Albans a full school-week later, on Friday 9 February. The writing is tiny and compressed on to two-thirds of a sheet of unlined Basildon Bond.

Dear Steve,

I am very sorry about the hopeless phonecall. I realised both during it and afterwards that I wasn't saying what you wanted me to say. I suppose it was partly because I didn't understand you, although now I can see it. That letter expresses my mood then & now, which is one of total depression, total boredom and above all frustration because it won't end until I see you in 2 weeks. Even then, I wonder. It will surprise you to hear that I think of you, you are the one unpolluted spot of me (how very dramatic) but it is true. I am very guilty that I don't write & that when I do it is unsatisfactory – you must have understood that, Christ, there is nothing to write about. This hasn't, I suppose, been going on for so long as it feels it has. Now I will have to humiliate myself by telling you the cause of my malady which you must know is work. I am doing – by agreement – the exams starting next week by dictation. Also, because I can't write I am finding it impossible to learn the work anyway, and because such attention is drawn to me I can't quietly give up. So you see we are back to the old work-fixation again. I was just getting it into proportion when I saw you last at the end of the holidays so it is a pity. Anyway the net result for you is that you are going out with someone who is treating you badly, because I am, and I am fully aware of it. Now it is up to you for you can chuck it in if you wish. I will remind you that as far as I am concerned you are still here,
with love, Grace.

This may be another case of Waugh's line about the value of being firmly and decisively wrong making its presence felt. I used to believe that people who guided their own lives were relatively rare. Most of us, I thought, were content to let events push us along, and if we occasionally took a decision it was because circumstances had already manoeuvred us into a position where only one choice was available.

Now I wonder if there isn't a more subtle and sinister influence at work. A belief in the inevitability of an event naturally implies that no decisions are necessary for it to happen, or that no decisions will prevent it, or, most often perhaps, that only the obvious decisions dictated by the weight of circumstance will have any purpose at all. But suppose the original belief is mistaken... Your mind, committed by its treacherous belief in the inevitability of something that isn't in the least inevitable, will lead you from one false action or decision to the next until eventually the expected event comes to pass. The belief holds you in thrall and directs any influence you might have over events. You yourself bring the event about, not God or fate or tea leaves in the bottom of a cup. It's hardly overstating it to say you caused something to happen merely by thinking about it. How does that differ from paranoia?

Indecision is regarded as a sign of a weak character, but it's more likely a natural part of the human condition. Its opposite, a capacity for decisiveness, is so rare that 'decision-makers' are highly prized and correspondingly rewarded. And yet all we're talking about here, surely, is that some people don't mind confrontation and some would rather avoid it. Being decisive will generally involve upsetting someone.

This letter cried out for some sort of decisive response and I proved unequal to it. My requirements of this relationship were simple and modest: I wanted to retrieve those long evenings of summer 1972 when we lay in each other's arms on the McGoldricks' settee, listening to music, kissing at length. To that end, my strategy (such as it was) sought to avoid antagonising her. To defer the recovery of those evenings was preferable to losing them altogether.

And so I did not chuck it in. Nor did I propose a way of going forward that we could both be happy with (and that might help resolve her feelings of guilt).

I could simply have booked into a hotel – thanks to the Christmas post – and surprised her with an unannounced visit. But the idea did not cross my mind. The confidence was beginning to seep out of me and a feeble focus on damage limitation was already starting to replace it.

No, instead of doing anything constructive I tried to get the affair back on to an even keel by returning to the style and tone of previous letters and, in effect, pretending that nothing had happened.

In my defence I would claim that, in effect, nothing had happened. But that just goes to show how shallow my understanding of the situation was, and it points to a more individual character weakness. Others may share it, but I have no way of knowing: in a troubled or even moribund relationship I yearn for a normality (as I perceive it) that helped cause the trouble in the first place.

I used to work with a Canadian who had served in Europe in his country's armed forces. During a simulated attack by the armies of the Soviet Bloc on what was then West Germany, he told me, the Nato troops guarding the frontier found their fall-back positions already overrun by the Warsaw Pact forces before they could reach them. The positions I have hoped to retreat to have been similarly ill-chosen and untenable. The word, I think, is 'hapless', although to a certain generation it conjures up an irrelevant image of Billy Bunter.

LETTER 25

Perhaps my indecision was the appropriate response, if only for a while. A pause of two days, and then this, from St Albans on Sunday 11 February.

Dear Steve,
As you are the only person who I suspect will be pleased, I feel obliged to tell you that my rejection from Bristol arrived this morning. I am crushed, of course, but no doubt will recover.
To compensate I read your letter again, and yet again, resisted the temptation to look up 'allegories'. It was a very good letter because it made you seem very near, which is what it should do. About the group, I wasn't going to mention it again 'cos pparently the tickets were sold out, although Craig says he is going to try to get us some. You got four of the letters right, it was the STRAWBS. Are you ashamed now? He said he'd write for tickets for Genesis, but I don't know if he's been successful yet. My father comes back today – I said that because I just heard my mother telling my brother – I didn't realise it myself. That is terrible, I feel guilty.

The reason I might have been pleased to hear of her rejection by the University of Bristol was that Bristol a year earlier had made me an offer. You see? We were back to normal, gently poking fun at each other, comfortable with our feelings.

On the other hand, she felt she had to explain why she had mentioned her father. That's not good. But she could have left him out of it altogether. He doesn't really go with the rest of the paragraph. Perhaps that's the point.

I saw Beth yesterday, she looks blooming – really much, much better. She went out with someone she met at the rugby club last Saturday – last weekend – which sounded amusing as he lives in

Station Rd & they were able to compare notes about Mark
[indecipherable surname, double-barrelled]
I am going to stop writing this for the moment, but before I do I
must tell you that I feel a tremendous surge of gratitude towards
you in me. (That is hopelessly expressed.) You make me feel very
happy & calm. I feel tranquilised & as if I want to cry. I wish you
were here very much. But at the same time I want everything to
end, I don't want to do anything any more. It isn't lethargy, more
like relief I think. Oh God I don't know.

The plodding uniformity of my moods prevents me now, as it prevented me then, of making head or tail of this. Once, decades later
(the night Eric Cantona launched himself feet-first into the crowd
at Crystal Palace), I ruined the serenity of another evening by failing to find anything calming to say to "a tremendous surge of guilt".
Here we have a tremendous surge of gratitude (a tepid emotion, I
can't help but reflect). And despite the surge, which prompted the
revelation, she ends on a note of utter hopelessness. What is obvious now, though not then, is that the hopelessness would outweigh
the gratitude sooner or later. We are into the territory of one step
forward, two steps back; but I was innumerate.

Just quickly reading through the above the next day (Sunday)
makes me wish v much that I felt like I did then now. It was
very momentary. What have you been doing? I have been trying
to imagine you there, with no parents or sisters. To what extent
can you do what you want? It must be strange to begin with. You
sound generally much happier about it now than you did last
term.

Just so. Here is the hesitant step forward, and the exchange teeters
towards safer ground away from the mires into which she is prone
to stray. Unfortunately, she too lacks confidence. In February, five
months into my university life, it has apparently just crossed her

mind that I am away from home. I doubt that's how I saw it then. I can be fairly sure, though, that the phrase 'I have been trying to imagine you there...' would have given me pause for thought. I had been trying for weeks if not months to lure her to Sheffield so that she would not have to try to imagine me there.

I notice an increasing petulance, now, in the way I express this point; I imagine the same deterioration of manners took place 44 years earlier.

Last night I babysat for the *[indecipherable – a family name, single-barrelled]*. I don't like it very much. Would you dislike me if I told you it is because the children revolt me? That is horrible, I know. What Dostoevsky says about children – *[indecipherable]* – is still what I think. But those children have adult minds. However they despise me because I cannot be bothered to tell them to shut up when they go upstairs & don't get into bed & scream & shout to each other. I used to make a fuss & then for a few minutes they would listen. Now I tell them frankly that they can do what they want. They are petrified of their father, but their mother is as bad as me. And the reason – the main reason – why they actually revolt me is because they are obsessed with food (she's going neurotic S thinks). But no. They really are. I have found out by deduction that they aren't supposed to eat loads of biscuits etc, & when their parents are there they don't. But what happens is, that I work in the kitchen & they watch TV. They come in one after the other – they sidle in would be a better word – making polite conversation and hoping I won't notice as my back is towards them, & eat. When/if I turn round they stop guiltily & stare at me pleadingly. It is truly driving me mad, it would you too if you were there. I suppose I should try to stop them but why? I realise this has taken rather a long time to explain & it couldn't be a more trivial subject, but it was my main preoccupation for 5 hours yesterday, & is regularly for 2^{1}/$_{2}$ hours every Thursday. I am seriously considering chucking babysitting in, except that it is worth it for the money, I suppose. God I must find something to like in the children, I am badly intolerant. You, I think, would approach it quite differently but having said that I now doubt it.

I wonder what she had in mind from Dostoevsky? I just Googled 'Dostoevsky children' and was directed to this at www.brainyquote.com: "The soul is healed by being with children." I don't think that can be it.

Would I have handled it differently? No. I had done my share of baby-sitting and had concluded that the less I had to do with the infants the happier I was.

Will you be coming down for Ian's one concert? Were you one of the people who complained? I really wish I'd thought of it myself. Perhaps you could abduct him, even, & drive him in a fast car back to Sheffield. He could share your room, although my opinion of him would go down if he plays bridge. You are bound to have something in common. Like an attitude of mind, for example... (I don't know what I'm talking about but instinct often [indecipherable]) He could teach you 'Inside' in the back of a van driving to Blackpool to visit his Aunty.

At the moment I am looking at your photograph; I don't too often because otherwise it will be too much of a shock when I next see you. Love to Gavin, Lesley & Anne my darling, Grace.

Jethro Tull were to have played Wembley on 28 and 29 April, performing *A Passion Play*. In the event the gigs were cancelled on the eve of the first show when Ian Anderson was diagnosed as suffering from nervous exhaustion. The concerts were rescheduled for late June. Things change, don't they. I didn't go.

LETTER 26

We are entering those echoing halls of the past of which, in the present, there is nothing hopeful to say. Silent and deserted are they, their walls bereft of decoration, the dust undisturbed by dancing and revelry. Protective sheets cover the furniture like so many corpulent, immobile ghosts. The caravan has moved on, the sceptre has passed into stronger hands.

The 27th letter left St Albans on Monday 12 February, a postcard-sized neatly trimmed piece of graph paper with a lined side. On the envelope, by the way, the combination of stamps to the value of three pence was different for the fourth letter running. Had I been a philatelist specialising in British standard issue, they would have been a rare treat.

Dear Steve – Thank you for your letters. If the parcel was untidy it was 'cos it was wrapped up in the waiting room of the railway station while under scrutiny (ill-disguised) from a young girl. (That was because it was an impulse.) 2 things of note happened yesterday a) I phoned B who sounded alive; & b) Maureen's birthday which I only remembered about when it was too late to phone her. Craig said he would write for tickets for the JT concert at Wembley in April; he sounded OK – but I expect you know better than me. I am writing with one of Smith's new line of retractable ballpoints – it is very good, I recommend them. Did you mean that you would arrive about 10.30 on Friday? If so don't bother to confirm, I will meet you. It is a beautiful day outside today, just like summer from inside. I hope Monday morning finds you well – Grace xxxx

LETTER 27

I made no reply. There was neither the time nor the need for one. When I found myself once more in Hertfordshire, after such a prolonged and at times barely endurable separation, it was with the calmest sense of confidence.

It is difficult, then, to convey my subsequent confusion. How might I express the depth of the unease to which I immediately fell prey? At first I could detect only the appearance of love behind a lifeless mask. And, failing to recognise my love, I choked back accusations and simmered instead with unvoiced and inarticulate complaints. Now I believe I can understand the depth of your despair too, concealed beneath the cloak of its silence and grim practicality.

Disdain? Coldness? No, nothing at which I might feel aggrieved; nothing against which I could even struggle; and sometimes I hesitated, suspecting that my misery might be self-inflicted, so profoundly subtle was the cause and so deftly did Grace feign not to understand it.

What, when you examine it, did I have to complain about? Her welcoming smile was as sunny as ever; never had she shown herself more considerate; on the first day I was almost taken in. What did it matter, after all, if she had done something with her hair that hardened the features of her face; if an ill-chosen top of a depressing colour and unpleasant to the touch rendered discordant the otherwise delicate rhythm of her body... there was nothing there that could not be remedied on the following day, I thought myopically, either through her own choice or at my suggestion... I was more affected by her busyness, her determinedly chatty brightness, so unaccustomed between us, and where I feared I saw more resolution than spirit, and – I hardly dare to say it – more politeness than love.

And so the hours trickled away, hours from which I had promised myself so much happiness. I contemplated their flight with a kind of stupor. On the eve of my departure, Grace came to sit with me and I could not help but return to my discontent and its dark causes.

"But what can I do about that, my friend," she said evenly. "You are in love with a phantom."

"No, not a phantom, Grace."

"With a creature of your own imagining."

"For heaven's sake! I haven't invented anything. You were my friend. I remember you. Grace! You are the woman I love. What have you done? What are you turning yourself into?"

She was quiet for a few moments, running her fingers over the cuff of her shirt, keeping her head lowered. Then she said: "Stephen, why will you not simply admit that you love me less?"

"Because it isn't true!" I cried with indignation. "I have never loved you more!"

"You love me, and yet you are disappointed in me," she said, trying to smile and shrugging her shoulders.

In the afternoon, for want of anything more stimulating to do, we took a walk. The town's tidy, well-heeled, bourgeois streets provided no inspiration. Walking became traipsing and the distance between us, metaphorically, took on a physical expression. Eventually, on a corniche parallel to the High Street and not far from Craig's house, we lost the ability to talk to each other altogether.

We stopped at random. Sitting on someone's front garden wall we were silent for minutes on end as the light faded and Mercury, the messenger of the gods, retreated towards the thermometer's bulb. This was not a companionable silence, of the kind a long-married couple develops while they sympathise telepathically. It was oppressive. Later that day, at the concert, there would be no need – indeed no possibility – of talk. But the hour augured badly for the days ahead.

It was a night of historic significance and all I can think about is my unhappiness. There was something in my demeanour that whole weekend that she could easily have mistaken for sulking.

Historic? It was the last time Grace McGoldrick and I went anywhere as a couple. It was the last time I saw Genesis play live. It was the last time I went to the Dunstable Civic Hall, which was knocked down to make way for an Asda superstore in 2000. It was the day the music died. But the creator of the blog history-is-made-at-night said: "So Dunstable shoppers, next time you're in Asda pause to remember that this also has been one of the wonderful places of the earth." That's not the way I remember it.

As for Genesis, their piece most widely discussed on the Internet by weary drunks at 3am is *Supper's Ready*, off the *Foxtrot* LP, which the band performed that night. On the below-the-line section of the relevant YouTube page Groovy Carl doesn't mince his words: "The greatest song in the the (sic) history of the world." And what does Igor Maxwell have to say? "For me is THE GREATEST and is over." We can only guess at what Igor's native tongue may be. As for Wolfgang Berens, there is something strangely prophetic about his verdict: "One of my lovely songs, verry strong and faithfull. It's a Musik of the revelation." It is indeed. The apocrypha first, then, followed by the revelation.

Two of the concerts from the February 1973 tour were filmed and yielded material for *Genesis Live*, the band's first live album. On the sleeve, Peter Gabriel is wearing the Magog headdress from the central section of *Supper's Ready* – but *Supper's Ready* itself was left off the album because of its length.

They performed at Sheffield City Hall on 17 February. I was in the audience. It was one of the most exciting concerts I have ever been to, viscerally exciting. As a generation we had a tendency to exaggerate our enjoyment of concerts – to be critical would have been to play into our parents' hands, bolstering their belief that the very word 'concert' was inappropriate and that nothing likely still to pass as music 50 years hence would be involved. That was 44 years ago now. If I do not still listen to *Foxtrot* occasionally in six years' time, it will be because natural causes have retired me.

The *Foxtrot* tour finished in Dunstable on 26 February. I was in the audience then too. It was a rather different occasion.

At the entrance to Dunstable Civic Hall a rascally bouncer attended by the cur Erebus lounged. Three-headed, Craig and Grace and I filed past them. No filigreed detail of sound escapes from the hall, but seepage shimmers on the auditory horizon like the glow, on night's skyline, of a distant town a range of hills away. Within the hall tumult resolves itself into its constituent parts. Waves of sound billow from the stacked speakers across the elliptical auditorium and crash against hardwood walls. Bellowed conversations create a backwash swishing over shingle. Rock music playfully harmonises the clashing rocks.

Volume is the trademark of this generation, of music first, then (in a more decadent phase) of hair. A concert exposed its young people to four hours or more of exceptionally loud music. There was something mildly addictive in the lingering buzz in the eardrums the following day, perhaps akin to drinking strong black coffee for the first time. Certainly the appeal must have depended on something other than love of the music. When you break the evening's entertainment down, a typical audience might be interested in no more than 25% of what they would hear (and feel, in their gut, and reverberating in their bones). The preliminaries, the back-up band and any new, unfamiliar material played by the main attraction may be discounted except insofar as these pieces served to tenderise the senses of the listeners. When, at last, something they recognise is played, the exhilaration is heightened by a carefully engineered rush of relief. It is a brutal bruit et lumière. The rolling mill of a steel plant comes to mind.

Absorbing the noise people stand around in clusters, glancing about themselves, waiting. There's the something of the atmosphere of a railway station or a ferry port, with no telling when the next transport will leave and no prospect whatever of making yourself heard above the station announcer. The time printed on the tickets is no more than a rough guide; the individuals pottering about on the stage give a better indication. Until they disappear, nothing will happen.

Off-stage, fashions come and go with the generations but types remain and the usual cast is present: the gypsy girl, the lost boys, Gnat King Cole, one or two passable King Charles I impersonators, Rapunzel, Rimbaud in season, Napoleon in rags – cheesecloth and ashes wherever you look. Miraculously, nobody we know is present. We form our own group of three, which will only dwindle figuratively to two, I and my guide withal, if Grace and I achieve an unlikely rapprochement. Unhappily, I am already in a place of quivering air where no light shines at all.

The hall, by contrast, is moderately well lit; enough this early in the evening to amplify any anxiety I might have about my appearance, a careworn weariness exaggerated by the need to seem unconcerned. The heat is stifling. It's February and I'm not dressed for this.

Conscience makes a belated appearance as a substitute for injured pride. I owe Craig for the tickets, for the ride to Dunstable (wedged among woofers and tweeters in the back of his van) and for the introduction to Grace McGoldrick in the first place and I can't find anything at all to say, far less anything clever. I try to pull myself together but the only solution I find is a rather forced politeness. I have a revelation of what the strained courtesy of the weekend betokens. It hardly matters now.

We nurse drinks – pomegranate juice, I hope – as time creeps by. I usher some of it along by telling the gloomy nature of the Genesis playlist, revealed to me nine days earlier. First up, a song about a desolate post-apocalyptic earth viewed by an alien visitor; next, an attempted rape explaining the origin of the word 'hermaphrodite'; then a light-hearted tale of eviction; the decapitation of a paedophile; the threat posed to Britain's flora by alien species; and finally, *Supper's Ready*, of which all that can be said with certainty, if you're asking what it's about, is that it is about 23 minutes long. Alternatively it may be about Judgment Day. If Craig and Grace hear this catalogue of woe – from their point of view, it's possible that the movement of my lips is the only indication that I am talking – they give no sign. Craig in particular does not propose a joint to cheer us all up.

The light and the recorded music give way briefly to infinite blackness and near silence. The support band – String Driven Thing – strikes up. Suddenly the hall is lit in flickering reds and yellows, with large, colourful and jerkily mobile shadows cast on the cavern walls. String Driven Thing's chief distinction, as indicated by the name, is a violinist; he contributes an occasional embellishment to their conventional folk-rock but his main impact is as a swirling rhythm section. It gives the music a shrill quality.

Somewhere in the hall, though in a parallel universe, this subterranean horror is mirrored by a sunlit Hyperborean kingdom where two young people, content in each other's company, are loving the music, the event and each other. If I work hard enough, if I can only find the key, I can guide us there. But I am lost, irretrievably; the requirement to work at this is so distasteful that I approach it halfheartedly, the clock ticking away. Something is dying and will not be resuscitated.

The volume relents just a little bit. I manage to say something at close to a normal pitch in your ear. "Can we go back to the foyer and talk a bit – we're missing nothing here."

The area beyond the auditorium is populated by tatterdemalion shades from which all the colour has leached. You too have a deathly pallor and it occurs to me that I must look ghastly. This doesn't help. Combined with my sense of being obviously and annoyingly needy, the idea that I must look dreadful unnerves me. I have the confidence of a whipped cur. And yet I still feel as though there is a tone I could strike that would make everything all right, at least for the next two hours. Inside the hall the noise is crushing, elsewhere in the building the bowels of municipal architecture have not moved in decades.

The plain truth is that I don't know how to talk to you if I can't talk to you in the intervals between kisses. Our conversations – outside the letters – have always been in low voices, mouth close to ear, head cushioned by shoulder. Without that access of intimacy I can't think of anything to say.

Outside, visible only as vague shapes through glass-bricked walls, people head for Bedfordshire; Dunstable is in sodium-tinted darkness. This is the last point at which I might reasonably run away; there's a motorway junction barely two miles away leading to refuge in Sheffield. We go back into the hall to drink the cup to its lees.

A flash of insight, false or otherwise, persuades me that the parallel universe was nothing other than Sheffield City Hall, nine days earlier, with the same performers but a notably different crowd: one person fewer. I had to get Grace to Sheffield – there was nothing else for it. This simple plan, sketched with childish simplicity, contends with the misery lying across my mind like a blanket of fog. No, not a blanket, with its inference of comfort, it's a gravitational field, preventing thoughts or feelings from ranging more widely, breaking out into a light in which they might be examined.

The evening advances. String Driven Thing give way to Genesis. The only real difference this makes to me is that the end of the concert, which I dread and pray for simultaneously, is growing closer. On the stage Peter Gabriel will soon don the Magog head. The whole performance has something of the dark and sinister feel of a Viennese masked ball for Tarot characters. Garish colours flicker through the hall, casting the shadows of grotesques, Grendel pirouetting, across the walls and on to the moulded ceiling. From the speakers the Gabriel Hounds approach. Half sick of shadows, I withdraw myself into the dark recesses of the hall. Time signatures dog my footsteps into the gloom. A goose plods heavily across my grave without benefit of wings, honking. All that concerns me for the next few minutes is to preserve one part of this benighted evening for myself – everything else is tainted. All the concerts we have attended separately, wishing only that the other was there to share...

The moment passes in a crashing flurry of notes. Synchronised with the stage lights, my future life flashes before my eyes. I foresee an endless series of dark and confusingly noisy rooms in which I struggle unsuccessfully to resolve a recurrent mystery – how to regain a lost or at least carelessly mislaid emotional response? Ratiocination is no answer to this. Passion, it dawns on me, half-wit in the half-light, is what has been missing. The word has never appeared in any of your letters. It has not been absent from our love, I insist to myself, although it is true that restraint has been a more dominant feature. What savour can be retained in a love when passion is consistently subordinated to discipline?

Not for the first time that night I sensed I was at the wrong concert. At the microphone was a young man made-up and dressed to look like an old man, stooped and broken, pleading but not expecting to be heard; what I needed was Jumping Jack Flash insisting that love, sister, was proximate; certainly no more than a kiss away. Before the revelation ran away from me and in a final attempt to retrieve the situation, I placed my hands on your shoulders and tried to kiss you and my heart was going like mad and no, you said, no, I won't, No.

The following morning at Watford Gap services, faced with a small but growing knot of fellow freeloaders, I accepted a lift with a driver who warned me he was turning off at the M45. Not thinking too clearly and having no idea where the M45 was, I took the lift to get away from the queue. The M45 turned out to be little more than a mile up the road and, being a modern junction of two motorways, it involved, of course, no roundabout.

The truck driver dropped me on the hard shoulder. My position was illegal and most of the traffic was passing at 70mph – certainly, nothing was going to pull up for me there. I scrambled up a bank and through a hedge and found myself beside a road (the A5, as it happened – the road that ran through Dunstable). To the left it seemed to head back in the direction of Watford Gap – as indeed it proved to do, after 20 minutes' steady though increasingly agitated walking. A penance, if you will.

On Wednesday 7 March Grace posted her 27th letter. A week had elapsed since the lost weekend. Apparently I had tried to fill it. Here, as ever, the absence of my side of the correspondence is profoundly frustrating.

But it would be fraudulent, all these years later, to try to recreate it. I can remember only one phrase. Railing at her refusal to defy her parents by visiting me, I wrote about the flaw in the Jablonski's hospitality: a shortage of "hot and cold running chaperons in every room". No doubt I was pleased with it when I wrote it. That being so, I deserved all I got.

The letter is long and contentious but I won't interrupt it. The postmark read St Albans, like all the rest, but I believe this one was mailed from Desolation Row.

Dear Steve,
Thanks for your letter. My weekend was good, yes, but the reason I didn't write was becos' I was uncertain of my attitude towards you (& yours to me). I wrote on Monday but didn't send it.
   I dislike v much being called deceitful - & even now particularly by you.
   Because of your general tone I will tell you what I didn't want to tell you, although it only disguises my final position, as you will see. Do you remember the conversation we once had about the stability of our respective families? I think I told you then about the difficulties between my parents. Their characters are v divergent anyway. However the main bone of contention was my father's job which involved going abroad a lot. Since his nervous

breakdown after Philip was born mummy has had a history of nervous trouble – recurring depressions. They mean that she simply can't stand it when daddy is away.

The original reason why we moved from the North was for d to change his job. It was soon obvious however that he would still have to travel abroad, so the arguments continued on & off. It was especially bad just before we moved from Edgware. Do you remember my telling you about finding daddy with his head in the gas oven? It was very late at night, and I was 11 years old. I have never seen a man cry before.

Perhaps I am being needlessly sensational; or perhaps that is less than what many people have to put up with. I don't know. But it has certainly made a deep impression.

In about the last 4 years it has been much better, at least as regards Daddie's job – depression is incurable. He is supposed to go away once a year which mummy can just about cope with. However this year, as you know, he went to Japan etc & on his return was told he'd have to go abroad again, this month.

The atmosphere at the moment is bad. When you were here it was a pretence. Now it is quarrels morning & evening, on & on. It really does make me go cold inside because it seems so like when I was younger. I don't think their marriage will go 'cos mummy relies on Daddy so much. But I don't know what will happen to her health if he can't get another job. Maybe my parents' attitude isn't going to change, but perhaps I'll feel more like arguing with them when things are less miserable.

Why did you think I didn't want to come? Work? Can't be bothered? Money? Your 2nd home not good enough for me?

(If you unconsciously think those then it is pretty bad.) Yet you say that you assume I want to see you? Surely the two ideas are mutually exclusive. Perhaps I am lazy? Which do you really think?

I have to come to my own conclusions also. You see I have decided that if I really loved you I would come to Sheffield & risk any number of arguments and bad feeling. Nothing, not even normally good reasons, would prevent me.

So we return to the compromise again. I didn't want to kiss you at Genesis, & I felt that you were going to ask why then. If you had it would have happened then & not now. And on the Tuesday you called me indulgent. My god that was the word you used and shouldn't it have felt wrong? It's got to be a pretty awful relationship when it is an indulgence for me to say goodbye or touch you or whatever. That kind of mediocrity is what we are in now. My fault of course, & possibly (you think?) because of the hopeless example of my parents. Anyway I refuse to drift apart which is what we were doing, I cannot stand being allowed to do what I want because you will put up with me. I will have no feeling for you of any value if that continues. That is why it is worth it for me at any rate.

It is cruel by letter I know. Perhaps it will seem more real to you as written, & less so as I am far away. That is what I want you to feel as it is what I feel now. But above all it is true. I am afraid you will revert to being a stranger very easily, but I deserve it if that happens. At least I will be free of guilt. You from worry. I mean it in the best way. I wish it was you who hurt me like this, you must have realised that. Now I have hurt myself. Your anger with me & perhaps dislike of me may stop you from being upset. I hope so truly. I am sorry if no. I am sorry that what I once gave you (& never anyone else before) I cannot seem to give you for always.

That is all.

Grace

Please convey my thanks to the Jablonskis, I didn't realise what she was conceding before, it was very nice of her & for God's sake I don't feel superior. How could I?

Typing that 44 years later, I still find myself affected by it – a sudden chill unrelated to the temperature in the room, followed by a flush around the eyes and a sense that my head is floating adrift of my shoulders. Not sickness so much as tension grips my gut and when I stand I am aware of a slight weakness in the knees.

I went downstairs, poured myself a glass of red wine and watched a particularly fine episode of *The Simpsons* – one where the opening sequence plays with scenarios from other comedy shows. In 1973 I probably smoked a cigarette, by courtesy of Gavin; that hasn't been an option for 12 years now, and it would be foolish to take up smoking twice in a lifetime for the same reason.

Now, I don't have to find a response. Unfortunately I did then. All I was fit for, immediately, was to feel sorry for myself and express myself mainly in complaints: broadly, how could she do this to me? For months she had been saying she loved me. It was a conversation I had with myself, repeatedly, and the conclusion didn't vary: that what we had should have counted for something.

To Grace I could muster neither argument nor counter-proposal because I was drained of self-assurance. All my confidence depended on Grace loving me. Now that she didn't I had nothing to fall back on. I could find nothing to recommend me. There might have been copious material for an appeal in her earlier letters but either I never thought to re-read them or could not face them, knowing that what they represented was over. The horror of this letter absorbed all the light of its predecessors and I could see only the darkness of the future.

Those are the melodramatic terms in which I viewed my position. Put simply, I was powerless. Having doubted from the very start that I was worthy of her, now I realised I had been right all along and I had expected to be dropped. No purpose could have been served by trying to deflect fate. Hence the snappy ripostes I devised in the succeeding months were far too late to be snappy and I kept them to myself.

I achieved no further insight. The letter showed me what it might mean to be literally lost in thought. If you think in words, your inner life becomes a monologue to which your thoughts tirelessly supply the next line; to be lost here means being unable to compose the next line and thus not being able to see how to proceed. If you think in images, you'll feel yourself in a maze, the walls of which grow higher and darker, and all you can do is curl up at their base and hope to sleep it off.

As for what her letter says, I can shed little light on specific complaints. I can't remember why I called her deceitful, or (a more flattering version I choose to accept) how I inferred it. There is only one genuine possibility: I was disappointed and frustrated by her reluctance to visit me in Sheffield. I must have claimed to have coaxed out of her some kind of commitment on which, as I saw it, she had reneged. It seems unlikely in the extreme that she ever made any such commitment. Nothing in her letters nor in my memory supports that interpretation. On the contrary, she consistently reminded me of how little prospect there was of her visiting me. It looks as though I simply overplayed my hand. I found myself free to repent at leisure.

Nor can I offer anything on the subject of my 'general tone' but I fear the worst. If I was capable of accusing her of duplicity I was capable of anything. I may have lost all sense of proportion and indulged in some smart-aleck sniping. Clever nothings with barbs would cease to be nothings, however clever I might have thought them.

As for why I thought she didn't want to come to Sheffield, I would have thought that quite obvious: she could not face her parents' disapproval. All the rest of the letter's references to her parents seemed utterly irrelevant to me. Not to her, clearly.

Some months earlier I might, I suppose, have embarked on a series of discreet confidence-building affairs with my fellow students. As Mrs McGoldrick almost said, the opportunity might never present itself again in quite such a promising way. Not only would that have built up a store of self-confidence to draw on if the need arose, it might also have furnished a ready-made replacement. Because I was in love, the idea never crossed my mind. Love isolated me, made me utterly dependent and then, laughing like a drain, cut me adrift.

Years later, when the matter was of academic interest only, I sought to make money out of it. I wrote up as a feature a ploy that involved elaborate deception and, effectively, doing nothing, and touted it around the teen magazines, where I found no takers. It appears in what might be called an appendix except that it is placed unusually well forward of the back of the book.

The best response, unavailable at the time because the appropriate *Simpsons* script had not been written, is inspired by an exchange in Moe's Tavern when the landlord has lost the love of his life:

Carl or Lenny: "You need to make a bold, crazy, romantic gesture of the kind that looks like it might blow up in your face."

Moe: "What if it blows up in my face?"

Carl or Lenny: "With your face, who cares?"

What in the event I did was worse than nothing. I took the literal approach. Not having seen it spelled out in her letter, I wrote back to ask if she was indeed dumping me.

LETTER 28

The last letter is postmarked Tuesday 13 March, St Albans, 2pm. The handwriting is as steady as I had seen for some time.

Dear Steve,

Your letter didn't arrive until today, so much for 3p stamps. Our lack of communication seems to have reached record heights. I don't see how I could possibly find your letter amusing, nor how you could have been writing it with a smile (5mins later...) I take that back because as I have just remembered according to many learned sources there is humour to be found in everything. I am easily lead.

I am more sorry to have confused you than I can say. I was thinking of writing the second part of that letter for so long before I actually did that I felt you would read it knowing already what I was saying. It is so much harder for me now, even more than it was then, because now I could change what I was saying to what you are hoping it was. But no, I am dumping you, & we are finished. I am glad you realise it is a tragedy for me also. I cannot understand, really, how it was that you have been so 'obtuse'. After the tone of my last letter how could we have gone on? You admit the mediocrity but I 'please' you still without trying – too bloody true it's without trying. O Stephen don't you see the weight of guilt that I have that I don't try? Everything – us is revolving around me. I cannot stand it, & now ironically it is I who have to dictate the end. Of course it will be very false, it is already, because I still like you more than anyone, but that may not last. But it has to end now 'cos, I repeat, it can only get worse.

Some parts of your letter I don't understand. I won't go through it now. I do want to see you, but naturally only if you want to see me. The Golden Egg is an admirable place for it to be, trust you to suggest it. When?
Grace

There was no meeting in the Golden Egg. Thus there was no further discussion of parts of my letter, nor of anything else.

I don't remember the content of my letter but I can recognise its dread falsity from her response. I had tried to maintain a stiff upper lip. I would not whine nor complain nor plead. Amid all these negatives, what by contrast I would actually do is not so clear. I would make light of the situation where I could. It makes me wince now to consider how artificial it must have seemed to her.

In my defence, I was trying to avoid hurting her or generally making matters worse – primarily by not lashing out. The erstwhile champion of passion had put that firmly back in its box. Cheerfully perjuring myself and anticipating many future arguments with other people in other circumstances, I implied that harsh words could, despite what we had thought, be unsaid. The air could be cleared. After the rain, the sun might burst through and steam rise from our sodden garments. Allowed to remain implicit and hence hidden, this lamb failed to emerge from the thicket.

APPENDIX

You must feel free to flick over the next three pages – they add little to the story but they impose a pause before the conclusion, and there's a very modest geographer's joke.

I wrote this some time after the event and hawked it round one or two magazines, with no success. It never occurred to me to try the *Cob's Pen* with it.

It refers throughout to letters. Might it also apply in the modern era to mobiles? Perhaps. Just as a letter lies uncollected on the doormat of an empty house, a mobile phone will occasionally be turned off, left behind or its battery allowed to expire.

It's the worst day of your life. The Love of Your Life (Loyl, an irresistible acronym), your soul mate, the one you'd hoped to grow old with, has just dumped you – by letter.

Your immediate response, as tears sting your eyes and you struggle to get to the last sentence (which inevitably expresses the pious, vapid hope that you can remain friends), is to talk to her, argue, plead, try to change her mind. And if you succumb to this temptation it will truly be the worst day of your life because there will be no way back from that, especially the pleading.

Think about it. This is a letter we're talking about. Some time has passed since Loyl wrote it – probably two, perhaps three days. In her mind the fait is accompli and she has moved on. She will be prepared for your tears; she will have hardened her heart. To drop you by letter, after all you've meant to each other, Loyl must have hardened her heart some time ago.

No, only a cool head is going to get you through this. Your only chance of overturning her decision is to absorb the dreadful news calmly and then do nothing.

Above all, you must give her no indication that her message has reached its palpitating target.

Instead, you must adopt a strategy and stick to it. Your main aim is to delay for as long as possible the day on which she is confronted with the full horror of her pusillanimity.

The fact that Loyl resorted to a letter gives you one crucial advantage. Had a telephone been available or a personal visit practicable, surely she would have used one or other. That she didn't indicates a certain geographical distance between you as well as the gaping chasm of insensitivity. She isn't likely to call or drop in. You do not need to move immediately – the vagaries of the post give you a day or two to play with.

Your strategy, then, should include the following steps:

● First, go to the nearest brassy seaside resort and send her a postcard: "Taking a few days off after exhausting Best of 33 snooker tournament, to visit Auntie Flo. Stick of rock follows." That's all.

● Second, you can return home and resume your life. The 'few days' are deliberately non-specific. They further reduce the risk of her belatedly visiting you and they move the inevitable confrontation over her letter into an indeterminate future. Life will have lost some of its savour, naturally, but the fact that you are back in control to a certain degree should soften the blow.

● Third, after about a week go to the nearest National Park and send a second postcard: "Called in to the Peak District on the way back, to blow out the cobwebs. Stick of Millstone Grit follows," or some such.

Once again you have extended the deadline. It's possible that you will not return home for another 'few days'. Her letter will by then have been sitting there like a ticking time-bomb for anything up to two weeks. Loyl may begin to experience some misgivings. She won't necessarily have had second thoughts, but her defences will be weakened. Nobody can prepare herself daily for a difficult but necessary interview every day for two weeks without losing something in intensity.

Besides, you haven't finished yet.

● Fourth, a week or so after the second postcard, get a friend to phone her with the news. What news? You might well ask. After all, nothing has happened for two weeks apart from a little light duplicity on your part. But she doesn't know that.

So the news is whatever you want it to be. The aim is to play for time and possibly sympathy. You might, for example, take your inspiration from Step 3. Have your friend tell her that you sustained an injury in the Peak District and are in hospital. Perhaps you were laid low performing an act of modest heroism – plucking a struggling, waterlogged ewe from a flash flood, say. The main thing is, you're being looked after, your parents have taken charge and when you're fit to leave hospital you will go back with them to recuperate.

This will deepen her quandary. As far as she knows, you remain ignorant of her letter. Instead you are in hospital, looking forward to an award for bravery from the National Union of Farmers. What sort of vindictive creature is she?

We can't be absolutely sure. But the time has almost come to give her a second chance.

Be careful to impress on your friend the importance of hinting that your discharge from hospital is imminent – you don't want Loyl trying to visit you there, since she won't find any record of you. But you won't gain very much time from this ruse, because otherwise your parents would have to become involved. No, two or three days later, you must visit her unannounced. Your explanation is that someone called in at your flat to pick up the post. They found her letter.

This is where you will no longer be able to rely on a ruse. You will have to talk about what she wants in a simple, direct, grown-up fashion. Which is how it should have been in the first place.

You may or may not talk her round. If you do, celebrate the reconciliation; if you don't, nothing is lost. And you've given yourself something else to think about for several weeks, which is how the healing process works, isn't it?

EPILOGUE

Disappointed lovers with a weakness for the golden age of the silver screen will sometimes fall back on what they might refer to as The Casablanca Consolation: "We'll always have Paris."

But the poignancy that makes the film so wonderful is precisely that Rick and Ilsa no longer have Paris. They – and perhaps Ilsa in particular – have changed. Paris, with the Wehrmacht high-kicking along the Champs Elysées like a hallucinatory Folies Bergère chorus line, has also changed. What Rick and Ilsa had is gone, irrevocably.

"So what will we always have?" Grace might ask, if we were to meet again and I were to reject the suggestion that we would always have York railway station.

"Why, Grace, the world and all that's in it."

The moment is what matters. What Rick and Ilsa will always have does not depend on a time or a place. It needs no context. It might even be diminished by dragging Paris and hackneyed romantic associations into it. The intimate contact, however fleeting, with one other person contains much that's good that life has to offer.

The moment can't be infinitely extended and so you cannot have it always, but you have the experience of it. You know it exists. Like a crystal formed under pressure in the depths of geological time it transmits its message into the future. It exists, furthermore, independently of the world. It doesn't depend on geography; indeed it holds the world at arm's length, if only for a moment.

And here, by the way and at last, is the refutation of Michel Quoist: love returns us to a childlike state and the age of the lovers is therefore irrelevant.

Another shortcoming of Paris revealed by the case of Casablanca is that the romance of Rick and Ilsa can only have been brief. Given more time, their memories of the city must surely have become frayed around the margins as those memories expanded to include moments that were less than perfect. Years of excessive smoking, drinking and growing misty-eyed at the sound of *You Must Remember This* would surely have taken their toll. Sentimental lovers for whom the coup de foudre explodes in north Yorkshire will eventually, imperceptibly, find that 'always having Pickering' becomes 'always having bickering'.

In a long relationship, love occasionally goes missing or grows stale for a period. Human foibles are cumulatively annoying, in their predictability as much as in the exasperation they cause. Grace did not know me long enough to find herself having to leave the room rather than scream with frustration as I crossed my legs at the ankles and made my shoes squeak, or drummed along to an advertising jingle, or whistled tunelessly. By bringing the chapter to a close when she did, she made it possible to look back on that time with a certain pleasure – almost pride.

It's not unlike the margins of science. Most of science proceeds by observation and testing, but parts of it – astrophysics, for example – depend largely on imagination. Gravitational waves, the Higgs boson, dark matter, quantum entanglement... Meanwhile, at the other end of the scale, life inside an atom seems to resemble a series of Russian dolls, where each layer peeled off suggests the existence of another. An atom, then, is a speck of dust floating in the light of the film projection, containing all that is possible.

Or, to put it another way, all around us are people who lead lives more or less completely mysterious to us. Their thoughts, concerns, priorities are their own. Each of them is a small universe contained within their skins, an infinite number of variations on a theme.

I wonder idly what became of Grace, what sort of life she has had. I don't regard that as morbid or self-indulgent, although I acknowledge it is probably the kind of speculation that only the lover abandoned will entertain. The one who cuts the cord will not, generally speaking, give much time to reflection about his or her victim's fate. Having shed the ballast they will be more inclined to look firmly ahead in the manner of a Soviet-era poster-girl. Let the dead bury their dead.

When you terminate a marriage or an affair you have to regard it as having run its course. That being the case, there is little point thinking about it further. It's the affairs from which you emerge feeling dissatisfied, feeling they still held potential that will now for ever be unexplored, that prompt speculation. This is the loser's prerogative.

But there is something troubling about the idea of potential unrealised. It is wasteful, and waste in general is an offence against life. Every light bulb left burning, every leaking pipe, every doctor's appointment carelessly missed is two fingers to those in the world who don't have such luxuries. In a world of limited resources, everything wasted is something denied to someone else.

Might that apply beyond the physical realm? It depends, I suppose, on whether you think that all resources are finite. Is the amount of love in the world unlimited? As the population grows, do the potential reserves of love grow proportionately? It would seem harsh to argue otherwise; you would imply that more people could expect less of life's bounty before they'd even got the wrapper off.

It's easy to see that a growing population competing for, say, a limited supply of fresh water will find less to go round, but surely that wouldn't necessarily be so in metaphysical regions. Unless, perhaps, the urgent requirement for water left people less disposed to love their fellow man.

If not a fixed quantity of love available to the population as a whole, how about for an individual?

I thought for a while afterwards that Grace had left me suspicious, cautious and incapable of committing myself fully again. That may have been true initially, but from a broader perspective I think the reverse is the case: that she crystallised a fundamental aspect of my character, which is that I am happiest when I have someone to love. The romantic life, then, can be seen as a succession of attempts to find the most deserving recipient of one's affection. Unfortunately, as Jefferson Airplane so thrillingly pointed out as long ago as 1967, the truth must first have been found to be lies for this to be fully evident. It is the truth that is left damaged while love persists beyond the object of it: a Platonic ideal of love, not an obsession with any given young woman.

Might a man disposed to fall in love and fritter his emotions away repeatedly be guilty of draining a resource better entrusted to someone less mercurial?

Such a man, you might say, needed help. He isn't likely to find it. On the contrary, in our emotionally incontinent times his behaviour will begin to look more like the rule than the exception. All around him, the media presents largely or entirely fictional accounts of people finding excitement and happiness through true love. The Ministry of Happy Endings, a pervasive psychological institution built up over the past 20 years, deploys numerous nudge mechanisms: couples grinning out of the Facebook profile pictures attached to the accounts of individuals, scripted-reality TV and chick-lit, the mythical status of Mediterranean resorts, the creation of the hen and stag industry.

The media has always exploited a general weakness for a love story; but the media has exploded in the past couple of decades and the weakness is often indistinguishable from mass hysteria. Some would date it to Princess Diana: an outpouring of grief on the part of hundreds of thousands of people, none of whom knew the poor woman. Or you might take it back to Beatlemania, when the response of young teenage girls to a quartet of lovable mop-tops was to scream themselves hoarse and generally to lose control of themselves. Or, before that, Lisztomania, and when Heinrich Heine coined the term he apparently meant it to imply a genuine mental illness.

By covering such phenomena, the media is already halfway to manipulating them. Mimicry is an important part of human behaviour; so too is the sense of belonging. To put it another way, if you see people acting in such a way that gets them on television, or that seems to command general approval, you're probably inclined to ape them.

This might be more or less harmless. Sticking a red nose to the grill of your car or veiling your Facebook picture with a French flag are visible tokens of right-thinking, which is a little Orwellian but not necessarily damaging. Such tendencies constitute, however, one more step along the road of making public feelings that used to be private and where, indeed, keeping it to yourself was regarded as a virtue.

Once you lose the sense of ostentation, and the natural horror of it; and you couple that with the growing frequency of events for which excessive, outlandish enthusiasm is demanded – every sporting event above a certain parochial level, every Star Wars film, every new piece of music by artists in their 60s or over – you risk being unable to identify what is genuinely worth getting excited about.

And if you get into the habit of displaying enthusiasm in excess of what you actually feel, or emotion of artificially inflated intensity, what do you suppose happens to your ability to express yourself? One answer is that there is no need to express yourself, because that's what emojis are for. Another, expressed with a suitable degree of excitement, is likely to emerge at a pitch so high that only dogs will be able to hear it. Or you may reflect and agree that in the process of pretending a range of emotions you don't actually feel, an authentic human response has been diluted.

We are almost back to St-Exupéry's people whose emotional illiteracy prevents them understanding a love letter. Now, though, the risk comes not from a surfeit of worldly goods but from the devaluation of genuine emotions.

So although the idea of love being a finite resource is ridiculous, it may very well be that there isn't as much of it around as may appear. There is no scientific expression to cover its conservation.

You can't say: "If energy, why not love, compassion, ratiocination and so on?" The world is effectively a closed system but hearts and minds are not. Imagination will roam as far afield as it chooses.

A computer scientist once took me to task over something I had written for a newspaper. I had been mocking the presumption of computer scientists working in the field of Artificial Intelligence: if philosophers down the ages had been unable satisfactorily to explain the workings of the human brain, I wrote, why should a bunch of computer scientists expect to understand and then reproduce it?

To demonstrate the flaw in my argument, the professor presented an equation that, he said, modelled human thought. Unfortunately I can't reproduce it on this keyboard – it is riddled with sigmas (upper and lower case), square brackets, ranges of values, and variables the professor didn't always trouble to identify. I didn't reply. It seemed such obvious nonsense that to tell him so would have been akin to calling him unhinged. Perhaps a similar equation could have modelled that idea and he would have understood me without taking offence.

If emotions and suchlike are not limited in the way that deposits of iron ore or reserves of hydrocarbons are, why would I feel a twinge of guilt at failing to make as much of the opportunity with Grace as I might have done? Because the waste then is personal and the potential left unfulfilled is my own. Because I loved her and gave up too easily. Also, of course, because control is always difficult to relinquish.

That crystal transmitting from the earth's core might have a second function. When a relationship ends, a residue of emotion is left with no object on which to fix itself. Perhaps the world absorbs love that has become surplus to a relationship's requirements and pulsates with it, more or less strongly, at a regular frequency. Some will be capable of responding to it, others not. By responding they do not draw on the world's supply, depleting it, but they increase it.

The latest scientific thinking about black holes asserts that objects drawn into them lose their identity. Scientists express the theory with such flagrant disregard for plausibility that it seems rude to ask for their evidence, so no-one does. If a BBC reporter and a sack of potatoes of the same weight were both sucked into a black hole, they say, and if it subsequently coughed them up, the material would be homogenous – although some sort of metadata 'fingerprint' might linger at the margins, recalling their earlier state.

Here's an image to represent my recollection of those far-distant days in Sheffield in the spring of 1973: I picture myself in a cinema where the story unfolding on the screen (in black and white, befitting the era) is blurred, to correspond to the quality of my memory; but the light from the projectionist's box cuts sharply through the darkness, and in the swirling beams (people are smoking) each beautiful scintilla of sparkling dust is a moment with Grace Alexandra McGoldrick. They are myriad.

Or, instead of a cinema screen, the light is falling in parallel planes through a slatted blind from the bright new morning outside, on to the warmth of a rumpled bed. This is an illustration of wish-fulfillment grafted on to later experience, but the twinkling particles of dust carry the same irresistibly positive charge.

Or a different context entirely: it is a warm summer's afternoon and I am sitting, propped against the base of a tree, reading a letter. Sunlight filters through the leaves and shadows dance across the paper. From a distance, glancing in, the sun flashes on individual leaves as a playful zephyr rustles the foliage. High above the meadow a lark sings.

It isn't particularly complicated. On the contrary, it's trite to observe that without the dark, light is meaningless. Without the possibility of sadness, pleasure would be tepid indeed. It's hard to read *Paradise Lost* without eventually sympathising with Satan. There must always be contrast, antithesis, balance. And in return for the privilege of waking into each new day, the day demands something in return.

I didn't see it that way at the time. It occurs to me that I made a deplorable song and dance about being dropped by letter.

To be honest, Grace had no realistic alternative. She had no means of phoning me: the only available telephones at my end didn't take incoming calls. And she could hardly visit me to deliver the news in person. It would have taken a very perverse sense of obligation to respond at last to my invitations only to end the relationship. She might, I suppose, have waited until my next visit – but the way 1973 was working out that could have left us with several months of increasingly difficult letter-writing to fill.

If I am to pursue this policy of brutal clarity, I have to acknowledge also that she did the right thing by ending it. There was little alternative. She could see that clearly at the time; it took me some time to catch on.

She might have cited any one of a number of grounds.

● DURABILITY

We were nominally a couple for about seven months. You could make a persuasive case for five, given that we spent no more than two unhappy days in each other's company in the first two months of 1973. Either way, it isn't a long time.

And during those months, I estimate that we spent about 21 days together. I've known loaves of supermarket bread that have lasted longer. Granted, one of Dennis Hopper's marriages was over after only eight days, but his ex-wife later had the grace to say: "I will say this about Dennis Hopper. We were married for eight days and truly... they were the happiest days of my life."

The strange, long-distance and intermittent nature of our relationship had a number of consequences.

The relationship never developed. On the rare occasions that we saw each other – weekends at her home, usually – time was always too precious to risk wasting it on things that normal couples do.

I am fairly sure we never went shopping, nor became addicted to 1972's equivalent of *Downton Abbey*, nor bickered about the housework. Instead, not having seen one another for several weeks, we spent the first few hours rediscovering the simple physical pleasure of kissing and hugging; the last few fretting about imminent separation; and of those in between I have no clear picture at all.

It troubles me still that I can remember so little of what we did together. Between July 1972 and February 1973 we spent at least seven Saturday evenings together and I can account for only the first of them. Others are mentioned in her letters but I can't recover any convincing images from those references. I am fairly sure we never stayed at home to watch *Doctor Who*, *The Black & White Minstrel Show* and *Match of the Day*, but I can provide no alternative prospectus.

Our growth was stunted too by the fact that we were largely restricted to letters. That might not necessarily have been a bad thing had I just been capable of reading a letter. Instead, as I may have mentioned, I read Grace's letters selectively, with limited comprehension and seldom more than once. As a consequence the passages that might be described as 'introspective' soared over my head and I gained no cumulative sense of her despair. In *La Porte Etroite*, Alissa no doubt succumbed to moments of dark uncertainty. I would have skimmed over those passages, since I could not understand the French expressions; as it turned out, I wouldn't have understood them in English either.

● PROSPECTS

Nor, had we somehow struggled through the dark days of February, was there light at the end of the tunnel. From her perspective there must have appeared to be nothing but tunnel. At best another seven months would have to be negotiated before Grace would leave home to go to university. Then, life might have changed – but not before.

In the event Grace had to postpone her exams for a year because of the handwriting problem. The unlit tunnel extended itself like

Pinnochio's nose. Where we failed to hold it together even for a couple of months with the idea that she would soon be free, in fact another 18 months were to pass before she broke free of the gravity of home to go to university.

And what would have happened had we managed to stay together until the summer? Would we have gone away on holiday? It hardly seems likely. If a weekend in Sheffield, chaperoned by a strictly Catholic Polish émigrée, was out of the question, an unaccompanied fortnight in Skegness would never have been contemplated.

I exaggerate. I should have done better than Skegness; but giving this more thought, now, I wonder. People's horizons were so much more circumscribed in those days. I doubt I would have suggested the Hippy Trail because we were scornful of hippies. So where else? Salzburg for her, Edgbaston for me?

Which brings us to a third impediment:

● Compatibility

Grace had questioned our compatibility in one of her letters. I regarded it as a sleeping dog and, uncomfortable in its presence, decided not to prod it.

Because the first point to insist on under this heading is that you only fret about compatibility if you're already unhappy and you're trying to locate the source.

The second is that if you're not happy, you can find evidence of incompatibility so easily that it is effectively meaningless. We're all different; whether those differences amount to incompatibility is entirely subjective.

There was, however, a greater depth to my anxiety on this score. As noted, I regarded Grace as more worldly than I. She was also more cerebral. I was trying to be both but I was aware of my limitations. Three examples (of the limitations, not necessarily of my awareness of them):

– I was 30 before I could pronounce Aeschylus
– When I finally won the *Guardian* Prize Cryptic Crossword after

decades of trying, my winning entry contained two undetected errors

– Walking a girl home through Weston Park in Sheffield one night, we passed the statue of a seated gentleman, a Victorian iron-master no doubt, identified on the plinth simply as Elliot. "Which Elliot?" she wondered aloud. "George," I replied confidently.

My generation was sensitive to the charge of pretension. There was a higher level, at which one became a poser or, tellingly, a poseur. Disposed to take an indulgent view I didn't regard myself as either: I was merely trying to become the kind of grown-up that I wanted to be. But my choice of words tells its own story, doesn't it? She may have felt she didn't have the time to wait for me to emerge, perhaps as a dowdy moth, from the gaudy chrysalis I was working hard to construct.

Besides, at one time she believed me to be special, but as time passed I revealed myself, in person and by letter, to be a sullen and possibly lecherous teenager like any other. A switch was tripped and I couldn't simply open the fuse-box and reset it.

● INSENSITIVITY

When Grace described finding her father in the act of suicide, I can clearly recall thinking to myself: "Well, that's horrifying, but what's it got to do with us?" It's no excuse to say that I was distraught. It would have been obvious to all but the most black-hearted that it had everything to do with us.

Grace's mother was prone to depression and her father was a failed suicide and I wanted her casually to defy them. I wanted far too much. My experience up to that point of observing parental rules for the sake of a quiet life was of no comparable value. A quiet life at the McGoldricks was a far more serious matter.

● CONGENIALITY

On a lighter note... This sub-heading suggests Sandra Bullock and it's no accident – the days of the great Hollywood screen goddesses are long past, but I have a soft spot for the star of *Miss Congeniality*, *Gravity*, *Speed* and the utterly ridiculous *The Net*. Congeniality isn't even the right word, but it will have to do because 'gregariousness' is too clumsy.

Although I didn't notice it at the time, Grace was very much more gregarious than I. Her letters record an astonishing number of friends and an impressive devotion to the idea of friendship. She set a lot of store by spending time with people and trying to make them comfortable. Sometimes, no doubt, this was accidental: Grace was constantly bumping into people in the street, on public transport and on foreign holidays. More often it was by inviting them in, visiting them or accompanying them to events. In the case of some of her friends – Maureen and Tony, for example – you could almost chart their lives through autumn and winter 1972 in Grace's letters. Under the circumstances it is extraordinary that she hasn't bumped into me several times over the past 40-odd years.

I, on the other hand, have seldom had more than one friend at a time, others being disqualified by distance, carelessness or, as the years go by, the Grim Reaper. As a result, I have exactly the same number of friends now as I did in February 1973 – two, and they are the same individuals.

That doesn't have to mean anything, but in me it implies a certain laziness, a comfort in familiarity and, probably, a tendency to repetition in conversation. Not being gregarious I can't imagine what it's like to have a number of friends. Had we spent longer together, I suspect I would not for very long have been able to disguise my impatience with the amount of Grace's attention her friends demanded, and contention would have been the result.

● Sex

Precisely because there was none, it should have occurred to me to wonder whether this aspect of compatibility troubled her too. Perhaps at some subterranean level her reluctance to visit me in Sheffield was inspired by anxiety about sex.

If so, and if she could have seen the state of the packaging on my increasingly well-travelled condoms, she would have felt herself vindicated. Perhaps also she had seen footage of Hendrix playing the electric guitar with his teeth, or had read some Henry Miller. It is easy to imagine, on reflection, that she thought it a doubtful pleasure on which to gamble domestic harmony.

Or, a cheerless thought, perhaps she thought it a sin. The photograph I have is of young church-goers on a sponsored walk; Grace and I first felt a pressure of the hand in a church hall; she read Michel Quoist. Could Grace actually have been Alissa? Perhaps I was missing something that was blindingly obvious all the time. Although the last good friend I lost never spoke of religion to me – of Chaucer, Gilbert & Sullivan, Newcastle United, yes, but religion, no – his funeral was surprisingly High Church. So you never can be completely sure.

Had I thought calmly about all this at the time, I would have spared myself a good deal of unhappiness. Unfortunately I was too busy feeling sorry for myself.

For a time I behaved as if the world were diminished by what had happened. Grace and I had failed to fulfil our potential and life on earth was poorer as a result. Love was the most complete and persuasive explanation for human life that I had thus far encountered and we had frittered it away.

I gave myself airs. The world's indifference was crushing and I sought revenge on it by reciprocating. I paid little attention to the world and certainly took no pleasure in it. Every day, I cut off my nose to spite my face and every night my face grew a new one.

I speak figuratively of course, but there were unexpected real physical consequences. I could not bear to look at my face and so I avoided mirrors. If a reflection took me by surprise nothing untoward happened; the sky did not fall in. But I felt woebegone and suspected that I looked woebegone too, a suspicion that needed no confirmation from reflective surfaces.

Also, I would find myself stopping in the middle of a perfectly ordinary action – picking up something that had fallen to the floor, for example – and remain still, as though in suspended animation, ready apparently to pass the rest of my life in this attitude. It was not that I was suddenly immobilised by an incoming tide of miserable thoughts. On the contrary, there was comfort in inertia. An ostrich burying its head might experience the same sensation.

There was no comfort, however, in the emptiness physically located in my gut, as though the roots of a tree had been removed from it. The actual location is less easily isolated: according to tradition, my heart was broken, but that would not account for the feeling in the pit of the stomach. Perhaps, then, the soul is located in the digestive tract.

I can guarantee I tormented myself for long periods over what had gone wrong. I tormented myself further with speculation over how, with timely intervention, I might have corrected it. The process is futile but it has to be endured.

In Sheffield in March 1973 I began the long, dreary process of adjustment to my reduced circumstances.

Much of this took place in the Star & Garter on Winter Street and, nearby, in the bar of the Students Union. The symbolism of a street called Winter, in March, with frosty wind making moan through the empty corridors of my life, needs no labouring.

The Star & Garter had more along those lines to offer. Its interior was distinguished by a vast mural of dancing girls presenting their flounced derrières to an appreciative lounge bar. The danceuse in the middle had only one buttock but it spanned the full width of her hips. It was as close to eroticism as I was to come for some time.

The only practical change in my life, however, was the loss of the daily prospect of a letter in the carved rack in Mrs Jablonski's hall. To replace that, cigarettes proposed themselves at a beggar's rate of exchange which rose, slowly but surely, to 20 a day.

My claim to have first taken up smoking at this time (and to have found it consoling) doesn't bear close scrutiny. A memory surfaces in which I am riding down the A5 on the Tiger Cub with a cigarette in my right hand – a memory that must predate Sheffield. The air rushing over the handlebars at 40mph burnt the cigarette down to my knuckles in moments, so perhaps it was merely an experiment, an error following on a trial. In March 1973, however, I was ready for a deeper commitment. The inhalation of smoke, nicotine, tar etc took the place in my life of Grace's kisses. That exchange sustained me through three decades, long after Grace was forgotten. Drinking to excess had never held much attraction; dry cider lost most of its appeal after the first quart. But I took readily to smoking, lying in bed and missing lectures, and discovered that dreams can be astonishingly vivid in that dozing state between breakfast and lunch.

Gavin and I passed the time between (and often during) lectures in a variety of ways. I have already mentioned the crossword, *Callan* and the snooker table. As a by-product of smoking, we also developed an art form derived from the striking of matches on strips of sandpaper. It was abstractedly expressionist and, invariably, geometric, and what it expressed was the futility of attempting to rescue anything meaningful from a lost cause. We rarely maintained our concentration through the entire life of a box (average 40 Finnish sticks) and therefore our designs became disfigured by random strokes.

Students of niche segments of industrial history will recall the 70s as a time when sandpaper on matchboxes was slowly yielding to a striking surface based on red phosphorus: we seldom found that sort of canvas satisfying enough to hold on to, and the boxes often went the same way as the expended lucifers. And yet in later life, presented with international travel, distinguished hotels and high-class restaurants, I found myself picking up matchboxes and not throwing them away. As their number mounted into the hundreds and presently the thousands, I had to acknowledge that I was a collector.

Collecting things I had previously been apt to discard, carelessly, suggests an impulse to atone for earlier wasteful behaviour. I can't quite rid myself of the idea that Grace and I were not only negligent of each other's feelings but of the global reserves of a vital resource. We failed to make the most of an opportunity – surely a woeful conclusion whatever the context. The sense I'd had of our love as something with an independent existence, an entity for which we were responsible and were obliged to nurture, drew me back to ideas of ourselves as more than mere lovelorn teenagers but as stewards of a spiritual flame. By taking insufficient care of each other we had allowed it to go out.

Might it be coaxed back into life with other partners? Certainly: another partner represents a new opportunity and renewed potential. The water flowing under the bridge is different. The bridge itself is different. The flame, however, with the mystical properties of all fire everywhere, requires only fuel and a spark.

In common with the cliché of disappointed lovers everywhere and throughout time, I found the world's lack of sympathy startling. When I stepped out of Mrs Jablonski's front door (which was actually at the side of the house, opening into a northern ginnel), I expected cold drizzle, grey skies and people heavily rugged-up making their way to another weary day of toil at their deeply uninspiring coalfaces.

When nothing of the kind presented itself – it was, by contrast, a rather bright, pleasant early spring in Sheffield – I felt the world had let itself down by going out of its way to slight me.

Its cheerful determination to carry on as if nothing had happened led me to conclude that, from its point of view, nothing had happened. I was left with two possibilities: that the world loves a lover but diplomatically ignores a loser; or that the world takes no notice.

It seemed, at least, to confirm the world's objective existence outside my head. The egocentric world view of a child is reinforced by first love. It can then be a difficult habit to lose, especially when you are aware of erudite philosophical tracts that suggest life is a dream and we dream it individually. The world's indifference is such a firm slap across the face that no dreamer would sleep through it.

If Grace and I were to meet again, I imagine an exchange littered with conditional clauses – simply because the chance of such a meeting seems remote. The cautious dialogue Clint Eastwood and John Vernon conduct towards the end of *The Outlaw Josey Wales* might provide a model. Several of their lines are prefaced by qualifiers: "If I were to speak to Wales, I'd tell him..." etc. In their case, film buffs will recall, discretion obliges each to pretend he does not recognise the other because they would otherwise have to shoot it out. It isn't an exact template for what I'm talking about.

No, Grace and I would chat easily over a small Americano in one of the coffee shops springing up along the High Street, as though the founding of Lloyds of London might be re-enacted at any moment. If such a conversation were to take place I am certain she would query the title I've chosen. The character quoted from *The Wild Geese* is, after all, a cad and a bounder. "Could you not have found something more... suitable?" she might ask. "Something more direct, perhaps."

"I would have liked *Alias Grace* but that was taken," I would reply. "*Grace Elegy* might work, or *Grace Anatomy*, but they would have been too clever by half."

"And in any case," she might point out, "they would have confined you to the name. You were wise to leave names out of it. 'Grace' has such overtones. But I wonder about the project generally... don't you think what you've done rather reinforces what I said about you putting me on a pedestal? Did *One Hundred Years of Cholera* cross your mind?"

A pause. "Or how about *Grace Reigns*?" she might add, trying to return to the spirit of the exchange.

"What?"

"The last words of Mr Honest."

"Again, what? Mr Honest? Is this from a Tarantino film?"

Grace might roll her eyes and sigh. "*The Pilgrim's Progress*, for goodness' sake."

"Who would be Mr Honest in that context?"

"He who would valiant be."

Despite the proverbially plentiful fish in the sea, love does not grow on trees and first love by definition is irreplaceable. Had I pursued this line of thinking at the time, I would probably have been even more melodramatic about my loss. If we leave aside for a moment the passing of my first love and the conventional ache in my broken heart, I was back at square one. At such times it becomes difficult to tell amour and amour propre apart.

The loss of a girlfriend would oblige me to begin the quest all over again, but this time – you would think – with a more realistic understanding of the parameters. Not a bit of it. How can experience be of any value if the circumstances fidget restlessly and life keeps moving the goalposts?

In any case, I was unsure what to hope for. It seemed unlikely that I would find anyone like Grace again, nor that I might experience anything to match the intensity of my feeling for her. My senses would be dulled, my readiness to expose myself to the same degree of risk would be much diminished. I pictured life as the gradual accumulation of armour to protect oneself from impetuous amour.

The whole business is so random as to defy analysis. The consciousness I call "I" depends entirely on an accident of birth. Why these parents rather than any other, this life, these personal characteristics? Who knows? Without invoking the supreme puppetmaster there's no accounting for it.

The same must apply to first love. Why this young woman and not another, earlier or later, in a different place? It is so arbitrary. At a particular moment on a distant July night, she chose like an indulgent driving instructor to accept my hand signals and everything flowed from there. Had she chosen otherwise I would have gone to Sheffield, thrown myself unreservedly into life there, made a series of hopeless social mistakes out of sheer desperation in the first week of the first term (when I could have been doing the background reading for which there would never be the time again) and my life would have been completely different.

It's a pointless speculation. What actually happened can be expressed simply and in one of two ways, depending on whether you believe in fate: life brought us together and played with us until it grew bored and turned its nourishing care elsewhere; or, we moved into each other's orbits, danced slowly around each other and resumed separate trajectories as other gravities began to take effect.

The temptation to dramatise is strong, to make the affair important enough to justify my snivelling; and to try to balance the world's indifference at the outcome. But none of it, to be honest, amounts to very much. A problem is not severe, is it, when the solution involves nothing more complicated than passing the time until it no longer seems to matter very much?

Eventually, I met a young woman whose body was burning a hole in her pocket. She elected to spend it on me. She was using the contraceptive pill and my condoms were old and redundant, so we threw them away. It seemed to me to be a rite of passage that should be marked in some way, but in the event they just went into a swing-lid kitchen bin in a small flat in Leicestershire, unused and unloved and, presumably, destined to sensitolly lubricate a landfill site in an east England winter.

And subsequently I met a young woman who showed me what the view is like when you're standing within a rainbow. And the sun burst through, and perspective was restored or, as in the Renaissance, re-engineered.

I finally saw Grace in Sheffield two years later. She was there as Drew Redmond's guest and spent an hour or so with me in one of the coffee lounges. It was an uncomfortable interview for me and I suspect for her too. I chain-smoked. Film and television producers trying to reproduce distant eras for their costume dramas have to seek out panoramas without electricity pylons, streets without yellow lines, clothes without zips; the makers of dramas set in the 70s will have to make sure plumes of cigarette smoke gust abundantly across their sets.

Apart from the smoking I remember nothing of the meeting, except the recurrent and earnest wish that I had found the backbone to have declined the opportunity to see her. It would have been enough to pass a short message through Drew, to the effect that it would pain me too much to see her in my town as someone else's guest – but that she should on no account go home without seeing the Mappin Gallery, Weston Park, Rare & Racy second-hand book shop, the Star & Garter mural, the Arts Tower's paternoster lift etc, etc.

That meeting took place, as I say, two years later. Drew came to Sheffield a year or two behind me – I almost wrote "followed me to Sheffield", but that involves an unfair implication. Grace, as noted, did not become an undergraduate so promptly. She spent another year, partly in secondary education and partly, I think, at work in the local store, before completing her A-levels in 1974. The freedom that university life promised was deferred for another year and a half. It must have been a dreary, tedious time for her.

I wonder what Grace would look like now. I could fall back on her parents for some sort of time-lapse photo-fit but her mother, in my mind's eye, is just a composite of every battle-axe I've known since. I have a clearer image of her father – a tall, slender man with thinning sandy hair and something of the gait of a heron.

Neither image is particularly helpful. It is probably better to think of her as an eternal 17-year-old photographed on the grassy verge of a happy highway to which, ignorant of the road's location, I have no need to go again.

The end of love is of necessity an unbalanced, solitary experience: unbalanced because it must be rare that both partners will the end; solitary for the same reason. But that isn't necessarily where it ends for either one.

If you're the iron-willed decision-maker who called a halt, you'll find inevitably that as time passes the nature of your resolution changes. You'll remember what made it necessary and how urgent it felt at the time. Thus, there's a tendency to remember only the bad times. When I was in Australia, it was noticeable that the expatriate English were far more severe in their condemnation of the mother country than were Australians of much longer standing. The reason, it seemed to me, was that the expats had taken a firm decision in the recent past and found that denigrating England helped them to justify it.

When the dust has settled, your resolve won't fade to the extent of a change of heart but it may modify your memory of the lost lover. You may (let's say 'you' for convenience, to avoid cumbersome constructions involving 'he or she') begin to feel slightly guilty, wondering whether you treated your ex entirely fairly, feeling that perhaps she (let's say 'she') deserved a little better.

Well, she may very well have done. I'm sure we can all look back on moments where we dug our heels in over something that may subsequently not have seemed worth it. You simply have to continue to trust the judgements you made and the perspective you assumed.

If you don't, you risk carrying ancient errors forward into the present. Evaluating a current relationship, you may make comparisons: "If I wouldn't allow the otherwise blameless A the benefit of the doubt in such a case, why should the present incumbent, B, be granted more latitude?" Or worse: "B's behaviour is inexcusable – A never treated me like this." From here, it is a short step to getting rid of B too, and a pattern is established. Once you have steeled yourself to drop someone who has meant a lot to you, it becomes significantly easier the next time.

The passage of time itself is an additional factor. While B is failing to live up to the standards set by a mythical predecessor, time is passing and we are all growing older. No-one, it may occur to you, is going to give you that time back. The older you are the more pressing this consideration becomes and the less likely you are to exercise patience. Let's not talk about time being wasted: it's all a learning curve, isn't it? But who wants to reach the age of 60 knowing all there is to know about mediocre relationships neither partner had the wit to terminate?

Having neither seen nor heard report of her in several decades, speculation can only be idle on my part. However, I believe that it's reasonable to keep faith with my recollection of the person I was in love with, as revealed by her letters.

I have no doubt whatsoever that every word she wrote was true and that when she said she loved me she meant it. And while we're on the subject, let's scotch any idea that age and inexperience made 'calf love' the expression for what we experienced (or, in the immediate post-Donny Osmond era, 'puppy love'). You would have to insist on a very sophisticated definition of love to exclude us. We felt ecstasy, we constructed the world around each other and, eventually, we (I am extrapolating, of course) suffered. How much more do you want?

Granted, there were no thoroughgoing sexual shenanigans, but I'd argue that our continence in that respect is further evidence of how unexpectedly grown-up we were. We lacked opportunity, certainly, but not completely; we could have simply and hastily done it half a dozen times had we been prepared to sacrifice ideals for opportunism. We knew, I think, what one bite from the fruit of the Tree of Knowledge was worth. When you're as close to the wild geese as we approached, you don't risk alarming them with unnecessary noise.

All that being the case, what are the chances that she got it all into proportion and was able to put it behind her? Good, you'd have to say, if what I wrote earlier about the superior position of the one making the fateful decision is true. But that was based on my own later experience and sets of very different circumstances. You don't have to see much of life before you realise that one person's revelation is not apt to be much use to anyone else; that you cannot see the world through someone else's eyes, however well you imagine you know them. The number of variables, the number of moving parts in a relationship is so great that it is fatuous to expect to understand how it works. In other words, I don't know.

Specifically, I don't know what happened in the final two weeks before our ill-fated last weekend. If I wanted to be glib I'd say that her father, a butterfly in the rainforest, metaphorically fluttered his wings by leaving his toothbrush at home and on the other side of the world certain consequences ensued. I might then fall back on the wisdom of bumper stickers and tea-towels and assert that A Girl's First Love is Her Daddy.

But that's obvious nonsense. I wanted to see her in Sheffield and I made too much of it. My motives were not entirely impure: during the period of our correspondence, she had seemed happiest during her visit to Cambridge. I thought it plain that Cambridge provided two liberating surprises for her: it gave her a clear picture of how her life could be for the next three years; and it removed her in the short term from domestic pressures. A weekend in Sheffield, I reasoned, could have similar benefits. I underestimated the importance to her of academic performance and family harmony. Also, more to the point, I let her down badly by failing to see how much she needed me to understand precisely those aspects of her life.

Her handwriting is another topic for idle conjecture. Its quality was always variable. She first started switching from left hand to right and back again in her letters to me when her exams were more than six months away. Anxiety about exams, then, need not have been the only cause. Where to look for other contributory factors?

If it were a purely physical problem, three years at university in the mid-1970s could not be expected to have helped. She would have encountered the distinctive green-and-white striped paper of computer output at university but it would be 10 years or more before personal computers commonly took away the need to write things down on paper. The computer business had progressed beyond the point at which the head of IBM envisaged global demand for his product at no more than five units, but not yet to where the head of minicomputer giant Digital Equipment Corporation found "no reason anyone would want a computer in their home". There were typewriters, of course, but even the electronic ones required a physical effort and had been discarded as an answer by her school. Besides, with personal computers and word processing came repetitive strain injury.

If on the other hand (so to speak), the handwriting problem was psychological, university could have been the fillip she needed. Yes, it brings more exams and supposedly the pressure that goes with them. But a revelation many undergraduates experience, scouring their motley cohort for points of similarity in a desperate need to belong, is that they have one great accomplishment in common: they are all good at passing exams. They have to be, otherwise they would not be there at all. Once that is accepted, a student can slip into cruise control and achieve a moderate second-class degree with hardly any exertion.

There are passages in her letters that are still uncomfortable for me to read and difficult to pass comment on. It's impossible to write about mental fragility without sounding glib. To use the vocabulary itself looks condescending and patriarchal; in the 70s, the blanket terms 'neurotic' and 'highly-strung' were in common use and supposedly more sophisticated contemporary terms have a similar tone. A man cannot write about his partner's mental health without sounding deeply suspect; what point is he hoping to make? If my reference a number of pages ago to *Casablanca* insinuated the beautiful face of Ingrid Bergman into your mind, you might like to think of this as The Gaslight Gambit.

Grace complained often that I put her on a pedestal, imposing on her expectations that she could not live up to. That's an oversimplification but it isn't entirely inappropriate. Beth, soon after the end of days, asked me witheringly: "If Grace said: 'Stephen, throw yourself off that cliff,' you'd do it, wouldn't you?" and of course the answer was Yes, I would have done, without a backward glance.

Beth's implication was that I had become a doormat in recent times, and she was right. The sum total of my ambition had for a number of weeks been to become the kind of doormat that lay inside in the hall, not far from the sustaining warmth of a radiator. From there, I might eventually be rolled up and taken with Grace to university. If I could get that far, we might resume a more balanced relationship. As far as I could see, to be any more assertive about what I wanted in the meantime would probably see me left outside in the cold with the wolves and the muddy boots; 'insisting' would quickly have turned into 'issuing an ultimatum' and it would have been a feeble bluff.

From that point on I accepted Grace's decision without question. She no longer loved me. It was that simple. Feeling the weakness of my position I reckoned I was hardly going to regain her love by reasoned argument. Some argument might be legitimate, but eventually you have to take "no" for an answer. I remain unconvinced that a relationship, far less love, can be rebuilt by negotiation; perhaps, to all appearances, fences can be mended, but to what purpose?

In later years and other relationships, calculation became a factor, and the preservation of meagre dignity a priority. Later, I would make choices based on the idea that time was passing and could not be recovered.

In an attempt to retrieve a marriage I submitted to ordeal by counselling. All I wanted, I told the counsellor, was for us to be able to return to how things had been before. She pointed out that there could be little point in that, since something in the marriage then had ushered us into the mire in which we now found ourselves.

There was an undeniable logic in her observation but no practical help. When life is good it would be complacent to behave as though it will always be so; but by the same token, it could turn into a self-fulfilling prophecy to constantly scrutinise a successful relationship for possible flaws. What else can you do except enjoy it and treat each other with consideration?

To be dropped not for someone else but for your own inadequacy is damaging to the ego. Carlyle again: "The meanest Solecism, called upon to amend itself, will look first for another to amend." In this case, I did not have very far to look for an alternative explanation: Grace, like Alissa in *La Porte Etroite*, realised she was making me miserable and she sacrificed her prospect of happiness to free me to find my own. She knew there were going to be no weekends en fête in Sheffield; no holidays; few simple pleasures but on a deeply irregular basis; not much, in short, to look forward to. It was nobody's fault. It was simply the way things were working out. She had to call a halt because I lacked the backbone to do it.

That very same lack of backbone gave her an assurance of success. She could almost rely on my passivity. If I had argued the toss or refused to accept her decision or cast doubt on her reasons, she might have found herself in difficulties. But I did nothing. Knowing that there was a distinct possibility, if I opened my mouth, that a self-pitying whine would come out of it, I kept it shut.

The Cat and I have been discussing sacrifice. Normally I wouldn't tax her with this kind of topic – the risk of sounding shrill and accusatory is too great – but she has been unusually wilful. Her habit of clawing the sofa has long been a misdemeanour I'm prepared to live with. Though she plucks threads from its arm until the resemblance to Dougal in *The Magic Roundabout* cannot be ignored, it is, after all, as much her sofa as mine. But the carpet belongs to the landlord and he holds £1,500 of our money, largely mine, which makes it a different kettle of fish.

"So will you please stop that!" I try to keep the note of exasperation out of my voice, knowing that if she feels thwarted she will redouble her attack. I'm also conscious that I have just begun a sentence with 'so', a habit I condemn in other people.

The Cat stops that and looks at me in her habitually baffled fashion. Why? She doesn't need to say it. "You know full well why, you dreadful creature," I say. "Look!" I point to her claws and then to the filaments of carpet that give the floor a not unfashionable hint of stubble. "Will you for goodness' sake go outside and shred the bark off a tree or something?" Again, her bafflement is unfeigned. The door is closed. The cat-flap is locked against Charlie. She has no means of letting herself out. In any case, she has never in all her 20 years threatened the bark of a tree or, indeed, any conventional scratching post. In this instance, however, she is not entirely in the wrong.

It can't be denied that, from time to time, we need a break from each other. Lately, believing the Cat to be on her last legs and reluctant to leave someone else with the responsibility of managing her final days, I have not taken advantage of opportunities to give us such breaks. I can't say that to her, obviously, and particularly not since her course of acupuncture has made such a clear difference to her enjoyment of life (not to mention the use of her hitherto moribund legs). "I've sacrificed several holidays for you this year, dammit. Show a little appreciation." She hits this full toss away over the long-on boundary by reminding me with the merest flash in her eyes that she has never, in 20 long years, had a holiday, unless two weeks with Uncle Ian in 1996 counts while I was gallivanting around the Mediterranean. There may also be entered into the ledger the long, empty hours when Auntie Sue came in twice a day to feed her during other absences. And she doesn't need to mention her one and only night in a cattery, when we were both so traumatised that I vowed never to subject her to such a thing again. No, holidays had been a careless topic to raise.

Having established that she was not a well-travelled animal, she moved on with baleful gaze to list other sacrifices I had imposed on her. The removal of her reproductive function, for example. The lack of regular feline company. Marked lack of enthusiasm for her very rare hunting successes. In short, she summarised, it was hard to see what her life had been for except to provide me with company on my terms.

I could find no persuasive reply. The usual appeal to her better nature – that any number of Mediterranean cats would give their eye-teeth for her life – would not do. She was quite right. When she is gone I will miss her, but only on those occasions when I notice her. The rest of the time I take her for granted, as though she were in suspended animation when I am not there. Her life and her enjoyment of it has been my responsibility since the day she was selected from her Ivinghoe litter (because alone among her furry little brothers and sisters she had a flat face, like a cartoon cat that has run into a spade). A creature of few resources, she must have found time hanging heavy on her paws during those 20 years.

Initially I aimed to make sure I had all the letters transcribed, in case I ever saw Grace again. Some way into the exercise I changed the emphasis: I would find Grace and return the letters to her if the spirit moved me. Now it has become evident that neither plan will be fulfilled. The script I have been tentatively developing, 'If we were to meet again...', can be put to one side. We will not meet again. Grace died several years ago.

The news was confirmed to me on the telephone by a woman who worked with her 10 or a dozen years ago. Grace was loved and admired, helpful and inspirational, she said. "I think of her often, still," the former friend and colleague added, with a catch in her voice. Having imposed on this friend the obligation to revisit unhappy memories and pass on bad news, I cut the conversation short. It was, in any case, over.

All this came about through three of those peculiarities of the Internet that leave room for hope that intuition still has a place in the cyberspace era. Sometimes, an Internet search will produce a headline result that a visit to the website indicated will not confirm. Second, two apparently identical sites will offer information to surprisingly different layers of detail. And third, although information on the Internet is widely assumed to be 'out there' for all time, you can't always find it a second time, which naturally makes you wonder whether you invented its discovery in the first place.

I was aware, from my earliest searches, of a Grace McGoldrick who died in the early years of this millennium – when I was looking for marriages, the question of deaths came up as a macabre corollary. But I put this individual into the 'unlikely' category because she had been a paediatrician. Enough time had passed, of course, for extensive retraining but even so... from arts student to specialist medical practitioner is quite a stretch. Subsequently, any reference to this Grace seemed to disappear into the ether anyway: it turned up in no further searches and I couldn't trace it when I tried. I forgot about it.

However, it became abruptly relevant when I stumbled upon a second website offering company records. Unlike the site on which I had originally found Grace's residential directorship in north London, this one provided employment details for the directors. Here, the Grace McGoldrick with the right middle name and the right date of birth was described as a doctor.

It remained to find her. When I sent the search engine to look for an online register of paediatricians it returned with no record of a Grace McGoldrick. But it did produce an indirect reference: the name of another doctor whom, it said, had worked with Grace McGoldrick at a clinic in the London area.

On going to the site indicated I found nothing that matched the headline result; no such employment history nor any reference to either person. But this second paediatrician was notable beyond her professional sphere: she had attracted the attention of the local press and hence of the Internet search engines by quitting London to set up an arts centre in west Wales. I emailed her via the centre's website, and she phoned me back later the same day. It wasn't a long conversation. There was no doubt we were talking about the same person. Grace would have been in her mid-fifties when she died. It was cancer.

In the vague hope of finding a memorial at which I could leave flowers, I visited the church where the McGoldricks had been among the congregation in the 1970s. Rather than roam at random along the cemetery's mossy avenues, I went first to ask directions at the offices attached to the new church hall.

I found myself standing in what may have been the exact space I had occupied in the summer of 1972. While I was contemplating dust, residues and the displacement of molecules, the registrar consulted her records. She was brisk but friendly and gave me the impression that it was the most interesting question she would be asked that day.

There was no Grace McGoldrick on her lists – hand-written, on paper, in defiance of the soulless spirit of the age. There were, on the other hand, references to two people who from their ages at death may have been Grace's parents. The registrar offered me Christian names. I had to admit that I knew them only as Mr and Mrs McGoldrick. She indicated to me where I might find them in the cemetery but warned that there was no memorial as far as she knew. "Sometimes people add them later," she said. Perhaps people had intended to but had been prevented by circumstances.

The cemetery lay across the road from the church and stretched down a slope towards a high, tangled hedge. Beyond the hedge, the unmistakable (and, in the light drizzle, incongruous) sounds of tennis broke the silence.

Halfway down, a low wall ran across the site and memorial plaques formed a regular pattern on the brickwork. Some were illegible beneath lichen; others were hidden by ivy; none that I could read bore a name that meant anything to me. As I turned to go, a brindled cat emerged from the shrubbery a dozen yards away and stopped to consider me. Apparently satisfied, it trotted off along the line of graves.

If we had met one more time, there was only one question I would have wanted to ask. If I had spoken to Grace again, I'd have asked her: "How was it for you?"

She might have approached the gratuitous ambiguity of the question with caution, as though suspecting an agenda: "What exactly do you mean?"

The temptation to respond by quoting Marlon Brando would have been strong. "Whaddaya got?" But she might not have seen *The Wild One*. The film would have fallen into the Unacceptably Violent category. Besides, it would have led the exchange into a pointless new direction. So I might, continuing to play recklessly with tone, have said: "Whatever" but that would sound so needless-ly dismissive as to discourage her from answering at all. Therefore the plain, honest and straightforward reply must be: "Life, Grace. Nothing more."

Acknowledgements

With many thanks to Leslie Tate and to Gilli Barratt for their encouragement, advice and editing; but any mistakes, typos or errors of other kinds in the final text remain my own.

Thanks also to Lance Crozier for the cover and for his typographical expertise.

Translations and paraphrases from *Citadelle*, by Antoine de St-Exupéry, and on page 245 *La Porte Etroite*, by André Gide, are my own and the same responsibility for any errors applies.
　　The verses quoted (with a change to the second line) on page 230 are from *Hero & Heroine* by The Strawbs, written by Dave Cousins, (P) A&M Records 1973. Efforts to locate the sound recording copyright owner to obtain formal permission to reproduce these lyrics have failed. I would be happy to make good this omission in future printings.
　　The extract from *The History of the Peloponnesian War* on page 179 is from the Penguin Classics edition, translation by Rex Warner.
　　The extract from Alexander Solzhenitsyn's Nobel lecture printed on page 235 is from *The Guardian*, date unknown.

About the author

David Guest has been a journalist for over 35 years, working for most of that time as a freelance writer and editor in diverse areas of the media. He has also been a computer programmer, an ice-cream man and a board-game designer.

He was born in Lancashire and finished his formal education in Yorkshire. Apart from a period in Australia he has spent most of his working life in the south of England.

- 🅵 www.facebook.com/david.guest.9674
- 🅳 @DavidAlanGuest
- 🖱 d.guest@btinternet.com